Praise

'Don't you just want to grab this, switch off the phone and
curl up on the sofa? Winter bliss from Lulu Taylor'
Veronica Henry, top ten bestselling author of
Christmas at the Beach Hut

'Pure indulgence and perfect reading
for a dull January evening'
The Sun

'Told across both timelines,
this easy read has a sting in the tale'
Sunday Mirror

'Utterly compelling. A really excellent winter's story'
Lucy Diamond

'I raced through this gripping tale about secrets and lies and
long-buried emotions bubbling explosively to the surface'
Daily Mail

'Wonderfully written . . . this indulgent
read is totally irresistible'
Closer

THE LAST
SONG OF
WINTER

Lulu Taylor is the author of fourteen novels including six *Sunday Times* bestsellers. Her first novel, *Heiresses*, was nominated for the RNA Readers' Choice award. She lives in Dorset where she continues to find inspiration for her stories of families, secrets and the mysteries of the past.

THE LAST
SONG OF
WINTER

LULU TAYLOR

PAN BOOKS

First published 2024 by Pan Books
an imprint of Pan Macmillan
The Smithson, 6 Briset Street, London EC1M 5NR
EU representative: Macmillan Publishers Ireland Ltd, 1st Floor,
The Liffey Trust Centre, 117–126 Sheriff Street Upper,
Dublin 1, D01 YC43
Associated companies throughout the world
www.panmacmillan.com

ISBN 978-1-5290-9400-8

Copyright © Lulu Taylor 2024

The right of Lulu Taylor to be identified as the
author of this work has been asserted by her in accordance
with the Copyright, Designs and Patents Act 1988.

All rights reserved. No part of this publication may be reproduced,
stored in a retrieval system, or transmitted, in any form, or by any means
(electronic, mechanical, photocopying, recording or otherwise)
without the prior written permission of the publisher.

Pan Macmillan does not have any control over, or any responsibility for,
any author or third-party websites referred to in or on this book.

1 3 5 7 9 8 6 4 2

A CIP catalogue record for this book is available from the British Library.

Typeset in Sabon by Jouve (UK), Milton Keynes
Printed and bound by CPI Group (UK) Ltd, Croydon, CR0 4YY

This book is sold subject to the condition that it shall not, by way of
trade or otherwise, be lent, hired out, or otherwise circulated without
the publisher's prior consent in any form of binding or cover other than
that in which it is published and without a similar condition including
this condition being imposed on the subsequent purchaser.

Visit **www.panmacmillan.com** to read more about all our books
and to buy them. You will also find features, author interviews and
news of any author events, and you can sign up for e-newsletters
so that you're always first to hear about our new releases.

To Judy Sadleir
With much love

Prologue
BRISTOL
1948

'You must have an idea why I asked you here.' Vincent seemed cool and completely in control but there was, Jack noticed, the faintest hint of anxiety in the way one manicured fingernail, a pale and polished oval, smoothed along the tablecloth, over and over.

'Not at all, old boy,' Jack said easily. He pulled a silver case out of his pocket and extracted a cigarette. Putting it between his teeth, he struck a match and lit it. 'I assumed it was because of the excellent food.' He grinned at his own joke, for the food everywhere was terrible these days. He would no doubt order the fish, plentiful here in Bristol, and whatever they had to go with it. There wasn't so much that could go wrong with that as long as the chef didn't stew it.

Vincent stared at him across the table, his lips tightening just a little.

Jealous, thought Jack. *He's jealous of all of it.*

After all, the maître d' and the waiters had made it obvious that they recognised Jack, calling him Mr Bannock in unctuous tones even though the table had been booked

1

under Vincent's name. They had offered him the wine list and rushed to put an ashtray in front of him when he lit up. He could feel their eyes on him, and sensed the half-turns from diners at neighbouring tables, discerning the low murmurs of his name.

That was what had been most disconcerting about fame. It was like living in a chamber where one's name was constantly echoed in murmurs all around. *Jack Bannock. That's Jack Bannock. Did you see? Jack Bannock!* Sometimes, braver or ruder souls approached. He liked the shy, nervous ones, overcoming their natural reticence and good manners to approach a stranger. He liked the starstruck women and the blushing girls who said, 'I'm ever so keen on you, Mr Bannock. I do love your songs so much! "A Vale of Violets" is my favourite.'

Some even remembered his films.

'I saw *The Robber King* when it came out, and I thought you were super!'

Others preferred his musicals of sentiment and derring-do, with beautiful ladies and noble lords falling in love. Jack liked the lads who glowed with pleasure at meeting their hero. He didn't like the women who shrieked and pawed at him, who felt entitled to his time and actually thought he might be interested in hearing their life stories, who demanded autographs like a right. And he particularly disliked the sort who patronised him, usually men. 'I say, are you that crooner fellow? The film actor? Fancy. I suppose you get paid very well simply to show off? And all the girls throwing themselves at you! It's a cushy number you've got there.'

He was used to it all now. It was hard to remember a time when he hadn't turned heads and heard that whisper of his name wherever he went.

No one batted an eyelid at Vincent. No one murmured his name.

Well, what would they say anyway? wondered Jack. *'I saw you in that film, Mr Lowther! Weren't you the soldier at the back who got shot in the first reel? Didn't you play the cad in the card game who got thrown out for cheating?' No one knows Vincent. It's only because he's Grey's friend that he has any work at all, and God alone knows what Grey sees in him. He's not so bad-looking, I suppose. And useful.*

Vincent ran errands of all sorts for Grey, whose celebrity had made him far too recognisable for ordinary life. Which was, of course, exactly as Grey liked it.

'So, why did you ask me here?' Jack said, as Vincent said nothing.

'Later,' Vincent said, shaking his head only slightly to signal that they should say no more. The head waiter had appeared to take their order. A moment after that, the bread basket with its round, hard and almost tasteless rolls was put in front of them. Moments later, it seemed, the soup arrived and the sommelier appeared with the wine, which he naturally poured into Jack's glass to taste. It was some time before they were finally left in peace. Vincent had kept up a stream of talk in his low voice, all about the staging of Grey's latest show. It was going to be at the Palladium, opening in only a few weeks. Hester Arundel was taking the female lead, as usual, but she'd been ill over the last week and Grey was full

3

of anxiety that she wouldn't be up to opening night and a full run of – he hoped – many successful performances.

'This is all fascinating,' Jack said testily, finally tiring of the unstoppable chat as he sipped his soup. 'I know most of this in any case – Grey told me. What I want to know is, what's this lunch in aid of?'

Vincent smoothed a finger over his moustache, falling silent at last. He began to blink rapidly. 'Well, I've come to talk to you about Grey.'

'I thought you might have. The trouble is, I don't particularly want to hear you moaning at length about his failings. I'm sure he's working you just as hard as ever, but you do ask for it, Vincent. You know what I'm going to say. Stand up to him. That's what I do. He's as spoiled as a little princess but you shouldn't let him act the way he does.' Jack sipped some of his clear soup. It tasted of hot water and salt and vaguely of onion, and he wondered what it was supposed to be. He put his spoon down and pushed it away. 'I'm going to be seeing Grey later anyway. He's coming up this evening for our trip.'

They were going to drive into Wales, stopping off at Jack's home town on the way to the beautiful island of St Elfwy off the coast of Pembrokeshire.

'I can't wait to see the perfectly ghastly place you sprang from, *mon choux*,' Grey had drawled, little white cigarette held aloft. They were in his smart Belgravia flat, just the two of them, drinking martinis.

'I'm sure it's almost as bad where you made your appearance,' Jack retorted. They smiled at one another. They were so similar. Jack Bannock and Grey Oswald. Both musical, talented and charismatic, although of course Jack was the handsomest. 'I,' Grey would say tartly, 'have the genius, though.'

They kept a friendly tally of their successes. Jack's latest show was still running at Drury Lane, while Grey's at the Coronet had closed after a healthy nine-month run.

'My next will be my best,' Grey had promised. 'Still running in two years, just you watch.'

'Let's work on something together,' Jack suggested. 'Like the old days? Remember *The Seahorse*? How we wrote it on the island, with Vee looking after us?'

'Of course I do. It was magical. Will I get to write the lyrics?'

'Most of them.'

'All right. After this latest is done and dusted and has refilled my coffers. You know me, always on the brink of ruin.'

The truth was, they were both successful and well known. Both from ordinary backgrounds, they had each invented themselves, using their formidable talents to clamber out of their milieu and up to the bright lights of the city and the glamour of show business.

'Now, now,' Grey said, tapping his ash away. 'Mother Oswald is very proud of the little suburban terrace where she brought me into the world.'

'And you mustn't be mean about my parents either. Working down the docks is perfectly respectable.'

'The docks?' Grey shuddered. 'At least selling insurance is done in an office.'

Jack pushed him playfully. 'You frightful snob, you. We're both upstarts, as you well know. You keep my secret and I'll keep yours.'

'Always, my darling,' Grey had said, suddenly solemn, and placing a tender kiss on the end of Jack's nose. 'And I can't wait to meet your family, especially if they're all as beautiful as you.'

That was what this trip was all about: the family and the escape and perhaps the creation of a new and exciting musical. They usually had to keep their relationship hidden, but every now and then they had the chance to be together, alone and completely themselves. They were going to the island, their first trip there in years. It was all arranged. Jack couldn't wait. Veronica had promised that the place was theirs for as long as they wanted. He could almost taste the pure air of the island, and the salty tang of the sea.

'Well, that's the thing, old chap,' Vincent said now. He paused as the waiter cleared their soup bowls and the plates of pallid fish were placed in front of them. 'I'm afraid that Grey isn't coming.'

Jack blinked at him, not able to take in what he had just heard. 'What did you say?'

'He's not coming.' Vincent looked grave and suddenly didn't seem able to meet Jack's eye. 'He's asked me to tell you . . . that the whole thing is off.'

'What do you mean?' Jack had gone very still, his whole being churning with sudden panic. 'He's changed his mind about the holiday? But why?'

'Not just the holiday, old man. All of it. It's all off. He doesn't want to see you again.'

'What?' stammered Jack. He pushed away the plate of food in front of him. 'What? I don't understand.'

Vincent looked uncomfortable. Jack had the distinct impression that he had been relishing this moment and was now not finding it quite as much fun as he had anticipated. 'I'm sorry. Grey has changed his mind about all of it. The flat, the show, the holiday. He's leaving England today for the continent and he'll be gone until the show opens.' There was the faintest hint of preening as Vincent added, 'I'll be taking over in the meantime.'

Jack was horrified to find that his eyes were full of tears. He felt a great shudder of pain go through him. He had feared this, he knew that now. From the moment he'd lost his heart to Grey, he'd feared that he would be hurt like this. The tears spilled out over his cheeks and he wept, reaching for his napkin.

'I say, old boy,' Vincent said awkwardly. 'Don't take it so hard. You'll feel better in a day or two. Go and see your people like you planned.'

'When is he leaving?' Jack demanded.

'He's on the night ferry.'

Jack knew it well: the train that left Victoria late in the evening for the coast and was then boarded onto its own ferry, landing at Dunkirk in the morning to complete its run to Paris. He'd made the journey himself plenty of times in the old days, though not since it had started up again after the war. He leapt to his feet. 'Then I'm going to see him. He must be mad; he can't be in his right mind. He would never do this.'

'Don't be ridiculous. You'll never get to the station in time.'

'Yes, I will. You'll see.'

Jack wiped his eyes, threw the napkin on the table and turned on his heel, weaving as fast as he could through the tables and chairs and other diners. He was heedless now of the murmur of his name, or what anyone thought as he raced out of the restaurant and across the road to where his car was parked. He was thinking wildly of how long it would take to get to Victoria and the quickest route.

The tears were still blurring his vision as he managed to start the car and pull out, heading towards the road to London. He had been so happy, so full of that gleeful anticipation. A week or more with Grey, just the two of them. A time to plan their future and work out how they could be together without the world guessing their rather obvious secret. He had been lost in dreams of their time on the island, walking together to see the stacks where the guillemots danced. And now it was all over? Just like that?

It can't be, it can't be, he said to himself through clenched teeth, his knuckles white around the steering wheel. Then he felt a fierce determination. He would not let this happen. He would not.

The Rolls needed filling up on the journey and Jack realised he would only have enough petrol to get to London but not to return. He was at the end of his monthly ration. The trip back could not happen now, no matter what.

The attendant filled up the tank from the pump and, as he took the last coupon from the booklet Jack had handed him, said, 'I say, Mr Bannock, I'm one of your biggest fans.' He grinned shyly. 'I thought you were a treat in that American film you were in, the one where you played that creepy feller. You gave me the jitters.'

'Thank you, thank you.' Jack tried to smile. He must look a fright; his eyes were probably red and swollen. All along the road, the tears had kept coming as he'd wondered why on earth Grey had pulled out of their trip. He noticed that a woman in her coupé at a nearby pump had just clocked him and was going scarlet with excitement. 'I must be off.'

'Yes, sir,' the attendant said, handing back the empty coupon booklet. 'All done. Drive carefully, it's all you're getting for the next two weeks. And it's a lovely motor you've got there, I must say.' He put a reverent hand on the silver bonnet.

Jack threw the booklet on the seat next to him and revved up the engine. 'Thanks. Goodbye.'

He pulled out of the garage as fast as he safely could. He was only a short drive from London now. There was a chance of reaching Victoria before the boat train left, and he would do all in his power to get there.

He remembered nothing, afterwards, of that journey. His Rolls flew towards London, easily outdistancing the rest of the traffic, not that there was much of that. Private cars had been pretty much mothballed during the years of the war and people had learned to live without them. Petrol was still rationed, even if more generously than in wartime. Jack's Rolls Royce drew eyes wherever it went. He usually enjoyed the notice it attracted, just as he enjoyed the greater surprise when people saw that it was Jack Bannock at the wheel. He was always beautifully dressed, his black hair oiled and slicked, so that just a lock or two hung romantically over his eyes.

'You're the only man I know who wears stage make-up in ordinary life,' Grey would tease. 'Anything to heighten those soulful eyes of yours. The Italian ice-cream seller you're descended from must have been quite the looker.'

It was true. During his short Hollywood career, he'd been likened to Rudolph Valentino and the make-up artists had created a similar sultry look: kohl-rimmed eyes of melting dark brown, the lids darkened just enough to make him look tortured, his skin whitened to a romantic pallor . . .

'I'm sure it was enough to make you fall in love with your-self,' Grey remarked waspishly. He was, Jack knew, jealous of those matinée idol looks. Jack didn't have to utter a word on film to make legions of women fall madly in love with him. He just had to gaze soulfully into the camera, his head at the perfect angle that showed his Grecian profile and full lips, and that was enough.

'That was why you were such a success in the silent movies and not so much in the talkies,' Grey would claim cattily, but Jack just laughed. Grey had nothing like the same in the way of good looks. He'd seemed middle-aged since he was twenty-one, with his thinning hair and lined complex-ion. Although his eyes sparkled with intelligence and wit, they were pouchy and downturned. The stream of jokes and witticisms that flowed from his mouth could not conceal his thin lips and slightly weak chin. He would never stir the female heart as Jack did, nor the male heart come to that. Nevertheless, he had made a theatre and film career of his own, only playing romantic leads because he wrote them for himself and because somehow his pairing with Hester Arundel made him seem credible as a lover of women. She was beautiful – as women had to be, that went without saying – feisty and with a wit quick enough to make her a plausible foil to Grey. She had lent him the respectability that made his camp wit and waspish humour acceptable to the general public. It had made him a great success.

We are perfect together, Jack thought desperately. *Why, why would he leave me now?*

He drew up in front of the station, heedless of bus stops and taxi ranks, and leapt out of the Rolls. The night ferry left from platform two and he dashed there, breathless. He raced for the first-class carriages, knowing that Grey would never travel anything less, and as he pounded down the platform, he saw two familiar figures. The first had its back to him, but he knew the almost floor-length fur coat draped over the shoulders, the smart grey felt homburg with the scarlet grosgrain ribbon, the wide turn-ups on the trousers. It was Grey. The second figure, directing the porter where to take their luggage, was only vaguely familiar, a young man that Vincent had introduced as his assistant. Jack, panting and panicked, could not remember the name. Was he Herbert?

Something like that. But he was dark and brown-eyed, like a younger version of Jack himself.

This is Vincent's work, Jack thought. It was a thought barely formed in his mind but he knew suddenly and quite clearly that Vincent had been working on this for months, subtly coming between him and Grey. And now he had clearly succeeded.

No, thought Jack fiercely. *No*.

'Grey!' he called, waving a hand, and the fur-coated figure froze, then slowly turned to face him. 'Grey, stop!'

Now Grey was looking at him. The pale blue eyes were hooded and cold. 'Jack, darling,' he said in that thick-throated drawl of his. 'What a delightful surprise. Have you come to wave me off?'

Naturally he showed not one flicker of surprise, although seeing Jack on the platform must have been the last thing he expected. Beside him, the young assistant looked fearful but busied himself with the business of the luggage.

'I'll keep that,' Grey said, pointing at his vanity bag. It was, Jack knew, stuffed to the brim with the lotions and potions that Grey delighted in using every morning and night. 'I can't afford to lose what little looks I've got,' he would say to Jack. 'It's all very well for you, but those of us not born with the looks of the gods need to cherish what we were blessed with.'

Jack stared at him, breathless. Then he managed to say, 'But Grey, what on earth are you doing?'

'Doing, my dear?' The cool blue eyes had slid away. 'I should think that's perfectly obvious. I'm going abroad.'

'But our trip—'

'Ah, yes, our trip. I'm afraid that the bright lights of Paris have proved more alluring than an outcrop in Wales. I'm sure you understand.'

'No,' Jack exclaimed. 'I don't understand! Not a bit! Why aren't you coming with me? Is it all over?'

Grey's gaze slid over the other people on the platform and Jack discerned a trace of anxiety. Nothing was allowed to be said in public that might in any way give the game away. 'I don't know what you mean, dear boy. Over? Of course not, we're friends just as we always were. I'm very much afraid, though, that our gallivanting in the valleys will have to be postponed. I'm sorry.' He turned as if to board the train.

Jack, desperate, reached and grabbed his arm, slipping a hand under the drape of the fur coat to the fine wool jacket beneath. There was a human warmth there that, for a second, gave him hope. 'Don't go, I beg you,' he said. He had a sudden certainty that if Grey got on the night ferry train, he would never see him again. 'Please, please, if any of it meant anything at all to you . . . don't go.'

Grey was stock still again, half turned to board. Everything seemed to slow and stop, as he stared down at Jack's arm. He blinked just once, and then gazed up at Jack. The eyes were cold. 'My dear boy, what a scene. It's just a couple of days in Paris. I'll see you when I get back and we can talk it all through.' He looked over to his assistant. 'Hubert, I'm getting on the train. When you're done, come and open that champagne for me, will you? I could do with a drink. Good-bye, Jack. *À bientôt*.'

With that, Grey put one elegant shoe on the footplate of

the carriage and then was gone, disappearing into the sleeping car with one final cool look over his shoulder.

For a moment, Jack was going to follow. The train wasn't leaving for twenty minutes. But a guard in a peaked cap carrying a passenger list on a clipboard was walking towards him down the platform alongside the dark blue carriage with its smart gold lettering. He was looking enquiringly at Jack. 'Name, please, sir?'

Ironic, thought Jack grimly. *One of the few people who doesn't know me.* He thought for a minute that he would simply board, and find Grey in his compartment and force him to listen, make him explain. But he knew the stubbornness too well. Grey might have a weak chin but he was obstinate. There would be no reaching him, not today or tomorrow. Perhaps never. But there was some reason why it was all over.

Not knowing was almost as great a part of the torment as the fear that Grey was gone for ever.

'Do you wish to board, sir?' enquired the guard, trying to read Jack's expression. 'There's still time to say goodbye. The train isn't leaving for a little while.'

'No,' he said bleakly. 'I won't board. Thank you.'

He turned to go. He heard his name and hope leapt in his heart but when he turned, it was only Hubert walking towards him along the platform. He stopped a pace or two from Jack. 'I'm sorry,' he said, almost nervously. 'I wish it weren't this way.'

'What do you know?' Jack demanded.

14

'Nothing.' Hubert looked away. 'There's urgent business in Paris. That's all. But I know you're disappointed.'

Jack gave a bitter laugh and Hubert turned to go. 'Wait!' Hubert turned slowly back to face him. 'Will you . . . will you look after him for me?'

Hubert nodded. 'Yes. Yes, I will.'

'Thank you.'

Hubert stepped towards the footplate of the carriage, and pulled himself up. He boarded without a backward glance.

'So that's it,' Jack said to himself. 'That's it.'

He turned, ignoring the whispers and nudges of the people on the platform who recognised him. He didn't even look around when someone said, 'Oh, Mr Bannock, I'm such a great admirer!'

He was consumed with misery. His world had turned to darkness and filled with ashes. Nothing mattered now that his heart was leaving on the night ferry train for Paris without him.

PART ONE

Chapter One
VERONICA
1938

'We are lucky,' Billie said to Veronica. 'Our daddy is not like other daddies.' The sisters were sitting on the rug in front of the fire in the nursery, waiting for Gladys, the maid, to bring in their tea. 'He's so much more fun and interesting, isn't he?'

'I suppose so,' said Veronica. She traced the pattern in the rug slowly with the tip of her finger and looked at her younger sister's shoes, noticing that they needed a polish. 'I suppose we're very lucky.'

They both knew that they lived a spoiled life. Daddy and Mama never rubbed their noses in it, or told them to think of poor starving children and how fortunate they were in comparison, but the girls understood that life in their house in Hampstead, with everything done for them by a houseful of servants, and with every luxury they needed, made them extremely well off.

But I don't care about money, Veronica thought. *I just don't.*

'There's all this,' Billie said, 'and the island too.'

The island. Just the words lifted Veronica's spirits. It

always seemed to be winter in London: chilly grey days followed by dark, blustery nights, the lamps glowing through fog, the trees black and spiky on the heath, which they could see from the upstairs windows. Perhaps that was because they spent their summers out of town, on St Elfwy, and so summer meant the sea, the blazing sky vanishing into the far distance, and splendid isolation for weeks on end, living in the white house on the cliff with its view of the mainland across the channel, and with birds and rabbits for company. Mama would relax entirely without the big house to look after, reading and playing the piano and walking. Girls from the mainland would come over to cook and clean, and an odd job man appeared regularly to manage the repairs and the garden for them.

Daddy would stay in town for the most part, only joining them for odd weeks when he had some time off.

Don't get sunburned, he would write, in one of his jolly letters. *I don't like to see my girls getting boyish and brown – stay fair and fragile!*

That was all very well for Billie, who was exactly the fair and fragile sort. But Veronica loved nothing more than to be in her shorts, white shirts and sand shoes, clambering over rocks, netting crabs and sailing the little dinghy, the glare of the sun on the water making her scrunch up her eyes against it. The summer she turned ten, she had grown so annoyed by the long, thick, fair hair that make her head and neck so hot – and that tortured her by being curled with rags into ringlets – that she took a big pair of scissors and hacked the whole thing off, tossing the ponytail into the sea with delight.

There had been a lot of trouble over it, and she'd been sent to bed in disgrace and not allowed out for two whole days. It had been worth it. Since then, she'd had a short, wavy bob that turned white in the sun when she took off her cap, and a blunt fringe that fell over her fierce blue eyes.

Billie was right, Daddy was much more interesting than other daddies. He didn't set off for an office every day with a rolled umbrella, briefcase and bowler hat, like the ones they saw streaming to Hampstead underground station in the mornings. He was an actor and producer, at home most of the day when he wasn't rehearsing, heading off to the theatre in the late afternoon, and not returning until long after they were asleep. Often there were parties downstairs. How could they be expected to sleep while that was going on? The roar of motor cars, the footsteps on the marble floor of the grand hall below, the music floating up to the bedrooms. Gaiety and laughter and fun. No other house in their neighbourhood was ablaze until the early hours. Perhaps that was why Daddy had bought this place set back behind iron gates, in grand isolation. No one to complain.

In the morning Billie and Veronica would peruse the visitors' book on the hall console. Such glamorous names were scrawled there: stars of the theatre and music hall as well as lords and ladies and all sorts of impressive people.

Billie wanted to be an actress too. Mama had been an actress once, a refined lady in society comedies, but she had given it up to make Daddy and her daughters the centre of her life, and never seemed to miss her old profession. Billie ached to get on the stage and was always begging to play any child's part going, but Daddy wouldn't hear of it yet. Billie, he said, was too young to be a theatre brat but when the right play came, he would see if she would be suitable. Meanwhile, he relished setting them games of imagination and play acting, letting them create alter egos and other personalities, encouraging them to disguise themselves to fool relatives, visitors and servants and get away with it.

Veronica loved the games but hated the idea of the stage. The last thing she wanted was people looking at her. She was restless and yearning, and she knew that the answer to whatever it was she sought didn't lie in the theatre. She didn't think it lay in the ceaseless parties that Daddy and Mama seemed to enjoy so much either. But what was it she wanted? She wasn't sure.

And then Rupert had come to stay.

Rupert was a second cousin, and much older than the girls. They had not known him before now, as he was the son of Mama's cousin and had grown up in India when not at school. But now he had come down from Oxford and was keen to become a playwright. He had come to stay in order to finish his play and, if Daddy liked it, have it put on the London stage with Daddy in the lead role. A play produced by and starring George Mindenhall would guarantee an audience, and probably overnight success.

'Rupert will stay in the writers' room!' boomed Daddy. 'Until his play is finished.'

The girls were quite accustomed to this. Daddy had famous authors here all the time, men and women who often looked like nothing terribly special, but who set the public imagination alight with their stories. He offered up a room in his house as a refuge for them to finish their latest works in peace and quiet during the day, with glamorous parties and dinners to enjoy in the evening.

So Rupert came, with two suitcases, one with his clothes and one that contained a typewriter, and he tapped away in the writers' room nearly all day. When he wasn't writing, he was in the library, reading and smoking, or setting off for long walks across the heath in a full-length tweed coat, trying to find his inspiration. He didn't seem much interested in the parties but retired to his room after dinner to continue his work.

Billie thought he was boring but Veronica was entranced. She sensed an artistic soul that seemed to emanate from him like an invisible cloud. For that reason alone, Rupert was beautiful. How could Billie not see it? She claimed Rupert looked like a giant weed, but Veronica decided she liked his pasty looks. It was true he was lily-white and freckled, and had hair that was a kind of muddy red colour, but he had warm hazel eyes full of intelligence and heart. He didn't smile much but that was because he was contemplating the great matters of life and death, and anyway, he usually had a cigarette hanging from his lips, or dangling from his fingers, the butt twisted between his narrow fingertips as he read. He was romantically tall, with long elegant hands, and was always running his fingers through his hair until it stood up on end, which she found quite heartbreakingly charming.

'Don't you think he's got *it*?' Veronica asked now. She had just heard the front door slam and had leapt up from the rug, rushing over to watch Rupert dashing out on one of his perpetual walks around the heath.

'You mean, he's a peril?'

'A deadly peril.'

'I don't think so.' Billie shrugged. 'He reminds me too much of Daddy.'

'Daddy?' Veronica was amazed. 'He's not like him a scrap! And he's related to Mama in any case, so how could he be?'

Veronica thought Daddy was ugly. It surprised her that anyone would want to see him on stage, but then she saw him transformed through costume, make-up, wigs and moustaches and she had to admit that he was quite different. At home, he looked ordinary, with a jutting brow over his blue eyes, and a long face topped by a flat plate of heavy dark hair parted harshly down the middle and stuck back with grease. It was only the light in his eyes and the gaiety of his spirit that detracted from what Veronica considered his ugliness. How on earth could Billie think that angelic Rupert looked anything like Daddy?

'Well,' Billie said obstinately, 'you might like him, but he's not a peril to me, let alone a deadly one.'

A peril was someone very attractive, and a deadly peril was someone dangerously so. Crumbly people were beautiful or handsome, depending.

Billie was not particularly interested in Veronica's assessment of Rupert as a deadly peril. The two of them were always falling in love with unsuitable people and just as quickly falling out again.

At least Rupert's arrival gave them something to think about besides lessons and the boring round of life at home, even if he paid them scant attention. Something very tragic had happened to him, which perhaps explained how little notice he took of his cousins. Mama said both his parents were dead, and two of his brothers had been killed in the war, so no wonder he was preoccupied and seemed somewhat sad.

I'm sure I could cheer him up, if he'd just let me, Veronica thought. She kept an eye on him, following him around like a wraith but usually just out of sight. She tried to catch a glimpse of his writing but it was no good. He kept it locked in his room.

Daddy's newest play had been a huge hit, his biggest yet. The play, written by a friend of his, was about an evil man who kidnapped a girl and kept her hidden in order to have his wicked way with her. But strangely the man was sometimes gentle, soft and loving. The girl fell in love with him when he was like this, but hated him when he was cruel. It was a mystery until it was discovered that the man was in fact twin brothers, and she had fallen in love with the good one. Of course, Daddy played both the twin brothers. And the pièce de resistance at the end was when the brothers duelled over the honour of the girl, and she had promised to marry the victor. The secret of the play was that in this fight, you had no idea which was Daddy and which was the stand-in, and which brother he was playing – although of course everyone knew that the good brother would triumph, somehow. And then they were unmasked, one after the other, and he seemed to be both of the fighters! All was revealed in the curtain call and the audience was nightly sworn to secrecy about how the trick was pulled off.

'It will run for years, just my luck,' Daddy would say gloomily.

'Don't be ridiculous, George,' Mama would say, gently reproving. 'Most actors would give their eye teeth for a part like that, for a hit! And a long run is a wonderful thing.'

Daddy harrumphed. He had a very short attention span and was quickly bored with the repetitive nature of his occupation. The same lines, the same drama night after night, and four afternoons a week. He was always keen to move on to the next thing.

'Do it for now, dear,' Mama said calmly, sewing rhythmically on her embroidery. 'Perhaps they'll let someone else take your part on in due course. But it would be foolishness to give it up when it's so successful.'

Veronica watched Daddy. Mama let him take charge all the time. Her whole life revolved around him. Yet sometimes, very quietly, she told him what she wanted and he almost always obeyed.

Daddy said suddenly, 'I'm planning a gala night in the new year. Once Christmas is over, we will need to reinvigorate our ticket sales. If all goes well, we'll have royalty coming – the Duke of Kent.'

'How thrilling,' Mama said politely.

'It certainly is. The girls must come. Billie, Veronica, don't you want to come and see the play? And the duke?'

Billie looked up, excited. 'I should say so! Perhaps the duke will fall in love with me.'

'You're fourteen years old,' Veronica said, 'so he'd better not.'

Mama said placidly, 'The Duke of Kent is married, dear. I thought you knew that. He and his wife already have two children.'

'Oh, what a shame,' Billie said thoughtfully. Then she cheered up. 'Perhaps he'll bring some handsome lord as his equerry and he and I will exchange passionate glances and fall in love.'

Daddy said, 'I shouldn't think being married would stop the duke. He's got himself in plenty of hot water already.' He chuckled.

Mama shot him a freezing look and he stopped laughing with a careless shrug. Billie got up, went to her father and put her arms around his neck. 'Dear Dads, do say we can go to the gala, and will there be a party?'

'I shall host a gathering at the Savoy!' declared Daddy, seizing Billie's hands in his. 'It is the very least that would be expected. What do you say, Dodo? Ball gowns, glittering jewels, stars of the theatre and the handsome duke?'

'A dream come true,' Mama said, calm as ever.

But Veronica thought it sounded awful.

'I say, are you going to follow me around *all* the bally time?'

Veronica leapt back, but it was obviously far too late. Rupert had spotted her loitering in the hall behind the bust of Augustus and peeping out from behind his marble epaulettes. He turned from the front door, where he had been about to exit in his long tweed coat, an orange knitted scarf twisted around his neck, and strode towards her across the marble floor, frowning.

'Come out from behind there. Why on earth are you hiding like this?'

These were more words addressed to her at one time than he had ever said before. He barely noticed her at meals when the family were dining together. He grunted occasionally in the direction of the sisters if they passed him in the house. Now, though, he sounded cross.

Veronica crept out from behind the bust. He was gazing down at her, hazel eyes narrowed.

'Well?' he said. 'What's going on? Are you kids spying on me or something? Is it a game?'

'Yes,' she said quickly. 'Just a game. We get so bored. So we're pretending you're an enemy agent and we're keeping tabs on you.'

'I see.' His face cleared a little. 'I did think you girls haven't enough to do. Don't you have lessons?'

'Of course,' Veronica said stoutly. 'But they're only in the mornings. The rest of the day, we lounge about a bit. Our poor young minds are restless with lack of activity.'

'Don't you read?' Rupert asked. 'You learn a lot from books. This is the time you should be reading all the classics. Get them under your belt while you've got the time before they start forcing you to go to those dreary parties every night.'

'Yes, we read. But you can't read all day, every day. We have to do something else occasionally.'

'True, I suppose. I have to get a break from my writing so

I know what you mean.' He looked thoughtful. 'Look, why don't you come out for a walk with me? Fancy it?'

'Do I!' Veronica said. Her heart started racing with excitement. 'Yes, please.'

'We'll have a stride on the heath. It'll do us both good.'

She raced for her coat and outdoor shoes.

They made their way over the cobbled forecourt in front of the house, out of the side gate, and along the street to the heath, which lay conveniently close to them. Veronica knew it as well as her own garden; she'd walked on it almost every day they were in London from early childhood, when nannies and nurses took her and Billie to the playgrounds and the boating lake and all the other wonderful places. As they went, Rupert smoking heavily on cigarette after cigarette, Veronica talked breathlessly, telling him about her life and what it was like to feel so aimless most of the time.

'I hate being a kid,' she confided as they went. It was heart-stoppingly exciting being close to him, and she felt electrified, as though her very hair was lifting with the static. He was like a soulful poet, and he was listening to her, drinking in what she was saying and asking her questions about herself: the nursery, the governess – 'She's called Miss Hopkins and she's frightfully clever but so starstruck by Daddy; it's so embarrassing the way she goes all marshmallowy when he comes in' – and the way her days unfolded.

'I just live for summers really,' she said. 'That's when I feel most free. On our island.'

'Island?' He glanced at her, interested. 'You have an island?'

29

'Only a little one.'

He laughed, and she felt little sparks of light inside her. 'Only a little one!' he echoed. 'Where is it?'

'Wales. Pembrokeshire.'

'Oh. I was imagining a little jewel in the Med, off the coast of Italy or something, somewhere hot and beautiful.'

She felt a tiny bit hurt, as though her island were being insulted. 'It's a beautiful place! Do you know Wales?'

He shook his head. They were following the path across the heath but she was barely aware of it, focusing only on Rupert's proximity, the swing of his tweed coat and the ringing sound of his shoes on the path.

'Well, it's lovely. And it is often very hot! I mean, it does also rain a good deal, and the storms can be terribly dramatic. But we have lots of simply lovely days, where the sea and sky are blue and the wind is gentle . . . and oh my goodness, the birds! Guillemots and puffins and gulls and sweet, sweet manx sheerwaters, clouds of them. And you should see the rabbits!'

'That does sound charming. Fancy. I had no idea you had an island, on top of all this.' Rupert waved a hand back in the direction of the house.

'One of Daddy's impulse purchases. He saw it advertised in *The Times*. And apparently there's a sort of feudal title that goes with it. He's the King of St Elfwy, or so he claims.'

Rupert laughed loudly, a proper bellow. 'There's no end to his vaingloriousness, is there? King! Of a rock off the coast of Wales.'

Veronica suddenly didn't like the condescension in Rupert's

voice. For all of her own thoughts about her father – and she knew he was a conceited show-off – no one else was allowed to say such things.

'It's just a joke,' she said with a touch of frostiness. 'He knows it's very silly. I wish I hadn't said anything.'

'There, there,' Rupert said, chucking away his cigarette butt. 'Don't be offended. I'm tremendously fond of your dad. And he's been jolly kind to me, and promises to do more. Don't worry, I wouldn't be disrespectful.'

'Oh, I don't mind,' she said airily, but feeling secretly reassured. 'He's an old duffer sometimes, that's for sure. Shall we go over to the bandstand? There's a tea place there. We could get some and a currant bun.'

'Why not? And you can tell me more about Miss Hopkins.'

She never wanted it to end, but before long they were heading for home. The light was fading, the mist was coming down and street lamps were beginning to glow. She knew it would be time for tea very soon.

'Thanks for taking me out, I've had ever such a good time,' she said as they went into the house.

'You're welcome.' He smiled at her. 'I've enjoyed it too. We'll do it again sometime.'

'Yes, please.'

'Perhaps Billie can come too.'

'Oh . . . yes, perhaps she could.'

That put a dampener on it, she thought, going upstairs. But still. She wanted to hug herself with excitement. Rupert was wonderful, just as she had thought. Truly interested in her. And around him she felt a thrill like she had never felt before. It made her think of the gorgeousness she had experienced when they'd been taken to the circus. The excitement had been overwhelming. When they went into the big top, she had felt as though she might burst, or melt. And this feeling was a little like that but focused utterly on Rupert. She felt she wanted to touch his hand, bury her nose in his red hair, be close to him. Perhaps even have him kiss her.

The thought made her gasp and her stomach twisted into a tight, hot knot that was equally pleasurable and sickening.

The nursery door opened and Gladys put out her head. 'There you are, Miss Veronica! Tea is ready and getting cold. You'd better wash your hands sharpish. Miss Billie's already started without you.'

'I'm here, I'm here. Keep your wig on,' Veronica said, deflated to be a child again when a moment ago she'd felt like a woman. 'I'll wash my hands at once.'

Chapter Two

Why did winter last so long, and summer go by in such a flash?

Life in London stretched from October to April, or even May, before they started to spend time on the island. It was true that the family did go away on holidays at other times. Veronica had a glorious time skiing in November, taken away by her best friend Mary and her family for a week, and oh, what fun it was. The girls were allowed to dance in the evenings, although mostly with each other. Veronica found she loved to dance. As soon as the band struck up, she was itching to be on the dance floor, even with Mary as her partner. The older men and women looked so glamorous. There was something enchanting about a couple dancing. It seemed to be the best way to spend time with a man: fun, wordless, joyful, exhilarating, both partners equally vital to the success of the dance. She watched the men in their white tie and tailed coats whirling the glittering, gleaming women around the floor and it looked like heaven.

If only Rupert were here, she thought, trying to imagine

him taking her in his arms, and the two of them foxtrotting around the dance floor. She loved to foxtrot; it was her favourite dance. She and Mary could dance the simple version, a waltz with a spring in its step, but she envied the better dancers with their fancy footwork. When the band started playing her favourite song – 'You're Drivin' Me Crazy' – she had to get up and dance along, even if she had no partner. Mary's mother wouldn't allow her to dance with the smiling men who came up to ask her. She was only allowed to dance with Mary's father and he didn't like to dance, so that was a no-go.

If Rupert were here, they would have whirled around together, with eyes only for each other. At least, that was what she liked to think.

Glamorous as it was to spend days on the slopes and then stay up late and dine in the hotel ballroom each night, Veronica was glad to get home. She was tired out by all of it, and also missed her family. She had written home almost every day, and Daddy had sent her very funny letters, one of which was full of drawings of the awful punishments she would get if she started getting close to any boys.

You and Billie are my angels, he wrote. *My girls are not allowed to be devoted to anyone but their dear old dad! So don't grow up yet, little Véronique. Do you understand?*

But it was Rupert she thought of most. He was the one she wanted to get back to see. He had taken a lot more notice of her since their walk together and they'd gone out several more times. She had wickedly pretended that Billie was busy and not even asked her sister, and so had managed to keep

Rupert to herself, as they strolled over the heath, up to the bandstand and the tea room, and back again. He told her about his play, which sounded extraordinary. It was a ghost story about a man who had been deserted by his wife, and she had taken their child with her. He was heartbroken and could hardly bear it. And then they came back. They hadn't really left him at all, it had all been a sad misunderstanding. After a joyful family reunion and many plans for the future, he awoke to find them gone again. And the police arrived to tell him that his family were killed in a train crash a week before. They had not been real at all. Their ghosts had visited him.

It gave Veronica a chill when she heard it, and she was sure it would be brilliant.

When she got back, she was disappointed to find that Rupert wasn't there. He had gone walking in the Lake District with some university friends and would not return until after Christmas, perhaps not even until the end of January.

Everyone was delighted to see her back, and Daddy made her tell him every detail of the skiing holiday, every scrap she could remember. He loved to know about her life. His happiest times were sitting in his big armchair in the drawing room, Veronica sitting at his feet so that he could gaze down at her as she chattered away, telling him everything.

'Has Rupert finished his play?' she asked, unable to prevent herself turning the conversation to him.

Daddy grunted as he lit his pipe and sucked on the end a couple of times to make the tobacco glow. 'Irritating boy. He's taking for ever. I haven't chucked him out because your mother is fond of him and I do like the sound of his play. But if he never finishes it, what is the point? I'm losing my patience with him.' Daddy fixed her with one of his intense blue gazes. His eyes, shaded by his heavy brow, could seem particularly piercing sometimes, as though he could see right into her head. 'He hasn't been talking to you, has he?'

'Oh, not much,' she said quickly, sensing that her father would not like this at all. 'Just in passing, you know.'

'All right. Good,' he said. Then his face brightened. 'Now. My gala night is all planned. It will be just after new year, to brighten those miserable January days. You and Billie are coming and are to have new dresses. It's going to be the most splendid occasion. Now, don't make that face. You'll enjoy it. You'll see!'

Christmas that year was lavish, although Daddy spent most of it at the theatre. The house always looked its most wonderful then, with the great fir tree in the hall smothered in decorations, and all the chimneypieces swathed in holly and ivy. There were several parties, including one for the children to include all of their friends and relations, with an actual Father Christmas handing out presents, and all sorts of treats and goodies. Veronica couldn't take her usual pleasure in it. She felt too grown-up for all of that now, and she missed Rupert, not least because thinking about him had provided such a distraction from her usual boredom. And she was depressed that he wasn't going to be at the gala. She wanted to see him dressed up to the nines, like the men in the Swiss hotel ballroom. She knew it would be bliss to dance with him and she yearned for it in the way she had longed for a birthday or an outing when she was just a child. There was something more tingling about the excitement she felt now, but it was the same sort of thing.

Daddy was right. The gala performance of his play was a spark of light in the dog days after Christmas and Veronica was surprised to find that she was actually looking forward to it. A night out in the theatre – a treat for most but ordinary for her – was perfectly nice, she loved getting lost in drama and stories, but a party afterwards usually filled her with dread. Perhaps she was growing up a little since her holiday with Mary, for it didn't seem as bad as she would once have thought.

The dressmaker had made her and Billie silk gowns with elegant cowl necks. Billie's was short, just over the knee, but Veronica was permitted the elegance of a full-length, grownup gown, in a lovely silvery colour. She knew that it suited her, the colour making her skin look pearly, giving her blue eyes and fair hair an icy quality.

'It's not fair,' wailed Billie. 'Why is my dress short and a hopeless pink, when Vee's is so sophisticated? And she's got lovely shoes. Look at my clodhoppers!'

Mama told her that Veronica was sixteen, but Billie was still a child and should be glad she was permitted along at all.

The gala night was exciting. The women sat together in a box opposite the grandest box of all, able to see the handsome duke taking centre place, surrounded by an entourage of important people. They stared at him.

'Isn't he rather short?' whispered Veronica to Billie.

'Not for me,' Billie whispered back. 'And he's perfect in every way!' She sighed.

He was good-looking, but Veronica found the pale blue eyes, the sharp features and pallid colouring were not her cup of tea, despite the air of royal glamour. Besides which the duke had a look of languid boredom, his eyes moving restlessly as though unable to find anything of real interest. Apparently none of the gorgeously dressed women gazing up at him adoringly from the stalls, or across from the circle, held any appeal for him. He took no interest in the box opposite.

'We're just kids to him!' muttered Billie crossly.

'Of course we are,' Veronica replied. She felt overwhelmed by the crowds and suddenly grateful to be still in the safety of childhood, even if only just. All around her, gorgeous women glittered in jewels and silks, so much of their skin exposed despite the furs and gloves, their hair styled elaborately, their faces made up.

What an effort, Veronica thought. *Is this what it takes to be loved?*

The women had taken infinite pains, while the men were dressed identically in their white ties and tailcoats. Why was that? Why all this work for women to be beautiful and the men hardly had to try at all?

She felt glad of her youth, being excused all that. Did it lie in her future, though? Was it inevitable?

Is this what I will have to do to win Rupert? she thought in dismay. How much simpler if he could fall in love with her before that all started. But he hadn't noticed her yet and perhaps he wouldn't until she looked like the women in the theatre.

The lights dimmed and the curtain rose. The play was a corker, full of rousing scenes that gripped the audience from the very beginning. Daddy was wonderful, of course, lavishly costumed and managing to get a great deal of humanity from his somewhat cardboard cut-out characters of twin brothers. Even Veronica began to believe in the purity of the love between him and the beautiful heroine.

The girls stayed in their box for the interval, but the royal box emptied so that the duke could be given cocktails and cigarettes in a private room.

Mama said, 'I hope he's enjoying it. It would be such a fillip if he were.'

'Of course he is!' exclaimed Billie. 'It's wonderful! Daddy is splendid.'

'He is good,' agreed Mama. 'It's actually rather a while since I've seen him act. They said he was trailblazer, you know, when he first came to prominence. A quite new form of acting. Before then, there was lots of artifice, lots of declaiming and facing the audience. Daddy liked it to be natural and real. The audience connected with him, and believed him, believed he was as human as they were. That's his genius.'

'But the play is very silly,' Veronica murmured.

'Perhaps it is,' Mama said, sitting back in her red velvet chair. 'But we are here to be entertained, not improved, so we will enjoy it for what it is. Look, girls, do you see? Sybille

39

Handforth is over there. You were named after her, Billie – a great woman and a great actress. I appeared with her in *Lady Windermere's Fan* at the Hudson many years ago. She was magnificent.'

The royal party returned, the second half began, and the play took off. Everything impressive had been saved for this dramatic climax: the fights, the effects, the gorgeous costume of the heroine's wedding dress. The sight of her standing from embracing her wounded lover to reveal the front dyed scarlet with blood made the audience gasp. The speeches between the lovers had the audience sighing and snivelling, and emotions were so excited by the end that one man was overcome and yelled, 'Kill the cad! Kill him at once!'

The ending was a wonderful piece of melodrama. The revelation of the identical twins made everyone gasp and applaud wildly – although there was only one brother for the curtain call, and that was Daddy. He took his standing ovation graciously, turning to bow to the royal box. Mama was delighted to see the duke on his feet, applauding heartily, a wide grin over his face. The royal ennui had been lifted. The news of this would boost ticket sales, without a doubt.

Daddy was still taking curtain calls when Mama bustled the girls out of the circle and away to the waiting car, which would take them to the Savoy for the gala. They would arrive before the crowds with time to freshen up.

In the ladies' room at the Savoy, Veronica ran a brush through her hair and then left Billie and Mama patting theirs carefully in place to make her way towards the mirror-lined ballroom. Glass and crystal glittered and shone in the lights, a band was preparing to play and waiters stood about, ready to serve the drinks, but no one else had yet arrived from the theatre. She ventured in, feeling daring.

Here I am, all alone.

She caught sight of her reflection in one of the mirrors opposite: a slim, pale figure. She ran one hand over the smooth, cool silk of her dress and with the other touched the strand of pearls at her neck.

Am I a grown-up now? I look almost like it.

She was filled with the sense of being on the brink of an adventure, at the edge of a forest with many pathways ahead and she had to choose carefully which one she would take.

The tap of shoes on the parquet floor behind her made her turn. She gasped. Standing before her was the most beautiful man she had ever laid eyes on in her life.

He stood just inside the ballroom, hands in pockets, the light making his oiled hair gleam. Not overly tall, he was elegant to the greatest degree but it was his face that drew the eye. He was absurdly handsome, with classical looks, full lips and lustrous dark hair. More than anything, it was his eyes that made him so irresistible-looking: dark, melting and framed by coal-black lashes and the straightest of dark eyebrows.

He's the deadliest peril I ever saw.

As soon as she thought it, she felt guilty. *What about Rupert?* But that thought made no difference. She could only stare at the gorgeous man. He returned her gaze, smiling at her, then walked gracefully towards her, his polished patent evening shoes making a satisfying click on the floor.

'Well, hello there,' he said. His voice was light but musical. 'And who are you?'

'I . . . I know you!' she said, surprising herself.

'Do you now? Who are you? Because I don't think I've had the pleasure of making your acquaintance.'

'I'm Veronica. I'm . . . I'm my father's daughter.'

He laughed. He was closer to her now and, if anything, more handsome the closer he got. The beauty of his dark brown eyes was mesmerising. What gave them that quality? The long dark lashes? The straight brows? Or the fact that they were the colour of melted chocolate? 'Your father's daughter!' he said. 'Well, that narrows it down.'

'George,' she said helplessly, completely undone by his nearness. She could hardly string two words together. Everything she had felt for Rupert now seemed childish and silly, a crush. The great lightning bolt that had just hit her, the one that made her feel faint and yet alive, was surely love. 'In the play.'

His face cleared. 'Oh! Veronica, George's daughter.' He laughed again. 'Then I do know you. But you were much younger when we met, just a child. You're a young woman now.'

'Yes,' she said simply. Only an hour or so ago, she had been terrified of womanhood. Then, all alone, after only a few minutes, she felt as though it was closer than ever. And now she was desperate to be a woman, at least to this man. But how could she hope to have any of the allure of the ladies in the theatre, with their ripe bosoms and sophistication? She had never been more aware of her skinny hips and flat chest. Her hair was still just a thick blonde bob, not styled into curls, and she wore no make-up, with only the strand of pearls for jewellery. She didn't waft in a cloud of scent, wrapped in furs, dripping in jewels. She didn't have powdered cheeks, luscious red inviting lips or nails the colour of blood. This Adonis could surely have any woman he wanted. A mixture of elation and despair coursed through her.

He looked at her quizzically. 'Do you remember my name?'

She searched her memory desperately. 'I . . . no.' She began to blush. 'I don't. I'm so sorry.'

'Don't be sorry. I like it.' He laughed again, not in the least offended. 'I'm Jack. Jack Bannock. How do you do?' He held out a hand and she took it.

His hand was warm, smooth and he didn't grip her but held her with gentle confidence for a brief second. His touch affected her from head to foot, setting something spinning wildly inside her. Then she remembered something.

'You're an actor. I saw you in a film.'

He shrugged lightly, letting her hand go and pulling a silver cigarette case from the hidden pocket at the back of his tailcoat. 'Ah, yes. My film star phase. I expect you saw *The Robber King*?'

'Yes! That's right.' That was how she knew him. She could not remember meeting him when she was a child but she recalled the smouldering dark appeal of the passionate hero of the film. She had seen it three times. That was this man, quite different in his white tie and tails. Jack. She was looking into those eyes right now, the ones she had seen on the screen, projected high above her, in giant intimacy so that she could read every emotion. She had watched him take the heroine into his arms and kiss her. It had been something that had almost made her sick with feelings she did not understand.

Just then, she saw Mama and Billie coming into the ballroom. She had seen them just a few minutes before, and yet it felt like a lifetime since she'd left the ladies' room and come here. Her moment alone with Jack was over.

Mama looked apprehensive when she saw that Veronica was talking to a strange man but as she approached, Jack turned towards her and her face cleared. She looked pleased. 'Jack! It's been an age!'

'Dodo. What a joy.'

Veronica felt herself shrink back to girlhood in the presence of her mother. Mama and Jack began to talk, their voices fading to a babble in her mind. The odd sentences came through but almost as soon as the spell of isolation was broken between her and Jack, the room began to fill with guests. The party had begun.

'What's wrong with you?' Billie whispered, coming up to her sister. 'You looked like you should be on the fishmonger's slab.' She mimicked a stunned expression. Then she caught sight of Jack. 'Oh goodness, it's only the Robber King! Isn't he just crumbly? No wonder you're in awe!'

'Yes, very crumbly,' Veronica said weakly.

'A deadly peril if ever I saw one,' Billie said in a confiding voice.

But Veronica felt too drained to say more.

*

The party was beautiful, that was certain. There was much fuss when Daddy arrived, leading the duke into the ballroom and making the introductions. The cast of the play were assembled inside the door, and the duke moved slowly down the line, exchanging a few words of congratulations, shaking hands and accepting bows and curtsies. Then, the formalities over, the duke was taken to the table of honour, the band struck up and the party properly began. Veronica only had eyes for Jack Bannock, but he was in great demand, summoned over to the duke's table and asked to join them for champagne and the smoking of many cigarettes.

Veronica and Billy watched the proceedings while they lounged at their father's table. They were the only occupants as everyone else had gone off to dance or join other tables. Occasionally people they knew came over to say hello, but even the arrival of Sybille Handforth, the grande dame of the theatre, magnificent in sable furs and a silver lamé gown, to speak to the girls could not match the allure of the handsome man across the ballroom.

And then Jack looked over and caught her eye. He lifted a hand to her, smiled and waved. The Duke of Kent followed his gaze and looked over too, and murmured a word of enquiry to Jack, who answered it. Then Jack stood up, bowed politely to the prince and took his leave. He walked towards the table where the girls were sitting.

'He's coming over here!' hissed Billie excitedly.

Veronica watched him advance, every step making him more radiant in her eyes. He reached her and gave the same small polite bow he had given the duke.

'May I have this dance?' he asked, as the band reached the end of the song.

Veronica gulped. 'Yes, please,' she said and stood up.

The band started their next number. The singer began to croon the lyrics. '*You . . . you're drivin' me crazy . . .*'

She was in Jack's arms. He was only a little taller than she was. They started to foxtrot together, moving in perfect time, Jack leading her elegantly as Mary had never been able to. It was just as she dreamed it might be with Rupert but a hundred times better. No, a million times better.

Jack gazed down at her, smiling. His liquid brown eyes seemed to see her in a way that no one else ever had.

So this is it, she thought, dazed. *This is what it is all about. I'm in love.*

Chapter Three

The funny thing was that at the exact moment Veronica lost interest in Rupert, he seemed to have a much greater interest in her.

Previously, her life outside the schoolroom had been largely taken up with the quiet but intense pursuit of him. She made it her business to keep on top of all his movements, all the time. She even had a notebook called *The Rupert File* in which she recorded all her findings, as though he was some kind of science experiment. No loving mother or doting nurse or dedicated detective could have taken more interest in the most minor doings of cousin Rupert. In it were recorded what he had eaten at every meal when she'd been able to observe him, the times and durations of his walks, the number of cigarettes he seemed to have smoked, and every detail about him she could glean from their conversations, however minuscule. She also wrote at length about her feelings for him, as well as stories, dreams, fantasies and schemes for their future life together.

Then, after the royal gala at the Savoy, the book became

worthless. She had no understanding at all of how she could have devoted so much time and energy to Rupert when all she had felt was the silly hero worship of a child. It had merely been a dress rehearsal, a trial run for the real thing. The real thing was the love she felt for Jack Bannock. *The Rupert File* was put in the cupboard of her bedside table, where it remained untouched, gathering dust.

Around the end of January, Rupert returned to the house, declaring himself ready to finish his play by Easter. He seemed, the girls thought, more confident than he used to be, and appeared more often at family dinners and in the drawing room afterwards to talk to Daddy, or help Mama wind her embroidery silks, or to stretch out on the rug in front of the fire to make jokes with Veronica and Billie, despite Daddy's disapproving gaze.

Veronica didn't mind that. Rupert was still good company and a nice enough young man to spend time with – goodness knew there were few enough of them about – but she no longer had any interest in following him around and monitoring him. She didn't hang around the hall at the time he went out for his walks, hoping he might ask her along, but was breezy and friendly as usual. She thought that she appeared outwardly just the same, and so she had no idea how he sensed a change, or even why he would care, but he did seem to care. As time went by, he appeared to be looking for her, waiting for her, expecting her eyes on him and discomfited when they were not.

One dull February afternoon, there was a knock on the nursery door, and it was Rupert.

'Hello, Vee,' he said. 'I wondered if you wanted to chum me for a walk on the heath?'

Billie and Veronica stared at him. This was unheard of. He had never done such a thing. Veronica had always put herself in his way in order for him to invite her along, and he had never sought her out.

'Oh,' she said, taken aback by his appearance. 'All right. If you're going.'

Billie was not invited and she said nothing as Veronica disappeared off to get her coat and change her shoes.

Once they were out of the house and walking together, Veronica was glad she'd come. But how very strange it was to feel nothing but amiable companionship. A fortnight ago, she had been convinced she would gladly die for him, that life was nothing without him. Now she wondered if he had any other coat but that shabby tweed, and found his pale complexion, light eyes and reddish hair unappealing.

'You seem a little old for the nursery,' he remarked. 'Aren't you sixteen now?'

'What? Oh – yes. Seventeen next month. We ought to call it something else. The sitting room, I suppose. But it's always been the nursery, it's what we're used to.' She shrugged. 'What's in a name?'

'Well . . . quite.' Rupert walked on, smoking thoughtfully. Finally he said, 'Listen, don't get me wrong, but you seem a little different.'

'I do?' She was interested in what he might say, because she felt different. And in her head she was thinking, *Yes, he's right. I'm too old for a nursery. I'm a woman now.*

'A bit standoffish, if I'm honest.' Rupert gave her a sideways glance as they walked along the path. It was grey and foggy and the pallor of the day made Rupert look grey as well. 'You've always been my friend, haven't you?'

'Have I?' she echoed. She was thinking, *This is strange. He didn't seem to notice me much before.*

'Yes. We've been the best of pals, you know that. So come on. Have I offended you?'

'No.' She was surprised, wondering why he thought this must be about him. But perhaps that was natural.

'I must have. You're giving me the cold shoulder like anything. And I must say, it's not very nice of you.'

'I'm sorry,' she said at once, contrite. She might not adore Rupert any more but she certainly didn't want to hurt him. It was just rather odd that previously he had seemed utterly unaware of her devotion but was now hurt at its removal. 'I didn't think I was giving you the cold shoulder.'

'Usually you're jolly keen to come on our walks. We're always chatting and having a joke or something. And now you may as well not even be in the house for all the interest you take. I don't think you should blow hot and cold like that, you know. It's not kind.'

'Oh. Yes, you're probably right. I've just been distracted,' she said. 'There's a plan for me to go to Paris, to a school there. You know, they want to attempt to make a proper girl of me, soften me out and give me some French refinement. I think it sounds awful.'

Rupert stopped suddenly and turned to face her. His

expression relaxed and he smiled at her. When he spoke, the slight tone of petulance had gone. 'Ah, now I understand.'

She blinked at him. 'You do?'

He reached out and took both her hands in his. His hands were hot despite the cold day, his touch almost burning into her skin. Once she would have died with joy at this moment. Now she thought of Jack's warm, smooth hand holding hers as she'd danced with him. Something had changed in her as he had taken her in his arms and whirled her around the ballroom. She'd felt something elemental shift and that she'd been given a glimpse of something eternal and beautiful that was both terrifying and the most wonderful thing in the world.

She knew what it was, of course. It was sex. The thing that she and Billie had been fascinated by ever since Mama had told them how babies were made and what their own destinies would one day be. They called it silly names between the two of them, part of their sisters' vocabulary. 'I can't wait to go to St Ives,' Billie would sigh. 'So much fun to be had in St Ives.'

'If you don't mind leaving with a sack of kittens,' Veronica would reply, and they would both understand what they meant and collapse in giggles. It could be called something else entirely the next day.

How mysterious sex must be. What made one person the kind one wanted to go to St Ives with, and another not? It could not just be looks – although of course Jack was the most handsome man she had ever seen. What was it? And how was it that she had desired Rupert, and now she did not? She had no idea. She only knew that the desire, once so fervent, was dead and gone and would never come back. There was someone else, and to him, she had given herself, heart and soul – and, she hoped, body too although she was hazy about exactly what that required beyond the mechanics.

Rupert was still gazing into her eyes, clutching her hands harder and more hotly. 'You're miserable that we're going to be parted.'

She had been trying to give him an excuse. Now she had made it worse. 'I'm not sure about that—'

'That's why you've been avoiding me. I understand. Listen . . . I've been a blockhead. I haven't really understood what you've been trying to tell me but I do now. You have feelings that you don't understand and I've been terribly insensitive. But I get it now.'

She felt dismay land in her stomach like a rock. 'I can't think what you mean.'

'Oh, come on now, Vee, don't play games. You've been leading me on like anything. Well, I've been meaning to tell you for some time now. I feel the same.'

Rupert was gazing down at her, his pale eyes aglow for once. They had not one eighth of the melting soul in Jack's eyes. Veronica said clearly, 'Please let me go. I don't feel anything.'

'I like the modesty act but we both know it's a big pretence. You haven't been able to take your eyes off me for months. You've got what you wanted. I feel the same. So, what are you waiting for?'

She felt like a fisherman who had gone to catch a trout

and landed, by mistake, a whale. He was right, she had been leading him on, but she couldn't admit it, that was impossible. She would have to front it out. 'I don't want you, Rupert, I'm very sorry.'

'You can't tease, Vee. You girls ought to learn that. Teasing gets you into trouble. Didn't Dodo tell you?' With that, he suddenly jerked her close into his arms and landed his lips on hers. She felt them firm and heavy, pressing hard on her mouth and then, to her horror, the tip of his tongue slid between her lips. She pulled away as hard as she could but he put his hand on the back of her head and she found she couldn't get away as she'd hoped, so she twisted her face away and his tongue was wet on her cheek. As she did that, she pulled back her foot and with all her might kicked out at his shin, landing a fierce blow there.

'Ow, you little vixen!' he cried, letting her go and pulling away.

'Don't ever touch me again,' she hissed at him, wiping her face with the back of her hand. 'Do you hear? Never again.'

She turned to run, seeing a man in a hat pulled low over his eyes laughing at the sight. He said, 'Lovers' tiff, eh!' as she passed, but she didn't reply, simply ran on, heading for home.

Any pity or guilt towards Rupert was gone and she was filled with disgust for him. What had he been thinking?

At home, she said nothing of it to Billie but burned with anger and shame whenever she remembered the filthy feeling of his tongue sliding between her lips. She heard the front door slam half an hour after she'd got home, and shuddered to think of him back in the same house.

That evening Rupert did not come down to supper.

Veronica went to her parents afterwards, as they sat in the drawing room, her mother sewing and her father reading. 'I think I would like to go to Paris, please,' she said. 'As soon as possible, if I can.'

As soon as possible turned out to be some time, as she couldn't start until the new term, but to Veronica's relief, Rupert packed up his things and departed for another long walking holiday, this time in Italy, and the typewriter went with him.

Billie hung over the banister to watch him go. Mama kissed Rupert farewell before he climbed into the waiting taxi, but Daddy didn't bother with anything beyond a brisk wave from his study. Veronica didn't come out of the nursery until the taxi had roared away over the cobbles, taking Rupert to Victoria station, even though Mama had called for her several times. She pretended that she hadn't heard.

'So Rupert isn't your favourite peril after all?' Billie remarked, coming back into the nursery.

'I never liked him really,' Veronica said airily, aware she was lying. She hadn't told Billie about the horrible kiss and the kick. It was too shaming. 'I was only practising.'

That felt true.

Billie flung herself down on the rug next to her sister. 'Anyone can see who's caught you now. That crumbly Jack.'

Veronica blushed but could hardly deny it. She had spent her pocket money on a gramophone record of Jack Bannock singing popular love songs, and she listened to it endlessly in the nursery. It was on now. She would stare at the record sleeve as the disc spun round.

'*My heart is like a vale of violets,*' he sang in his gentle baritone. '*A vale of violets for you!*'

Billie raised her eyes heavenward and wailed, '*A vale of violets for YOU-HOO-HOO-HOOOOO.*'

'Don't spoil it,' Veronica said crossly.

'Spoil it? I bet you hear it echoing in your brain even when it's not playing. The rest of us certainly do. I'm surprised you haven't worn it out.'

Veronica threw herself back on the rug and stared up at the ceiling. 'I can't help it. I think I adore him.'

'So that's why Rupert's been parked, I suppose.'

'Yes. But it was nothing really, I can see that now.'

'You'd better not tell Daddy about your pash,' Billie said. 'He thinks you're a fan, that's all.'

'I am!'

'Bit more than that.'

Veronica rolled over onto her stomach and gave her sister an agonised look. 'I just want Daddy to invite him here. I've waited and waited and he simply hasn't.'

The play had become a success all over again after the gala evening and the pleasure the royal party had taken in the show. It was booked out for months, and Daddy was cock-a-hoop with the box office receipts. Lavish parties were the order of the day again, and although Veronica stayed up late scanning the arrivals, all dressed up under her dressing gown and ready to go downstairs if Jack Bannock arrived, he never did appear. To assuage her longing, Veronica could only play her record and spend farthings on the picture postcards they sometimes sold in the post office of film and stage stars. But she had every one they sold and there'd been nothing new for a while. She was hungering for the sight of Jack with a physical ache. If only he were in a play so that she could go along and see him in person. But there was no news of him.

'You never know,' Billie said with sympathy. 'He might turn up here one of these days. But of course, you can hardly ask.'

They both knew that Daddy would take against Jack Bannock if he thought that Veronica had a crush on him. He had been so obviously happy to see Rupert go. He had also stopped inviting the girls to the theatre as often as he once did. He had noticed how grown-up and pretty they had looked at the gala, and suddenly was much keener on keeping them at home, preferably in the nursery.

'I suppose all I can do is hope,' Veronica said, and she got up to put the needle back to the beginning of her record.

They were sitting around on a sunny Sunday afternoon and Daddy was relishing his freedom from the theatre with large whisky and sodas while he read through a stack of typed papers. As she worked at her embroidery, Mama told Veronica about the arrangements for her stay in Paris.

'You'll be living and studying at the *école* in the Rue de la Pompe. There are many other girls, I'm sure you'll make lots of friends.'

Veronica blinked at her mother. Friends were not something she knew a great deal about. Perhaps if she'd been

to school like other girls, she would have a whole gang of
them, but as it was, there was really only Mary, who lived in
Kent and whom she saw rarely. She was better friends with
Gladys the housemaid, who was not so much older than
she was, than anyone else but Billie. The thought of friends
scared her. She needed her family and she longed for romantic love. What were friends for but interfering and weighing
one down?

'Mademoiselle Laurent will meet you at the station off the
boat train. You'll be travelling with the Stuart-Smiths; their
daughter Amy is going out too.'

She sounds perfectly awful, thought Veronica, quite
unfairly.

Daddy snorted.

'What is it? Do you have something against the Stuart-
Smiths, dear?' Mama asked mildly.

'Who? No. It's this pile of tripe.' Daddy threw the typed
page he was reading onto the floor and brushed the whole
pile after it. It fell with a thud, the pages fanning out as they
hit the rug. 'Rupert's play. He has sent it to me from Lake
Como. Such nonsense. A fine idea, but the execution! Quite
terrible. What a shame. I thought he had promise.'

'We're talking about Veronica going to Paris.'

Daddy looked stricken. 'Don't. I can't bear it. Are you
sure you want to go to that dreadful place, Vee? Full of
ghastly Frenchmen. And Frenchwomen. The French, generally. They've entirely taken over.'

'It's only for a term,' Veronica said diplomatically. 'Just to
improve my language.'

'Veronica's going to learn to *être une femme*,' Billie put in helpfully. 'She'll come back all elegant and *soignée* and doing her hair all day long.'

'You know all this, George,' Mama said. 'You agreed with me that it's a good idea.'

'I didn't realise it was so soon.' Daddy looked sulky and then pleading. 'Are you sure you want to go, Vee?'

'Yes,' Veronica said, although she wasn't really that sure. Most of the time she dreaded it but it seemed like an answer to dreaming her life away on the nursery rug listening to Jack Bannock singing hopeless love songs to her.

Daddy slapped the side table next to the sofa with an open palm, making the dangling crystals on the lamp chink together and the ornaments rattle. 'I can't believe I forgot. I need to go to Paris. I can arrange to go at the same time. That's decided. You'll come with me, Vee. We'll go together.' He grinned at her, his blue eyes bright. 'Won't that be lovely?'

Mama sighed. 'Oh, George. I've made all the arrangements.'

'Then unmake them. What could be nicer?' He reached over and grabbed Veronica's hand. 'We will have tremendous fun. You'll see.'

It was decided that there was no time to go to the island that Easter, not when there was so much to sort for Vee's trip. She was taken on endless journeys into town to be bought clothes of the most boring and dowdy kind, a nice little hat to go with her thick wool coat, and very sensible shoes. Veronica didn't really care much, but it was obvious she wasn't going to learn to be a woman, as Billie had joked, but to brush up her French and study grammar, literature and poetry. Whatever she came back with, it wouldn't be Parisian polish. Nevertheless, as the trip grew closer she found she was looking forward to it.

She missed the island, though. Her birthday was usually spent there, in a day of joyous freedom, when she could row out in the dinghy, watch the birds with her binoculars and sunbathe on the rocks by her favourite little beach. If it was warm enough, there would be birthday cake outside in the afternoon, with bunches of beautiful spring flowers to decorate the table.

'We'll spend the whole summer there,' Mama promised. She took the girls for tea at Fortnum's for Veronica's birthday instead, which Billie liked very much but Veronica felt was nowhere near as lovely as being on the island.

'Oh, I can't wait,' she said longingly. 'Days and days on our own, with no one to bother us.'

'You're a strange fish, Vee Mindenhall,' said Billie, shaking her head. 'Very strange indeed.'

It was certainly exciting to be going to Paris with Daddy. She felt quite like a grown-up. They boarded the boat train at Victoria, a porter wheeling away their luggage as they found their first-class sleeping car.

'We can sleep almost the entire journey,' Daddy said. 'Pity the poor folk in second class. They have to get on and off the train at the ferry.'

'Why?' Veronica asked, puzzled. 'What happens to their bit of the train? Why can't they stay on it?'

'They load our carriages onto the ferry but leave theirs here. Ours get hitched to the French train on the other side, but they board the second-class carriages there.' Daddy grinned at her. 'Lucky us. Aren't you glad that Daddy can look after you and spoil you like this? With your lovely new luggage as well.'

He had insisted on buying her a smart leather suitcase with her initials on it, which was taken away to be stowed in the baggage car, and a travelling case full of what Mama called 'necessaries', which she kept with her for the journey.

Daddy was in great spirits, and seemed to enjoy the fact that he carried his celebrity with him wherever he went, like a coat that he could not take off. Even when people said nothing, the light of recognition in their eyes showed that they had noticed him. Some, of course, either did not know him or hid it, but plenty did.

They went to the dining car before bed so that Daddy could have a whisky while Veronica had a cup of weak tea. The small tables with their pocket-handkerchief tablecloths seemed like something from a nursery. They were almost finished when a middle-aged man came up, smartly dressed, with a carefully trimmed moustache and beetling brows. He put his hand out to Daddy. 'Old man, how are you? What a pleasure to see you again. It's been a while since you've been on the links.'

'Yes, indeed,' Daddy said politely, shaking the hand briefly.

'All well, I hope?'

'Very well, thank you.'

'Good, good. Give my best to your lady wife. Hope to see

you for a round one of these days.' The man nodded, smiled, revealing crooked yellow teeth, and walked off, swaying slightly with the movement of the train.

'Who was that?' Veronica asked.

Daddy laughed. 'I have no idea. It happens from time to time. Someone believes they know me, and imagines I must be from their office or their golf club or their old regiment. They don't wish to be rude so they acknowledge me hoping I won't notice that they haven't used my name. It's a harmless little trick and I play along, as they are keen to get away before I rumble them.'

Veronica laughed too. 'But it must be awful, everyone knowing who you are. I can't think of anything worse.'

'I rather like it,' Daddy said. 'It makes me feel as though I've made my mark on the world.' He gave her a keen look. 'And what do you want from life, my child? Don't you want to be known and recognised?'

'Oh no. If I had my way, no one would ever look at me unless I wanted them to. My idea of heaven is to live somewhere like the island. Then I could do what I liked with no one to stare at me at all.'

Daddy seemed quite pleased with this answer, though he said, 'Perhaps Paris will cure you of that. You never know.'

The train rattled through the night and Veronica hardly slept, while Daddy snored in the berth below hers. She felt the shunts and heard the rattles as the train was run onto the ferry taking it across the Channel. She must have dozed off for some time during the crossing, but she jerked awake when they were disembarked in France. She lifted the blind ever so slightly and peered out of the carriage window, but could see nothing in the early morning darkness. She knew they were on the French side now, as the train was moving again, and after a while she got up and went to get dressed in the WC at the end of the carriage.

Daddy was awake and dressed as well when she got back and he suggested breakfast. 'We'll be in Paris at nine or so. Some coffee will wake us up.'

The dining car was almost empty. They found a table and had ordered breakfast from the waiter when someone came swaying down the carriage and took the table next to theirs. Daddy peered over, curious, and Veronica followed his gaze. The man opposite was extraordinarily neat, in a beautiful grey checked suit with extremely sharp shoulders, a silk shirt and a purple patterned cravat shimmering neatly at his neck. His short brown hair was combed flat and very shiny, but sticking out the tiniest bit at the back. He did not have a handsome face – it was too long, his nose and ears too big, his bottom lip too protruding – but an interesting one that gave the impression of an intense life going on behind the pale, downward-turned eyes. He looked about thirty, though it was hard to tell; he could be any age from twenty-one to forty-five. As soon as he slid into his seat, he pulled out a silver case and extracted a fat white cigarette, which he lit at once. The grey pungent smoke wreathed his head and fought with the smell of kippers in the air.

Daddy leaned over, excited. 'Grey? Hello there!'

The man looked across without interest. Like Daddy, he

seemed accustomed to the attentions of strangers. But as soon as he saw who was speaking, his eyes lit up. 'Well, what do you know? George Mindenhall. The great, the celebrated, the triumphant George. Goodness, what joy! Fancy seeing you on the cattle truck to Paris.'

He had a soft, throaty voice with the hint of a rasp, the accent tight and clipped.

'Come and join us!' Daddy said ebulliently. 'This is my daughter, Veronica.'

'Charmed.' Grey bent his head in Veronica's direction. 'But I'll stay here, George, I'm no fun to be with. I've been awake all night, writing a play.'

'How on earth do you write on a train? I just can't do it, with the noise and the motion.'

'Oh, it's quite easy. No need for pen and paper or blessed typewriter, not at first. I write it in my head. That's how it happens, you know. I close my eyes and summon the muse. It all comes to me in an intense few hours and then I start bashing away, putting down everything just as I saw it play out in my mind. To be quite honest, it rather terrifies me. I can only imagine it's a little like being possessed. Or possibly being some kind of medium in constant conversation with the spirit world. So exhausting.' Grey sighed, and Veronica noticed that he did look awfully tired. The waiter arrived with their coffee and he ordered a pot of his own. 'That's why I need to get to Paris, so I can hole up in my hotel and write it all up as soon as I can before it's gone. I never write half so well at home as I do when I'm travelling.'

'What's it about?' Daddy said, interested. 'Is there a part for me in it?'

Grey laughed, and Daddy looked offended but tried to hide it. 'I'm afraid not, dear George. You know me, I write the best parts for myself and the play is entirely aimed at the young.'

'I can't think what you mean,' Daddy said.

'You know very well. You're a crowd pleaser, I'm a crowd shocker. You deliver good old-fashioned melodrama and I present high chic with laughs and a healthy dose of eroticism – modern stuff. Not better, just different.'

'I suppose you mean that your actors spend a great deal of time in their nightgowns,' Daddy said stiffly.

Grey burst out laughing and pointed his cigarette at Daddy. 'That's exactly it, George, you've got it in one.'

Veronica was amazed at the other man's audacity in putting her father into a box that did seem a somewhat inferior one compared to modern eroticism. But Daddy seemed not to be as infuriated as Veronica thought he might be.

'The public do seem to like it,' he conceded graciously. 'I'm well aware of that. You must be raking it in, Grey.'

'We must make hay while the sun shines, one never knows when the tempests will come and spoil the crop. But yes, things are going well. My last is still playing on Broadway and in London, with a show opening in Sydney too. I'm meeting some American producer in Paris who might want to film it. Lots of lovely lolly in the film world.'

Daddy looked interested again. 'I'm meeting a producer too. Irving Winger from Chromium Pictures.'

'That's the very man.' Grey stubbed out his cigarette. 'How funny.'

'Shall we get together in Paris? A cocktail and a chat perhaps?'

'Let's,' Grey said. 'I'm at the Louis Dix. Send me a message.'

The waiter was approaching with a tray laden with food.

'Ah,' Grey said. 'Your breakfast. I shall leave you in peace. We will meet anon in Paris.' He stared suddenly at Veronica and she had the strangest feeling that he had been very aware of her all the time that he and Daddy had been talking. 'Have you considered joining your family profession? How about an acting career, hmm?'

'Er . . . no,' Veronica said. 'My sister has, though. She longs to be an actress.'

'I can see some of your mother in you,' he said, in his clipped way. 'Your eyes have a special quality: direct, transparent, sincere. We look for that in actors; it's very important. You have the looks, with that strong facial structure. You should think about it.'

Veronica stared at him. No one had ever talked about her in such terms before. What was a strong facial structure?

'Veronica is going to school,' Daddy said firmly. 'She won't be going on the stage.'

'Pity,' Grey said, reaching for another cigarette. 'Those kippers look rather splendid. Waiter, I shall have the same.'

And he turned to a notebook he had put on the table and did not look over again.

Chapter Four

Paris was beautiful and exciting. Veronica hadn't meant to be enchanted but it was impossible not to be enraptured by the elegant houses, the wide boulevards lined with cafes and bistros, and the delightful parks. In the days before Daddy left, he didn't take Veronica to her school in the Rue de la Pompe, but kept her with him. She had a room off his suite in the grand Hotel Marly, opposite the Tuileries Garden and a few minutes from the Louvre, and while he was busy she roamed the streets around the hotel and visited the museums.

From what Veronica understood, Daddy had come to Paris and rented the palatial suite to impress the film producers who might make a movie of his hit play, and perhaps even cast him in it. She could guess that it was not likely. Daddy might look young on stage, where his dyed black hair and thick make-up could create an illusion of youth, but there was no way that he could look on film like anything other than a middle-aged man. The hero would have to be young and handsome, like Jack Bannock. But Daddy might be able to be a co-producer and make some money that way.

Veronica made the most of her freedom while she could. Soon she would be locked up in the school, her days measured out in lessons and activities while they tried to teach her to be a cultivated lady. She read books, she knew lots of things. Wasn't that enough? She only hoped it would be more interesting than it sounded. She suspected it was just a way to use up her time and get her ready for some sort of life in adulthood, which no doubt meant marriage.

As she wandered the streets of Paris, she became fascinated by the people. She walked past huge cafes with dozens of small tables outside on the pavements, aproned waiters flitting between them with loaded trays. The avenues were broad and grand, with motor cars chugging up and down, avoiding the horses and carts wheeling along at their own slower pace. Down by the river were endless book stalls and art stands, with people stopping to browse. She observed men in coats and hats, children in their school uniforms and sensible coats; but it was the women who interested her the most. There were mothers with children hanging off their hands, plump nurses taking their charges to the park and to school. She saw housemaids, shop girls, housewives bustling into the stores, and working women in plain suits and sensible shoes. Sometimes she saw nuns, and once some peasant girls from abroad in embroidered full skirts and clogs and strange headdresses. But it was the fashionable Parisiennes she found most entrancing. She gazed at graceful young women wearing long coats, smart heels, sometimes draped in furs, stylish hats perched on their coiffured hair. They seemed to know some elusive secret to a perfect life. In the hotel lounge, where Veronica loitered at times with her book, drinking a tangy citron pressé for as long as she could spin it out, she watched ladies in silk dresses and pearls sitting at the little tables, their faces perfectly made up, talking to one another, or sitting with smart gentlemen. Veronica was sure they were being witty and sophisticated and alluring in a way that was utterly mysterious to her.

She remembered Billie saying she was going to learn to *être une femme*. Be a woman. Billie seemed to know how to be a woman without being sent abroad, and Veronica was sure that Mama had needed no lessons at all. But it seemed that she would need to learn lots of time-consuming tricks and chores to make her hair sit in polished curls and her lips gleam scarlet and her eyelashes curl darkly on her cheeks. It reminded her of her night in the theatre. It all looked like so much work.

What she would really love most would be living on the island. She imagined being in the large white house on her own, with just the birds and the sheep for company, exploring the ruins and sailing her dinghy when she wasn't reading her books and thinking about life. All of this complex and demanding world of being a grown-up would be kept at bay. On the island, even Daddy and Mama seemed to revert to being young again. All the trappings of life in the city and in the theatre, the social round and the obligations, rehearsals, performances, anxiety about ticket sales, all fell away. Everything became simple and straightforward, just about being alive and part of nature and being one's real self: simply breathing and existing.

But for now she was watching wildlife of a different kind: the women of Paris, like beautiful birds themselves. There was one woman she had seen three times in the hotel lounge. She was, to Veronica, utterly exquisite, with dark hair and a porcelain complexion made more startlingly perfect by contrast with her scarlet lips. She seemed to wear only black, with many ropes of pearls at her neck, but she did not look in the least funereal. She would be led by a waiter to a discreet table by a marble pillar where a handsome man awaited her. He would get to his feet, kiss her hand and position her chair for her. They drank coffee and, once, champagne.

The woman was Veronica's dream of what she could be if she tried hard enough. Exquisite and perfect as a painting, she was slender and graceful, and seemed unruffled.

Not like me, Veronica thought darkly. *I'm fierce and sturdy and there's nothing to be done with my hair, it will always be thick and wiry. I can't glide through life like that, I have to stamp and climb and stride. But how wonderful life must be to have what she has.*

She was sure that the couple was not married. They arrived separately and left together with an air of anticipation. There was an intimacy and intensity about them that spoke of love but not marriage, though what the difference was, Veronica did not know. She only knew that the easy familiarity, the effort at tolerance and the amused affection between her parents was entirely missing here.

As she watched them, Veronica tried to imagine them making love, but it was such a powerful image that she had to banish it from her mind.

Daddy had taken her to lunch and had retired upstairs to sleep, and Veronica was kicking her heels in the lounge with her book. The beautiful dark-haired woman was sitting at her discreet table, but quite alone this time and drinking tea instead of coffee. Veronica was peering at her from time to time over the top of her book, wondering if the woman looked more like a painting by Sargent or by Ingres, when she saw the waiter approach her with a note on a silver platter. The woman took it in her fingertips, opened it and scanned it, before saying a few words to the waiter, who bowed and left. Then she looked up and stared directly at Veronica, who immediately dropped her own eyes and pretended to be lost in her book.

After a moment, though, she could not resist looking up, and the dark-haired woman was gazing back at her intently. The moment they locked eyes, the woman lifted her hand and beckoned a finger towards Veronica, who looked around to be sure it was her that was meant. The woman nodded slowly at her, and so Veronica slid off her seat and walked across the lounge towards her, book in hand.

'You are English,' said the woman with a strong French accent as Veronica reached her.

'Yes, that's right,' Veronica said, thinking she had never sounded so English. 'How do you know?'

'You look very English and you are fair and you're holding an English book. What is it?'

'*A Tale of Two Cities*.'

'How appropriate to read that in Paris.'

'Have you read it?'

'Oh, yes. In French, of course. I have also read it in English, but I am not so very good that I could appreciate it perfectly and enjoy the story.'

'Gosh, but your English is wonderful! I'd not like to try my French on you.'

'Well, that is only to be expected. We French understand that sadly we must learn English to get on in the world, but we comfort ourselves that it is probably better than hearing our beautiful language butchered.'

'I suppose there is that.'

'Why don't you sit down and tell me your name?'

'My name is Veronica Mindenhall.' She slid obediently onto the chair opposite. The woman was even more beautiful close up. She had the kind of perfect face that Veronica had only seen on the screen and looked as though she was somehow glowing from the inside. Her eyes were a dark, dark blue that was almost purple, the smudged dark shadow on her lids making them look like bruised amethysts.

'Why are you not at school, Veronica Mindenhall?'

'I'm on my way to school,' Veronica said in a martyred tone. 'I'm going to Mademoiselle Laurent's academy in the Rue de la Pompe when Daddy can be bothered to take me there.'

'And until then, you are whiling away your hours in one of the most expensive hotels in Paris, reading Dickens in the lounge all alone.' She laughed. 'What an unusual schoolgirl you must be. What is your father doing all this time?'

'Very important things,' Veronica said vaguely, unsure how much she should give away of her father's business. 'In the suite. Meetings and so on.'

'And so on,' echoed the woman before laughing again. 'How amusing you are. Will you have some tea?'

'May I have hot chocolate?'

'But of course. So much nicer. We shall both have some.' The woman beckoned over a waiter with the merest lift of one arched brow and ordered the chocolates in rapid French.

'What is *your* name?' Veronica asked when the waiter had departed.

'You can call me Irène, I think that is easier.' She pronounced it 'Ee-ren', which sounded much prettier than the English version.

'Aren't you meeting your friend today? You usually meet the man with the thin moustache when you're here.'

Irène stared straight at her. 'You're very direct.'

'I don't mean to be rude,' Veronica said hastily.

'That's quite all right. You're not rude. I was meeting him, but I've received a note to say that he cannot make our rendezvous after all. So I am all alone for an hour or two. I ought to go shopping but I have an appointment at Chanel later and I don't want to think about dresses for the entire afternoon. Besides, I am intrigued by you.'

'I say, your English is marvellous,' Veronica said sincerely.

'Thank you so much. It is a good thing to speak another language. I will be honest, we spoke several languages at home, and English was one. And of course I was made to study it. You should try to learn French when you are with your mademoiselle, make the most of your time. It is very becoming. Italian is also good to know, but do not bother with Spanish or German. That is my advice.'

Veronica was filled with a desire to learn French at once. Anything to please Irène.

'Ah,' Irène said, 'here are our chocolates. While you drink yours, I want you to tell me all about yourself, right from the start.'

It was only when she paused for breath that Veronica realised how long it had been since she had properly talked to someone. In conversations with Daddy, she had to be careful, always on her guard to make sure that she said nothing that might upset him, and there was quite a lot in that category.

Irène, though, listened thoughtfully and sipped on her hot chocolate while Veronica gulped hers in between her breathless paragraphs. Despite her intention to be discreet, she had soon told Irène a great deal about her family life, her father's profession and her own hopes and dreams.

'I am fascinated,' Irène said, when Veronica had ground to a halt. 'I know no one who acts for a living. It is not something we do. Writing, yes, very respectable if one must work. Painting, yes, as long as one is extremely talented and one creates great art. Music – perhaps. And there are respectable professions if one absolutely must. But not the stage. Is it possible to be on the stage and be a gentleman in England?'

Veronica was hurt. 'Of course. The theatre is not like music hall or pantomime, you know. It's a proper art form.'

'I do not know what you mean by music hall but I assume you are talking about the difference between comedy and opera. There is, of course, a great distinction.' Irène shrugged. 'Don't be offended. It's my ignorance and no reflection on your father. There are great men of the theatre, but I tend to think of the writers, directors and designers . . . not the actors.'

'Daddy directs plays, and produces them,' Veronica said quickly.

Irène nodded. 'You have convinced me.'

'What does your friend do then?' asked Veronica, still feeling defensive. 'The one you meet here all the time.'

'Oh! He does nothing. That is what a great many of my friends do. They are rich, you see.'

'How can they be rich if they do nothing?'

'That is the great mystery. Money makes money and if you have enough, you task others with looking after it and making more. It is a great privilege, of course. And men have arranged things so that they pass the money on to each other, father to son, uncle to nephew. Some women are heiresses, but usually women are left with less than the men, so most of us must find a man with money if we are to live like humans.'

'Oh.' Veronica had never thought of all this. She knew that Daddy made the money but that Mama enabled it by caring for him and for their home and daughters. She had only just begun to think about what independence would mean for her, and how she might earn a living, but she also knew that there was the safety net of Daddy's success, the houses they owned and, now she thought of it, no brother to take it all away. But could she really rely on Daddy and his money all her life? She would have to support herself at some point unless she married and she simply could not imagine that. She felt a sudden insecurity, as though she had been walking on thick ice and then heard, somewhere beneath her, a distant crack. 'Will you marry your rich friend then?'

'Sadly not. I am afraid he is already married.'

Veronica blinked at Irène. She had guessed that they were not married to one another but she somehow hadn't imagined he had a wife already. 'Is he?'

Irène gave her a sideways look. 'Come. You are not exactly a child, even though you have that naive quality of an English schoolgirl. You must be sixteen?'

'Seventeen.'

'Then you are probably aware that there any many kinds of relationships between men and women, inside marriage and out of it.'

'I suppose so.' She thought of how she had once heard Mama shouting and crying late at night, berating Daddy for a friendship with an actress at the theatre. She hadn't wanted to hear it and had shut it out and tried to forget it but that was when she had first become aware that the bonds of marriage were not as sacred as she thought. Of course, it was obvious that there must be love outside marriage. After all, she would give all she had to have an affair with Jack, married or not. But even so, it was hard to shake the great belief that marriage was the rightful end of all love affairs, a place of safety for men and for women. 'Will he leave his wife for you?'

Irène looked shocked. 'Of course not. The mother of his children? He would never do something so disgraceful and I would not want him to!'

'Then . . . what will happen to you?'

'Ah, that is the question.' She smiled but her amethyst eyes were suddenly sad. 'These arrangements are hard where there is love, you see. Easier where there is none. I'm sure that Philippe and I will part before too long. I must find someone else to love, someone who is not married, and then it will be my turn to become a respectable wife and mother, and to learn how to turn a blind eye to my husband falling in love with young women like me.'

Veronica gaped at her, appalled. 'You make it sound inevitable.'

'Oh, it is inevitable.' Irène shrugged. 'It is the way of the world.' She leaned forward. 'You must make the most of your youth and passion and allure while you can.'

'*Être une femme*,' Veronica said, now feeling gloomy. Irène's message seemed to have taken her back to the idea of womanhood as a life pre-ordained, a struggle and a compromise and a sacrifice. 'That's what I have to learn, apparently. And now I see why.'

Irène laughed. 'Of course. Now, if you have nothing else to do, why not come with me to my appointment? It can be your first lesson in how to *être une femme*. If it is successful, perhaps I can set up an academy of my own.'

*

76

Veronica left a note for Daddy at the desk to be taken up to his suite, and then went off with Irène.

'The atelier is quite nearby,' Irène said, as they stepped out into the street. 'We will walk there.'

They strolled together through the city, Irène pointing out important shops and the entrances to the passages, the covered shopping alleys that looked like secret corridors of treasure. Veronica was proud to walk next to her elegant new friend, although she felt more of a bumpkin than ever.

'Ah, here we are, the Rue Cambon. Have you heard of Mademoiselle Chanel?'

Veronica shook her head.

'Well, stay quiet and listen. Prepare to watch an artist.'

They arrived at a grey-stone terrace of townhouses, with the ground floor a glass-fronted boutique. Low white awnings over the windows carried the name 'Chanel' in flat black capitals, while on the wall by the double-fronted door was a black sign with the same lettering in white.

'Is this a dress shop?' Veronica asked.

'A shop and a workshop and a design studio. Inside you will find all sorts of masters and mistresses of their craft. That is why we call it an atelier. Now, we are right on time.'

When the door was answered, they were led inside to a simple yet luxurious interior of white marble, a staircase curving away to the upper floors. Irène and the smart woman who met them in the hall chattered away in rapid French as they ascended the stairs and Veronica followed, looking about her as she went. On the next floor, they were led into a comfortable room carpeted in a velvety beige with long windows over the street below. There were alluring racks of dresses and jackets, a curtained changing room, lots of mirrors, and elegant sofas and chairs lined the room, with tables alongside dominated by vases of white flowers. Everything was white or black or a kind of honey colour, and the overall effect was clean, modern and the most stylish thing that Veronica had ever seen.

She loitered quietly against one wall, drinking it in, while Irène went to the racks and began to flick through the clothes, still talking rapidly and evidently with pleasure to the lady who had led them up.

The next moment, the door flew open and a small, slim woman came in. She was simply dressed in a plain black skirt, a white shirt open at the neck where ropes of pearls were twisted, and a soft white cardigan with gold buttons, the sleeves pushed up to the elbow. It was ordinary enough and yet she looked, to Veronica, extraordinary. It was not even her clothes that were most compelling; beyond their obvious elegance, she had a strong face, with a long, pointed nose and sharp chin, dark hair worn short in polished dark waves, and intense brown eyes under strong, straight, slender brows.

As soon as this woman had entered the room, the atmosphere changed to one of reverence and fear in equal parts. She was followed by two ordinary-looking women in aprons who carried baskets and had tape measures around their necks, a calm man in a suit wearing glasses, and another, more harried-looking younger woman in a suit, who had a large notebook, sketchpad and a collection of pencils.

Veronica pressed herself back against the wall, hoping to

remain invisible, and at first this seemed to work, as the new arrival was concerned with greeting Irène and then inspecting one of the racks as she fired questions at her staff. But suddenly the intense eyes were fixed on her, and Mademoiselle Chanel was gazing straight at her, her wide mouth fixed in a straight line, one brow lifted.

'Who is this?' she asked in French, which Veronica understood perfectly.

Irène explained in French that this was a new friend of hers, an English girl – might she stay and watch the fittings?

Veronica had no idea how she understood all this, when the French was as rapid as any she had heard that day.

'Hmm, English?' Mademoiselle Chanel stood back and regarded her carefully, one hand on a hip. When she spoke again, it was in English, delivered in her low tones, prettily tangled by her strong French accent. 'Yes, of course, I can see that. You cannot mistake the English.' She moved towards Veronica. 'Perhaps you know Lady Jean Campbell?'

'I'm afraid not.'

'Oh! Well, never mind.' She fixed her with another look. 'Are you related to Winston Churchill?'

'Not a bit.'

She shrugged. 'One never knows.' She seemed to lose interest in Veronica, and turned her energy and attention back to Irène. 'Now, mademoiselle, let me show you what I have created for you.'

The next two hours flew by. Veronica edged along the wall and dared to perch on an armchair so that she could watch the proceedings in more comfort. It should have been deathly dull to watch a dressmaker at work, but it was completely absorbing. Even Veronica, who never gave clothes much of a thought, could see that the articles that Mademoiselle Chanel handed to Irène were superb in their cut and subtlety, their fluidity and style. A dark-red wool suit set off Irène's dark colouring perfectly, the skirt narrow over the hips and long to mid-calf, the jacket nipped in at the waist; a cream blouse emerged in beautiful tiny pleats at the sleeves and neck. A plain black dress similar to what Irène was already wearing was made chic with a white pointed collar and matching cuffs, and a row of pearl buttons down the front. A dark blue sequinned column evening dress fell like an electric waterfall from Irène's slender shoulders to the floor, the fabric moving like silk as she turned in front of the mirror.

Each time Irène tried on a garment, Mademoiselle Chanel pushed her glasses onto her nose and frowned, then barked in rapid French at her assistants, moving Irène back and forth so that she could examine her from every angle. She summoned a seamstress, grabbed a tape measure or some pins and made some minuscule adjustment to whatever was being worn. Even though the change seemed so tiny, the garment would always look better in some mysterious way. Once Mademoiselle Chanel demanded her pad and quickly sketched out an idea for another glamorous evening gown, this time trimmed with feathers along the décolletage and at the hem, which Irène enthusiastically endorsed.

Time was getting on when Irène suddenly turned to Veronica. 'But we must have something for you! Mademoiselle Chanel, is there anything you think would suit my friend?'

She turned her sharp face back towards Veronica and retorted, 'She is a little young to be wearing Chanel!'

'It is never too young to find your style, to discover the power of fashion, surely, Mademoiselle Chanel? She is seventeen. It is the right time, is it not?'

'Hmm. Perhaps. She has a way to go. Come here, child.'

Veronica stood up and walked over to the slender Frenchwoman, who was still scrutinising her through those dark, intense eyes. She was in awe of the energy and artistry she had seen over the two hours, and although rather afraid of Mademoiselle Chanel's fearless self-possession and confidence, she was very drawn to her too. The direct brown-eyed gaze seemed to see right into her.

'And yet,' Mademoiselle Chanel said thoughtfully in her musical voice, 'you have something. A certain strength. Let me see. That fair hair, and those blue eyes – you are striking. Your looks would suit my summer designs. I'm dressing my clients for the autumn already but . . . Come, we will try something.' She turned to the gentleman who had quietly watched proceedings from the corner and commanded him to fetch something. While he was gone, Irène changed back into her day clothes and the things she had tried on were taken away to be given their final alterations in the sewing rooms on the top floor. The gentleman returned with clothes draped over his arms.

'This!' declared Mademoiselle Chanel, taking a dress from the pile. She held it up. 'Yes. This.'

She handed a navy-blue crêpe dress to Veronica and indicated the curtained changing room. Veronica disappeared behind the curtain and took off her lace-up shoes, woollen stockings, tweed skirt and thick jumper. What a yokel she looked in them, she realised. A pudgy schoolgirl. A child. Standing there in her knickers and vest, not even a proper brassiere yet despite being seventeen, with her skin pale in the sudden chill, she felt not like a pudgy schoolgirl but like a nymph. The pudge was her thick clothing. Underneath she was slim. She took the blue dress and unbuttoned it, then slipped it over her head. It was light but carefully constructed with a double lining that gave it a fluid, smooth look. At the neck, a round collar was completed with careful, almost invisible navy embroidery. Tiny navy ornamental buttons ran in a double row down the front to a belt in navy-blue crêpe, and the skirt fell to her knees with pleats cut into both sides so that the front looked straight. The hem was edged in more of the invisible embroidery. The sleeves fell below her elbow and buttoned at the embroidered cuffs. It was so simple and yet also the most beautiful dress she had ever put on in her life. It hardly mattered that she had bare legs and feet.

Irène put her head around the curtain. 'Oh. *Oui. Oui, oui.* Come out and show Mademoiselle Chanel.'

Veronica stepped shyly out into the salon to be met with the strong gaze of Mademoiselle Chanel again as she scanned her up and down. At last she said, 'It is just right. You suit it perfectly.'

'We will take it,' Irène said happily. 'Veronica can wear it home.' She looked to the head of the atelier. 'Please package up her old things, madame.'

Veronica gasped. 'But I can't!'

'But you can,' Irène said firmly.

'I highly advise you accept the kindness of Mademoiselle Irène,' Mademoiselle Chanel said crisply. 'Such offers are rare. And I am prepared to let her buy this dress, even though it is, strictly speaking, not finished.'

Veronica could not think what was not finished about it, but she said nothing. It was clear no one was going to listen to her.

Irène and Mademoiselle Chanel talked quickly in French, embraced, and the designer walked out of the room, followed by her small entourage, while Veronica's things, except for her stockings and shoes, were taken away to be packed. She felt that the beautiful white box with the Chanel wording on it, and the stiff bag in which it came, were both far nicer than the things inside, which had come from the Army and Navy stores last autumn.

Just before they left, Irène took Veronica to stand in front of one of the many mirrors. They looked so contrasting: the elegant dark-haired Frenchwoman and the fair, blue-eyed girl. She was still in her Chanel dress, but now with lace-ups and woollen stockings, and the coat she had come in.

'You are very pretty,' Irène said. 'But you do nothing to heighten it. You do not believe in it. I think you do not even care about it.' She opened her bag and took out a small tortoiseshell-backed hairbrush. 'I've been longing to do this.' She quickly ran it through Veronica's thick hair, applying hard and rapid strokes until the hair beneath it grew shiny and malleable. She issued a quick command to an assistant and was soon handed some pearl hairpins. With these, she deftly pinned Veronica's hair into place. Then from her bag she took a powder compact and a lipstick before smoothing powder over Veronica's cheeks and applying a slick of red over her lips, which she rubbed almost completely off with a fingertip, leaving the hint of a blush there. 'It's a start,' she said, looking quizzically at her handiwork. 'But can you see the effect?'

'Yes,' Veronica breathed. A quite different girl looked back at her. This was not the skinny, barefaced girl in the silk dress who had stood alone in the ballroom of the Savoy. This was a young woman with sophistication and something like beauty. The dress brought an indefinable quality, despite the solid woollen coat over the top of it. She saw her eyes glowing. *Is this really me?* she thought. Then she thought of something and her face fell. 'But how can I pay for all this? Daddy will have a fit when he finds out I've bought a Chanel dress!'

'Don't be silly,' Irène said, putting away her lipstick and compact. 'I would never have suggested this if I meant for you to pay.'

'You can't buy me things like this!'

'Don't worry, my dear, I won't. Philippe has an account here, naturally. And he has one at the Galeries Lafayette too, which is lucky, as that is where we are going right now to get you some decent shoes and stockings. And perhaps a coat. I'm afraid that one is scarcely fit for the bonfire.'

Chapter Five

Veronica was worried how she would explain her new clothes to her father but in the event, he did not even appear to notice that she had them.

When she returned to the suite, elated with the silk stockings and dark blue shoes that Irène had bought her in the Galeries Lafayette – a place of immense wonder and charm, full of indescribable luxury and treasures – she was also horribly aware of the bag she was carrying that gave away where she had been. But Daddy didn't notice anything at all. He was far too taken up with fretting about the fact that Grey Oswald was coming over that evening, wondering what to have waiting for him.

'Perhaps he is a cocktail man,' Daddy said, picking up the detritus of the day from the table. 'He seems very much a drinker of martinis, doesn't he?'

'I suppose so,' Veronica said, taking off her coat and putting it, along with the guilty bag, in her bedroom.

'Well, I shall play it safe with champagne. One can never

go wrong with that. Pol Roger, I think. I'll telephone down now for them to bring it here.'

Veronica watched him curiously. It was true that she had been struck by the special aura of the man on the train but she had not expected someone in Daddy's position to be quite so affected by him. 'Who is Grey Oswald?'

Daddy stopped clearing away papers and scripts to look at her reproachfully. 'Oh, Vee. A daughter of mine and you don't know who Grey Oswald is?'

'Of course I know something about him.' She walked to the sofa, enjoying the sensation of wearing her new dress. It was so light and liberating after her heavy wool things. 'He's written quite a lot of super plays, hasn't he? Very daring things. He acts in them too.'

'That's right. He writes society comedies – brittle and bright and very witty. But really, Vee, his success . . . it frightens me. He is so prolific, so influential. He's leading the way into whatever new world is waiting for the theatre. He's the future.' Daddy looked downcast suddenly. 'I have to admit that I'm the past.'

'No!' exclaimed Veronica.

'Yes . . . yes, yes.' He brightened. 'But perhaps an alliance with Grey will keep me at the forefront of things a little longer. And perhaps I can learn something from him too.'

'I should think he'll be learning things from you,' Veronica said loyally.

'Ha! I doubt it. But one never knows. Anyway, it's still rather exciting that he's coming to us for a drink when he is no doubt in high demand. Come on, help me stuff this all away and then we'll be ready.'

Veronica helped her father clear away his papers and then she retreated to her bedroom to brush her hair again, and repin it with the lovely little pearl slides. Then she took out the tiny bag containing the things Irène had bought her at the Galeries and removed a small gold compact, a gold lipstick with a column of waxy red inside, and an even more intriguing palette of dry black paint, which, when moistened, could be brushed through her lashes to darken and stiffen them. It seemed quite ridiculously decadent and an outrageous demand for attention to put such things on her face, but Irène had seemed to think it the bare minimum of what she should do.

Now she sat in front of her dressing room mirror and carefully tried to do what Irène had managed so effortlessly: a patting of the creamy powder over her face with the little puff; a smear of the red on her lips, which she pressed together, and then damped down with a tissue. She finished with a brush of the black stuff through her lashes and the tiniest sweep through her fair eyebrows.

'Well,' she said, staring back at her reflection, noting the darkened lashes and brows. 'It does work after all.'

She looked older and prettier and more alluring. That was obvious. Standing up, she pivoted on the heel of her new shoes, and admired the spin of the blue dress as the crêpe flared out.

This morning she was a schoolgirl, and this evening a *belle* in Chanel.

How suddenly things could change.

The loud rapping at the door of the suite brought her out of her bedroom in time to see Daddy open it to Grey Oswald, who stood in the doorway, a picture of a stylish English gentlemen in his three-piece Prince-of-Wales-check suit and scarlet tie with matching silk pocket square. He wore a smart hat, and around his shoulders was draped a chestnut-brown glossy fur stole. His wide trousers ended in sharp turn-ups and the shiniest of leather shoes.

'Georgie boy,' he exclaimed, and then said in his clipped way, 'What a delightful sight you are. But not as delightful as that bottle I can see chilling in the ice bucket. Make haste and pop it, won't you? I'm dying for a drink.'

'Grey, do come in.' Daddy stood back to let him enter the room.

'I say, what a view of the dear old Tuileries. How much does this set you back a night, George?' Grey went over to the long windows and peered out, pulling out a cigarette to light as he did so.

'Not as much as your suite at the Louis Dix, I suspect,' Daddy said drily.

'Ha! You're probably right. But it's all work, isn't it, old boy? All for the career. We must let these Hollywood ruffians see that we know how to live in style. They might have the loot, but we have that. Don't you agree?' He turned back to the room, his small eyes twinkling and his thin upper lip drawn back in a smile.

He's not at all crumbly, Veronica thought, as she came out into the sitting room, *but there's something very magnetic about him.*

'You remember my daughter, Veronica,' Daddy said, indicating her.

'Of course.' Grey perused her with the sharp eyes that had the quality of being able to absorb everything in a second. 'The fierce little thing with the face. But you've changed, my dear! Isn't that dress new?'

'Yes,' she said awkwardly and flicked a glance to Daddy, who was busy with the bottle in the ice bucket.

'Ah.' He seemed to grasp everything at once. 'And very nice too.' Under his breath he added, 'As it should be, considering where it's from – if I'm not mistaken. And someone has taught you to paint a little as well. Paris has worked its magic on you rather faster than I expected. How interesting. More and more I can see that you do indeed have a face.'

'I'm more than a face,' she said tartly, though she was secretly very pleased that Grey had noticed her new look. He was a man of taste, that was obvious. He had seen immediately who had designed her dress, and that made her feel even more grown-up.

'Of course you are. And I'd love to hear how you got your hands on that little number later.' He spoke again at his normal volume. 'But oh, George, how divine – champagne!'

*

They sat and drank champagne in the suite, Grey holding forth in a stream of witticisms and gossip, with Daddy occasionally joining in or taking the conversational reins for a while before Grey deftly took them back, all the while puffing on his stubby white cigarettes. Veronica sat and listened, enjoying the rapid chatter while she sipped on her own small glass of champagne. The golden liquid prickled on her tongue and quickly made her feel fuzzy and slightly happy and sleepy at the same time.

'And what are your plans for the evening?' Grey asked.

'Veronica and I shall have supper downstairs, I expect,' Daddy said.

'I am sure there is no better company in Paris,' Grey said courteously, nodding to Veronica, 'but perhaps you could do me the honour of accompanying me to La Vieille Ferme nightclub? Have you heard of it? Ridiculous place, really. The floor is covered in straw, the tables are in little pens. The waiters are in peasant clothes, wine in flagons. It's all a novelty; it will be gone in a few months, or restored to sanity at least – if someone doesn't accidentally burn it down, with all that straw scattered everywhere. Anyway, for now, it is the hottest ticket in town and the revue is quite something apparently. I've been invited to go along and see some singer strut his stuff on the stage. Someone angling for a part in something, I expect, but Hester is a big fan. Why don't you come with me?'

'Ah.' Daddy looked torn. 'What a wonderful invitation, Grey, but I'm afraid Veronica . . . a schoolgirl . . . I don't think—'

'Nonsense, George. She looks twenty-one. Go and put some more lipstick on, dear, and we'll go out. The dress you're wearing is more than pretty enough.'

Daddy looked as though he was wavering. 'I suppose she does look quite mature with her hair brushed.'

'Oh, yes please.' Veronica jumped up, eager. Then a thought came to her and she said in dismay, 'But my old coat! I can't go out in that.'

Grey reached for the fur stole he had draped over the back of the sofa. 'I believe I have the answer to that, my dear. My little bit of squirrel will serve very nicely, I think. Now, is that the end of the excuses? Because I am rather keen on getting myself some filet mignon and a martini *tout de suite*, even if you're not.'

Veronica had not thought that the day could become any more exciting but now she was in a taxi, sitting between Grey Oswald and her father, the soft fur of Grey's stole tickling her chin. The lights of Paris twinkled, the river shimmered with their reflections, and the Eiffel Tower was lit up, looking like a rocket made of gold net piercing the sky. Perhaps there was something to be said for the social whirl of a glamorous city.

The taxi arrived only a few minutes later, and soon they were being ushered past the velvet rope across the door to the Vieille Ferme – 'Don't get excited, it's there for effect,' Grey murmured as they passed the rope, 'they let any old person in, I'm afraid' – and then they were led into a nightclub with tables set, just as Grey had said, in little wooden pens with gates to them. Bales of straw were set along the side of the room and more straw was scattered on the floor. Lanterns glowed on the tables, most occupied by chic-looking guests in evening clothes, very much at odds with the farm theme, although most seemed to be enjoying themselves.

They were led to their table by a waiter in a strange puffy white shirt that dropped almost to his knees, leggings criss-crossed with leather straps and clogs. They filed into the pen to sit down at the table bedecked with a red-checkered cloth.

'Absurd and disgusting,' Grey said as they sat down, his small eyes suddenly hard. 'One hardly dare light a cigarette. I expect the food is filthy too. One doesn't come to Paris for something like this.' He sniffed. 'I rather wish I hadn't let Hester talk me into it.'

Daddy summoned a waiter and, in French, asked him to sweep away the straw around their table. 'It's a hazard,' he explained. 'Understand? Dangerous.'

The waiter disappeared and came back with a broom so that he could sweep away the excess straw.

'It's a start,' Grey said, lighting up a cigarette. 'Thank you, George.'

They ordered dinner and were halfway through their food when the lights dimmed even further, and the stage was suddenly illuminated. A master of ceremonies came out onto the stage and the curtain rose to show a small band sitting at the back. On stage, the farm motif was dropped, and the band were dressed in black tie. The man on the stage, in white tie and tails and heavy stage make-up, was clearly there to warm up the audience but his patter mystified Veronica. She couldn't understand any of his French, although plenty of other people were laughing at whatever it was he was saying. Before long, though, he introduced someone, and the audience applauded with anticipation.

On strolled a small woman with coppery hair rolled into fat sausagey curls pinned back against the sides of her head, and with dark red lips. She wore a black satin dress with dramatic fringing at the sleeves and hem and sturdy high heels. She was clearly a crowd favourite already and launched into a series of rollicking songs delivered with a raspy, vibrating singing voice.

'Hideous, isn't she? But she has something,' Grey acknowledged, as they listened. 'Slightly too raucous for my liking. And no good for a musical. She's pure cabaret with all that implies.'

Veronica had no idea what he meant, though Daddy agreed enthusiastically and gave his own opinion, which happened to be the same as Grey's.

After the French lady singer left, there was a pause. They had finished their supper and the plates had been removed. A martini and a large flagon of wine had eased Grey's fears of a fire, as he was smoking away, and the whole room was full of smoke and the buzz of conversation, which died away as the master of ceremonies emerged again for another routine of jokes.

'I think this might be the act we've come to see,' Grey mused. 'Let's hope so. The joy of the farmyard is distinctly waning.'

The little made-up man on the stage was closing his

93

remarks, and as the band prepared to strike up, he said, '*Mesdames et messieurs – Jacques Bannock!*'

'Ah, yes, that's the one,' Grey murmured. 'The Robber King himself.'

Veronica gasped. She had been feeling quite sleepy after her dinner and a glass of red wine on top of the champagne, but now astonishment jerked her awake and before she had time to take on what was about to happen, her adored Jack was strolling onto the stage.

He looked, of course, quite perfect in his evening clothes, just as he had on that night weeks ago. If anything, he was more handsome under the stage lights, his eyes as meltingly gorgeous as they had been when he had smiled at Veronica and danced with her on that magical night in the Savoy ballroom.

What more could happen today? she wondered, as her heart fizzed and thudded. *What could be more perfect than to see Jack?*

'One must admit, he is a looker,' Grey murmured, leaning forward across the checked tablecloth.

'He can sing too,' Daddy remarked.

'Can he now? Well, let's see.'

Jack moved with grace and confidence around the stage as the band played the introduction to his hit 'A Vale of Violets', and the audience burst into anticipatory applause.

'Haven't you heard him before?' Daddy said in surprise. 'They even know him here.'

'I saw his little film, but I avoid cheap music,' drawled Grey, but the sharp light in his eyes gave away his interest.

Jack sauntered slowly to the back of the stage where his microphone stood. As the band reached the end of the long introduction, he turned, opened his arms and began to sing his famous hit.

Oh! thought Veronica with rapture, feeling his voice coat her as though she was being dipped in chocolate. It was ten times more beautiful than on the gramophone record, and replete with more richness, timbre and allure than she could ever have expected.

Oh, Jack, she thought, gazing at him with shining eyes, filled with that mysterious feeling that she knew was love. She watched, utterly absorbed as he moved about the stage, taking his microphone stand with him, the black cord snaking after him. He sang with fabulous ease, owning the room and everyone in it. No one could look at anyone else, or listen to anything but the honeyed tones of Jack's voice.

The song came to an end, and the audience applauded and cheered with delight.

'*Merci!*' Jack said into his microphone. 'I'm afraid my French doesn't extend much beyond that. You're very kind. If you can bear it, I'm going to sing again. This is one of my favourite songs, written to mark a special day in my life. It's called "Fear No More".'

'Oh, this is lovely,' Veronica said to Grey. 'It's one of my favourites.'

She was fizzing with excitement and pleasure at Jack's nearness, at being able to gaze on his handsome face and listen to his voice, and be near him. Then she noticed that

Grey had gone very still, his hand holding the constant cigarette poised over the ashtray. His gaze was fixed on Jack, full of an intensity she felt quite frightened of. He looked almost fierce, and very far from the languid, witty Grey of earlier. His mouth was set in a thin line, a deep crevice lay between his brows, and hollows had appeared in his cheeks.

Veronica looked away quickly. She didn't like Grey's expression, though why, she did not know. She looked back at Jack, who was bringing 'Fear No More' to the orchestral bridge, and while the band played, the trumpeter wailing a riff on the tune, he strolled to the front of the stage to smile at his audience. Almost at once, his eyes fell on their table, close as it was to the stage, and he recognised Daddy immediately, smiling and touching two fingers to his forehead in a gesture of salute.

Then his eyes met Grey's. As Veronica watched, she saw a look of surprise sweep rapidly over Jack's face, and then a start of recognition. The expression on his face looked almost like a question and then showed apprehension. The band reached the end of the musical bridge and Jack missed his cue, only by a few seconds, before he took up the next verse and sang again. But he had stopped walking about the stage. Now he was focused on that one table, where Daddy, Veronica and Grey sat together. He finished 'Fear No More' and, in a voice of languid loveliness, he said, 'This song is a love song despite the melancholy name. It's called "The Last Song of Summer".'

The band struck up the plaintive minor-key melody and Jack began to sing.

'*When you left, those years ago, you took the sun with you,*
And when you left me all alone, you took my meaning too.
I'll always think of our lost love,
When I hear the last song of summer . . .'

Veronica had never heard this song before and, as Jack said, despite its melancholy sound, there was hope and the promise of return in its lyrics. Every summer might end but it would lead to the next one and better days would come back, bringing happiness with them.

But she could not respond to the song as she had hoped. Jack's voice remained enchanting beyond anything she'd ever heard but all she could do was watch as Jack sang the entire song to Grey, never taking his eyes from the other man's face. It was as though the rest of the world, including her, had ceased to exist.

A chill seemed to grip her as she realised.

So that's how it is.

She felt totally and completely hopeless.

After Jack had left the stage, Grey seemed very keyed up, his fingers shaking slightly as he lit yet another of his stubby cigarettes.

'Come, we'll go backstage,' he said, standing up. 'I can't bear this farmyard another minute. The sooner this place closes, the better.'

He was striding for the side door before they had barely had time to stand up themselves.

'Grey can be somewhat determined,' Daddy said, as he and Veronica followed. 'And I think he believes he has found someone rather special in Jack.'

'I think so too,' Veronica said in a small voice, but Daddy didn't hear. She followed, lost in her own misery as they made their way backstage, Grey somehow making it clear they were allowed to go to the dressing rooms so that no one stopped them. They passed the red-haired woman singer as she headed out wrapped in a fur coat, a cigarette in her red lips, accompanied by an ugly man with a sharp moustache with whom she was arguing loudly.

The next moment, Veronica was following Daddy into a large dressing room where Jack was already changed from his dinner clothes into smart grey trousers and was buttoning a white shirt at the cuffs. Grey was perched on the wooden bench below the bare lightbulbs of the make-up mirror.

'We simply won't take no for an answer,' Grey was saying. 'Let's leave this filthy place and get a drink somewhere civilised. I think you and I have a lot to discuss.'

'Do we?' Jack said lightly. He seemed to be focused on his cuffs and then choosing a tie.

'I can't think why our paths haven't crossed before,' Grey said with a smile. His voice was less brittle than normal, a touch of something husky in its timbre.

'They have, I think, you just didn't notice.'

'How ridiculous of me. I must have been ill. But they have now, and we must make up for lost time. I believe you and I should work together.'

98

'Should we?' Jack raised one eyebrow at Grey. 'We both write songs. We both write musicals. We both sing. Surely we are competitors, not colleagues?'

'Well, we will see about that,' Grey replied. 'Tie that tie, dear boy, and let's get out of here.'

Daddy coughed. 'Jack, a marvellous performance. Congratulations.'

Jack turned, slightly startled as though just realising that there were other people in the room. 'George! I had no idea you were coming this evening.'

'Neither did I.'

'But I'm so glad you did. Always a delight.' Jack finally turned his gaze to Veronica. 'Hello, dear child. How are you?'

Veronica stared at him, miserable. She had felt all her happiness drain away in the last thirty minutes. The fun of her new clothes, her sense of being stylish and attractive and grown-up . . . it had all turned to ashes. She was nothing to Jack and never would be. And now he had made it plain. She was a child. 'Very well, thank you.'

'Good, good.' He turned away as if he'd barely heard her.

Daddy took her arm. 'I'm going to whisk Veronica away. She's really too young to be out this late in any case. You two go and enjoy your business talk.'

'We will speak very soon, George,' Grey said absently, his eyes following Jack as he moved around the room, fetching his jacket and smoothing his hair.

'Goodbye, George, and thanks for coming,' Jack said. 'You too, Veronica.'

'Night, boys,' Daddy said, and he began to push Veronica gently towards the door.

'Goodbye then,' she said. 'Goodnight, Jack. Goodnight, Grey.'

'Sweet child!' Grey said. 'Goodnight. See you again in London, no doubt.'

'What about your fur?' she asked suddenly, starting to pull it from her neck. 'I must give it back.'

'Keep it, dear girl! Keep it. It doesn't signify at all. And it suits you much better than it suits me.'

In the taxi on the way back to the hotel, Daddy held her hand gently as if to comfort her.

'Did you understand?' he asked her.

She nodded, not wanting to talk about it.

'It's normal in our world, you know that.'

She did know it. Daddy had often spoken of the men and women in the theatre who preferred to love others like themselves. She and Billie had called them seahorses, but they had forgotten why. They had enjoyed speculating on who was and who wasn't at the parties at home.

'Are you shocked?'

'No. Of course not.'

'Good. Good girl. It's just the way of things. You must be tired. We'll be back at the hotel soon.'

Daddy didn't seem to understand why she might feel crushed.

I'm an idiot.

Why hadn't she guessed that Jack was a seahorse? It

was obvious now. And that meant that he would never, ever love her.

Oh, lucky Grey. If only Jack had looked at me like that, sung to me like that!

She put her forehead on the cool glass of the window as they drove back through Paris. How late it was.

But I will always love him, she thought. *I can't help it. Even though it's hopeless. There's nothing I can do about it.*

Chapter Six

The women at the next table were talking about their cooks, Veronica realised, and complaining about the standard of what they were preparing.

'Her soup is perfectly disgusting,' one said to the other. 'Great globs of grease floating in it, lumps of gristle. It's peasant food!'

'My dear, Agatha is the same. She cooks as though she hates us.'

Veronica giggled into her cup. After nearly six weeks at the academy, she found that the confusing babble of French all around her was resolving into something she could understand without trying too hard. Her lessons must be doing some good, she realised.

Irène said, 'What is so funny?' She loved to laugh and very much liked Veronica's jokes.

'Nothing really. I'll tell you later.' She indicated the women at the next table. 'Something I overheard.'

'Fascinating. I hope it was about love affairs. So that is enough about all the lovely things I have seen and done this week. How is school, *ma chérie*? Any interesting stories that will amuse me?'

'Boring,' Veronica said glumly. 'I don't like it much. Mademoiselle Laurent still adores me of course.'

'Oh, she does? I hadn't realised she had taken her fondness for you quite that far.' Irène looked at her a little wickedly over the top of her teacup. Once a week, she liberated Veronica from school and brought her for tea in the hotel where they had first met. Sometimes they went shopping, although there were sadly no more outings to the atelier and boutique of Mademoiselle Chanel, but most often she and Irène simply chatted. Irène seemed to find her endlessly amusing as Veronica recounted the stories of her school days and the girls she shared her lessons with. 'However, I'm not surprised your teacher adores you. But how far do you permit her to adore you?'

Veronica laughed. 'What do you mean?'

'Do you let her . . . kiss you?'

'What?' Veronica stared at her, astonished. 'Kiss me?'

'Well, schoolgirls can often create a passion for a teacher. Or another girl . . .' Irène lifted a slim black brow. 'Is that you, perhaps?'

Veronica felt her cheeks redden but she tried not to show that she was embarrassed. She liked to think that she was sophisticated and then Irène would say something that would make her feel like a clumsy child again. Mademoiselle Laurent adored her because she was clever and wrote interesting things but there was no sense of anything else. She couldn't imagine wanting to kiss her either, although she

103

was a handsome woman, still young and with an intelligent intensity that was appealing and attractive.

'No,' Veronica said firmly. 'I'm not like that . . . I mean, I don't believe there's anything wrong with it, but . . .' She knew that there was at least one romantic relationship at school, where the intensity of emotion and the need for physical closeness went beyond the bonds of simple friendship. It didn't bother her; she envied people finding that reciprocated need in one other. While some of the other girls would have been sickened or appalled by it, Veronica was not. She knew, however, that the world at large felt differently and that girls who loved each other would have to keep discreet about it when society was so firm in its expectations that women would love men, marry them and bear their children. She said now to Irène, 'It doesn't bother me a bit if that's what people want. But it isn't me.'

'I already know that,' Irène said with a slight shrug, putting her teacup down. 'I can tell you will love men.'

Veronica was embarrassed again, as though she was somehow being somewhat traditional and boring, even though the idea of loving men – whatever that meant – was still so strange and darkly exciting, an adventure waiting for her at some future point still not known. She was embarrassed by both her normality and the almost painful admission that she desired something that ought not to be spoken of. She didn't know what to say. She couldn't admit to Irène that she was already in love with a man – and ironically with one who could never love her back.

'It is better to love, even though it is full of pain and woe, than never to love,' Irène said, gazing at her intensely. 'And if you love men, believe me, you will know that pain and woe. It's inevitable. But there is also joy – if you're lucky and find the right man. If you are unlucky, you will love where no joy is possible. I hope that is not the case.'

Veronica felt scarlet creeping up her neck. *She has guessed! She knows I love Jack and that he's a seahorse!* She felt mortified.

Irène looked suddenly concerned and reached out to take one of Veronica's hands. 'Has something happened, *ma chérie*? Has someone already hurt you? Have they touched you?'

'No, no,' she stuttered, aware she must be bright red. She wanted to explain but didn't know how.

'Wicked men will try to use you,' Irène said. 'Do not let them.' She rubbed her fingers over Veronica's hand, then looked earnestly into her eyes. 'If you wish to know what it's like, I can arrange it.'

'Arrange what?'

'For you to experience love . . . the way it should be experienced.'

Veronica gaped at her.

'I know you think it's outrageous. But it is done for men, you know. They are taken to women who can school them in the art of love, so that they know what it can provide and how to give pleasure themselves. So it should be perfectly acceptable for you, a woman, to be taught the same lessons. Better that than you're taught lessons that are harsh and unkind, that might perhaps scar you for life and make you unable to enjoy yourself ever again.' Irène looked knowing. 'Let's say you are only ever given vegetable soup, cheese and bread to eat your whole life. You would stay alive, perhaps even like it . . . but you would never know the joy of eating the finest food in the world, all the exquisite flavour and choice, the art of cooking, the pleasure and sophistication in the finest things . . . the enjoyment that marks a life truly well lived.'

Veronica stared, taking in what Irène was saying. It seemed extraordinary, and yet also . . . what she said made sense. Veronica had always had the romantic view that there was only one person who could or should be intimate with her, and that experience would be ecstatic – quite naturally and without practice – because they were the right one. But why should that be true? Perhaps it would be safer and more sensible to learn the ropes without the emotional intensity of falling in love. She was deeply curious about what it would be like, and had thought about it a great deal, ever since Rupert had arrived in their house. But then . . . 'Would it be right?'

Irène laughed lightly. 'Right? What do you mean?'

Veronica realised that Irène was always challenging her notions, received from school and church and all the rest, about what was supposedly right. She was the mistress of a married man and was perfectly at ease with it. Now she suggested that women could take control of their bodies rather than wait for a man to select them. More than that, she was honest that plenty of men would attempt to use Veronica whether she liked it or not. What was right about that?

'I mean . . . I don't think I'm supposed to . . .'

'Supposed to? Why should other people tell you what to do with your life? What right do they have?'

'I don't know, I think it's just the done thing.'

Irène's face hardened just a little. 'I think you should forget these rules. They are made to control us women. Take your father. Do you think he's faithful to your mother?'

Veronica shook her head; she knew he was not.

'I am sure you wish he were, but you accept it. But is your mother faithful to him?'

'Of course.' She couldn't dream of Mama doing any such thing, and she saw at once what Irène was saying. Mama would be judged harshly but Daddy was not.

'Why is it right for him and not for her? If marriage vows are so sacred, then why is he allowed to break them and she not? I hope Philippe's wife has taken a lover too, it's only fair. You must be on your guard, *chérie*, against the double standards in the world. You must defend your freedom to be yourself and do as you please. Defend your liberty to think your own thoughts and determine your own destiny as much as you can. I sense that you already feel this.'

'I think so,' she said slowly. She thought of the island – its appeal was the utter freedom from the constraints of society to be herself. She remembered the day when she was only ten, when she had taken the scissors, cut her long hair and thrown the ponytail in the sea, revelling in her power to chuck it away. And she knew that if Rupert, when she had loved him – or Jack, if he had been able to love her – had offered to take her to bed, she would not have hesitated, no matter what anyone thought. If she had happened to love one of the girls at school, she would not have hesitated then either. Irène was offering her an opportunity that might not come her way again.

Veronica said slowly, 'You think you can find someone to . . .' She was about to say 'take me to St Ives' when she remembered how meaningless that would be to Irène. She dropped her voice right down. 'Someone who would make love to me properly?'

Irène leaned forward, her dark eyes candid. 'Oh yes. That is exactly what I am saying. I have a very kind and skilled acquaintance, a charming man, and he would be an excellent first lover for you.'

Veronica looked away. Despite what she had been thinking, she felt half scandalised and then ashamed of herself for feeling that way. After all, she was from the world of the stage and the theatre, the great and forgiving forum where individuality and self-expression were praised and encouraged. Daddy had always said that art was freedom. But here was Irène, not from that world, offering her an experience that she knew would horrify Daddy. No matter how much freedom he had himself, he was not so keen on that freedom for his wife and daughters. As Irène had pointed out, there were limits for women.

'I . . . I don't know. I'm not sure,' she said slowly, still feeling beetroot in the face.

'You don't have to decide now,' Irène said. 'Think about it.

And we will see. Now, let's talk about something else. What are you reading? Did you start that book I gave you? I want to hear everything you thought about it.'

Later, when Irène had bid her farewell and gone her way, Veronica walked slowly back in the direction of the Rue de la Pompe, scuffing her shoes along the pavement as she went, lost in thought. She looked, in her woollen coat and sensible shoes, what she was: a schoolgirl. And yet she wasn't quite that. She knew it. Sometimes men who passed her in the street looked her up and down, occasionally muttering something under their breath as they went past – she did not understand their French but knew it was something obscene. They also knew that she was not a child any more. One man, striding past, had reached out and pushed a hand quickly onto her chest, squeezing her hard where he touched her, before moving swiftly on. She'd gasped but before she could protest he was some distance off. Only the tingling pain in her chest told her it had actually happened. It was violating.

I will never know what it's like to love Jack, not physically. I'll always love him in my heart and soul but there'll not be anything else. Perhaps I should accept Irène's offer and let it happen. Find out the mystery. Because I haven't a hope of falling in love now I love Jack.

The more she thought about it, the more sensible it seemed.

Her life in Paris was soon to come to an end. She had already asked if she might stay on after the end of term – and Mademoiselle Laurent had talked vaguely of an art tour of Italy for some of the girls, which sounded exciting – but

Mama had written back to say that the political situation was far too unstable to stay in Paris, let alone go to Italy. Veronica would have to come home. That meant she would have to decide quickly.

*

Dearest Vee,

How is life in Paris, you lucky, lucky, lucky blighter? If it weren't for the war they say is coming, I'd have been allowed over but now they won't even talk about it. Blast it all! I'm going to be stuck here, I just know it.

But guess what? I'm luckier than you are right now. Because guess who Daddy and Mama had over here last night? Only your Prince Charming, Jack Bannock. He is so crumbly that I do know why you're so in love with him. It's only when you see him in the flesh that you remember how divine he looks. The thing was, he was with that awful Grey. The ugly one with the craggy face and cravats and endless cigarettes, who talks like a pretend person, not like a real one. Even his jokes, which are funny, sound as though he carefully wrote them all earlier, even though he couldn't possibly have. It's as though he's made up. Anyway, they seemed to have a fine old time and stayed up very late making cocktails and Grey played the piano and Jack sang, which I have to admit was very fine (I was on the stairs of course). They are writing a show together, which is supposed to be the next big thing. Daddy is cock-a-hoop because they persuaded the Chromium picture people to make a film of his play but now they are arguing if he is too old to be in the film. The film people want someone younger, like Jack – who won't do the films any more, he says.

Don't be jealous that I saw your darling. You after all get to be in Paris and drink tea with la divine Irène. So it's all fair.

But darling . . . do you think Jack is a seahorse with Grey? Because that is what it looked like to me. I'm sorry if you didn't guess. But perhaps you did . . .

See you soon. Can't wait.

Lots of love,

Billie xxx

Veronica screwed up the letter and threw it away, sobbing.

On Sunday mornings, the girls walked to the nearest Protestant church for the service. Mademoiselle Laurent did not come, but Fräulein Dorfmann, an older German lady who taught languages, accompanied them. Afterwards, their Sunday treat was to go to the Bois de Boulogne for ice cream and the chance to wander free for a while among the woods and lakes of the park.

All the way through that morning's service, Veronica felt sick. At any moment, she was sure, something dreadful would happen. The roof of the church would be split by lightning or the aisle would crack and sunder and she would be sucked down into the bowels of the earth as punishment for her wickedness.

Then her sensible, rational voice would start scolding her.

111

You are being ridiculous. There are far more wicked people than you, probably sitting in the next aisle. You have done nothing wrong and whatever it is you do will not be wrong, if you don't hurt anybody.

Besides, she was quite sure that what it was that Jack and Grey must do – surely kissing at the very least – was considered much more wicked than what she was planning.

This was her last chance. The summons home had come. The train had been booked and her journey back with the Stuart-Smiths was all arranged. She had no idea what awaited her once she left Paris. All plans were on hold. They would have to see what happened next.

We will go to the island first, Mama had written. *And after that, who knows?*

That was what had decided her. The world she knew was about to be rocked to its foundations, anyone could tell. Now, with the trees in the full blossom of late spring, the skies blue and bright, there were soldiers on the streets of Paris, along with an air of nervousness and apprehension, a sense of something approaching and the desire to clutch at the last vestiges of peace and happiness. Veronica was not immune to it, and nor were the other girls. There were plans afoot of one kind or another.

The service droned on, and she thought to herself, *If war does come, I might be dead in a year. And I can't die without ever going to St Ives. And if I'm only ever to go once, it had better be a decent trip.*

She had written to Irène:

I've thought about what you said and I think you are right, it makes sense to learn the ways of the world while I can. Can you arrange it for me? Perhaps when we have tea on Sunday?

Irène had sent back a note:

Mais oui, chérie. *Leave everything to me. And don't be scared.*

Of course she was scared. She had been terrified in the bath this morning looking down at her slim, pale body with its almost flat chest, wondering if she would pass muster. She vacillated between being desperate to call it off, and being relieved that the decision was made and all she could do now was go with it.

All morning, she had been dry-mouthed and speechless and now, as the service began to near its end, she was almost frozen with terror. Irène had made the arrangements, and outwardly all looked as normal. When the service ended and they all filed out, no one would perhaps have noticed that the slender girl – she had lost weight in Paris – in her wool coat, a little too heavy for the weather, had eyes wide with apprehension and shaking fingertips. They walked in two wobbly lines to the Bois. This was their favourite time of the week, when they were allowed to escape for just a little freedom, although it was well understood that anyone infringing the precious privilege would lose it for all of them.

When they arrived at the grand cafe that was their

rendezvous point, it seemed that half of Paris was out, drinking coffee or pastis or wine at the cafe tables, walking in the sunshine, or taking children to the boating lakes or to the zoo and other amusements.

As soon as they arrived, Veronica could see that Irène was already waiting at one of the tables, a demitasse in front of her. She was wearing a pale spring coat of lavender wool and a hat with a jaunty lavender ostrich feather in it, the light colour setting off her dark looks beautifully. She called and waved. '*Véronique, ma chère!* I am here!'

'Fräulein,' Veronica said, her voice coming out strangely gruff, trying to get her teacher's attention as she looked over the lines of girls, counting heads. 'Fräulein, my friend is there! Mademoiselle is expecting me for tea, as usual.'

After a moment, Fräulein saw Irène waving. She was already a familiar figure after taking Veronica out on several Sundays. 'Yes, go, go, go. Be back on time, Veronica!'

It was that easy, Veronica thought, as she walked towards Irène's table. That easy to walk out of childhood and into womanhood. Now the mysteries, whose call she had first felt with Rupert and then with Jack, and that seemed packaged up with all her fears of not being quite enough, or perhaps being too much, those mysteries were about to be revealed to her. It was overwhelming, terrifying . . . But – she looked around at the many couples promenading, sitting at tables, chatting and flirting – the mysteries had been revealed to many, and they had lived to tell the tale. The women who had several children had clearly done it more than once. It could not be that bad.

'My little one, you look terribly pale,' Irène said, frowning and taking her hand. 'And you're cold! You're frightened.'

'No! I mean . . . yes.' Veronica sank into a metal bistro chair, feeling sick again.

'There is still time to say no,' Irène said gently. 'In fact, you can say no at any point. No one will be angry.'

'I'm fine,' Veronica said, feeling braver but mostly because Irène had given her this way out if she wanted it.

'Good. Come, we will go and meet André. You can get to know him a little first. It will make things easier.' Irène stood up and waved to Fräulein Dorfmann, who was still trying to manage her charges as they began to scatter off across the park. 'Goodbye, Fräulein! I will bring her back safe and sound, you'll see.'

They walked out of the Bois and towards the Champs-Élysées. 'We will meet André at a nice little brasserie before we go to the apartment,' Irène said, as casual as if they were arranging a simple lunch.

Veronica found her voice leaving her once more. She felt wobbly and unsure again, but decided the best course was simply to follow Irène with the obedience of a little dog, and listen as she chattered on about the races at Deauville where Philippe was taking her for shopping and gambling and socialising.

What am I doing? she asked herself. But then she remembered that her heart was broken. Jack didn't love her and never would, or could. Life was changing for ever, with the war that seemed all but certain. What did she matter? What did any of it matter? This would be her blow against oblivion and her attempt to take something from the chaos that seemed about to engulf them all.

'Here we are. Follow me.' Irène led her under the dark green awning of an anonymous-looking brasserie. Inside, the walls were pale pink, hung with art deco prints of the city. A waiter came forward, Irène spoke in quick French and he led them towards the rear of the restaurant. Veronica stared at the prints as she passed, trying to keep her thoughts on anything but what was to come.

'There he is,' Irène said quietly as they approached a table at the back. 'Now, see, doesn't he look nice? And he doesn't bite.'

Veronica looked past her to where a young man was standing up. He was very smart in a dark blue suit and waistcoat, a red pocket square and a silk tie of dark blue diamonds and as soon as she saw his face, she felt a wash of relief.

What have I been imagining? she thought.

She realised she had been expecting a sort of hairy beast of a man, almost slavering at the sight of her. Instead, this man was much younger than she expected, and he looked slightly shy himself. He was handsome, as Irène had promised, with very fair skin, light brown eyes and dark hair slicked down neatly with oil. A slim moustache traced its way over his upper lip.

He looked, she thought, just a little like Jack. Nowhere near as exquisitely handsome and without the melting chocolate eyes, but still . . . reminiscent. She was still terrified, of course, but this would, she felt, make it easier.

'André!' Irène offered her cheeks to be kissed rapidly three times and then turned to gesture to Veronica, standing awkwardly behind her. She spoke in English. 'May I introduce Veronica? She is the friend I told you about.'

'*Enchanté*,' André said, bowing politely. 'Please, join me.'

He stood away so that Irène could take her place on the dark green banquette, and the waiter held out a chair so that Veronica could sit on it. When they were all sitting, she was facing Irène and André like they were a little inquisition.

The waiter returned almost instantly with menus.

Irène took one. 'Now, first, lunch.' Her dark blue gaze slid to Veronica. 'You must eat, even if you're not hungry. And wine, too, I think . . .'

Veronica said nothing. She had never felt so awkward in her life, unable now even to look in André's direction, but staring desperately at the print on the wall above Irène's head, or at the tablecloth, or at the water carafe. Anywhere but at André.

Irène did not rush her. She ordered a meal for them all, of which Veronica managed a mouthful or two though she tasted nothing, and the wine, which was a little easier to swallow, and so she consumed a glass over the lunch. She managed to answer a few questions – André politely asked her how she was enjoying Paris and about her school – and to join in the conversation a little, but mostly she sat in silence, trying to keep her composure as she listened to André and Irène talking easily about art galleries, concerts and the doings of their friends.

Finally, when tiny cups of black coffee were sitting in front of them, Irène leaned in towards them both. 'Now, my sweets. We know why we are here, and I think it is time for our little

arrangement. Veronica must go home before too long, you
know.'

Veronica managed to lift her gaze for a moment to the
young man opposite, half fearing he would be laughing, but he
looked earnest and quite nervous himself. She was relieved and
then almost felt a bond between them even though nothing
had happened, with barely a word exchanged between them.

'Yes,' André said, 'that would be best.'

His voice, now she listened properly, was gentle and soft,
almost boyish. Could he really be the sophisticated lover that
Irène had promised? He did not look that much older than
she was.

'Then come, let's go,' Irène said, and summoned the waiter.

The moment had come at last.

They left the brasserie and walked a little further on before
Irène turned off the boulevard and led them to a tall house
of the kind with large flats on each floor, built around a
concealed courtyard. The concierge barely looked up as they
passed through the doorway in the gate, and into the courtyard before mounting the stairs.

'No lift!' Irène said cheerfully as they went upwards, passing the grander apartments on the lower floors. They were
not quite in the rooftop when she came to a halt in front of
a shiny black door and pulled out her key. Inside was a neat
and rather beautiful apartment, more of a garret, furnished
sparsely but with style.

'My bolthole,' she said to Veronica, as she led them in.
'André, you have a key, do you not?'

'Of course,' he said with a bow.

Irène was being bright and gay and keeping the atmosphere as light as she could. Veronica's heart was thumping hard, and not from the climb up the stairs. She felt clammy and sick.

'There is everything one could need,' Irène said cheerfully. 'The little bathroom, the kitchen, and of course my bedroom. You must see the view! It's quite wonderful this high up. Come on.'

She led them into the bedroom. It was as plainly furnished as the rest of the flat, with a simple double bed made up in white sheets and ivory blankets. Lamps stood on either side, on two wooden tables painted bright red. A red and pink armchair in the corner, a towel rail, a small bookshelf and an armoire were the only other items of furniture. Irène stood by the window and gestured towards the view. 'You see? What a view of the Eiffel Tower! It doesn't get better. Having said that . . .' – she pulled the curtains shut – 'perhaps a little more atmosphere is best.'

Veronica released a shaky breath as the room sank into gloom.

'Now,' Irène said smoothly. 'I'm going for a walk. I'm going to leave you two sweet things here and you must amuse yourselves. I will be back in an hour or so, that is really the most that can be done. Don't worry, Veronica, André will look after you, I promise. *À bientôt!*'

And she strode out of the room and away, the front door shutting behind her in an instant.

They were alone.

Chapter Seven

It was not what she expected.

Before this afternoon, she had imagined a kind of tortuous doctor's appointment performed by a forceful and hairy giant, which she had to tolerate as best she could and perhaps, *perhaps* get the faintest inkling of what its potential could be if she were in love with the performer of the deed.

She had not anticipated this small, neat man with his immaculate hair and slender moustache, well dressed and sophisticated. He was a world away from the hulk she had feared, and much more like herself than she had expected. That alone made her less fearful.

And she had not anticipated that André would be so delicate. They stood together in the gloom of the bedroom and he talked to her softly as he gently helped her out of her coat.

'May I unbutton your dress?' he asked politely.

'Oh yes, please do,' she replied. She felt his fingers shake just a little as he undid the buttons until it slipped down to the floor, then he helped her step out of it. She felt the cool of the room on her skin and it goosebumped, but he ran a smooth hand over her bare arm and warmed her. She had expected to flinch, but his touch was reassuring and calmed her instead.

He looked earnestly into her eyes. 'You are very beautiful,' he said gently, 'and you are doing me a great honour. I will go to the bathroom and undress, and you can do the same, if you still wish it. Do you?'

She nodded quickly and he left her alone to take off her underwear and climb under the cold covers of the bed, where she lay, trembling, her heart thudding. It was not terror, though. There was a great excitement coursing through her and she clutched the pillow hard, feeling like she wanted to weep or shout, but she just lay there.

André returned with a towel wrapped around his waist. He was slim, like her, a soft scattering of dark hair over his chest, and as soon as she saw his naked torso, she shut her eyes tightly. She felt him climb into the bed beside her and she trembled.

'You can open your eyes, you know,' he said softly.

'I don't want to. I'd rather feel than see.'

'You can do both?'

She shook her head.

'Very well. Whatever you please. May I touch you?'

'Of course. That's the point, isn't it?'

'Perhaps. But I need to be sure. I won't do anything you don't permit.'

'I'm here, aren't I?' She knew she sounded tart but she couldn't help it, it was the nerves.

'All right.'

121

The soft hand was on her arm again and then stroked across her collarbone, over her shoulder and onto the other arm. She shivered.

'You don't like it?' he asked, concerned.

'Yes . . . I mean, no . . . I like it.'

'You are trembling. Don't be scared. May I kiss you?'

She thought briefly of the unpleasant kiss she had had with Rupert, the tongue forced between her lips. It had changed what she had imagined kisses to be: the passionate but static press she saw in films. But with André, it might be something else entirely. 'Yes,' she said firmly, her eyes still screwed shut.

She felt him shift closer to her. The warmth of his body was pleasing, along with the weight of him as he leaned into her. A hand stroked her hair.

'So pretty, your hair,' he muttered. 'Very blonde. Very English.'

Then he ran his smooth palm down her cheek, turned her face a little towards him and put his lips on hers. She felt the soft line of his moustache on her upper lip and cheek and a tremble in his breathing.

She pulled away and opened her eyes. His light brown ones were close to hers, his face so near she could see the freckles and marks on his pale skin, and the dark moustache. 'You're nervous too, aren't you?'

'Of course,' he said, and smiled.

'But you're a very capable lover, aren't you? That's what Irène said.'

'Well, she shouldn't have said that. No, I am not. I mean, I might be but it is not what I believe about myself. But I

122

am a man, and you are an innocent and beautiful girl and you want me to be your very first experience of love. I am honoured and also . . . of course, nervous.'

'Is it your first time?'

'Not . . . exactly.'

'Not exactly?'

'Well, I have made love. But not like this. Not with someone like you.'

'How old are you?'

'I'm almost twenty-three. And you?'

'Seventeen.'

'Then the time is right for us. We will learn more together. Now . . . will you let me kiss you?'

She nodded. He smelled sweet and tangy, like lemon and honey mixed together. She closed her eyes again and now he moved much closer to her, pressing his weight on her, and began to kiss her, slowly and gently and yet insistently so that when she instinctively opened her mouth to him, it seemed like the most natural thing in the world. There was no invasion, nothing repellent, but sweetness. And everything that followed, to her intense surprise, felt exactly the same: sweet, delightful and natural.

'I would not be so rude as to ask you impertinent questions,' Irène said, as she walked Veronica back to the academy an hour later. 'But I trust it made you happy?'

Veronica nodded. After they had finished, they'd lain together, pounding hearts pressed against each other, their skin clammy with a sheen of sweat, and regained their breath.

He had kissed her again, and thanked her, then reminded her of the time. There had been just enough time to wash, dress and hurry downstairs to meet Irène on the boulevard below. André had taken her hand and squeezed it, smiling at her under his hat, and said, '*Au revoir, mademoiselle*, you were so charming. *Merci*.' Then he had gone.

She blushed because she couldn't help it, overcome with the sense of having joined the great union of womanhood now, with secrets and mysteries explained and shown to her. She was, of course, still a novice, but she knew now.

'Good. I knew that was how André would be.' Irène grabbed her hand. 'I told him to look after you and take precautions too, of course, against pregnancy. But I didn't need to. He would have been just the same, no matter what. I wanted you to have that, my sweetheart, rather than be ruined by a painful or frightening experience. And I am very happy if that is what you had.'

'I did.'

'Good. Very good. My last gift to you before you go home.'

Irène wrote to Veronica the next day. The letter was by her plate at breakfast, and she opened it and read it, the other girls around her chatting and squabbling.

Dearest girl, I have heard from André. He found you exquisite and likes you very much. Would you like to see him again? I know you have only a week or so before you leave but your tutoress may be open to my taking

124

you out to see some of the culture of Paris, as you are
not going to be having much in the way of lessons. In
fact, telegram your mother and ask if you can leave the
school and stay with me for your remaining time . . .
that will make it easier. If you wish, that is? Write and
let me know as soon as you can.

   Irène

Veronica released a shaking breath. The letter shook in her trembling fingers.

'Are you all right, Vron?' asked the girl next to her. 'You've gone awfully pale.'

'Yes, oh yes, I'm fine. I must just ask Mademoiselle if I can telegram home, that's all. I'll do it now.'

Daddy and Mama already knew of Irène because Veronica had needed their permission to go to tea with her. She knew suddenly that they would be perfectly happy for her to spend these last days with Irène and that if they telephoned to discuss it, Irène would soothe any anxieties or concerns quite perfectly.

Veronica got up and went to find a card to write her telegram, then got Mademoiselle's permission to send the maid out with it. She spent an anxious morning waiting for a reply. It came at lunchtime.

SPLENDID IDEA. GO AHEAD. ONE CONDITION:
ONLY SPEAK FRENCH. BE BACK FOR JOURNEY
HOME AS ARRANGED. WILL SQUARE WITH M'SELLE.
FOND LOVE.

Well, oh my, Veronica thought as she read it, eyes wide. *Oh, my, my, my*.

Irène's apartment was exactly as Veronica had hoped it would be. Decorated in the style of Louis XV, it was a riot of ivory and gold, with gilt mirrors, pier glasses, Chinese cabinets and plenty of flounces and bows.

'Philippe says I am his Pompadour,' Irène said, coming to meet her after the maid had answered the door and taken her coat and suitcase. 'So it is appropriate that I live in her kind of style.' She laughed. 'It is not really to my taste, I am a simpler person than this, as you saw from my hidden apartment. This is a little character I like to play: the feminine, frou-frou, scented mistress. And it makes Philippe happy.'

'So that apartment is yours?' Veronica asked, overwhelmed by the ornate furniture, including pink silk sofas on spindly little gold legs. The thing that surprised her was the very large amount of books throughout the hallways and rooms; not unread leather-bound ornaments, but real books that looked as if they had been studied: literature, art, history, biography . . . the titles were as wide ranging as a bookshop's, and not just in French and English but also in German and Russian. Although Irène was clearly cultured, this showed a whole new side of her character at odds with the bows and frills and gilt of the apartment. It was much more of a piece with the garret.

'Yes, the little apartment is mine and just as I like it. Very plain, very quiet and calm. This place is rented for me by Philippe. I am a kept woman, you know! I shall be allowed to keep the furniture, if he decides to release me. It shall be my compensation. And there is jewellery and some other nice little things to provide my pension from him.' She shrugged. 'The lot of the mistress. Of course, if I leave him, I must abandon the furniture, but I shall keep the jewels, that is understood. Perhaps that is why he buys me so much.'

'Do you think he will leave you?'

'In time, I'm sure he will. Although I must say, he does seem very loyal. Quite the most faithful and enduring of my lovers. I'm sure he'll be around for a while yet.' Irène smiled at her. 'Which is flattering of course.'

Veronica watched Irène sit down on one of the sofas. She was so effortlessly elegant, wearing a navy dress and jacket that Veronica suspected was the work of Mademoiselle Chanel, and with ropes of pearls at her neck. 'I can't imagine anyone wanting to leave you.'

'Of course not. It's my job to be enchanting. The only problem is that some people are enchanted that you would rather were not. Not Philippe, he's an angel. Now. How exciting that you are here! We are going to have fun.'

'You're supposed to speak French to me,' Veronica reminded her.

Irène blinked. 'What nonsense. I will practise my English on you, that is much better. I rarely get the chance.'

'You don't need to practise, you're perfect.'

'And you are sweet.' Irène blew her a kiss. 'And tonight . . . a rendezvous?'

Veronica blushed. She had been thinking about André nonstop since Sunday afternoon. She had been caught dreaming more than once, remembering their encounter in vivid imaginings that left her almost gasping and filled with a strange new hunger. She had longed to do it again, from start to finish, but with more understanding, more relish.

Irène smiled at her now. 'I can see you would like that. André is very happy to hear that you are staying here and that there will be more opportunities for meetings in my little garret.'

Veronica felt bold and rash but also timid all at once. Was she really going to do this? It was surely very wicked. And yet Irène did not think so, and it did not feel wicked. She was still astonished by how it had felt the very opposite.

'Yes,' she said firmly. 'I would like it.'

They returned to the little flat that very evening. André was already there, less formal than last time in casual clothes that still looked, to Veronica, very elegant: loose wool trousers with turn-ups, a shirt and a tie under a bright red sweater. Veronica had taken care over her appearance, wearing a pale green silk dress lent to her by Irène, which flattered her fair hair, neatly brushed into glossy waves that Irène had coaxed out of her wiry locks with potions and curlers and a hair dryer.

His eyes brightened when she came in with Irène, and he greeted them both with kisses to the cheeks.

'You look very charming,' he said appreciatively, looking at her dress and then her face, expertly made up by Irène, of course. 'Very *soignée*.'

'Thank you.' She smiled at him, thinking, *We have made*

love and we are going to do it again. Then she felt deliciously grown-up, as though a key had clicked in a lock and released it, opening the door to life beyond.

This time there was a bottle of champagne waiting in an ice bucket, and they sat down to talk and share a glass while remaining apparently oblivious to what was about to happen. After a while, Irène made her excuses, put on her coat and left. As she went, she said, 'Now, bring her home, won't you, André? Whenever you wish. There is no hurry now that there is no worry about the school.'

'Of course,' André said, bowing slightly to her as she left. Then he closed the door and they were alone.

He turned to look at her and smiled. A surge of pleasure ran through her.

'I like you,' she said spontaneously. 'Very much.'

'I like you too. You're more beautiful than I remembered, and I thought I'd remembered you very well indeed.' He came over and pulled her into his arms and kissed her hard and thoroughly. This time she was ready and willing, and keen to lose herself in the kiss, and for him immediately to take her to the little bedroom. But he pulled away, smiled and said, 'Let's talk first.'

He went over to a gramophone in the corner, switched it on and put on a record of soft orchestral swing music, and poured them both more champagne, before sitting on the small sofa. 'Come.' He patted the seat next to him. 'Tell me about yourself, Véronique. We have leisure now. Let's enjoy it.'

Although she longed to go to the bedroom, she liked that he wanted to know more about her, and this was surely prolonging the delicious anticipation. So she sat next to him and began to tell him a little about her life at home: her father's career, Mama and Billie. He asked the occasional question to keep her talking and, as she did, she missed them all quite suddenly.

'Your family sounds interesting. Irène told me you had a curious background. But I've heard that the English are all quite insane.' He laughed and lit a cigarette from a packet in his pocket.

'Insane!' echoed Veronica, and she laughed. 'Not insane. Normal to me, but of course, the theatre lives by its own rules.'

'I'm sure it does.' He offered her the packet of cigarettes and, after a moment's hesitation, she took one, let him light it and inhaled. Immediately she was lost to a fit of desperate coughing. André bashed her on the back, as he took the cigarette from her and stubbed it out, laughing. 'A little more practice, I think, my dear.'

When she'd recovered, wiping away tears, she said, 'I suppose that's spoiled my glamorous lady routine.'

'Perhaps. But you are all the more enchanting for it.' He stubbed out his own cigarette, then pulled her close, stroked her hair and held her hand; she began to lose herself in the excitement of his proximity again.

He started to kiss her tenderly, tasting of champagne and cigarettes and his own essential maleness. She lost herself in the pleasure of his kiss and when he began to embrace her with greater intensity, she was more than ready to go to the little bedroom with him.

Afterwards, they dozed and slept, woke and embraced and slept again.

'We'll go back in the morning,' he said.

'Good.' She tucked herself close to him. 'I don't want to leave here. I want to stay.'

'So do I.'

She woke again in the cool grey blue light of early morning, and when she moved, he woke up too, and made love to her again. The previous slowness and languor was replaced by urgency and something she had never known before: a mutual and intense passion. She didn't close her eyes this time. Instead, they gazed at one another throughout, serious, utterly focused on one another, each taking the other to a new pitch step by step.

What is this? she wondered, although her thoughts were fuzzy and distant, as if coming to her through vast starry space. *What is happening?*

I had no idea it could be like this.

They walked back together through the almost empty streets when it was still early. He kissed her outside the door to Irène's apartment.

'Goodbye, *chérie*. You are so beautiful and adorable. Can I see you tonight?'

'Yes, I think so. But can't you stay with me today?'

'Sadly no. I have other commitments, you know. Till tonight.'

Veronica watched him go, then made her way up to the apartment where the maid let her in. Irène was still asleep and would be until mid-morning. Veronica was exhausted and wanted to rest but there was no way she could sleep so she took a long bath and then lay on her bed, staring into space and dreaming until at last she slept a little.

Irène took her to the Louvre every afternoon to look at a different painting. Today it was *The Raft of the Medusa* by Géricault, a frightful vision of suffering in the wake of a shipwreck. Veronica found it was almost too much to look at. Her emotions and everything about her seemed heightened, as though several layers of skin had been shaved off, making her desperately sensitive to the world. Touching a coffee cup was almost too much for her. The feeling of hot liquid on her tongue was overwhelming. Walking along the street with Irène was like being put in charge of a powerful and magnificent motor car that she was learning how to drive. Her body was something new and strange, and her experience of it had completely changed.

In front of the painting, finding the human misery within it too much, she burst into tears.

'Darling!' Irène hugged her. 'What is it? I'm sorry, is this too harsh?'

'I can't bear it,' Veronica sobbed. She buried her face in the soft fur of Irène's stole. 'Why do we have to suffer? Why can't life be simple and lovely when there is so much to enjoy? Why must people be so cruel?'

'Ah, my sweet girl.' Irène hugged her more tightly. 'Life is cruel. There is sadness and suffering. That is why we must take our joy where we can. Come on, let's go. This painting was perhaps a bad idea. Let's go and see something joyful instead. I know. The Dutch domestic. Vermeer. We will find comfort in maids pouring out water and women playing the piano and the quiet of afternoon sunlight. I think that will be the answer.'

When they emerged from the Louvre, Veronica was indeed calmer, but for the first time she was aware of aspects of the city she had previously been sheltered from in her school in the Rue de la Pompe and her walks in the Bois de Boulogne. There were signs she had not seen before, directing citizens to bomb shelters. There were people everywhere, not just soldiers, but dazed-looking families huddling together, clutching suitcases, and small children in the parks and on the boulevards. Everywhere there seemed to be ragged poor people of all ages, some begging on corners or sitting in doorways. Sad-eyed women in dark headscarves and shabby dresses held out their hands for coins.

'Refugees,' Irène said sadly. She had already put coins into many eager hands, murmuring words of comfort as she did so. No matter how much she gave, there were dozens more desperate for a little help. 'They're pouring over the borders from Germany and Czechoslovakia. Life is very difficult for them now.'

'Jewish people?' Veronica knew that there was violent antagonism towards the Jews in Germany.

'Yes, and anyone the German government would object to, and those who want to flee from conflict and war.' She looked sombre. 'But Paris might not be far enough. We shall see.'

'What do you mean?'

Irène looked at her meaningfully and then said, 'I don't know what to say when you are so heightened in your feelings at the moment. But remember what I said. Liberty, freedom to think and to speak and to do – they are vital to us. These things are very important. They are worth fighting for, worth sacrificing everything for. Imagine a world where you are told what to think and you are punished if you think differently. It is not so very far away either.'

'You mean . . . Germany?'

'Yes. And other places. Where there is no liberty. No art. No literature. Everything must be sanctioned by others. It is hell. It is *The Raft of the Medusa* every day.'

'Oh.' Veronica felt a pang of horror as she remembered the frightful suffering. Each person in the painting had been so alone, so desperate. When she spoke, her voice was high with tension. 'Is that what's coming?'

'Not if we resist. Not if we give every ounce to stop it.' Irène squeezed Veronica's hand. 'But this is not very cheerful. Let's not think about it. We shall have fun while we can.'

That evening, in the little garret, Veronica and André talked for longer. She sat nestled under his arm and told him more about her life and this time about the island.

'It's called St Elfwy, and it really is the loveliest place in the world.'

'And you own this island?' he said, clearly intrigued.

'Well . . . yes, I suppose so – as much as you can own anything like that. It isn't really something you can possess. I wish you could see it,' she said, missing it with a rush of intensity. 'It's so long since I was there. In fact, I've never been away so long in my life. It's so beautiful there. It's wild and natural and full of birds and creatures and plants. It's so free, even though you are trapped there, by the sea. You're also protected because no one can touch you. It's somewhere you can be entirely yourself.'

'A place like that sounds like heaven right now.'

She turned her face up to him. 'Let's go there! Come with me, we'll go to Wales. You take the road to the west and you carry on and on, until you're in glorious Pembrokeshire. And then . . . at last, you see St Elfwy, sitting across the channel, a gorgeous green jewel in the turquoise sea.'

André smiled at her, running a finger down her cheek and gazing into her eyes. 'I love your blue eyes, so intense when you feel passionate. Your island sounds marvellous.'

'Then let's go!'

He laughed. 'I can't think of anything nicer, and being with you would be perfect.' Then he sighed. 'But of course, that's only a dream.'

Veronica leaned her head on his shoulder. 'Really? We can't make it come true?'

He held her hand and squeezed. 'You know we can't. So we must make the most of the time we have left. You're

135

leaving the day after tomorrow. This is one of the last times we will be together.'

She felt suddenly desolate. 'I can't believe we met less than a week ago. It feels like a lifetime.'

'It has been a beautiful interlude in our lives. But we always knew it was going to be short, didn't we, *chérie*?' He spoke gently but firmly.

'Yes. But I didn't expect this. I like you so very much, absolutely everything about you.'

'And I you. But if I'm being realistic, I know it's easy to like someone in these circumstances. We are outside normal life, you know. It is a sweet dream. That is why we must enjoy it for what it is. And not ask too much of it.' He kissed her softly. 'I don't want you to feel any pain. That is not what we are doing. We are here for pleasure alone.'

He began to kiss her again and soon she had forgotten about the island, her family, the pain and suffering in the outside world, and everything but the intensity of his touch and the pleasure it brought her.

The following night was their last night together before Veronica had to return to school and then make the journey back to England. Once more, she spent the whole night with him and this time, they slept all night in one another's arms, waking to make love and then to sleep again, until it was time to get up and return to Irène's apartment.

After she had bathed and dressed, she waited in the sitting room while he made coffee for them both. As André emerged from the little kitchen, holding two small cups, she was over-come and burst into tears.

André's smile vanished. He put down the cups and hur-ried to embrace her. 'Now . . . come, Véronique! Please, my dear . . . Why are there these tears?'

'Because I'm in love with you, of course.' She cried harder and hugged him tightly. 'And I don't want to leave,' she said, between sobs.

'Of course.' He rocked her gently. 'I'm afraid that it was inevitable you would feel like this. Perhaps I should only have seen you that first time. I knew that it would mean so much more to us both if we continued. But . . .' He stood back to smile at her. 'I couldn't resist you. I love you too, my sweet, but we both know that it is a love of time and place and circumstance, and we will never be able to make it more than that. You know that?'

She nodded. She did know it but she couldn't help how she felt: giddily, desperately, thoroughly, physically in love.

He pulled her with him to the sofa and they sat down close together. He gazed at her, his expression solemn. 'Per-haps it sounds callous, but that was the point of this. I only finished my military service last year. When war comes, as it is bound to, I will be called to join the army again at once. And then who knows? There was never any chance for us, you understand that?' André gripped her hands, looking hard into her eyes. 'That was why we did this. To take just a moment of joy before the world sweeps us up and away for ever. You have given me a gift I will cherish all my life, and I hope I have given you the same.'

'You have, you have . . .' She sniffed and tried to smile. 'I wish it didn't have to end.'

'The end was in the beginning.' He kissed her again. 'Let's keep our memories. And if you are in Paris again one day, who knows?'

'I don't know anything about you!' she said desperately. 'You've said hardly anything.'

'It was better that way. You feel things very much, Véronique. I don't want to make it harder for you. You can always reach me through Irène. Now, come, dry your eyes. Let's have our coffee and then we will go home.'

When they said a swift farewell outside the door of Irène's building, Veronica knew that André didn't want to draw it out and make it painful for her.

'Good luck, sweet Véronique,' he said, kissing her cheeks. 'I hope we meet again. I will never forget you. And thank you for the joy you brought me.'

As he turned and walked away, she felt the strangest sense of knowing him better than anyone in her life, and of not knowing him at all. He had said so little. She knew nothing of what he did or where he lived. She knew intimate details of his body, how he sat, how he liked his coffee, and how he laughed when she told him a funny story, but almost nothing else. And now, after the passion of the last few days, he was striding briskly away and into that unknown life from where he would most likely never return.

She remembered what he had said, as she bit her lip, screwed her eyes shut and fought off tears. Then she ran inside and up the stairs to Irène's apartment.

Later, when she had packed and was ready to return to school, Irène came to find her. 'Darling, I cannot go with you to the school. Philippe needs me today and I must go.' She sighed. 'I'm afraid that we are all about to lose people we love one way or another. Will you be all right if my maid Sophie takes you back?'

'I can go alone, I'd rather do that,' Veronica said. 'It's not far and I know the way.'

'Very well. Before we say our farewells . . .' Irène went to a console table and collected a small velvet purse. From it, she took a set of two keys linked together by a red ribbon. 'These are keys to my little garret. I want you to take them. Just in case you ever need it. I have keys of my own of course. And André also has a set. I am sure that you never will need them, but just in case life brings you here again . . .'

She pressed the small set into Veronica's palm and then smiled, but this time in a pained way.

'I don't have much family. My friends are women like me. I have no children. Your friendship is something quite new for me and I have enjoyed it a great deal. I want to care for you, *chérie*, if I can.'

'You gave me a wonderful gift,' Veronica said shyly. 'You gave me André.'

'Yes,' Irène laughed. 'It was a risk! But something told me it was right.'

'Why a risk?'

'A risk to your happiness. I knew André would be kind and sweet and I knew you would likely fall in love with him, which I think you have, just a little.'

Veronica blushed and looked away. She had hoped she appeared more sophisticated than that, a woman of the world who could easily have an affair that served a purpose and didn't involve her heart. But she had not been able to.

'Yes, just a little,' she admitted after a moment. 'But I don't know anything about him. It's very strange. He let me talk and didn't say much about himself.'

'He is reserved,' Irène agreed.

'Can you tell me about him?'

'Of course. Anything you want. But I think it's best that I do not.'

'How do you know him? Is he a friend?'

'More than a friend, *chérie*. He is my brother.'

Veronica walked back through the city, carrying her suitcase. No one gave her a second glance; the streets were full of people with suitcases.

At least I know where I'm going, she thought, feeling suddenly spoiled. Here she was, weeping over a man, when thousands had nowhere to live and no knowledge of their future.

She trudged towards the school, every step taking her back to the old life, where she was a schoolgirl being told what to do by teachers, an innocent and a child with no power to make her own decisions. Well, she had taken her power and she had made her choices and she did not regret them, even if it meant the pain of loss and separation.

But how strange . . . that all that time, he was Irène's brother. Now she thought of it, he looked like her – the same almond-shaped eyes, although brown where hers were that bruised blue – dark hair, delicate features, and grace and beauty.

Oh, André, she thought, longing for him suddenly. Then she pushed that out of her mind.

There is a journey home to make. I'll see Mama, Daddy and Billie. And perhaps . . . at last . . . the island.

PART TWO

Chapter Eight

ROMY

Present Day

So there's the boat, Romy thought, and she felt a jolt of surprise at how small it was, bobbing about on the swell below her.

Of course, she had known that she would be crossing the mile stretch of peninsula to St Elfwy by boat. How else? There was no bridge and there was never likely to be – but she'd imagined a great ferry, like the one that had taken her family to the Isle of Wight when she was a girl. Back then, her father had driven the car over clanking ramps into the belly of the ship. They'd left it jammed among all the others in the lower hold, and clambered up metal staircases to the exciting level of the cafe and the doors to the seats outside. She and Florence ate crisps and watched the seawater churning far below. Huge white gulls with aggressive yellow eyes would approach along the prow, ready to pounce, occasionally darting for the packets, once even stealing one straight from Romy's hands and disappearing with it, scrunched blue foil glinting in its talons.

Just my luck, she thought. *Flo never got her crisps nicked.*

She wondered why she had imagined a huge port, an enormous ferry, lots of people, here on the edge of west Wales.

Of course it wouldn't be like that. But even so . . . I didn't expect this.

The taxi that had brought her from the station had got as near as possible to the coastline, but now there was a flight of steep stone steps down to the water, to navigate along with all her luggage. At the top, she paused, feeling a little dizzy. Below her, she could see a bright yellow motor boat tethered to the stone quay, bumping against the weathered buoys strung along it.

'You're not exactly travelling light, are you?' said the taxi driver, panting slightly as he came up loaded with bags to add to the pile next to the steps.

'It's everything I need for quite a while,' Romy said quickly. 'Sorry it's so much.'

She could almost hear Flo rebuking her. *Don't apologise, Romy! You're paying him. You've got to stop feeling so guilty for everything.*

Flo had been very against the idea of the island. She had made it plain that she thought it was the very last thing Romy should do.

'I just don't think you're in the right mindset. I don't think you're anywhere near recovered,' she'd said.

'This *is* my recovery,' Romy said stubbornly.

And in the end, there had been nothing Flo could do about it.

'There's still more to come,' the driver said, heading back to the taxi.

Romy wondered if she should start taking bags down to the boat. She hadn't factored in all these elements. In her mind, she'd had one stage: arrive at the island by boat.

But it had been so much longer and more difficult than all of that. She had turned down offers of lifts and was now regretting it. Instead, deciding on strict independence, she'd travelled by taxi and train but that had just meant that she'd relied on the help of strangers instead of friends, which was much more stressful. She'd been supposed to be travelling light and yet bag after necessary bag had been added to her luggage pile. Then, after managing to get herself and all her luggage off the train with the help of the guard, she'd found her taxi and asked to be taken to the local supermarket. Rather than the brightly lit, well-stocked outlet of some major chain, she'd found a quirky place that also served as a post office and petrol station, stocked for holidaymakers rather than residents. There were lots of beach games, disposable barbecues and beer, but not so much in the way of supplies. She saw that a return trip to the mainland would be needed sooner rather than later. That shop had added another three bags to her haul, plus a couple of ten-litre bottles of water.

The drive to the coast was fifteen minutes. It had seemed like nothing on the map but when the taxi roared along tiny winding roads away from civilisation, past the last lonely farmhouses and cottages before they arrived at the dead end and the staircase down to the sea, Romy realised how alone she already was. And she wasn't even at the island yet.

Just then someone emerged from the square cabin of the yellow motor boat onto the deck and then vaulted lightly over the side onto the quay. They looked up, saw Romy standing there and waved. There was a vague shout but most of it was carried away on the wind.

The figure came along the stone quay and bounded up the steps as though the steep climb were nothing at all and, a moment later, a young man in sturdy boots and waterproof over-trousers held up by straps that clipped over a thick fishing jumper was smiling up at her, his long brown hair blowing all over his face.

'Hey, are you Romy?'

'Yes,' she said, smiling gratefully, relieved to hear her name. The stranger was suddenly a friend.

'Great. I've been expecting you. Shall I help you get your stuff down?'

She blinked at him. 'You're Australian,' she said almost wonderingly.

'That's right. They've been letting us visit for a while now.' He grinned again and started loading himself up with bags as the taxi driver puffed over with the last haul of luggage. 'Thanks, mate. Can you bring that lot down for us? We'll be done in one or two trips if you can.'

The taxi driver, startled, obeyed, and went after the younger man as he headed off down the steps. Romy put on her backpack and started after them, balanced by a heavy bag in each hand. She warded off dizziness by staring at each step as she went until she finally stepped onto the quay. The yellow motor boat bobbed on the lightly churning water. Out of the calm of the harbour, the swell was picking up, and the sea flashed turquoise, blue and then a sullen grey.

At the quayside, the taxi driver was waiting meaningfully by the pile of bags. Romy put down her things and scrabbled in her pocket for the fare. It was a large one, with the trip from the station, the stop at the shop and then on to the coast and, of course, she owed him for carrying all that stuff, so she rounded it up generously. He seemed mollified.

'You've got my number,' he said, handing her a small business card. 'I'm Geraint. You can ask for me if you want. I'm not so busy this time of year.'

'Thank you,' she said gratefully. She'd not considered the practicalities of returning to the mainland. Another thing her fuzzy mind had just assumed would be easy. But now she knew there was a good fifteen-minute drive to the nearest shops, she realised a friendly driver was just the thing, and was glad she'd tipped so well.

The Australian emerged from the cabin of the motor boat where he'd been stowing Romy's things. 'How much more?' he asked.

'Just this,' Romy said, showing what was left as the driver headed for the steps. 'I'm amazed you brought so much down in one go.'

He shrugged with a laugh. 'It wasn't that much really.'

'What's your name?'

He grinned at her, showing a row of unusually even white teeth. Perhaps it was the proximity of the sea, but he seemed to have a slightly piratical look, with his long brown hair and stubble. 'I'm Jesse,' he said. 'Good to meet ya. Ready to get on board?'

'I suppose so.' She still felt dizzy from the descent. Now

the boat swayed in front of her, much higher out of the water than it had looked from above.

'Come on. Pass me your stuff.'

She slipped off the backpack and he leaned over, swinging it away from her with one easy motion into the back of the boat. He put out his hand for the other bags, and when they were gone, he reached out his palm for hers. She took it and felt his power travel into her and suddenly she had the strength to jump up, grab the side rail and swing herself up and through the gap in the railing onto the little vessel. Once on board, she could see the rows of plastic seats that filled the interior.

'You're my only passenger today,' Jesse said. 'Usually I've got a few more than this, but tourist trips are cancelled for the next few days. The weather's a bit iffy.'

'Oh.'

'Don't look frightened, we'll be fine. We're heading straight over and I'm dropping you there. Easy.' He reached for an orange life jacket. 'But I need you to wear this anyway.'

He helped her put it on and strap it around her waist.

'Great.' He grinned. 'I'll bet you all the fish in the sea that you don't get a drop of water on it. But you know, safety first. Right. Are we ready?'

She nodded, and felt the significance of the moment. She had left the mainland. She was on board the boat. She had been so taken up in the journey, and the problem of the luggage and getting on board, that she hadn't even properly looked at their destination. As Jesse went into the cabin and started up the engine, which roared into life, she turned to look out across the sound to where the island sat, craggy and beautiful against the grey sky, its low cliffs stained by the sea and the countless birds that nested on them.

She leaned against the railing as Jesse reversed the boat out and away from the quay before turning it round to face the island. Next to her was a life ring, a large red circle with black letters printed on it: *Ynys Elfwy*. Elfwy Island. St Elfwy Island, to give it its full English name, though most people just called it Elfwy. It sounded sweet to Romy's ears – Elfie. Small, manageable, almost childlike. A pet island. Quite different from the way she had thought about it up until now. She felt that in some ways she already knew it very well, but that was in its film incarnation. On screen it was an oppressive, frightening place, dour and menacing in black and white. And of course, in the film it hadn't been called St Elfwy but creepy Stix Island. When she'd first seen photographs of the real island online, it had been quite startling to see it looking still and calm and enchanting in the light of summer. Rather than the palette of grey in the film, it had appeared like a haven of colour: the pinks and purples of heather and thrift, emerald-green carpets and khaki tufts of grass, scatterings of white and yellow flowers. The cliffs glowed orange and red in the summer sun and the sky seemed an endless canopy of blue under which the birds swooped and floated. It had enchanted and obsessed her beyond her ostensible reason for going. How could anyone be unhappy on such a place?

Now, on this cool May day with a promised summer yet to materialise, it looked far from tame. It looked glowering and lonely, something left in the swelling sea as though sent to Coventry by the mainland for bad behaviour. As the boat chuntered out of the natural harbour, away from the quay, she felt the power of the waves increase and the boat rolled forwards over them. The engine roared more loudly as Jesse revved the engine and the wind, briny and thick, started to whip at her hair, picking up strands and flinging them over her face until she brushed them back. She clung to the rail as the boat jerked over the swell.

'The tide will be on the turn soon,' yelled Jesse from the cabin, which was open to the small deck. 'Millions of litres of water sweep through this channel. The current is something else. See those rocks?' He waved towards a chain of pointed outcrops jutting out of the sea like a series of knobbly dark fingers. The largest was more like a tiny island. 'Those are the Ragged Maids and the big one is called the Bloody Countess. The water churns between them like they're the blades of a food processor. You don't want to be shipwrecked on one of those. You'd be cut to pieces.'

Romy felt the power of the water under the vessel, surging and moving beneath them, and was seized by a sudden rush of uncertainty. The sea was another thing she hadn't really factored into her imaginings, except as something at a safe distance. The crashing of waves onto a shore, the romantic glitter of sunlight on a mirror surface, the gentle swell of tides ebbing and flowing. Not millions of litres of water on the constant move, swirling and churning between her and the mainland.

'The island doesn't have a lighthouse, but it probably ought to,' Jesse was saying. 'There's one further up the coast nearer to the main port, for the big vessels out at sea. Sailors in the channel just have to know in advance about the Ragged Maids.'

She nodded and brushed more hair out of her eyes. She looked into the cabin to see that Jesse was staring at her, still smiling but with an appraising look in his eyes.

'If you don't mind me asking, why the hell are you going to stay on a godforsaken place like Elfwy? Are you mad about birds or something?'

She grinned. She wasn't going to tell him the reason, she still intended to keep that to herself. 'Not particularly.'

'Well, that's all there is out there. You and about a million birds. Some seals. And the warden. But he's a right misery guts. You don't want to spend more time with him than you can help.' He looked suddenly concerned. 'Are you really sure you want to go over there? You seem too nice and gentle for all this.'

She felt tartly offended. 'I'm stronger than I look.'

'You'd better be.'

He turned back to his controls. 'Look, up to you. Whatever makes you happy. I would go crazy in five minutes, but other people love all that hermit stuff.'

Romy said nothing, but gazed out over the steely coloured sea, watching the island grow larger with every moment. It didn't take long before they were across the channel and in the calmer water around the island. Birds soared and swooped all around the cliffs and in whirling formations overhead.

We're nearly here! Romy thought, suddenly excited.

The island had taken on real-life proportions as they got closer. Now the cliffs – small from a distance – rose above them. The island had heft and reality now, and it didn't seem so mad to want to live on it. Jesse brought the engine down to a purr and they moved slowly towards the island, skirting the east side to the landing place. It was not particularly pretty – a brutal concrete jetty thrust outwards into the water of the natural harbour, with rusted steel hand railings – but it was obviously practical. Jesse steered the motor boat up against it, and emerged rapidly from the cabin to throw a rope around one of the landing bollards, before shutting off the engine and leaping onto the jetty to fasten the rope tight and anchor the rear of the boat in the same way.

'This is it!' he declared, giving her his best pirate grin. 'St Elfwy!'

He put out a hand and she took it gratefully, as she stepped carefully up from the bobbing boat onto the firmness of the jetty.

'Here I am,' she said, almost wonderingly. She was standing on the actual island, seeing it with her own eyes rather than through the camera lens. She thought of the scene of the heroine landing at this very jetty – though not in its current state – unaware of what lay ahead. A tingling excitement fluttered through her.

'Yep, you're here all right. Shall we get you unloaded? Where are you going to be living?'

'Clover Cottage,' she said happily. She'd been lured by that pleasing name.

'Oh yeah,' Jesse said, without much interest. 'I know it. It's a bit of a hike. We'll probably have to do two trips, unless you've got the tractor?'

'No,' she said, mystified, wondering if it was something she was meant to bring with her.

'I guessed not. It's kept in a barn by the main house but you'd have to get permission to use it. Come on, let's load up and we'll get on up there as best we can.'

A few minutes later, loaded up with luggage, they set off up along the jetty and clambered up a set of concrete steps that had been constructed on the cliff side. As they got higher, Romy saw a stone wall and behind it the familiar white facade. *So there it is. The very place.* She pointed at it. 'Does anyone live there?'

'Cliff House? Yeah. The warden. Didn't they tell you?'

'Well, I knew there was a warden here. Not where he lives.'

'He's got a stronger stomach for it than I have. No wonder he's such an oddball loner.' Jesse made a face. 'I know it's all make-believe, but I find that place bloody creepy. I wouldn't want to spend a night in it, if I'm honest.'

'Oh?'

He gave her a sideways look. 'Don't you know about it? About the film?'

'Oh . . . yeah . . . vaguely. So is Clover Cottage close by?'

'Bit further up the hill, I'm afraid. Come on.'

They reached the top of the steps and Romy found herself suddenly in quite a different place. The sea was below them now, and a green plain sloped away before them. Cliff House was off to one side, its blank windows facing the mainland, and now she could see the beauty of the island top. It was rich with birds strutting and waddling about, and the bobbing tails of rabbits loping about on the grass. In the distance she could see the wavering lines of stone walls, clumps of stone ruins and the slate roofs of buildings. 'Oh, it's beautiful!' she cried.

'Yeah, it's nice,' Jesse agreed. 'But it's lonely. Don't forget that.'

He led her along the cliff path, then turned to the west and they joined a stony pathway that led through the soft island grass to a low stone wall with a gate in it. Behind that was a cottage built of rough grey Welsh stone shot through with veins of coppery orange and white. Its roof was black slate spotted with lichen and lumps of moss, the island colours melting it into the background, camouflaging it from the mainland.

'Clover Cottage,' Jesse announced. 'Home sweet home. I mean, I think you're insane. But whatever floats your boat.'

'It's perfect,' Romy breathed. The house was like a picture book illustration: two storeys, and five windows – two up, two down and the fifth over the front door. Two chimneys at either side completed the symmetry.

'Let's get in. I want to put this stuff down.' Jesse kicked at the gate and it squealed as it opened under his weight. 'Salty sea air. Terrible for metal. Terrible for most things, come to that.'

Romy followed him up the short path. A thought occurred to her. 'I wonder where the key is. I never asked!'

'I don't think that's going to be an issue,' Jesse said, putting down some luggage and opening the front door. Then he smiled at her. 'You first.'

'Thank you,' she said gratefully. She had wanted to be first inside; it mattered. Just inside the hall, standing on dark stone flags, a table held a welcome box and an envelope with her name on it in bold letters: *Romy Stevenson*. The key for the cottage front door hung on a string over the mirror above the table, but it looked little used. Romy dropped her things and pushed open the nearest door. It led into a little sitting room, with a stove in the fireplace, and assorted, mismatched furniture that appeared many years old. The sofa, though, looked squishy and she liked the faded chintz and pale peach cushions, still with an old sheen of taffeta. A large red rug softened the stone floor, and thick curtains hung at the window, which would once have been wooden sashes but were now draught-excluding glass and anti-rot PVC frames. They were the only unpoetic note in the simple, old-fashioned room but Romy had a feeling she would be glad of their modern qualities before too long.

She spotted the table in the corner with barley twist legs, a cane-seated chair in front of it and a lamp with a dusty marbled paper shade. A desk. Just waiting for her.

'It's perfect,' she declared.

'Perfect?' Jesse eyed her with amusement. 'For what? Going quietly mad? Come on, what the hell are you doing here? We get film buffs, bird spotters, religious nutters and tortured artists.' He suddenly beckoned her to the window. 'Come over here.'

Romy went over to join him. Jesse pointed out of the window at a bird sitting on the fence. 'What's that?'

'Er . . . not a seagull . . .' she said after a moment.

'Right. So you're not a birdwatcher. You know this is one of the most famous bird sanctuaries in the country, right?'

'Of course,' she said indignantly. 'And I had to sign a contract about all the rules when I took on the cottage.'

'That leaves religious nutter, tortured artist or film buff.' Jesse stood back and regarded her quizzically. 'How do you feel about the Singing Caves?'

She blinked at him. 'Umm . . .'

'Right, there's never been anyone here who doesn't know about the caves who isn't a religious nutter or a movie obsessive. So by a process of elimination, you have to be a tortured artist.' Jesse looked around. 'No sign of an easel. Or a violin.'

'I'm not an artist. At least, not like that. I'm a writer.' She felt suddenly a bit of a fraud. 'Well, trying to be one.'

'Whoops!' Jesse made a comical face. 'I forgot that one. The seeker of silence in order to forge a work of genius.'

Romy felt a little offended. Everyone else had taken her project seriously. They might have been dubious about her intention to spend weeks living alone on an island off the coast of Wales, and they might have worried about her state of mind. But no one laughed at her desire to spend some time getting inspiration for her work.

'I'm only kidding,' Jesse said, seeing her expression. 'What are you writing?'

'A kind of history, I suppose you could call it.'

'Okay. Do you have to be completely isolated and really

uncomfortable to write? 'Cos I kind of prefer a nice warm pub and pint by the fire when I'm doing my emails. But what do I know? I'm a dozy Australian who operates boat tours and a water taxi service for a living, and I've barely read a book in my life. Marvel Universe is my second home. So ignore me.'

'It's fine,' she said, mollified. 'I suppose it might seem a bit eccentric to stay here on my own.'

'I've gotta be honest, I'm a bit worried about you. It's tough living out here on the island. I just wonder if you have any idea what you're going to be up against.'

'I'll be all right,' she said stoutly. 'I'm tougher and more experienced than I look. And I don't mind being alone. Besides, I had to assure the trust that I was mentally fit to be here.'

Jesse gave her a sideways look. 'Yeah. The infallible test. Look . . . I'm gonna check in on you a bit, okay? And gimme your phone.' He took it when she handed it out and deftly typed in a number, pressed call, and then ended it. 'Right, you've got my number and I've got yours. Let's keep in touch.'

'Okay.' She felt a little uneasy for a second, surprised at how easily he had got her number, but then comforted. It couldn't hurt to have a friend to call on if she needed one.

He handed back the phone. 'Right, I'll go back and get the last of your luggage.'

'I'll make some coffee,' she said, realising she hadn't yet seen the kitchen. 'If I can find it.'

'Sounds good.' Jesse let himself out of the front door and went loping off down the path.

Romy watched him go. Jesse seemed like a good guy. He'd been a bit mocking but she believed he was honestly concerned for her welfare. It had to be a positive to have someone on hand looking out for her.

As though there hadn't been plenty of people looking after her already.

'I want you to stay close to us,' Florence had said, clearly unhappy that Romy was moving so far away. 'I hate the idea of you being in the middle of the sea, on your own.'

'It's what I want,' Romy had said obstinately. She hadn't been able to explain exactly why. But when she'd first seen the description of the island, a word had jumped out at her. *Sanctuary.*

She realised that was exactly what she wanted.

The island had been a religious sanctuary centuries ago. Now it was a bird sanctuary, as well as a place for those who needed its quiet and beauty and isolation.

Maybe it's a place where I can be safe. A place where I can do the work I really want to do. After all, it inspired Veronica Mindenhall. Maybe it will inspire me too. I hope so.

She laughed ironically at her own thoughts.

So many people must have nightmares about this place. I'm sure it's the last place most people would come for peace and security. Whereas I'm escaping my own nightmares.

And perhaps, she thought, *they won't follow me here.*

Chapter Nine

While Jesse finished unloading, Romy spent an enjoyable half an hour rootling through the kitchen, checking out the equipment and putting away her supplies. When Jesse came back, the fridge and cupboards were loaded up, she had made a list of a dozen things she'd forgotten, and the coffee was freshly made.

Jesse saw it on the table as he came in, rubbing his hands. 'Ah, thanks, that's exactly what I need!'

'It's the least I can do. There are biscuits if you're hungry. And I've managed to unpack a bit as well.'

Jesse sat down at the scrubbed pine table and picked up his mug. 'There's a freezer out the back in the outbuilding. All the cottages have them. You'd be sensible to put some stuff in it. If the weather turns, you might be cut off from the mainland for quite a while.'

Romy glanced out of the window at the bright blue sky, where clouds skittered past on the breeze. It was hard to imagine the weather turning so grim but, of course, it must. 'You're right. I thought I had plenty but I could probably do with a bit more just in case.' She sat down opposite, and picked up her own mug. 'I'm really grateful for your help.'

'No worries.' He sipped his coffee.

'Where do you live, Jesse?'

He nodded his head vaguely in the direction of the mainland, though it could not be seen from the kitchen. 'Did you see the lifeboat station?' Romy looked blank and he laughed. 'I can't believe you didn't notice it. It's right there by the quay. People come from all over to have a look at it. It's pretty famous.'

She thought back to her climb down the steps. She'd been focusing on the descent and on getting to the island, but now she remembered seeing an odd sort of building. 'Oh, do you mean the warehouse on stilts with the sort of slide coming down from it?'

He laughed again, more loudly. 'Ah, yes, I guess you could describe it like that. That's where the boats are launched from in an emergency.'

'Do you live in there?' she asked, puzzled.

'No. I do not live in a lifeboat station. Honestly, you clever book types can be a bit dim sometimes. Actually, I live a few fields back behind it, in one of those caravans you see all over the place here.'

'The mobile holiday homes? Those pale green ones? I had noticed a lot of them about.'

'They're very popular. Most of the campsites have them, and anyone with a back garden or a field big enough puts in one or two, then charges holidaymakers a pretty penny to stay in them over the summer. People near the beaches can make a lot of cash that way. I'm living in one that belongs to the Old Chapel. They let me rent it cheap 'cos I'm there all year round, and they're a charity as well.'

'It must be cold in the winter?'

'Not really. They've got heating in these days, a nice little gas fire. Proper curtains. It's fine. You'll have to come and see it, if you like.'

'Yes, that sounds nice.' She couldn't imagine wanting to leave the island soon, but she could look in when she did. 'So have you lived here long?'

'About two years.' He grinned. 'I was travelling the world, getting some experience. I ended up out here when someone told me the surfing was epic. And it was great. I spent a brilliant summer being an instructor and got together with a local girl. I didn't have plans, so decided to stay a while. And I'm still here.'

'That's romantic.' Romy smiled at him.

'It would be. If the girl hadn't decided she wanted to see the world and gone off.'

'Oh no! Where is she?'

'Australia, I think,' Jesse said, and grinned. She wasn't sure whether to believe him.

'I'm sorry.'

'It's fine, we weren't meant to be. What about you? Where are you from?'

She put down her mug. 'Bristol. Do you know it?'

'Sure, I've been there. Great city. And not too far away.'

'It feels quite far away now,' she said, looking out of the

window and seeing only the grassy island top and the flash of blue-green sea in the distance.

'I bet.'

'But that's the point.' She picked up her mug again and sipped her coffee. 'I've had enough of the city for now. I need to get away.'

'For your work? And are you going tell me anything about this book of yours?'

She looked over at his pirate grin and enquiring brown eyes. 'Maybe I will. But not yet. I'm not quite ready.'

'Intriguing. You've got me interested. I think you're keeping something quiet. You'll have to tell me next time I'm here.'

'Do you come here often?'

'Is that a line?' he said playfully.

She flushed and laughed awkwardly. 'I can't believe I just said that. But I mean . . . I mean, do you come over from the mainland?'

He waved her discomfort away with his hand. 'Don't worry, I know what you mean. I do some of the boat tours that go around the island, and occasionally I'll bring pre-arranged parties of birdwatchers over for a few hours. And I'm a taxi service for anyone that wants it. And I also do occasional film tours, when I have enough people who are interested.'

'Film tours?'

'Yeah. Have you heard of that horror film, *The Last Song of Winter*? It's got a real cult following. I'm surprised if you don't know it.' Jesse went on without waiting for a reply.

'You get a lot of people who want to visit the island for that reason, they want to see the place where it all happened. The trust doesn't like it, though. Birdwatching, yes. Film obsessives, no. But I've been allowed to bring over a couple of tours a season, as long as I guide them and keep them on the straight and narrow. I can take them to the caves on the boat – they're always really keen for that – and to a couple of key locations.'

She nodded, wondering what to say. There didn't seem much point in pretending to know nothing about the film but she also wanted to keep her work to herself for now. She wasn't ready to start sharing. So she said nothing.

'The Singing Caves really get them going,' Jesse confided. 'They are incredibly spooky.'

'You'll have to take me there then,' she said lightly.

'Sure, any time. It's the best bit of the tour, to be honest. They always want to go into Cliff House but that's strictly forbidden. The old grouch who lives there hates anything to do with the fans.'

'He doesn't let anyone in?'

'Nope! No way.'

She nodded, filing this information away. Her instincts to hide her interest in the film from the trust had been right.

'So when do you start writing?' Jesse asked.

'Tomorrow, I think. Once I've settled in. It shouldn't be too hard to get into it, with all this peace and quiet.'

'Quiet?' Jesse rolled his eyes, shaking his head. 'It's pretty noisy here. You'll find out.' He put down his empty mug. 'Right. I'd better get back before the tide turns.'

Romy thanked him again for all his help as she let him out of the cottage, watched him go down the path and then shut the door behind him. She stood with her back against it, gazing into the hall, and sighed, suddenly exhausted.

Despite what Jesse'd said about the noise, there was a sudden startling silence. She was alone. Really alone.

I haven't been alone in so long.

For the last year, she hadn't been left alone at all, not really. Her family hadn't allowed it. It was for her own good, they said. She knew it was because they cared about her but it was oppressive. She became desperate to get some space to herself, and she had needed something to provide not just a fresh start but also a goal. The book had been something she'd been planning for some time, ever since she'd been forced to abandon her PhD. When she'd seen that it was possible to actually stay on St Elfwy in one of the remaining habitable properties, she had been overcome with excitement at the thought of being there.

The website had explained that the island was primarily a bird sanctuary. Supervised day trips were allowed for bird-watching purposes, but holidays were not. Instead, retreats were permitted as long as they followed strict guidelines. Each applicant had to apply separately and be accepted on their merits, so it was quite difficult for a couple to go together, unless both fulfilled the criteria. Families were not allowed. Dates for the stay could be applied for, but in the end they would be allocated. There was a strict contract to be signed to make sure that rules around island wildlife were observed.

At first, Romy had assumed that the retreats must be based around birdlife but she soon understood that they could be anything, and the testimonials were from many different people, some following spiritual goals, some artistic or literary. Some wished to rebuild and repair the ruins, as a kind of practical therapy. What none of them did was connect the island to the film that had been made there in the 1960s, which had made it so famous. Nor was Veronica Mindenhall mentioned, except briefly on the About page, where Romy read:

St Elfwy was for many years the private property of the Mindenhalls, a distinguished theatrical and literary family that included Veronica Mindenhall, who spent considerable time here during her life. The island later became a bird sanctuary governed and managed by the St Elfwy Trust, but with the stipulation that creative work must be encouraged annually, with retreats offered to artists, writers and artisans, among others.

The more Romy had browsed the site, the more excited she'd become. The island was beautiful, and in a part of the world she loved. The cottages available were delightfully old-fashioned in the way that most appealed to her, with their quaint shabbiness and spare comfort. The thought of sea air and sun and solitude invigorated her. The cobwebs would blow out of her mind and perhaps some of the darkness would go with it. But better than that, it couldn't be more ideal than to write her book in the very place it was set.

Full of enthusiasm, she started to fill out the application page, only to see that she had missed the final submission date by a fortnight. She was surprised at the depth of her disappointment as she stared at the unforgiving date on the screen.

So it wasn't meant to be after all.

A reckless feeling possessed her.

I'm going to try anyway. Why not? What can I lose?

Feeling reckless, she sent it off, following up with an email apologising for her late application and asking if it might possibly be considered. The date of the notification for the successful candidates was still some way off, so perhaps she might be lucky.

An email popped into her inbox a week later, and she expected a standard thank-you-but-no reply, telling her the final date was the final date. Instead, she had a polite request for more information about the book she was writing and a more detailed CV.

Due to unusual circumstances this year, we are prepared to consider late applications. However, we must make sure that you're aware of the remote nature of the island, and the enforced isolation. You can be cut off from the mainland for long stretches. Although we provide modern internet services, these can be prone to interruption when there are circumstances outside our control. Because of this, we do ask that you complete a psychological profiling test, as we are only able to offer

this opportunity to those who have the necessary mental robustness to undertake it and profit from the unique atmosphere and beauty of St Elfwy Island.

As soon as she saw that, Romy felt anxious. A mental health test? She was afraid that she wouldn't pass.

Even if she did, she still had to persuade her family that she was fit to live on the island.

'This is what is going to bring me back,' she promised them. 'It's going to mark my new start.'

Her sister Flo had been worried. Romy had lived with her and her family for some time after she'd been released from the hospital in west London, and then attended as a day patient for a few weeks longer. 'I just worry about you,' she said bluntly.

Romy laughed. They'd been sitting in her sister's kitchen while Flo dashed about getting the children's supper after a long day in the surgery. She was always doing a million things at once. 'You don't say!'

Flo seemed to have spent most of her adult life worried about Romy one way or another. It had been Flo who pointed out to their parents that Romy, aged sixteen, was too thin, too wired and too addicted to exercise to be functioning in a healthy way. Until then her parents had simply seemed to think that Romy had a speedy metabolism and hadn't noticed that she was up at four in the morning to use her skipping rope or do push-ups or go for a run or a cycle. They were full of admiration for her top grades and her desire to always perform at her best, and didn't yet seem to see that the idea of failure or being any less than perfect would send her into a flat spin of panic.

Flo had noticed, though. And she had persisted in noticing and trying to get Romy to see it too, for years and years before anything had begun to change. By then, she didn't have to convince their parents, or anyone. It was obvious that Romy was ill.

'I don't like you setting yourself impossible goals,' Flo said firmly.

'Says a mother-of-four GP who manages an entire family and writes medical articles and keeps up an Insta following of half a million.'

'I'm not ill, Romy,' Flo said. 'I know I'm an overachiever and a perfectionist. We both have that streak. But I keep on top of it – just – and you haven't been able to. That's not a judgement, it's just a fact. I'm worried that writing this book might trigger you again.'

'Anything might,' Romy said with a shrug. 'I can't stop living in case it stops me living.'

Flo laughed. 'Good point.'

Romy smiled over at her sister, feeling the usual warm glow whenever she made her sister laugh. Flo was right, they were so similar. They looked very like each other: warm brown eyes that turned down slightly at the far edges, very straight brows and lashes, and freckles scattered over the long noses they'd inherited from their father. But Flo had an edge, a star quality that Romy felt she lacked. Flo glowed on camera, on her Insta feed and YouTube channels in a way that didn't seem fair considering how hassled she generally was. Romy felt she was better suited to libraries and study rooms, behind her glasses, long brown hair twisted up into a knot except for a strand that she twisted round her forefinger when she was thinking or reading. 'I'm really passionate about this project, Flo. I honestly don't think I can concentrate on anything else until I've done it.'

'Okay, I get it.' Flo bent down, took a large dish out of the oven, steaming and bubbling with melted cheese, and bellowed, 'Kids! Supper!' Then she glanced back at her sister. 'But don't get obsessed.'

'Sure!' Romy said lightly. Like it was that easy.

Flo stopped bustling for a moment and fixed her with a serious look. 'You'll need to get Caroline's permission. You can't go unless she says it's all right.'

Romy nodded. 'I understand.'

'I don't want you to think we're treating you like a child. This all comes from a place of caring about you.'

'I know.' She smiled at her big sister. 'And I'm grateful for that. I really am. I'm going to do whatever it takes so that I can do this – if they accept me, of course.'

Romy's next task was to get Caroline to pass her as healthy enough for the challenge. She felt a little guilty about the picture she painted of St Elfwy to her therapist, implying that there was more of a thriving community there than was strictly the case. She described it as an artists' retreat, with day-trippers constantly visiting to see the bird sanctuary and the remains of the monastic community that had once lived there. While it was true that boats circled the island several times a day in the season, taking tourists to spot birds and seals and admire the rock formations of the island, and gaze out towards the spreading ocean on the far side, the island wasn't quite as vibrant and populated as Romy implied.

'It sounds amazing,' Caroline had said. 'Lucky you, I'm envious! It sounds the perfect place to get this book written.'

'I know, it really is.' Romy felt a small tremor of something that was a sense both of power and of anxiety. She felt powerful because she had misled Caroline and Caroline, despite being an experienced therapist, had believed her. And the anxiety was because of how seductive that feeling was. As she talked to Caroline, she hadn't thought she was lying, or even misleading or exaggerating. She had completely believed what she was saying as she said it, even though part of her knew that she was purposely exaggerating.

It's a tiny thing, she told herself. *I'm aware of it. That's the main thing.*

They had agreed that Romy beginning her work would be an important milestone.

Romy has made great strides, Caroline had written in her report. *She is not showing any major psychological issues beyond what would be normal for her situation. I believe that the time is right for her to rediscover her independence and learn to become self-reliant again. With the right network of support and a firm contract of behaviour to abide by, she should be able to cope with island life and I think that it will be an important step in her full recovery.*

This was enough to secure her family's agreement. She must have passed the psychological tests for the trust, because not long after she filled them in, an email arrived accepting her application and offering her some dates for her stay. She took the first available window, too delighted and excited to wait any longer.

Romy shook her head in disbelief as she stood in the hall of Clover Cottage. She was really here, after all this time.

So now, I have to do it. I have to write this book of mine.

Her laptop and notebooks were carefully packed into her special backpack, which was in the sitting room, next to the bobble-legged Edwardian table that she had already decided would be her desk.

She went in to make sure it was there. Yes, there it was, safe and sound. She knew exactly what was inside: the power pack and plug, the laptop, the mouse, the notebooks, the pens and pencils, the sticky notes and the highlighters, and some reference books. She had collected a great deal of her research as web notes.

Just then her phone pinged and she saw that there was a message from Florence.

So have you arrived then??!!??

Romy smiled at it. It was a comfort in some ways to know that Florence was in her house in London, probably about to set off to get the children from school, and thinking about her.

Yes! she wrote. **Safe and sound. It's gorgeous. I'll send some pics and check in properly later.**

V glad to hear it. Have you done your form for today?

A slight crossness tensed her shoulders but she tried to shake it off. She knew the score. It was part of the condition on which she had been allowed to come over.

No. I'll get online and do it asap.

Romy saw a pink file on one of the shelves near the television and went to pick it up. It was full of information about the cottage and the island, and on the very first page was the password for online access.

I guess everyone wants this first of all.

Grabbing her telephone, she found the network and entered the code. Her phone attached to the signal and a raft of notifications appeared, most queries from friends and family to ask how her journey was going.

She went to the window and snapped a view of the island beyond. For a moment she was tempted to put it on Instagram and drafted a post:

Beautiful Elfwy! I've just arrived. I'm so excited to be here, and to start settling in to my cosy cottage. More pics to follow soon.

Then she remembered her promise to Florence and deleted it. No social media allowed. Instead, she set about getting her laptop set up on the table and also connected. Then she sat down, put on her glasses and accessed her online form, filled it in and shut down the page.

She had to do it. If she did as she was told, then she would be left in relative peace. She had promised she could be trusted and Caroline had convinced her family that the days of compulsive lying were over.

Then she sat back in her chair and let out a long sigh.

So here I am.

She picked up the file again and started to read carefully about everything she needed know about the cottage.

It was late afternoon before she had finished finding her way around the cottage, unpacking her things and making up her bed with linen and Welsh blankets from the airing cupboard. Someone had been over in the last day or two to clean the place and switch on the heating and hot water provision and all the appliances, so the linen was fresh, the airing cupboard warm, the fridge cold, and the tank full of hot water. Romy took pleasure in carefully folding away her possessions, deciding on where things would live and tucking them neatly into place. Everything felt new and ripe with possibility. The stay in Clover Cottage stretched ahead of her, unsullied and still full of unrealised dreams.

When everything had been put away, she decided she would go out for a walk while there was still time. Since she'd arrived, the day had softened into a warm and balmy afternoon. Birds chirruped and the wind was dancing through the long grass tops. She pulled on a jacket and stepped out of the cottage. The air was full of birdsong and everywhere she looked there were birds and more birds. She recognised gulls, blackbirds and sparrows, of which there were many, but there were dozens more kinds that she did not, large and small and in a variety of colours. There were birding books in the cottage, and the trust had sent her a sheet all about the different birds who made the island their home, so that she could obey the various rules around their safety. It had all seemed very common sense – essentially she was not to disturb the birds in any way. Well, she hadn't brought a rat or a cat with her – two of the species forbidden on the island – and so she didn't think she would present much of a danger to the birds as long as she kept a respectful distance.

As she began to walk towards the cliff path, she sensed that the island was alive with avian activity. Everywhere she looked were dozens and dozens of birds nesting on the cliffs and rock stacks, packed wing to wing, and the noise was tremendous.

So this is what Jesse meant.

Around the colonies, more birds fluttered and there was a general sense of organised chaos but also a febrile energy.

They must be nesting, she realised. *I suppose it's that time of the year.*

For a while, she stood and watched them, overwhelmed by the sheer number of birds she could see in the small patch of cliff she was looking at. There was something astonishing in the mass of creatures, all following the same instinctive urge to mate and breed and raise their chicks. What was it all for? What did they achieve except to continue the cycle of life and death, and just . . . be birds?

Maybe there's a lesson there.

She mentally laughed at herself already taking some life lessons from her surroundings, then stuffed her hands in her pockets and walked on, keeping her distance from the nesting colonies, not just to leave them in peace, but also to avoid the ceaseless chatter.

As she rounded the top of the island's highest point, she saw the ruins of the old abbey spread out before her. There had been a monastery foundation here for several centuries, the monks running a mostly self-sustaining community, trading for what they needed from the mainland. The island was not far off the pilgrim route from Ireland to Canterbury and they often welcomed travellers on their way into Britain. The monks had planted gardens and created the freshwater lakes that could apparently still be seen today.

The Church had owned the island for many years after the monastery had been disbanded and the monks scattered in the wake of the rule of a particularly cruel abbot. It had been leased out until bought in the thirties by the Mindenhalls, who had eventually transformed the island into the bird sanctuary and retreat it was today.

Here on Ynys Elfwy, the birds are returning in ever greater numbers, the information sheet had informed her. *Our puffin colony is small at only around two thousand birds (a thousand breeding pairs) but it is growing. We remain a safe and secure habitat for the rich traditional birdlife of these islands: manx shearwaters, storm petrels, guillemots, oystercatchers, stonechats, kestrels, rock pipits, choughs, cormorants, shags and of course gulls of all kinds – and many more.*

Romy stood looking at the dark grey remains of the ruins. It was hard to imagine a thriving community living and worshipping here, tending animals and gardening and running a religious life, as it seemed so bare now. All that was long vanished.

All the endeavour and work. What's left of it? A few old stones.

And yet, there had been another sort of life left for these ruins, when the film crew and actors had arrived in the sixties. The remains of the monastery had provided an eerie, unforgettable backdrop, and here she was looking directly at it, completely unchanged from those days. She almost expected those terrifying ghost monks to emerge from inside the ruins, their faces hidden in the shadows under their cowls, their hands tucked into their sleeves, the dreadful ropes knotted at their waists.

Romy shivered. *I'll wait until another day to explore. It's getting dark.*

She looked behind the island to where the sun was moving downwards towards the western horizon, setting the sea ablaze with glittering light and turning the rocky islands into dark blobs. The evening breeze came off the sea with a brisk chill to it. She would go home the way she'd come and leave the rest of the island for tomorrow.

Turning, she began to head back on the same path. There was not much danger of getting lost on a place as small as this – although it was bigger than she had realised now she was here. The circumference must be several miles.

A movement caught her eye and she glanced over to her right, to see a dark shape standing on top of the wall, a pair of binoculars pressed to its face, apparently gazing out to the sea. She felt a sudden jolt of fear, and then calmed herself.

It had to be the warden. Richard. He must have come back from town.

Now that her eyes had adjusted, she could see it was a man, dressed all in black, with a shock of white hair ruffled by the strong breeze, but he was too far away to make out many more details. He must have seen her. Surely he'd be alert to the presence of anyone else on the island? No doubt the trust kept him informed about people coming and going, he would have been expecting her . . .

Romy stood still for a while, wondering whether to approach, or even whether to wave at him. It was a strange kind of etiquette. How to introduce herself to a complete stranger who was now her nearest and only neighbour?

As she watched, he moved slowly and deliberately, turning away so that his binoculars faced away from her and towards the other direction.

Well, there's my answer, she thought. *He doesn't want to know right now. And fair enough. He's busy. Perhaps he's counting birds or something.*

She turned back towards Clover Cottage, enjoying the sounds of the birds twittering and chirruping in the hedge walls and the noise of the waves rolling in from the channel.

In the little kitchen, Romy began to make her supper. The stove was an old-fashioned storage range and she was relieved to find it was electric. According to the pink file, the island had been electrified in the eighties, when a cable had been sunk across the channel from the mainland.

Romy took out her electronic scales and measured out

the ingredients for her meal, totting it all down to log later. It was a simple meal of lentils, roasted vegetables and cold chicken that she'd brought with her, along with a rich dressing of epigenetic herbs blended in oil and a scattering of mixed seeds.

She put some music on her tablet, lit two candles, sat down at the table, took a photograph of her food to send to Flo, and started to eat.

It wasn't so long ago that no one would have trusted her to do this: to make her own dinner, rich in variety and nutrients, and then to sit and eat it. But she was determined to show them that things had improved, that she was better and that life had finally taken the turn she needed it to.

Pushing her plate away, she felt replete and then, just for a second, there was an instant of panic. For so long, she'd taught herself to hate and fear the sensation of being full, and here it was again, dangerous and yet insidiously seductive.

She concentrated as Dr Birley had taught her: breathing in and out very slowly, bringing herself only into the moment, using all her awareness while tapping an index finger lightly on the skin between her thumb and forefinger on the other hand. After concentrating for a moment on the here and now, she repeated a small mantra several times and felt her anxiety begin to lift. She didn't have to follow her routine to the end, or repeat it, before her sense of calm returned.

Romy breathed, pleased with herself. She had had her first tiny challenge and easily beaten it. That was a very good sign.

She cleared up, and then considered doing some work as it was still early, but she couldn't be bothered to start anything now after the long day of travelling and settling in. That could wait until tomorrow.

In the little bedroom with its sloping roof, Romy went to the gable window tucked under the eaves and looked out. The view was ravishing, the deepening blue sky pricked with stars, the horizon with a band of lavender pink where the sun was disappearing. She saw a few black shapes against the dark sky, then a long skein of birds, soaring or flapping through the air, began to approach, bulging out or disappearing to nothing, moving silently through the air in a great flock as they glided in from the sea to the island. Then they were passing over the roof of the cottage, heading inland.

That was beautiful, she thought. *I wonder what they are.*

Just as she was getting into bed, she heard the calls begin, cutting through the night sky, a raucous chatter and crowing, not beautiful at all. Long cries sounded on top of the general noise, like wails of sorrow or regret.

Romy pulled the covers up and listened for a while, assuming the cries would die away, but they were just as noisy and intense after half an hour, perhaps longer.

She felt the first warning signs of prickling palms, a dampness at the back of her hair. She reached for her headphones. They were concealed inside a softly padded silk headband that she could wear all night without any discomfort. Pulling it on, she used an app on her phone to play gentle music designed to calm her mind and lull her to sleep.

Within moments, she had closed her eyes and drifted away.

Chapter Ten

Romy had already planned her routine. She had written it out and stuck it up in the kitchen, pinning it to a cork board there. Schedules were safety these days. 'Control what you can control,' Dr Birley had said. He was all about getting her unruly thoughts where they needed to be: out of the mastery of her mind, reduced to the bullying little nothings they were, and then expelled.

'Why do you need control?' Caroline would ask her. 'Maybe you just need to let go.' Caroline focused on understanding why her thoughts were unruly in the first place.

It was confusing sometimes, managing all the ways in which people told her to get better.

It's like my medication, she thought, as she swallowed her pills for that day in the tiny bathroom by her bedroom. *Sometimes I wonder if I'm taking so many that they're cancelling each other out. Or perhaps I only need some to counter the ill effects of the others.*

She looked solemnly at her reflection in the mirror, noticing the way her long brown hair fell on her freckled shoulders. She was tempted to see her many flaws but instead said out loud, 'I'm beautiful as I am. I'm alive and I'm loved.'

She dropped her last pill into her palm and swallowed it, putting the negative thoughts about her medication out of her mind. Last year she had ceased believing she needed her medication, deciding that she was well again, and stopped taking it. That had been a serious mistake. She had promised she would never make it again. The only way was to be accountable to herself and stay in control and part of being in control meant routine.

First thing in the morning: exercise.

That was one thing all the therapists and doctors had agreed on. Exercise would help to regulate her.

'Within reason,' Dr Birley had said. 'We don't want to see the obsessions return.'

During the worst of her exercise addiction, Romy had exercised so hard she had actually broken her leg.

So exercise was going to be a run around the island, maximum twice, or a long and leisurely walk, maximum three times around the island. Then it would be breakfast, then work. She would do a good solid morning of work every day, and then eat lunch, and then she would explore or go back to the mainland or just amuse herself in some way until the day was reaching its end.

She stared at her routine, suddenly wondering if it was going to be enough to fill her time for the two months she planned to be on the island. It didn't look so very much. Would she get a bit bored?

Then she reminded herself: she had a lot of work to

get through, she would not be bored. And if she needed company – well, there was Jesse, for a start. He was very friendly.

She changed into her running things and went out the back door, stretching a little in the bright morning sun. She breathed in the sea air and drank in the view. It was stunning. The sky was baby blue, little white clouds bobbing across it. The turquoise sea was dimpled with diamonds, and the mainland glowed green and yellow above the dark cliffs. The island was abuzz with life, birds hopping through the hedges and on the walls, singing and whistling, while the larger seabirds crowed and squawked, doing their curious dances and half-flights, jumping up and down in the fern and heather. After blocking out the noise all night, she had decided to run without headphones today. The chattering seemed less mournful and strange in the daytime – either that, or it was quite a different sound.

What are they all on? Romy wondered. The chattering excitement in the air amused her.

She started to run along the dirt track path that ran towards the outer edge of the island and then followed the cliffs around it. There seemed a vast number of birds everywhere, mostly on the ground, although many wheeled in the air around the cliffs or were heading out over the sea. Besides the large grey-and-white gulls that were everywhere, there were scores of chocolate-brown and white birds with bright eyes and slightly hooked bills, and darker, smaller birds as well. Running on the stony track was not easy, with hedgerow, dense fern and skeins of wildflowers encroaching on it.

Masses of daisies turned their white-frilled yellow faces to the sun, while the purple pom-poms of nigella stood upright on their slender stalks. There were banks of tiny flowers in yellow, pink and white wherever she looked. It was very different to the pavements and walkways she was used to in Bristol, but it was also enchanting. A new and delightful sight met her at every step and halfway round, she stopped at a gap in the hedgerow to gaze down the sheer black cliffs that tumbled down to the sea where the waves slapped and foamed against them. The air was sharp and salty in her lungs and the wind ruffled her hair as she stood there. She decided to stop running for a while and walk the last bit to the top of the island.

'Oh my goodness. This is so beautiful!'

She thought of the Mindenhall family, owning this place just for themselves. She already knew that Veronica had spent a great deal of time here, although the biography she'd read had been vague about what she had done during that time. She felt a sudden kinship with Veronica, thinking of her walking these very paths and feeling the same joy that she was feeling right now. 'Imagine this belonging just to you. I don't think I'd ever leave it.'

As she was saying this out loud, she wandered over the brow of the island and saw the abbey ruins again, laid out in front of her. People did leave, in the end, it seemed. Perhaps it wasn't really possible to stay after all, not for too long. There was a time when the island was the right place but, like the birds who left for the winter, perhaps it wasn't always so.

Well, it's right for me, right now. I'm sure of it.

She observed the ruins for a moment. They looked much less creepy in the daylight. She would have to go and have a proper look later. Then she continued on, stopping only when she got to the furthest point. Now she could see the rocky stacks that rose in the sea just beyond the island. Some geological movement or event millions of years ago must have left these wonky stone towers in the sea, flecked with guano and dotted with patches of pale grass, and with dozens of birds nestling on the narrow outcrops. Beyond the stacks, the open sea stretched out towards Ireland, a few craggy islands dotting its silver water. Romy felt as if she were standing on the edge of the world, even though a glance to her right showed the mainland thrusting out into the sea with rocky fingers and curving out into a point further up. Beyond, there was a big port, where ferries and ships brought in their cargo of goods and people, facilitating the endless movement of human trade and traffic.

She turned and carried on her run, jogging along the track and following its curve.

Romy had almost made her first circuit and was approaching the grey slate roof and tall chimneys of Cliff House when she saw the black-clothed figure walking up from its back garden. It was the same man as yesterday, the one with the white hair. She wondered what to do, slowing down to give herself time to think. She hoped he would march on his way to do whatever it was he wanted to do, when she realised he was coming directly towards her and, the next minute, he waved and shouted.

'Hello there!'

She waved back, too breathless to shout at that moment.

'Come over here!' He beckoned her towards him, so she started to jog along the path to where he was approaching her. As she got closer, she could see that his hair was not per-oxide but a natural white, as was the stubble that covered the lower half of his face. He had a round, almost soft-looking face, with full lips and a large nose, and green eyes under dark grey brows that contrasted strikingly with his white hair.

That's strange, I thought he'd be more craggy-looking, she thought. But perhaps that was some sort of imaginative association with the birds. He didn't look aquiline or beaky, but almost boyish despite the hair. As she approached, she smiled and waved back.

'Hello,' she said, still slightly breathless and aware of the sweat at her hairline and on her nose. Her ponytail hung damply down her back and tendrils of hair stuck to her cheeks and forehead. 'Very nice to meet you. I'm Romy.'

'Are you? Well, listen, Romy, what the hell are you doing, running through the bird colonies first thing in the morning?'

Romy stared at him, taking in his words. 'Oh . . . well, I . . .'

He stared at her with cold green eyes, brows arched in interrogation. 'Didn't you read the terms and conditions? You are supposed to stay away from the birds.' He didn't sound angry but oddly flat and emotionless. 'Don't you understand that? Because it's basically the most important rule there is.'

'I didn't disturb them,' she said quickly.

'How do you know?' He stared at her, his expression blank and his eyes still icy.

'I suppose I don't but it seemed all right. I didn't go that close to them. I wasn't aware of disturbing them.'

'You have no idea what's going on. This is a vital time in their courtship and mating rituals. I don't need you going around literally putting your foot in it.'

Romy gasped and flushed.

He went on, gesturing towards the cliff as he spoke. 'This is a bloody sanctuary and you've been given special permission to be here. You signed that contract. You've broken it already. You haven't even been here twenty-four hours.'

A wave of panic washed over her. She'd messed it up already? She'd been so happy on her run, so delighted with the birds. Had she really hurt them, like a child hugging a beloved chick so close they squeeze it to death? But it had seemed so harmless! She couldn't think of one bird she'd startled or sent squawking and fluttering up into the air.

'I'm sorry,' she said, going scarlet. 'I didn't realise. I won't run up there again.'

'You'd better bloody not,' the man said bluntly. 'Because your permission to stay here can be rescinded at any time.'

'Please don't do that, I absolutely promise I'll stick to the contract. I just didn't realise that running was a problem. I'll only walk from now on.'

'Right. Okay. Well, make sure you do. Because I don't like spoiled city women coming here and thinking they own the place. Understand?'

He turned on his heel and walked away, back in the direction of Cliff House.

Romy was appalled to feel tears stinging her eyes. She wanted to go after him and explain that she wasn't spoiled and had made an honest mistake, and that she was far from believing she owned the place, but she didn't trust herself to keep her composure. She'd probably start begging and weeping and making a fool of herself. Besides, he was marching off at a rapid pace and was already making strides back to the white house.

She set off slowly back towards Clover Cottage, having lost heart for any kind of running even though she was nowhere near the cliffs and the colonies. Instead, she started going over the rules around the birds in her mind. As she remembered, they hadn't been very complicated – more or less, just leave them alone. She remembered that she was particularly warned not to attempt to help any bird she thought was in distress, or prevent nature taking its course in any way.

> **If you see a larger bird preying on a smaller one, or a struggle taking place, do not attempt to rescue any bird. It is the normal course of things for larger birds such as kestrels, buzzards and gulls to hunt smaller birds and chicks, and to take eggs. We must allow this to happen, no matter how distressing it may seem.**

Romy had thought she could easily handle that. She didn't intend to approach the birds or interfere with them. It was a privilege just to be on this island with them.

She felt hurt, as if she'd been accused of wanting to damage or harm them in some way, when she felt entirely the opposite. And she still couldn't understand what she might have done wrong.

'Spoiled city women?' she said out loud. This phrase annoyed her for its sweeping generalisation and inherent contempt. That man didn't know the first thing about her and yet he had labelled and dismissed her. She hated that kind of prejudice.

Her upset began to be replaced by annoyance, not just at the way she had been spoken to, but also at the fact that the two of them would have to share these few miles of island for the next couple of months and he had already spoiled it.

What a shame.

By the time she reached the cottage she felt a little calmer but still shaken. This was not the best start to her time on the island, and she felt a black cloud of depression hovering nearby.

You've failed, whispered a little voice in her head. *That didn't take long.*

As she took off her trainers, she tried to turn to the techniques that Dr Birley had taught her, to banish the voice, and with the help of some breathing, she felt a bit better.

And didn't Jesse tell me that the man was a bad-tempered loner? she reminded herself.

On impulse she picked up her phone and quickly texted Jesse:

Thanks for all your help yesterday, I really appreciated it. I just ran into the warden. He's exactly the old misery guts you said! What a charmer! Speak soon. Romy.

Leaving her phone on the hall table, she went upstairs to bathe, then came down for breakfast. She photographed her food first, then sat on the bench outside the back door so that she could bask in the morning sunshine with her coffee and granola, and gaze out over the bright sea, listening to the chatter and chirrup of birdsong.

A message vibrated on her phone and she saw that Jesse had texted her back.

Ha! Sorry you met the resident grouch. Steer clear if you can. Let me know if you need anything or want a boat ride. Happy to take you any time. J x

The message made her smile. She had an ally. Her annoyance over the meeting with the warden faded and she put it out of her mind. She had no need to see or talk to him unless she wanted. She could still follow her plans, that would be fine.

'Right,' she said, getting up with her empty dish and mug. 'I ought to get started on the reason why I actually came here.'

She went through to the sitting room with a fresh cup of coffee and settled down at her desk, firing up her computer and getting out her notes. The folder was titled *The Last Song of Winter*.

Flicking through the pages and pages of her handwritten notes, she quailed for a moment in front of the great task. For a while, she'd been telling herself that as soon as she got to the island, she would finally be in the right place to make a start. That's what she had told everyone – the therapists and counsellors and doctors, and her family – because that's what she believed herself. That all she needed was the time and space, and it would flow from her.

But, of course, it wasn't going to be that easy.

She'd first seen *The Last Song of Winter* in hospital, a DVD playing on an abandoned screen in a day room. Someone had set it going and then disappeared. She'd been intrigued by the melodramatic nature of the film, the sixties horror vibe and the unusual location: an island in a stormy sea, where it was clearly cold and uncomfortable. As the events unfolded towards their grisly end, the island itself became a character in the drama, its looming atmosphere and craggy beauty a vital ingredient. The film was a mixture of the mundane and supernatural with a strangely beautiful soundtrack. When it finished, Romy had been astonished to find that she had not only been gripped from the moment she sat down, but that she felt strangely tearful and moved as the last credits played to the twang of the title song, a melancholy, minor-keyed tune that was haunting and lovely.

The following day she had gone back at the same time and watched the whole thing again. She watched it almost a dozen times during her hospital stay, and then she googled it. It turned out that *The Last Song of Winter* had quite a following, and that there were countless forums, channels, accounts and threads dedicated to discussing it. Many thought it was a hilarious, schlocky melodrama full of unintentional comedy; memes of scary ghost monks and the screaming heroine were favourites for this crowd. Another tribe were earnest and academic, devoted to analysing what they considered the ironic, almost satirical brilliance of the film and the artistry behind every shot. But the group that interested Romy the most was the one that thought this film was a metaphor for grief and depression, and who considered it both meaningful and beautiful, a combination of the noir and horror traditions, with a distinctly British flavour.

That was what had led her to Veronica Mindenhall. And here she was, on Veronica's island itself, and she could at last concentrate on the mystery that had intrigued her so much. How on earth had someone like Veronica become associated with this weird film? And what was it really about?

That was what she wanted to find out, and what she wanted to write about.

Now she flicked over her notes again, and logged into her online cache of research. She had to make some sort of start. She had told Caroline she would come back with the bones of a first draft, and Caroline had said that was a great goal. But now she felt lost and confused. How to begin? How to organise all her many, many notes and thoughts and ideas into something not just coherent but interesting?

I'll start at the beginning, she decided. *With what got me started on all this.*

The film was in her download file, and she clicked on the icon. The familiar haunting music played again as the credits started to roll and the film began with the portentous opening shot of great waves crashing onto the shore.

The shore that is only a few hundred metres away, she realised with a shock. The reality that she was here, on Stix Island – as she'd always thought of Elfwy before – gave her a sudden chill. She began to watch again, gripped in a new way now that she had walked along the same jetty and up the same steps as the heroine did now, giggling and carefree as she arrives on the island.

A few minutes later, the heroine was inside Cliff House. It was sparsely furnished, but there was a style in its complete plainness. For the first time, Romy noticed that there were subtle monastic references everywhere in the house – a gothic arched mirror, a pattern of crosses on the edge of a table-cloth, the knotted rope that kept the clothes airer suspended from the kitchen ceiling. Candles in plain sticks flickered everywhere, creating odd shadows on the uneven walls of the house.

Romy leaned forward and switched off the film. It was all a little too close for comfort. It was taking on a new reality for her. She would watch in bite-sized chunks, she decided. That was enough for today.

Reaching down to her backpack, she pulled out the slim paperback biography of Veronica Mindenhall, the only one she'd been able to find. It was called *Memories of My Mother, Veronica Mindenhall*, a stiff title that reflected the prose inside. It was a formal portrait of Veronica, told in a cool and factual style that gave little insight into exactly who she was, and yet very few facts either. No wonder it was such a slight piece. It didn't seem to know if it was written for family or for the general public and, as a result, it could please neither.

She opened it where she had last turned down the page, and took up a pencil so she could underline anything of interest that she hadn't already marked up.

My mother's time at school in Paris resulted in the fluent French that she kept for the rest of her life, and a love of the French, French food, culture and litera-ture that never left her. I often saw her with her head buried in a classic French novel or work of philosophy. In particular, she was a great admirer of the writer Marguerite Heurot, whose classic novel The Lover of Minette *was one of her favourites before it was gener-ally recognised as a masterpiece and before its author was awarded membership of the august Académie Fran-çaise. Naturally, she read it in French. That book would be published after the war.*

Not long after my mother's return from Paris in 1939, war was declared and life changed for everyone. Veronica, always reclusive, decided that, despite her youth, she wanted to spend the war years on St Elfwy, the island that had belonged to the family since her father had purchased it on impulse in the early 1930s, after seeing it advertised in The Times. *Here, she contributed to the effort in many different ways, all of which were her singular own.*

The problem with a book like this, Romy thought, was that it raised as many questions as it answered, and dropped tantalising clues without supplying the answers, and there didn't seem to be many ways to learn more.

But that's why I'm here, she reminded herself. *To find out more.*

She reread the paragraph, wondering why Veronica's daughter had devoted so much time to stressing her mother's interest in this great French writer.

'Oh,' she said out loud to herself. 'This is probably a riposte, because of Veronica's connection with the down-market film.'

After all, the movie had been regarded as trashy pulp fiction for many years after its release. Describing Veronica's tastes in literature had the purpose of making her look intellectual and learned. That must be it.

Romy felt pleased with this insight, and opened her notebook. She wrote: *Interest in Heurot. Lover of Minette. Favourite book???*

That's probably worth looking into, she thought. *At some point.*

She had a vague memory of reading the novel herself, the summer before she went up to university, but she couldn't remember very much about it. But then, she'd been reading so much in preparation for her degree course, it was no wonder.

Romy settled down to her laptop, and decided she would research the island as far back as she could.

This is the place Veronica loved. Now that I'm here, surely I'll begin to understand her on a deeper level? And that's got to help me understand what links her to the film, how it all came about.

To understand. That was what she wanted most.

Chapter Eleven

'Hi, chicken, how are you doing?'

Flo's voice came delightfully clear down the phone line.

Romy stood outside the cottage, her bare feet prickled by the stiff island grass, a jaunty breeze blowing around her and shaking the heads of the flowers growing over the garden wall. 'I'm doing really well.'

'Thanks for doing all your forms and sending the food pics. You are doing really well. Any issues?'

'Not yet!' Romy said chirpily. It was true. She was getting used to the wails and shrieks of the birds at night, and her noise-cancelling headphones helped with that, of course.

'You're not creeped out being on the island, where the film was made, are you?'

'No, it's fine. After you've watched it as many times as I have, it doesn't have the same effect.' She knew that this wasn't strictly true but she was managing her feelings around the film by watching it in small chunks and then writing down her notes before returning to it.

'So how is the writing going?'

Romy gazed out across the island towards the sea. The wind was whipping little white crests on the water, which was a petrol blue shot through with deep green. She could see tiny dots on the beach far away; the early morning surfers were up to enjoy the swell. The truth was, she wasn't that sure now that she had all that much to say about Veronica and the film. She was lacking something, some kind of connection, that her online research could not provide. 'Yeah, it's all going well. But I'm taking it easy. Not rushing.'

She could hear Flo bustling around as she listened. 'Good idea,' her sister said. 'Take it easy, rest and relax. Try to get to the mainland a few times a week, won't you? And let me know if you need a visitor. I've got to go, sweetheart. Loving your photos, keep sending them. It really is ravishing there, isn't it?'

'Yes, it really is. Bye, Flo. Speak soon.'

'Bye, darling.'

The phone went quiet and Romy took a deep breath of sea air, watching a swirl of birds overhead, hearing that ceaseless chatter of their cries.

'Right,' she said. 'Routine. Walk. Work.'

As long as she stuck to her routines, she would be all right.

Romy was absorbed by something she had found on the internet – a fresh account of the film by someone who had worked on it – when a loud rapping on the front door broke into her thoughts. She leapt up, suddenly frightened. Loud knocking was the last thing she expected at her island cottage.

She went to the door and opened it tentatively, guessing that it could only be one person. Outside, the warden was standing staring out at the view beyond the cottage as he waited for her to answer. In the instant before he turned back to look at her again, she saw that sitting on his shoulder was a large, glossy black raven, its claws gripping the shoulder of his dark jacket.

He turned to face her and the raven stepped slightly on its talons, to keep steady. It cocked its head at Romy, bright eyes glinting.

'Hello,' the warden said gruffly, frowning slightly.

'If you've come to shout at me again, I'd rather you didn't,' Romy said coolly. She had gathered her courage since the encounter the day before yesterday, and already decided that she would stand up for herself if she had to. 'I've reread my contract and you can be sure I'll follow it to the letter.' She went to close the door.

'Wait!' He put up his hand. 'Don't. Can you give me a moment?'

She looked around the edge of the door at him. 'Well?'

He looked awkward suddenly and took a deep breath before speaking again. 'Look, I was out of order. I've come to apologise.'

'Okay.'

'Okay? So you accept my apology?'

'How can I?'

'Er . . . what?'

'How can I accept an apology that I haven't received yet?'

He stared at her, frowning again, and then suddenly his

expression changed and he laughed. 'Good point. All right. I'd like to apologise.'

There was a long pause and she said, 'Go ahead.'

He shook his head and laughed again. 'You're like a terrier.'

Romy shrugged. 'If you want to apologise, then do it. You keep saying you want to but you don't seem to think you need to.'

'You're very literal. All right. I thoroughly and sincerely apologise for telling you off the other day. You're right, you weren't doing anything wrong. I got annoyed for other reasons and took it out on you. I'm sorry. Do you accept my apology?'

'You haven't exactly rushed over.'

'No. I should have come earlier. I had to go to the mainland yesterday. But I really am sorry. I've been feeling really bad about it.'

Romy looked at him. The green eyes, which had looked so cold before, had softened and were almost beseeching. Close up, the white hair had a subtle range of white and grey within it, and she could see his cheeks and chin were covered in soft white stubble as well. It had the effect, oddly, of making him look younger. But it wasn't only the warden looking at her, the raven had also fixed her with a still, beady gaze.

'Is this your familiar?' she asked, pointing at the bird.

He lifted a hand and gently touched the claws on his shoulder. 'This is Martha. She took a shine to me a summer or two ago and she's become my friend.'

'She's very fine.'

'Yes, a beauty.' He lifted his eyebrows. 'So . . . now it's my turn to pin you down. Do you accept my apology or not?'

She was thoughtful for a moment, remembering what Jesse had said about how grouchy and generally unpleasant this man was. At least he wasn't shouting now, though. Still, she didn't have much choice, bearing in mind the circumstances. 'I didn't much enjoy being shouted at, but I appreciate that you've come here. We have to exist almost alone in a very small space, so in the interests of a good atmosphere, yes, I accept your apology.'

'Good.' He smiled for the first time. 'In that case, why don't you come around for tea this afternoon? A peace offering.'

'Oh.' Romy was surprised. She hadn't expected that they would actually make friends. A courteous recognition of each other's existence was just about all she had anticipated and she wasn't sure she wanted anything else. But what harm could a friendly cup of tea do? She cast her mind over her schedule and knew that she had not yet put anything into her free time this afternoon.

'All right,' she said. 'Thanks. Just a quick one.'

He laughed. 'Yeah, you must be in a hurry.'

'I do have things to do—'

'I'm kidding, you do what you want. You don't have to answer to me. And I guess I don't need to give you my address either.'

Romy shook her head. 'I'll find it.'

'My name is Richard, by the way. You probably know that.'

'I'm Romy.'

'Yeah, you said . . . and they told me.' He smiled again. 'See you later, Romy. Any time from four p.m.'

He turned and walked off down the path towards the little gate at the front of the cottage, the large black raven still perched on his shoulder. Romy watched him go and then thought with a rush of excitement:

Oh my goodness. I'm going into Cliff House. The actual house. Today!

Despite her tingling anticipation of her visit to Cliff House, Romy found herself unexpectedly absorbed in her work, with the new account of the filming she'd found. She was keen to get down to the caves and see them for herself. She would have to ask Jesse about that, she thought, and made a mental note to text him later.

Then, with a gasp, she noticed the time and jumped up, feeling panicked that she would be late for the four p.m. tea date.

Stop.

The mental command Romy had learned to perfect. She stood stock still in the middle of the sitting room and concentrated on her breathing.

Now. Play it forward.

She imagined taking her time, getting ready at a slow pace, and watching as the minutes ticked away on the clock. She visualised leaving the cottage, walking slowly over to the main house and knocking at the door in a leisurely way. In her imagination, the clock said quarter past four. Her mind began to spin and her palms to prickle. She tapped the skin on her hand with her forefinger and breathed in long and slow, while she considered, *What happens next?*

Richard will be angry!

She told herself, *He will not be angry and, if he is, so what?*

I'll be disappointed in myself!

She said firmly, *You have no need. You make the rules. You are in control. You can decide what to do and when.*

She knew what Dr Birley would say to her. She could imagine him now, short and round and dishevelled, gazing at her over the top of his glasses, twitching slightly in that way he had. 'Be late, Romy. Go on! Be half an hour late! What are you afraid of?'

Not so long ago, her thoughts would have taken her into a nightmarish territory of death and disaster that she would have done anything to avoid, accepted any bargain to prevent. But now, after her treatment and her medication, she was more confident that she understood that these terrible events would not happen if she was five minutes late.

Breathing out, Romy opened her eyes, checked the time again and let the agitation wash away from her. She could control this now, and it was all important that she did. She could never go back to those bad old days again.

As soon as she had left the cottage, Romy felt calmer and her excitement about going to Cliff House returned. Before coming to the island, she had hoped that she might be able to go inside, but she'd known it was by no means certain. Hearing that visitors were not allowed in, she was sure this would be even harder than she'd imagined. But now she was on her way there. Black-and-white images from the film played through her head. How much would it have changed in all these years?

She took a circuitous path from the cottage towards the white house, taking her time as much as possible, not just to help break her addiction to rigorous timekeeping but also to breathe in as much of the sea air as she could. The view was so beautiful that she was beginning to feel that every minute away from it was a terrible waste, especially on a day like this. Gulls were on the move, their huge wingspans stretched out against the sky as they rode the currents in soft circles, wheeling around as they scrutinised the sea and cliffs for food. Other, smaller birds flitted around the cliffs, or jumped and hopped around the ground cover, exploring the heather and hedges. Insects and butterflies fluttered among the pink and white flowers. Out on the waves, there were boats on the move. She thought that she spotted the yellow craft that had brought her out the day before but it zoomed out of sight before she could be sure it was the same one.

I wonder what Jesse is up to . . .

She took off her light jacket, already too hot. It was very warm for May, but she guessed that tomorrow it could easily be freezing cold and dank. The sea could go from the cerulean, twinkling ripple below to a roaring, fierce grey torrent. That was part of the charm of this part of the world.

Cliff House was only a twenty-minute walk or so from the cottage, even if she took it slowly. She was glad that there was even this distance – if, by some miracle, she and Richard began to get on like a house on fire, she still wouldn't want to be too close. Privacy was the point of a place like this.

She was about to approach the front door when she saw that the back door was open, so she headed there instead. The garden around the back of Cliff House was beautifully kept, with tubs of bright spidery geraniums and soft petunias, and banks of rosemary and lavender. As she was admiring it, Richard came out of the house. He had taken off his jacket and was wearing a blue shirt over a T-shirt, with Martha the raven still perched on his shoulder, now making a raucous cawing sound as they stepped outside together.

'Shut up, Martha, you're bloody deafening me,' he said in a conversational way to the bird, before he spotted Romy. His face brightened. 'Hi! Thanks for coming. What do you fancy? Tea? Coffee? I've got one of those pod machines, you can even have a cappuccino or a latte if you want.'

'Thanks, I'll have a cup of tea. Just ordinary tea with milk.'

'Great, a woman after my own heart. Come in and I'll make it. Get off me, Martha, shoo, shoo!' The big bird fluttered up as he brushed her off, cawed and then took to the wing, flying off over the garden. 'Peace at last.'

Romy followed him into the kitchen, a large cool room with rough plastered-and-whitewashed walls and a floor of slate flags covered in old rugs. It was dominated by an electric range like the one in Clover Cottage but bigger. The cupboards were modern but plain, nothing was fussy. With a jolt of recognition she realised that, although the fittings were new, the room itself had changed very little from the one in the film. The clothes airer that had hung from the ceiling in the film had gone, but the kitchen table looked very much like it was the same one.

Her skin prickled and tingled at the strange sense of déjà vu mixed with the feeling of stepping into a dream world. 'What a lovely house. This room is wonderful! I suppose this belongs to the bird sanctuary?'

Richard went to fill the kettle at the sink. 'Yes. It's a bit institutional, but it suits me. Does the job. It's weatherproof, that's the main thing. Have a seat. Then we'll take the tea outside. I've even got biscuits!' He gestured to a plate of digestives on the table.

'Great, thanks.' Romy sat down. It was cool in the kitchen after the warmth of outside. 'How long have you been here?'

'Quite a while,' he said, setting the kettle on the range top. 'About five years now. That's gone quick. Feels like five minutes.'

'Have you always been keen on birds?'

Richard laughed. 'In a word – yes. I have always been very keen on birds. My favourite place in the world when I was growing up was Slimbridge. Do you know it?'

'The bird centre in Gloucestershire.'

Richard nodded. 'It all started when my dad took me to see a murmuration. You know, that extraordinary cloud of starlings, swooping and whirling in the sky. It's just one of nature's most incredible sights. At that moment, I fell in love with birds, and why they do what they do. And the more I know about them, the more astonishing they become. I can't really think of anything I'd rather do than be here, studying, monitoring, recording and protecting the amazing wild birds of this part of the world.'

'Is there still much to learn about birds?' Romy said, and then, seeing his expression, said, 'Sorry, stupid question.'

'No, no, I'm quite interested in it. It's never occurred to me that people might think we know all there is to know. In fact, we really only began to study the behaviour of birds quite recently. It was only in the 1930s that experiments started being done around here to find out more about where the birds went in migration, how they found their way back, how their breeding worked . . . And how to protect them from man, both in terms of hunting and in general ecological ways. Shipping companies used to dump oil around here, with awful effects on the birds – that's stopped. And not so long ago, chicks were slaughtered by the thousands, dragged from burrows, ploughed into the soil as fertiliser or used as bait in lobster pots. Eggs were used to make soap. The guillemots used to be hunted like pheasant, shot from boats by floating shooting parties. So we've made progress. But it's not over yet. There are still lots and lots of mysteries to find the answers to.'

'That's fascinating,' Romy said, shaking her head. 'Honestly.'

'It is to me. I'm glad if you can see it too. Right, kettle's boiled. Let's go outside and sit in the sun.'

The rosemary bushes in the garden gave off a warm scent, with bees buzzing around the blue-purple flowers. On the stone terrace was an all-weather table and chairs, where

Richard put the tray down. Romy had been reluctant to leave the kitchen, which she had surreptitiously been studying as hard as she could to reconcile with its appearance in the film, but it was lovely out here. She sat down opposite him.

'It's so peaceful here,' she said. 'Just so gorgeous.'

'Yes, you get used to the quiet – apart from the birds, of course. But it'll get a bit busier as we go through the season. You'll notice the boats skirt the island more often. They take the tourists on tours around it, pointing out the areas of interest, any wildlife that makes an appearance. It's particularly popular at seal pup time. If dolphins or porpoises make an appearance, even better. We've even had the occasional whale.'

'Jesse from the tour company brought me over,' Romy volunteered.

Richard made a face. 'Oh, yes. Jesse.' He poured out the tea into mugs.

'Don't you like him?'

'He's all right. Bit of a smart arse. Thinks he knows everything. And also he fully believes that his Australian charm is simply irresistible. I'm afraid I can't see it. Maybe it works on the girls but it doesn't work on me. Here's your tea, help yourself to milk.'

'He seemed very friendly. I liked him.' Romy poured some milk from the jug into her tea.

'Well, there you are. You're a girl. He comes here a few times a year to do tours. I try and make sure I'm not here. I can't bear the gawpers.' He shrugged. 'I don't know. I suppose Jesse's all right. There's just something about him that rubs me up the wrong way. I suspect he feels the same about me. So it's best if we avoid each other.'

She knew he must mean the tours Jesse gave connected with the film, but she had already decided not to mention it if he didn't. It wasn't a given that he shared the same reticence about it as the trust did, but there was no point in risking it. She decided to change the subject. 'So . . . the bird sanctuary is governed by a trust, and they own the island – is that right?'

'That's pretty much the shape of it, yes. The main aim is the protection of the wildlife, of course, primarily the birds. But there is also the element of encouraging artistic creation as well. So these retreats are awarded to various applicants every year.' He smiled over at her. 'I get used to mad artists and writers appearing here. Some of them do get on my nerves – the ones who don't respect the rules. The last bloke here was a nightmare, couldn't get it through his thick head that the birds weren't tame pets for him to coo over.' He gave her an apologetic look. 'I'm afraid you got a bit of the brunt of annoyance. I can see you're respectful.'

'That's okay. It's all forgotten.'

'And you're writing something, aren't you?'

'That's right. I'm planning to write the history of the religious community on the island, and how it came to be here.' It was something she had made up for her application, to conceal her real interest in the film.

'Well, it must be a good idea,' he said. 'The trust is very picky about who's allowed here. If they don't like the submissions, they don't pick anyone at all.'

'Do you get any say?'

210

Richard guffawed. 'The humble warden? What do you think?'

'So they just tell you who's coming?' Romy took another sip of her tea. 'I was so surprised to get my place, as I submitted so late. Maybe I was just lucky because they didn't like the other submissions. They certainly asked plenty about my book and everything around it.'

Richard nodded and said nothing. He didn't appear to be interested in her book himself. After a moment, though, he said, 'It's not everyone who sees the appeal of a place like this. What did you like about it?'

She hesitated, wondering how much to tell him about her backstory. He had softened from the aggressive stranger who had upset her so much into an ordinary man with a passion for birds and a talent for making a good cup of tea. She was tempted to start explaining that she was in recovery from an illness and this was part of her recuperation – a major step in being independent, learning to trust herself and, finally, after years of freeze, learning to think and work again. Then she decided that was a little too much information to hand over to a complete stranger. There was no need for Richard to know any of it. 'I just need the peace to write my book. I'm sure you get lots of people like me.'

'A few,' he said with a smile. 'When you've finished your tea, I'll take you round the island if you like. So you can see it from my perspective.'

'I'd like that,' Romy said. 'I'm a firm fan of learning as much as you can from an expert when you get the chance.'

'Sensible.'

211

She put down her mug. 'Any chance I can use your loo before we go?'

'Of course – just through the kitchen, door to your left once you're in the hall.' Just then there was the flap of large wings and Martha swooped down with a loud caw onto Richard's shoulder. 'Ah, here's my friend. She's wondering who you are, I expect.'

Romy stood up. 'I'll leave you to explain. Back in a sec.'

She went through the kitchen and out into the hall, where she stopped to look around, and gasped when she saw the exact gothic mirror that she had noticed the previous day in the film. Pulling out her phone with shaking hands, she opened it and snapped a picture of the hall and the mirror from a few angles. It felt sneaky but she knew she wouldn't be able to recall it properly later, and she might never get another chance. Then she went through the left-hand door, only to find herself in a narrow corridor lined with low bookshelves, the walls covered with framed photographs, the door to the lavatory at the far end.

'Oh my goodness!' she said, astonished. The photographs were of the Mindenhall family going back to the 1930s. One that drew her eye at once was of a man in a smart suit, sitting on what was obviously a chair made to look like a throne with cardboard and shiny paper, wearing a cardboard crown and holding a homemade sceptre and orb. He had thick dark hair and a jutting forehead, and a silly expression on his face, with his eyes crossed. A sign at his feet read *King of St Elfwy*.

This was George Mindenhall, of course. She recognised him from her research into Veronica. He had been a famous actor, a celebrity in his day who was pretty much forgotten now. The man who had bought this island on impulse all those years ago, and the reason she was standing in this house right now. He must have been very arrogant to award himself the kingship like this, although there was an air of self-mockery around the whole thing. Perhaps it was a family joke.

She stood and stared for a moment and then moved on to the next photograph. Her heart raced as she recognised Veronica Mindenhall, standing on a rock near the cliff edge, gazing out to sea, her eyes fierce and her blonde hair blowing in the wind. She was wearing a white shirt and wide-legged trousers belted in at the waist with a man's belt.

She could be out of the pages of Vogue! *Romy thought. Though I expect not in the thirties. What a look she has – that face!*

She pulled out her phone and snapped pictures of the two photographs and then realised she had already taken too long, so she reluctantly put the phone away and went to the loo. She had forgotten something vital: this house was not just the setting for *The Last Song of Winter*, it was also Veronica's home. She had lived here for years. Her spirit, and that of her family, was here too. It was just as important – if not more important – than the film.

Veronica lived here. It's her place.

On the way back, she took out her phone again and switched it to video, then filmed the wall slowly as she walked back, trying to get in as many of the photographs as she could. As she reached the end of the little gallery, she

stopped to switch it off and her eye was caught by the spine
of a book on the shelf below. It was an elegant pale and
small hardback, the title of the book in large Roman letters:
L'Amant de Minette.

The Lover of Minette.

The very book she had read about in the memoir. It was
one of Veronica's favourites. On impulse she pulled it out
and opened it, flicking through the pages. They were marked,
she noticed, underlined in pen and with comments scrawled
all over, and there was a sheaf of thin folded paper, obviously
typed on, tucked into the cover.

Knowing she had been away long enough, she took it with
her back to the garden.

Richard was far too polite to remark on her absence
but she said cheerily, 'Sorry, I got absorbed looking at your
bookshelf!'

'Ah, happens to the best of us.'

She held out the novel. 'I couldn't help seeing this. I loved
this book! I read it for my degree.'

'Oh, what did you read?'

'French and Philosophy. I'd just love to read it again. I
don't suppose I can borrow it, can I?'

A dubious look passed over Richard's face. 'I'm not
sure . . . Everything here belongs to the trust, you see. It's a
kind of museum in some ways.'

'I'll be very careful with it. And of course, I promise to
return it.' She smiled. 'But don't worry, I completely understand if you can't lend it.'

Richard considered for a moment. Martha, back on his

shoulder, fixed her with that black beady eye and Romy felt a pang of guilt. She'd already taken advantage of his hospitality by filming the photographs. Now she was trying to get more details about Veronica without admitting it. But what was the harm really? She'd tell him all about it eventually. 'Well,' he said. 'I guess I know where to find you and it! As long as you can return it to me, say, next week, I suppose that'll be fine.'

'Thanks so much, I appreciate it,' she said sincerely. 'I will look after it.'

'It's fine. Leave it here, and you can collect it when we get back. I'm going to put Martha on her perch, she knows not to follow me then. I'll leave the book on the kitchen table while we go on our walk.'

Fifteen minutes later, they were walking along the dirt path that led to the bird colonies. Romy felt completely at ease. It was hard to believe that only recently she'd been almost crying at the way he'd spoken to her. Now Richard was enthusiastic, friendly and very good company. Besides being interesting and articulate, he was also funny and charming in a way she didn't expect. The white hair had made her assume he was old but now she realised he must only be in his forties. Still a bit older than she was, but not ancient by any means.

'Do you ever leave the island?' she asked, as they approached the thickest bird colonies. 'I mean, for longer than shopping trips.'

'I don't like to, but I've got mandated times when I have

to go. Mental health and all that. Temporary wardens come in at those times. But I'm always here for this time of year because it's so exciting.' He grinned at her. 'It's mating season. The whole place is alive with courtship and breeding. Lots of shagging, in other words.'

Romy laughed awkwardly. 'Oh, right. Of course.'

He didn't seem to notice her slight discomfort. 'Right now, there's a huge amount of activity as the birds return to their breeding ground. They're seeking out their old nests, their old cliff spots and their old burrows. You'd be amazed what creatures of habit they are. Most of them are monogamous, finding the same mate again year after year. That's why this part of the year is so important. They're on the brink of mating, they're going through the preparations – hence all the movement and noise.' He pointed to the stacks, high twisting rocky towers that reached up almost as high as the island, but set further out to sea. 'See all the black-and-white birds? All packed together like that, shoulder to shoulder, out there?'

'The ones that look like penguins?'

'They're from the same family of auks. Those are guillemots. The locals call them eligugs. That's the Welsh name. They've been out there for a few weeks now, getting used to being close to each other again, the males and females getting to know one another before they mate. They preen each other and sit together, settling down into their spot ready to incubate an egg. After they mate, the eggs will appear a week or two later, very pretty pointed things though you'll be lucky to see one close up, or that isn't covered in guano.

And you will need to keep clear of the cliffs as much as possible once the eggs are laid. You can easily startle the birds off the nests.'

Romy stared over at the bird-covered stacks, taking out her phone so she could snap some photographs of the guillemots. 'They're so pretty!'

'Yes, and they are also pretty stupid – or so it seems. They balance on those impossible cliff towers and lay just one egg, which they keep up there, on the edge, sitting it on their feet and passing it from male to female to take turns brooding. Like slow, high-stakes football.'

'Don't they lose them over the edge?'

'Yes, they do lose a good number. But you'd be surprised, most survive. And of course, it's the stupidest birds who fail to ensure the survival of the egg – managing to stick it to the stack with guano so it can't be turned, or letting it fall down a crevice or just kicking it off the edge – so there's probably a bit of natural selection there as well.'

Romy remembered the curious night-time cries she'd heard. 'I've seen some great flocks of birds come in quite late, they make pretty raucous noises. I managed to tune it out after a while, but it sounded like they were going to go on all night.'

Richard nodded, smiling. 'I'll show you something. Let's keep walking.'

They walked on. On the stacks, the guillemots kept up a constant movement and loud chattering, sometimes diving or falling off the crowded tower, flying to a nearby rock and strutting in the sunshine before attempting to return to their previous spot. Romy laughed as she saw one bird dive-bomb back on, scattering several others in a bid to regain position. Crash landings seemed to be a popular method of winning back a lost spot.

Richard stopped at the edge of the path, pointing to a patch of sea not too far from the island. 'See that?'

She looked out in the direction he indicated and saw what looked like thousands of black-and-white birds, less intensely coloured than the guillemots, sitting on the surface of the water, floating silently, a speckled carpet moving with the swell of the waves.

'What are they doing?'

'It's called rafting. They're taking a mass rest. Just hanging out for a bit. Those are the manx shearwaters, or cocklollies.'

'Cocklollies! Eligugs!' Romy exclaimed. 'Such marvellous names.'

'They're at sea all day but they come back at night. They nest in burrows in the ground. At this time of year, like the guillemots, they're busy with rituals and dances and conversations. They need to get to know one another again. To learn to trust. To get back into the habit of loving.'

'Do they?' It had never occurred to her that birds might require such a thing.

Richard nodded. 'It makes sense, if you think about it. The mates won't have seen each other for almost a year. They've lived a solitary life since they left the colonies, to protect themselves as much as anything. They need to re-establish their bonds before they mate and become parents again. They start sorting out their old burrow together, lining it with feathers, making it nice for the chick. Getting in the mood.'

Romy shook her head. 'I just never thought of birds like this – that they might need to woo, and love and trust. Like us.'

'They'll take their time over their courtship – that's what you heard last night. It can be quite a racket. Once they've mated, the female zips back to sea, we think to stuff herself with fish in preparation for laying the egg. Then she and her husband take turns looking after it – they both have brood pouches. All very equitable.'

'They were so noisy at night,' Romy said, gazing at the mass of silent floating birds. 'Why aren't they making any noise now?'

Richard shrugged. 'They just seem to be enjoying their early evening. Taking a bit of time off the exhausting mating rituals.' He laughed.

Romy smiled too. 'You know, I had no idea about all this. I thought birds were . . . just birds.'

'We've only scratched the surface. Come on, let's head back. But if you're wondering what all the rioting is in the night – it's the shearwaters.'

They turned back towards the way they had come. The evening breeze had sprung up, cool and fragrant.

Richard said, 'They can sound a bit eerie at times. I hope they didn't spook you.'

Romy gave him a sideways look. 'I wasn't frightened.'

'Of course not. But just in case, why don't I give you my

number? For safety if nothing else? I can be right over if you have any problems.'

'Like what?'

'I don't know. You probably won't need me. But it can't hurt.'

'Okay.' She tapped his number into her contacts as he dictated it to her. Then she said, 'Thanks so much for the tea and the walk. It's been great.'

'You're welcome. I'm going over to the mainland tomorrow if you want a trip or need any shopping.'

She thought of Jesse, who had said he would take her. 'I'm fine for now, thank you. I'm still well stocked.'

'Okay. I go once a week at least. I can always let you know when.'

'Thanks, that will be very helpful.'

They walked back in companionable silence. At Cliff House, Richard went inside and came back with the novel, which he handed to her with a smile. 'Here you are. Enjoy it. I don't think anyone else is going to be in a rush to read a novel in the original French, so keep it as long as you like. Leave it in Clover Cottage if you want, I can always get it from there.'

'Thank you. And thanks again for the tour of the birds. I loved it.' She held the book, enjoying its smooth feel and the anticipation it sparked.

'You're welcome,' Richard said. 'Don't forget, you can call on me at any time.'

'Thanks, Richard,' Romy said. 'See you soon.'

She turned to go home.

That went very well, she thought. *I think we might be friends after all. Funny how things can change so fast.*

She walked quickly in the direction of home, eager to look inside the novel and see what the scrawlings were on its pages, and what was written on the folded sheaf of paper inside the jacket. Could this be Veronica's copy of *The Lover of Minette*? It looked old enough. It must be. It was in her house, in French.

Romy's heart raced with excitement and she quickened her pace.

At last I'm going to get to know something about Veronica herself. Something no one else knows. It's my first real connection with her.

I can't wait.

PART THREE

Chapter Twelve
VERONICA
1940

Veronica stood on the jetty, watching the little motor boat coming in towards her. She shielded her eyes with one hand and waved hard at the approaching craft. It was bright and windy, the stiff breeze flapping her trousers about her legs and cutting through her bulky fisherman's jumper.

'Hi there!' she called. 'Hello!'

There was the familiar figure on the boat, plump and short with a shock of fair hair, his expression set in its usual scowl. At first, when Jim had brought her over, Veronica had been frightened of him, and repelled by his face, which was droopy and ugly. But now she was used to him and appreciated his calm and reliability. She needed that. She depended on him now, far more than she ought to.

She came dashing down to the edge of the jetty with her collie Boris bounding at her heels. The eager dog rushed forward and back, swirling around her, his tail wagging at the excitement of the arrival. 'Calm down, Boris! Hello, Jim!'

Jim brought the little motor boat to a halt and tied it up. He scowled up at her through the bright sunshine. 'Good day, 'm. There's a swell out there, that's for sure. Glad not to be rowing today.'

The motor boat could not be used all the time, with fuel rationed. Journeys had to be carefully planned.

'Glad you made it,' Veronica said happily.

'I'm the last boat still here,' Jim said. 'Others have all gone, even the lifeboats.'

'Of course. The evacuation.' She was suddenly solemn. She had seen the lifeboats leaving the station, heading southwards for the coast of France, along with the fishing boats and the last of the old trawlers not requisitioned by the Admiralty already. Jim hadn't taken part in the rescue from the beaches, his boat had been out of action then. She was ashamed of how relieved she felt that, as a result, he was still here to come to the island.

Jim swung two large sacks up onto the jetty, then climbed up after them, bringing a leather satchel with him.

'Come up to the house, I'll make tea,' Veronica said, her heart lifted by the sight of the satchel. It surely contained treasure.

She strode back up the steps, Jim following behind with the sacks. All around, the birds whirled and called. On the slopes, she could see puffins in crowds, while gulls swooped back and forth overhead and oystercatchers whistled and chirped at their approach.

They walked around to the back door of the white house, as he refused to come in the front, and he followed her into the back kitchen where she bustled about making tea while he dumped the sacks near the pantry.

'Are you going to stay over, Jim?' she asked.

'Ah,' he said, which meant yes. 'In the old barn.'

'You could stay in one of the cottages, you know.'

'Barn'll do.'

The first time she'd seen where he'd intended to stay, she'd been shocked. The roof was barely intact, and there was nothing much there at all, except an old fireplace, a sea lantern, and a bed made of driftwood that looked distinctly uncomfortable. The barn smelled musty and smoky, and the corners were dark with mouse droppings. It didn't look at all like a nice place when there were other more comfortable places to stay. But Jim insisted.

'We fishermen always came here,' he said stubbornly. 'It's our place.'

That was from the time before Daddy had bought the island, when it had still belonged to the Church, though it had been long deserted. The old monastery was already in ruins long before then. It had been rented out as farmland for a good many years, and provided a place for shelter when the sea was too rough to make the homeward crossing the two miles across the channel back to the mainland.

'I'll walk with you there,' she said, 'then we can come back for tea. It'll be brewed by then.'

'Ah.'

They walked together the short distance from the house to the barn, going out of the back gate and crossing a stretch of grass rich with flowers. Above them, on the plateaus of grass and green fern, were hundreds of rabbits, staring down at them as they walked.

'Look,' Veronica said, pointing at them. 'Your traps should be full.'

'That'll be right. I'm gonna check 'em all after the tea.'

He went into the barn, and emptied out some things from his satchel, coming out a moment later with the bundle of letters she'd hoped for. 'These are yours, 'm.'

'Thank you, Jim.' The arrival of letters was one of the best days of the week. She took them gladly, savouring the potential. She would not read them yet, but would keep them till later. 'Come on then, let's have tea.'

Jim had brought a can of milk from the farm so there was the treat of the real stuff instead of the powdered she had to use when she'd run out. They sipped their tea and Jim said, 'I've got mackerel for 'ee and also sea trout.'

'Thank you, Jim. We'll work it all out when we see what we have in the way of rabbits and eggs.'

'Late in the season,' Jim said gruffly. 'Eggs nearly finished for the year.'

'Yes, but there should be some late clutches. Let's look anyway.'

After tea, they went out and walked to the higher point of the island, tramping over pink and white sea campion as they went. Boris had been left at home for this expedition, as the birds were nesting and should not be disturbed.

Jim pointed to a colony of small birds, brown-black on top and white below, standing in crowds among rocks and boulders on an outcrop high above them.

'Eligugs,' he said. 'Guillemots. They nest standing there like that, one egg each. Keep it on their feet, pass it back and forth, mate to mate. When it hatches, they have to guard the chick. Gulls take it in a mouthful if they're not careful. Then the chick jumps off the cliff with the father into the sea, where he'll teach 'em to swim and fly and protect 'em.'

She looked up at the colony, the mass of birds jammed together, barely a bill's space between them.

'I can look out some guillemot eggs later,' Jim offered. 'And razorbills.'

'If you like.'

'We'll look out the gulls first.'

They reached the plateau, thick with purple moor grass, bracken and heather, where the nests were easily concealed. Jim approached the nests, tramping hard in his fisherman's boots to scare away the squawking gulls. They rose up, their pink legs splayed, shrieking in protest and swooping back and forth as Jim made his way between the nests, looking for fresh clutches, lobbing stale eggs over the cliff as he went.

Veronica turned to look inland at the gentle slope of the island, alive with birds. She could see sparrows and dunnocks and stonechats, but they were only the ones she recognised – there were many more. She must ask Jim to teach her more about them. Everywhere were throngs of birds and the air was full of noise. The colours of the island filled her with a kind of calm bliss: the pinks and purples and greens and yellows of the grasses and flowers, the dark stone, the streaks of copper and green in the cliffs, the blue and white of the sea. From where she was standing she could see, further off and a little lower, the two freshwater lakes that supplied water to the house and cottages, where the seabirds washed salt from their plumage.

A few minutes later, Jim reappeared, this time with his satchel full of gulls' eggs. 'I reckon this is the last we'll get this year. Lots have gone over.'

'No more eggs,' she said in dismay. She'd got used to the bounty of gulls' eggs since arriving a month ago. 'You'd better bring me some chickens, Jim. Good layers.'

'You'll need a run.'

'Will I? There aren't any foxes here.'

'Kestrels will take 'em. And you'll need to keep 'em contained. I'll help.'

'Thanks, Jim.'

'I'm gonna check the traps now.'

'Fine, I'll see you back at the house. Shall I take the eggs?'

He nodded and handed over the satchel, then headed off to find his snares and check for rabbits. Veronica put the satchel on and strolled back to the house, her hair lifted and ruffled by the wind. It was warm, a sunny June, but still cool. But here, far from everywhere on the island, it was peaceful.

As she had this thought, she heard the roar of engines and turned to see a phalanx of planes approaching from the east. They soared over the mainland and banked right, swooping over the island so that she could see the RAF roundels on the underside of the wings. What were they? Lancasters? Fortresses? She had no more idea of how to identify these vast metal birds than name all the feathered ones that thronged the island. Where were they going?

She watched them roar into the distance, heading out over the Atlantic.

The war seems so far away and yet it is closer here than I ever imagined it would be.

She turned back towards the big white house, where her letters awaited her.

Her parents had refused when Veronica said she wanted to live on the island. She was far too young at seventeen, and she was not allowed to go there alone until she was at least eighteen, it didn't matter how much she begged and pleaded.

After she'd returned from Paris, it seemed like life had sprung suddenly into the most intense and joyful experience possible, burning with sensation, only to be doused to emptiness and misery immediately afterwards. Her spirits plummeted.

'What on earth is wrong with you?' Billie said. She had changed even in the few months that Veronica had been away. She had turned fifteen, and was taller and more grown-up. Like Veronica, she was fair but in the glossy way that Veronica could never manage, and had suddenly gained the curves and bosom Veronica lacked. 'Honestly, Vee. I'm so intensely jealous. You've just been to stay in Paris. You've had a marvellous time with a glamorous new friend, this lovely Irène who sounds like a dream. You can't think how much I'd like to meet her. You even went shopping at Chanel! And yet you're moping around like you had a terrible time.'

'Of course I didn't,' Veronica said. They were strolling together on the heath, enjoying the bright sunshine. The summer had turned hot and bright. 'I had a wonderful time. I miss it, to be honest. And I feel as though there's nothing to look forward to in life ever again.'

'That's ridiculous. You're not even eighteen years old. How can your life be over?'

Veronica shrugged. 'I don't know. But I can't bear it here. I really can't. I loved Paris but that's over. It won't happen again, not for ages. I just want to go to the island as soon as I can. I've missed it so horribly.'

'We'll be there soon, for the whole summer, just as usual,' Billie said in a comforting way. 'If you had to choose – Paris or the island – which would it be?'

Veronica thought, before lifting her face to the sky, spreading her arms and crying, 'Oh, I just don't know, Billie! Paris, I suppose. But only if . . . if it could be the same as it was then.'

Billie looked at her oddly. 'Did you fall in love or something, my Vee?'

Veronica flushed deep red and said quickly, 'I love Jack, you know that. My heart is still a vale of violets.'

'Hmm.' Billie looked suspicious. 'I wonder. I think something happened.'

Veronica said quickly, 'No, no . . . and anyway, I have to find something to do with my life. Something real. I want to try my hand at writing a play . . . or writing something. I don't know. I want some isolation, that's all, where I can be by myself.' It was hard to explain to Billie that she was desperate to get some peace and quiet and to absorb and digest what had happened to her with André. Her life had been shaken and changed and she would never be the same. But what was meant to launch her into a new life, into adulthood, had teth-ered her to a moment in time that could never be repeated.

She found herself unable to stop thinking about and re-membering all their conversations and all he had said to her; every inch of his body, the smell and taste of it. The sensation of making love to him. It filled her mind constantly, creating a simultaneous agony and joy that she could share with no one.

She had written a few times to Irène, desperate to ask for André's address, but she had always chickened out and ended up asking only that Irène would pass on her love. And Irène had said nothing about him in a way that made Veronica feel, sadly, that she was closing off the route between them. But that had always been the agreement. It was a transaction, not the beginning of a love affair. André had said the same.

But he also said he loved me. That it was circumstance that was keeping us apart.

She clung on to that with all her heart.

Billie took her hand. 'Listen, Vee, I can see you're missing Paris. But once you've spent the summer on the island, you'll probably be keen to come home.'

'I don't think so,' Veronica said firmly. 'I know I'll want to stay.'

'They won't allow it. Daddy will want to keep you here.'

'I'm sure he will, but I will just have to do my best, that's all.'

Veronica, Billie and Mama had spent the summer on St Elfwy as usual. For Veronica, it was bliss to return, and she had drunk in its sea air and revelled in its beauty, which was intense during those hot months. Even though Mama and Billie were there too, she had plenty of time to herself, to think about André and dream and write to Irène, who occasionally wrote back letters of almost studied frivolity and lightness, barely mentioning the war and only referring to André in passing.

The island did not seem to be working its healing magic in quite the way she had hoped.

'It's not quite the same here, though, is it?' Billie said, almost whispering as though she were murmuring a heresy. 'It feels different.'

'Of course it's the same,' Veronica said obstinately, but Billie was right. Preparations for conflict were everywhere. The RAF was setting up coastal airfields for the protection of the waters, the trade and fishing routes, and the skies were heavy with planes. The navy was preparing for war at sea, requisitioning the best and most modern vessels, leaving the fishermen only the oldest and least reliable craft. They were recruiting as many fishermen, trawlermen, lifeboatmen – or anyone who could sail or manage a craft – as possible for minesweeping, rescue and patrol duties.

There were nowhere near as many holidaymakers as usual. The atmosphere of serenity was quite changed, and they could sense it even in the isolation of the island. During their stays, they usually had various housekeepers to live with them: local girls who would take on a week or two of domestic duties, cleaning and cooking, to keep life comfortable. This summer it had been more difficult to find them. Some were already training for war work, others were preparing to take over the jobs that the men would leave empty. More teachers were required, more drivers, more workers generally, and the women were stepping up. As for the odd jobs, gardening and water taxi duties – Jim took them all on.

'It really is happening,' Mama said sadly, as they sat outside the white house in the long summer evenings. Daddy had stayed behind in London to work, so it was just the three of them, managing the cooking and cleaning between them. 'It doesn't look like it can be avoided.'

Veronica nodded, drew up her feet beneath her and rested her cheek on her knees. She felt too gloomy to speak. It was awful to think about herself at a time like this, but she felt a sense of great misfortune, to be entering adulthood just as the world convulsed into war.

Billie said, 'Flora Reynolds told me that her father says Germany can't win. They're weak, really. All this marching and shouting is just a front for being thoroughly hopeless. How can they beat us? Together with France, we're far stronger.'

'Perhaps you're right,' Mama murmured. 'I hope so. We want it over quickly.'

'Whatever happens, nothing will really change, will it?' Veronica asked with an edge of anxiety in her voice. 'How can it? It's the same year after year. The birds nest, mate, lay eggs, raise chicks. The seals come to nurseries. The seasons change. The flowers bloom. War can't change that.'

'I hope not, darling. I really do.'

'I don't see how it can,' she said. She understood obscurely that the island represented something eternal to her, where she could get some kind of deep reassurance against the vicissitudes of life. Perhaps that was why she longed to stay so deeply.

Mama said, 'Let's enjoy the peace while we can. After all, war hasn't started yet.'

Despite Veronica's attempts to stay, Mama had been firmly against it, and so at the end of August, they had shut up the house and made their usual departure, leaving at the same time as the last of the puffins, who vanished until March. Veronica liked the fact that no one knew where they went. Puffins seemed so goofy and yet off they went on their mysterious, untraceable voyage – like their pufflings, who paddled away one night without so much as a practice swim, learning to fly out at sea, and were gone for five years. It was believed the puffins travelled out into the Atlantic somewhere but no one knew for certain.

What a place to spend the winter, she'd thought when she'd heard this. *Fancy leaving the cosiness of the burrows and simply disappearing off into the cold, wild waters like that.*

She imagined scores of little puffins out in the deepest ocean, riding the giant waves during a winter storm, sucked upwards inside a massive curve the size of the Eiffel Tower, and sent rolling down again, inside the churning foam and water. What mad creatures they must be to spend a winter in such a way. Or perhaps they went somewhere else entirely, and whiled away the time on the calm of an ice floe somewhere. That seemed more puffinish somehow.

But if it were me, I would stay here and never leave at all.

It was desperately hard to leave the island, especially as

the weather was so glorious, with the heather in bloom and alive with bees and birds, the air full of song, the beaches covered in the little white cushions of seal pups, guarded by their large grey mothers. But Mama was obdurate. Veronica was to return to London with them. She was far too young to stay by herself.

As they headed back to the mainland in Jim's motor boat, she turned to take one last look at St Elfwy, her beloved sea jewel of an island, sick with missing it already.

I will come back, she promised herself. *I will. War or peace, I'll be back.*

But war had come, and a freezing winter that meant that even Veronica had felt relieved she was not alone on Elfwy. Life had changed. Daddy's theatre was closed at night and there were only daytime performances, so he fretted around the house, drinking too much whisky and talking about the glory days that were past.

'Can't you do things for the war effort?' Billie asked at dinner, where Daddy was already half-cut before the claret was served. 'That might give you a sense of purpose.'

'I'm doing enough!' Daddy said indignantly. 'Keeping my play going is a public service.'

'You could create something especially to entertain the troops,' Billie said. 'There's going to be a need for that. They're planning something on Drury Lane, I think. That's the word at the agency, Mr Cunningham said so.' One day, Billie had simply refused to do any more lessons, or to go to any kind of school at all. Instead, she had put her ambitions to be an actress on hold and gone out to find a job, pretending that she was a year older than she was. She had found employment with a theatrical agent, typing up letters and taking phone calls, arranging appointments and making tea – although her surname had probably not been a hindrance. 'You should do the same, Dads. Start planning something for the soldiers or to lift morale. We're going to need it.'

Daddy harrumphed. 'I'm too old for this. I'm past it. I'm not someone like Grey – he's finding all this very stimulating. Or perhaps it's just that he and Jack are enjoying themselves so very much.'

'Are they?' Veronica asked. She had been toying with her potatoes but now she put her fork down. Once, Jack's name would have meant everything but he felt like a distant dream to her now. She still adored his music but when she put on her records and listened to his beautiful voice, she saw André's face instead of his. Jack had been, she felt, a stepping stone to something else, an important process to lead her to something real – just as Jack had been a stepping stone from Rupert.

'Oh, yes, Grey and Jack are going great guns,' Daddy said with more than a touch of bitterness. 'They've written a show together, which they will both star in. Apparently it took them a matter of weeks to write and compose the whole thing.' He looked miserable. 'My life is over. I can't compete.'

The film deal with Chromium had come to nothing after all that effort. The play was too old-fashioned, the company had said. Wit and vibrancy, or sophisticated noir, was taking the ascendancy over melodrama.

Veronica had gone to Daddy's study later, where he was drinking more whisky and soda and smoking a fat cigar while looking at old play programmes. She'd sat down on his desk and lit a cigarette herself.

'I didn't know you smoked,' Daddy said crossly. 'You shouldn't.'

'You don't like it because it makes me look more grown-up. I'm not a child any more, Daddy, you must see that. I'm eighteen now.' Her birthday had come in the depths of the freeze, and there had been no jolly trip to Fortnum's this year. She didn't mind: she was an adult and able to make some of her choices at last. Daddy looked sad at this reminder that she was a grown-up, and she smiled. 'Come, Daddy, that's the way it had to be. As soon as I can, I want to go St Elfwy. I want to spend some time there, and here's why. I want to write. I've been trying and I think I can do it but I need some time to think and create. I want to write a play, and if you give me that chance, I will do my best to write a play for you. I can't pretend that I'll be able to produce anything like Grey would . . . but I think I could do something.'

Daddy stared at her, as though she had suggested something utterly outlandish. 'Write? You?'

'I have to find something to do. And that is what I think I might want to do. I have to find out if I'm any good at it, that's all.'

'I don't know,' Daddy said gruffly. 'I don't like it. It's a very iffy profession. You'd be better off marrying well. You're pretty enough, Vee, and you've money behind you.'

'I don't want that. I want to be independent.' She put out

her cigarette which was hardly smoked, set her gaze on him and bent forward. 'Let me. Let me write. My success will be your success too. I think I can do it.'

Daddy stared at her. She could see that what she'd said had chimed with him. Suddenly he opened a desk drawer and took out a wodge of typed manuscript paper. 'This is Rupert's play,' he said. 'The idea was wonderful. The execution terrible. You could work on this.'

'That's his idea!' she exclaimed. 'I can't take that!'

'For practice. What does he care? He has written to your mother to say he's joining the army. He won't have time for it now. Take it, use it and see what happens.'

She thought of Rupert and her childish passion for him. That seemed like a lifetime ago.

'Will you let me go to St Elfwy then?'

'I won't stop you. But you can only go when the weather changes. It will be too hard before then.'

She leaned forward and kissed him, jubilant and relieved at once. 'Thank you, Daddy. I mean it.'

Veronica could not have known what it would be like to live on the island by herself. Nothing was the way it had been. But she rather loved the new spartan quality of being alone there. She found she could manage without any domestic help, though it took a while to get used to it. It was a shock to realise that floors didn't clean themselves and that if she didn't wash the dishes, the pile only grew larger. For the first time, she began to cultivate a garden, growing vegetables. She would contribute to the nation's well-being with the food she could grow, the bounty of the rabbits on the island, and whatever else the island could supply. And she would write.

From the time she had arrived in May, life had taken on this quality of peace and beauty and a sense of purpose she had never known before. It was hard work but it made her happy. All day she cleaned, cooked, gardened and maintained her smallholding. In the evenings, behind the blackout, she lit the lanterns and wrote, sometimes working on the play and sometimes pouring out her heart about André, writing everything she could remember about him and then moving into fiction: stories of their reconciliation, their future, his life, wherever he was. It made her feel close to him when really, there was almost complete silence. Only the occasional forwarded letter from Irène even let her know he was alive.

Beyond all this, the war was gathering in a dark wave and she listened out for reports of what was happening in France with increasing anxiety. They had all been so sure that Germany would fail and yet it was succeeding, in the most miraculous way and at breakneck speed, crashing unstoppably through the forests of France, and out to the west and north, flinging the allies out of its way like toys. The rescue from the beaches of Dunkirk was the great effort to save the army that was now limping back on the flotilla of little boats that had still not managed to return home.

While Jim emptied the traps of rabbits, Veronica walked back into the kitchen. Boris had been slumbering beside the range, but now he leapt up to greet her, his tail frantic. The sacks of goods that Jim had brought were still sitting by the pantry and needed emptying. She must put the fish in the cold store, perhaps cook or salt them to preserve them.

But first there were her letters. She saw at once that one came from France and the handwriting was familiar, so she opened it quickly and saw it had been attacked by the censors, with whole lines missing under thick black strips.

My dear,

I'm writing this quickly. Forgive me if I do not say enough.

Paris has changed in the speed of light. Last month, life was much as normal – I even went to the opera with Philippe! Now . . . I do not need to tell you what is coming. There is panic. Everything has closed, people are fleeing the city in droves. I do not know what will happen. Philippe has gone to his chateau in the south. There is no place for me there, of course, but he has left me money. I shall not leave. I cannot think where I could go and I have no motor car in any case.

I must tell you something of André. He and I agreed for both your sakes that you would know nothing of him in the real world, which is why I have said nothing of note of him until now, but that was before all of this. He is a pilot in the Armée de l'Air – here the censorship kicked in, ruthlessly expunging Irène's words – *XXXXXXXXXXXXXXXX. I am told that André set out on a reckless mission of his own XXXXXXXXX but I do not know what happened after that. He has not been heard from but perhaps XXXXXX.*

242

There is a great likelihood that he did not return. I am so sorry, for you and for me. We both loved him.

The speed with which my world has changed is unbelievable and I do not know if I will be able to write to you any longer or what will happen. My beloved Paris is falling silent. But I will stay. I will shut up my grand apartment and go to the garret, I think.

I think of you often. Take care. I hope we will meet again one day. Remember what I said: liberty and freedom are worth giving everything for.

All my love,

Irène

Veronica dropped the letter and clutched the edges of the table to hold herself up. She stared into space, her heart pounding. André's name throbbed in her head; his face was before her mind more clearly than it had been in months, as though she had seen him only yesterday.

She tried to imagine him as a pilot at the controls of a fighter plane, and she saw it quite clearly in her mind: his pale intense face, the dark eyes fixed on his mission, guiding the soaring little craft to wherever he could do something for France's cause. What was his reckless quest? She had always known that under his calm and controlled exterior, his gentle ways and his tenderness with her, there was something very strong and she was certain he was brave.

Oh, André.

She thought of the hours in the little bed in Irène's apartment. In their time together, they had spent more time in one another's arms than not. That idea made her simultaneously joyful and agonised.

Taking a breath, she gasped and opened her eyes. They had been stinging with tears but now she spoke out loud. 'I won't cry. I don't know if he is dead. And if he is . . . then my hopes and prayers must be for Irène now.'

The letter had taken some time to reach her. The Germans had already occupied Paris, and if Irène was still there, then she was at their mercy.

My poor Irène. Please, please . . . be safe. But oh . . . André.

When Jim arrived with the haul of rabbits, a good two dozen hanging over his arms from leather strips, Veronica had regained her composure. She had read her other letters – news from Billie and Mama, a silly postcard from Daddy and letters from friends – and put the thoughts of André and Irène out of her head until she could take the time she needed when she was alone again.

Instead, she discussed with Jim – as far as he would discuss anything – the value of the rabbit haul, and settled with him for the goods he had brought her in exchange. Her vegetable garden, neglected for a long while and not planted, was still a work in progress and, having started so late, she had only managed to produce fast-growing lettuce and marrows so far.

'You'd better take me back to the mainland tomorrow, Jim, so I can go to St David's and do my shopping.'

'Ah, weather's good, tides are fair. We can go there and back in the day if you like, 'less it changes.'

She cooked them a supper of gulls' eggs and marrows, and they ate it sitting outside, and watching as the sun went down and dusk began to settle. Soon she would have to put up the blackout, but for now there was still enough dark blue light in the sky. The day birds went silent, the ground-nesters retreating to their burrows, and the rabbits bounded back to join them. The night birds began their calls and cries, the chirrups from rocks and walls. The storm petrels flew in from the ocean in a whirring cloud to flutter into their tiny crevices. And then the shearwaters, who lived on the wing over the sea during the day, began to soar in.

'Cocklollies,' Jim said, lighting his rough pipe and blowing out a cloud of pungent cut tobacco. 'Gotta be millions of 'em.'

The shearwaters shrieked and wailed as they came in to spend the night stranded on land, graceless and clumsy instead of nimble as they were in the air. It seemed to Veronica, as dusk fell, that they were bewailing all human wickedness and loss and death. A blade of pain took a path through her heart and despair drenched her.

She stood up in the gloom and gathered up the plates. 'I'll turn in, Jim. I'll see you in the morning to catch the tide.'

'Ah, mmm.'

'Goodnight.'

She went inside, hoping that when she had shut her window and the curtains, and the candles were out, she would have peace from the sobs of the shearwaters.

245

Chapter Thirteen

1940

The noise and bustle of the railway after the peace and silence of life on the island was, Veronica found, quite overwhelming. For weeks, she had been almost alone except for her thousands of bird companions, and the seals and porpoises, and of course Boris. Once a week, she crossed to the mainland, took her bicycle from where it was carefully stored by the shore, and rode to St David's for her fresh supplies. And then she went back, ferried by Jim, to spend her time gardening, walking, cleaning and doing the small bit of cooking she was able to. And, of course, she wrote. She had decided to take Rupert's play apart and then rebuild it somehow. But really, she hadn't the first idea. So she had taken up a book of Shakespeare's plays from the shelf in the sitting room and begun to read it instead, trying to find out the qualities of greatness.

For the first few days after she had received Irène's letter, she had been in a whirl of grief and tears, thinking and dreaming of André on his reckless flight to wherever he went. Then she decided she must stop, or go mad.

It helped her not to think about André and his fate, or Irène, trapped in the occupied city. There had been no further letters and she didn't expect any.

Then another letter had arrived.

Dearest Vee,

I'm so sorry but you will need to come home at once. Daddy has to have an operation and we are all very worried about him. They're going to remove a tumour next week. The doctors say it will be straightforward and it's most likely benign. Daddy thinks we're not to worry at all, you know what he's like. Mama is in a frightful state.

Can you please come back? They long to see you. Daddy would love it, I know. And so would I. Mama needs you.

Send to let me know when you will get here.

Bill xxx

Veronica had been surprised by the news, only because it was so very out of character for Daddy. She had imagined him going on and on and on, his great frame carrying him solidly into the oldest of age. As it was, he was only in his sixties, still young. While he had had a lifetime of perform-ance nerves, late nights, parties, cigarettes and alcohol, he had hardly lived the toughest of existences. He had enjoyed luxury and leisure not granted to many.

Daddy will be fine.

She knew that absolutely. She wasn't even sure if it was

worth going to the trouble of the trip back to London and all the expense, but she could hear that Billie needed help supporting their mother. What Billie had said about Mama worried Veronica almost more than the news of Daddy's operation. Their mother had always been so calm and strong, it wasn't like her to crumble in this way. She wrote back to Billie to say she would come, and began to make the arrangements.

There was something almost mythical about Veronica's voyage back. She awoke at dawn in magnificent solitude in the white house on the island, then made her way to the jetty where Jim was ready to take her across the water to the mainland. From there, a horse and cart was waiting as she couldn't take her suitcase on a bicycle or cycle in her smart city clothes. The ride to the station took two hours, then she climbed onto the trundling little branch-line service that would take her eventually to Cardiff, where she could change for the mainline to London. From Cardiff, the carriages were full of soldiers, the racks rammed with packs and equipment, and the air thick with cigarette smoke. From time to time, the train stopped for long and unexplained stretches, and no one said a word. Life was about this now: acceptance of how things were. A faith that somewhere, someone knew what was going on, and that all of it was for the best in the end.

Veronica sat back in her seat, trying to keep her hat low over her eyes so that she didn't meet the gaze of any of the soldiers. She didn't want to see their faces. Some of them of the right age and build reminded her of André, although he was not a soldier. She saw no airmen, for which she was grateful. She concentrated instead on *A Midsummer Night's Dream*, which she had brought with her in a slim blue leather volume. She tried to banish thoughts of André by concentrating on the text, mouthing it lightly as she went. It was familiar. She had seen it several times and, as a girl, had played one of Titania's fairies at Daddy's request. She'd only had one word but the experience had terrified her to the point of being sick, and then Billie, only four, had taken the role instead and done it brilliantly.

What makes this play so funny? Why are the lovers so poignant? What is it?

She tried to keep herself occupied with thinking and reading, as the train started up again and thundered along, taking her ever closer to London. At last, in the late evening, they were on the outskirts of the city, cutting along grimy rails and under metal bridges, the steam flying back mixed with soot and dirt, until they pulled under the curved iron-and-glass roof of Paddington station.

Veronica waited for the crowds to disembark first before she climbed down from the carriage. They were on platform one and she could see the station offices all along the opposite side. To her surprise, standing under the Telegraph Office sign was Billie, her face white and her eyes huge. When she caught sight of Veronica, she gasped and rushed forward, throwing herself at Veronica, who dropped her case just in time to catch her sister in her arms.

'Billie, what is it? I wasn't expecting you!' Panic gripped

her, tightening around her at the sight of Billie's stricken face.

'Oh, Vee, darling . . . I'm so sorry. You're too late. Daddy is dead.'

The atmosphere of the large house in Hampstead was so sad that Veronica realised she had not known how light and happy it had been until now. The whole place seemed to hang about them, heavy and empty.

Veronica took off her hat and put it on the hall table. She felt strangely calm, almost untouched. 'Where's Mama?'

'Upstairs. She won't come down or do anything.'

'And . . . Daddy?'

'He's at the undertaker's.'

Veronica almost laughed. It sounded like he was on a visit there to arrange something. And perhaps he was. She found it impossible to believe that he had died. Billie had said that he had never woken up from the operation and, in her mind, he might even still be sleeping, just waiting for the anaesthetic to fade from his system.

Billie took off her coat, still pale. Unlike Veronica, she had wept on and off all the way home. Now she said in a small voice, 'We'll have to arrange a funeral.'

'I suppose so. I'm sure Daddy would like a big send-off. Everyone he can muster.'

'What a shame he had to die in wartime, with so many scattered.'

'I should think an old gentleman of the stage will be one of the least grievous losses,' Veronica said tartly. 'Considering.'

Billie's eyes widened. 'Vee! You know what I meant.'

A tear rolled down her sister's cheek, and Veronica was remorseful. 'Forgive me, Bill. Of course he should have as good a funeral as possible.'

Nevertheless, there was something like bitterness in her heart that Daddy, who'd lived a good long life and seen his children grow up, would get a fulsome celebration, well larded with praise. And where was André? Forgotten, blown to pieces, lost in the rattle of bullets and the blast of bombs. With all his life ahead of him.

It made the memory of their nights together ever more tender.

Billie stood with her head bowed, her hands clasped in front of her, uncharacteristically quiet. Veronica went up to her and put her arms around her.

'Please forgive me, Bill. I'm sorry. That was cruel of me. I didn't mean it.'

Billie sniffed. 'It's all right. You don't seem to mind much, though. About Daddy.'

'Of course I do. But it's such a shock. Shall we go and see Mama?'

They went up together, climbing the stairs slowly, hesitating to face what they knew would be their mother's overwhelming grief.

Why can't I seem to feel anything?

Veronica wondered it often over the next few weeks, as she moved about the house, making arrangements and caring

251

for Mama. She felt as though she had stopped living when she left Elfwy and was now only existing in a numbness.

Mama's grief was terrible. She had been so restrained and ladylike for so many years, an elegant actress of drawing room comedies and polite farce. Now she was gripped with tragic intensity, lying in pieces on her bed, sometimes possessed by storms of tears that could grow to a shrieking hysteria and sometimes shaking and moaning quietly for long hours.

'What can we do with her?' Billie asked as they stood together outside her bedroom door, listening to the moans within. 'What will bring her out of this?'

'We need to get this funeral done,' Veronica said. 'She can't move on until it's over.'

They wrote to friends and family and put a notice of the service in the paper to alert those who had worked with their father. As it was, Daddy managed to make small headlines of his own, despite the devastation of the war news. Half of Europe seemed to have fallen. Countries were declaring war on one another as if it were some kind of playground game. Britain had been promised that the long, miserable, weary and costly endeavour had only just begun. Perhaps remembering the star turns and charisma of George Mindenhall would be a small distraction from all that.

It was decided to have the funeral at the church in Hampstead and the wake at the house.

'Then we will shut it up,' Veronica decided. 'Rent it out, perhaps. Or sell it, if we're allowed.'

'We could offer it to the War Office?' Billie suggested. 'I've heard that they're looking for large houses like this.'

'Really? What for? A hospital?'

'Not just hospitals and convalescent homes. There are lots of things they have to do. Training. Billeting. Planning and scheming. I don't know. All the business of war.'

'It's a good idea, Billie,' Veronica said firmly. 'It can be Daddy's last act of service. We'll donate the house for the duration, better than having to worry about it for now.'

'And what about us?'

'I'm going back to the island, of course. Now that it's mine.'

To her intense astonishment and delight, that was what the will had said. 'To my daughter Veronica, the entire island and estate of St Elfwy in Pembrokeshire, to do with as she pleases.'

In her turn, Billie had received the rights and income to all of Daddy's co-written plays, his image and representation, and dramatic and film work. 'In recognition of her love for the stage and my work upon it.'

Mama and the sisters each received a legacy of money, with an income for Mama for life, and the sale of the big house was supposed to buy her a modest place of her own. If they loaned the house to the government for now, there would still be money enough to take care of them all, just as Daddy would have wanted.

Veronica grasped Billie's hand, gazing into her eyes. 'Why don't you come with me, Billie? Bring Mama? We'll be happy there, the three of us.'

Her sister shook her head. 'No, Vee. I'm not like you. My life is here now. I want to stay in London. I love the agency. I'll live in the garden cottage. And you know Mama won't want to leave, she won't be able to imagine living anywhere else but here.'

Veronica knew she was right. And in any case, she was still in love with her isolation. 'Of course. The garden cottage is just right, if you're sure you'll be all right.' The small red-brick two-bedroom place at the far end of the garden, with its little fence and entrance gate, had once been for the gardener but he had left and it was standing empty. 'But surely it makes sense for me to take Mama to Elfwy with me?'

'Let's see,' Billie said. 'Let's see what she wants to do.'

By the day of the funeral, Mama was beginning to come out of her paroxysms of grief. She seemed to have moved to some sort of acceptance just in time to be able to rise from her bed and become something more like her old and elegant self: Dodo, the beautiful actress and loving wife to George Mindenhall, a legend of the stage. In her dramatic black costume, hat and heavy veil, she looked like something from a stage production, a leading lady making a grand entrance as she descended the stairs, pale but composed. At the bottom, she announced, 'I am ready.'

Veronica waited below, in a smart black dress, gloves and a black straw hat. In a flash she understood that Mama was not just grieving for Daddy, but for the end of her own existence as his wife. The starry, glamorous life they had shared, the huge and beautiful house, the thrill of the theatre, the staff

254

and gardens and invitations . . . it was all over now. Dodo was dying too, in a way. Her parents' world was almost vanished, melting away with every second that passed.

She and Billie went forward to support their mother, and together they walked along the cobbled Hampstead streets to the church, which was thronging with people – those attending the service and those come to stare at the famous actors and actresses close up. Press photographers and journalists hovered around, asking for comment, though they stood back respectfully as the Mindenhall women arrived. The church was as glorious as if it were not wartime. Sybille Handforth had arranged for mountains of white flowers to be sent from her grand garden to the church, and they had been beautifully arranged. Daddy's coffin was covered in an exquisite blanket of white roses that was rather comforting, as though it was keeping him cosy in a heavenly perfumed warmth.

Veronica was aware of very little during the service. She stood with Mama and Billie, thinking mostly of Daddy, how he was lying just a few feet away and the fact that she would never see him again. It seemed so unreal.

He just can't be there, she decided. *He can't. He's somewhere else. He's simply moved away for a while and left us to get on with it in his absence. And all this is just a pretence to keep people happy.*

That idea seemed to work. It convinced her and kept her balanced. But she could not, she found, listen to any of the readings or to the sermon, in case they upset this delicate balance she had created for herself. Only a few words pierced her self-imposed deafness, when a famous actor declaimed the speech from Shakespeare's *Cymbeline*, and in a great booming baritone announced: 'Fear no more the heat o' the sun! Nor the furious winter's rages . . .'

Fear No More.

With a start, she remembered Jack Bannock and the beautiful mournful ballad that he had sung that night in Paris. Like a flash she saw Daddy with her, sitting in that ridiculous nightclub, while Jack sang so beautifully and Grey fell in love, and she wore Chanel and thought she was heartbroken . . .

For a second, her control wavered. She felt the threat of tears and despair whirling just out of sight like a far-off tornado. Then she bit her lip, banished the memory and managed to carry on.

At the cemetery, the coffin was lowered slowly to its resting place. In a suitably theatrical gesture, white pigeons were released, fluttering upwards and away. Veronica watched them go, feeling that they were the things she had believed in most all day. Daddy, like a bird, had fluttered up and was waiting for her somewhere, not gone but waiting. A line from the play that she had read on the train that day before she even knew he was dead suddenly sounded in her mind.

My soul is in the sky . . .

It was from that silly piece of business near the end; the character was saying he was dead. But it was still poetic and beautiful – a soul, in the sky.

Yes, Daddy's soul was in the sky. Even while the vicar was

intoning the miserable liturgy of ashes to ashes, she didn't believe a word. He had flown upwards and was waiting to accompany her wherever she went.

When it was over, they began their walk back to the house to the wake, which was as lavish as rations – and Daddy's cellar – could provide.

Mama was walking just ahead with Billie when Veronica felt a presence on either side of her. Startled, she looked up to see Grey Oswald on her left.

'Is it very wrong to say you look exquisite?' he said, in his husky drawl. He picked up one of her hands and kissed it, adding, 'I'm sure it is. But it's true.'

Veronica looked to her other side and saw Jack, as handsome as ever, still able to make her heart skip a beat. Jack touched the rim of his hat to her. 'Condolences, my dear Veronica. You must be grief-stricken.'

'Thank you,' she said, pleased to see them. Of course they would be here if they could. She had thought of Jack in the church, but not seen him. It was a comfort to know he'd been there. 'How kind of you both to come.'

'How could we not?' Grey asked solemnly. 'I'm sure it made George very happy to know how important he was in the start of Jack and my very productive creative collaboration.'

'He really was what brought us together,' Jack added with a smile. 'I don't think Grey would have come – or at least stayed – if it hadn't been for you and George.'

'He was delighted,' Veronica said, a little untruthfully, but she was sure that they understood Daddy's theatrical jealousy had been a thing apart from his affection for them.

'George was wonderful all round,' declaimed Grey. 'And taken far too soon. But that is why we are celebrating him so much today. And plenty of champagne is the first step. Luckily I have some spare, and it should be at just about the right temperature now as well.'

'But we're going to back to the house,' Veronica said in surprise.

'They are. But we're not. Come on, we'll get back in a little while. But first, we're going to hail a taxi, if we can find one, and get you to ourselves for a moment.'

As they walked into Grey's luxurious flat, Veronica wondered why her life was so often these extremes. From the bare white house where she cooked and cleaned for herself, to this elegant, chic apartment, with every luxury that could be had in wartime.

'I hope you don't mind,' Grey said, as he went through to the large and light drawing room, decorated entirely in monochrome, the vases full of white lilies. 'I could, I suppose, have brought my champagne to the wake to share, but there's so little of the fine stuff left, it seems a shame not to drink it oneself, when it is, really, the fruits of one's labour. Don't you see? But I wanted to share it with beautiful you as well. And so did Jack, didn't you, Jack?'

'Of course.' Jack smiled at her while Grey bustled about to open the bottle chilling in the bucket. 'I really am most sorry for your loss. It's hard to imagine George gone. He was so full of life, so much larger than life. A one off.'

'Thank you,' she said gratefully. 'Yes, dear Daddy. He'll never be forgotten.'

'Not even if I wanted to!' exclaimed Grey, popping the cork and sharing out three glasses of golden bubbles. 'Let's toast the old rascal.' He handed Veronica a glass, gave another to Jack and then raised his own, lifting an eyebrow at the same time. 'To George, who gave me plenty of nasty moments, and lots of brilliant ones as well. He was his own man, and a bundle of talent and charisma and all the rest. Gone too soon, dear George.'

'Dear George,' they echoed and all sipped the champagne.

Grey added, 'To be honest, it is very bad timing. We were about to ask George a favour.'

'Oh, Grey,' Jack said, looking reproachful. 'This isn't the time!'

Grey looked abashed and put down his glass. 'You're right, Jack. I apologise.'

'Don't apologise on my account,' Veronica said, 'it's perfectly all right. What is it? I'd rather have something else to talk about, you know.'

Jack gave Grey a warning look but Veronica touched his arm to let him know that she didn't mind.

How funny that I can touch Jack's arm and feel so little, when I adored him so hugely.

Grey wandered about the room, gesturing with his cigarette and sipping from his champagne. 'Well, you see, my dear . . . Jack and I have to write our next show. For various reasons, we delayed and delayed, and then wrote something we both hated and inspiration has finally struck. But . . . there's a problem.'

Jack sat down and gestured to Veronica to take the chair opposite. 'You know how things are with us, don't you, Veronica? You weren't much more than a child when we met but that was a while ago now and, anyway, I'm sure you were not naive with growing up in the theatre.'

'You mean, you're in love,' she said frankly.

Grey laughed. 'Bless you, child, yes. We are.' He looked fondly over at Jack. 'Goodness knows what that heavenly lad sees in me, but it seems to be something.'

'You fool,' Jack said fondly. 'I'm crazy about you.'

'Well, there we are, that's lucky.' Grey perched on the edge of the sofa behind Jack. 'But it's not easy in this world of ours for men like us to be together. We need to live together to work together, especially quickly. You see, we now have more than one commitment – at least I do. So it's important we get this show written as quickly as we can. Well, it's nigh on impossible for us around here. We need to escape somewhere. Georgie often told us of his romantic hideaway off the coast. Far from prying eyes.'

'And I'm Welsh,' Jack put in. 'So it's particularly appealing.'

'Do you have a piano there?' Grey asked quickly.

'Well, yes, a little out of tune, but yes,' Veronica said, understanding. 'You want to go to St Elfwy.'

'A fortnight, no more than a month. That's all. Can it be done? Do say it could. We would love it so.' Grey's usually cynical eyes were suddenly soft. 'You don't know what it's like to have to hide a part of oneself like this, when one could be so happy.'

There was a pause and Veronica said softly, 'I don't suppose I do. Of course you can. I might be there myself but I won't bother you. In fact, I can move out to the cottage and you can have the main house. And I'll be at home with Mother a bit longer in any case.' She started to think of the details and how to get the place ready and how they would manage, when she felt warm arms around her and Jack was kneeling by her, enveloping her in a hug.

'Thank you, Veronica. You can't know. You really can't. What it means to us. What a gift it is.'

She laughed. 'You're welcome. It's easy enough to grant.'

He gazed up at her, those liquid chocolate eyes as heart-melting as ever. 'Is there anything I can do for you, Veronica? Anything at all?'

After a moment, she said, 'Yes, actually, there is something.'

Grey looked over, interested. 'Do tell us. Of course we'll pay.'

'No . . . not that. It's nothing, really, at least I hope it isn't.' She hesitated. 'Jack, I wonder . . . will you sing me "The Last Song of Summer"? It was so beautiful and sad, and will always make me think of Daddy.'

Jack blinked at her in surprise. 'Sing? Of course.'

Grey jumped up. 'And I'll accompany you.' He put down his glass and stubbed out his cigarette, before going to his white grand piano and sitting down. He ran his fingers over the keys in a ripple of sound, and then played the opening

261

bars of Jack's melancholy ballad. 'This is it . . . yes, this is the key. Ready, dearest?'

Jack stood up, took a deep breath and nodded.

Grey played and Jack began to sing, his beautiful voice filling the drawing room. On the second chorus, Grey joined in with the lightest of harmony, swelling out the song to its climax.

Veronica thought of Daddy on St Elfwy, striding about the island, declaiming his favourite monologues, shouting encouragement to the birds, sending rabbits bounding in all directions as he went. She remembered him laughing and telling her to row harder, as she tried to manoeuvre the dinghy around the island cliffs. She recalled how he adored to tease her and Billie, to make stupid faces and ridiculous jokes, how tightly he'd hugged them, how much he had loved them.

Oh, dear Daddy. So silly and vain and talented and selfish and wonderful. What would she do without him? Would he really stay with her, fluttering somewhere just out of sight? She hoped so. But she wished he had not gone, and she wished she had been able to say goodbye.

When they had finished, they looked to Veronica, their eyes full of sympathy.

Oh, she thought with surprise, for she hadn't noticed. *Oh. I've found my tears. They're here!*

For they were there, rolling down her cheeks, and she wept for Daddy as if she would never stop.

Chapter Fourteen

1940

'Well, what do you think?' Veronica called, standing up at the front of the boat and pointing towards the island. 'Isn't she lovely?'

'Lovely!' shouted Jack. He looked impossibly handsome, his black hair ruffled by the wind and his dark brown eyes bright. He wore a white shirt that billowed out as they motored through the water towards the jetty.

'Your very own island,' Grey yelled. 'You lucky girl. Aren't you spoiled?'

'Very,' she cried back.

The day was a beautiful one to show the island off. The sky was layered in shades of purest blue without a cloud, the sun was bright, and a merry breeze, strong over water, danced over the grasses and flowers. The island's dark, copper and white streaked cliffs were topped like a cake with a coating of sweet colour from the cliff-top thrift, the celandine and primrose, and white campion and scurvy grass. Heather and lavender added tinges of purple and grey. The white house stood, warmly inviting, at the top of the first plateau, the island rising behind it, and the cliffs and rocks and levels were full of birds, their music rich on the air.

Jim steered them over to the jetty and they docked, off-loading the luggage they had brought, and then disembarking themselves and the excited Boris, who had been staying with people on the mainland while Veronica was away and was thrilled to be home with her again. A few trips up and down to the house, and they had stowed away all their possessions. Jim was not staying this time but was keen to make the journey back and so was soon on his way.

'What a beautiful house,' Grey said as they went around the ground floor, taking a look. 'Spartan and yet comfortable.'

'We like it very much,' Veronica said, enjoying seeing the old place afresh through new eyes as the men explored the house.

'And this is your famous piano,' Grey exclaimed, going into the drawing room and seeing the old instrument up against the wall. He went over and lifted the lid.

'It's not quite like your wonderful grand,' Veronica said apologetically. 'But I had Jim bring a tuner over.'

With such renowned guests arriving, she had asked Jim to get someone to clean and prepare the house, and to make up the cottage that was in the best repair for her. Grey and Jack had said they couldn't possibly turn her out of her own home, but she had insisted, telling them that it was no trouble to her and that they deserved some time to themselves.

Grey ran his fingers over the keys and trilled out a melody. 'Yes. She'll do very nicely. Thank you, Veronica.'

'You know, of course, that Grey can't read music,' Jack

remarked, leaning against the doorway, his hands in the pockets of his shorts.

Grey laughed. 'It's true. I'm self-taught and it's all by ear. But it seems to work well enough.'

'As long as you've got me to write it down.' Jack grinned.

'That is a help, I admit it.' Grey sat down on the stool and began to hum along to some melodies. 'Did you bring plenty of sheet music paper and pencils? I can feel my inspiration cooking already.'

'Don't start yet,' scolded Jack. 'Let's unpack. And I must have some tea or something before we begin on the music.'

Veronica did not like to ask where their supplies had come from, for there were lots of luxuries in the boxes that they had hauled up with them from London, as well as two crates of wine and a great deal of gin and vermouth, and they had pooled their rations too to give a generous lump of butter, bacon, eggs, bread and enough tea to keep them going, although she was pretty sure Grey would have more tucked away somewhere.

'Come on,' she said. 'I'll stoke up the fire the girl lit yesterday and we can get the stove properly warmed up for tea.'

They drank tea in the kitchen, which was always the warmest room in the house, and even in August, the house was cool thanks to the thick stone walls.

'What are you doing here with yourself, Veronica?' Grey asked, lighting a cigarette over his teacup. 'I mean, it is pretty here but I find it hard to understand what a girl of less than twenty has to occupy herself with.'

Veronica shrugged. 'I've always wanted to live somewhere like this, on my own. Perhaps I have a depressive streak or something, I don't know. My family are theatre people and yet it's never been something I want for myself. I've always felt happiest on my own, with nature. I don't know what I'd do if I couldn't walk twice a day, striding out on the clifftops with Boris, watching the birds and the ever-changing sea and all its moods. It's more fickle than any girl, bright and sparkling in the morning and glowering and furious in the afternoon, calm again at night or howling with fury. Sometimes I lie out on the cliffs when the sea is raging and I can feel them shake and shudder with the force the sea is throwing at them, those violent waves! Then you feel like you're really part of nature.'

Grey was bemused. 'I love to travel, Veronica, and I love the world in all its contrasts. But give me a hot, serene climate any day. Give me constant blue skies and sunny days, and a balmy breeze and the sun to worship. That's my sort of life.'

'You might get that here for a while. But never really for long. But it's August,' she said, 'and that's often our best time. I have my fingers crossed for you. You can brown yourself in the sunshine with any luck.'

Jack sat back, taking one of Grey's cigarettes for himself. 'Well, I like this and that's all. It's home to me.' She smiled at him, almost hearing the return of his Welsh accent in the smooth lilt of his voice. 'I like my weather to be like an opera, not a nursery rhyme.'

'Tsk,' Grey said but smiled. 'Robber King. That's what you are.'

Veronica said, 'Come on, let's go out and I'll show you around the place.'

As she led them out, Veronica was properly struck for the first time that this was all hers now. Daddy had been King of St Elfwy, or so he'd told them. When they were children, Billie and Veronica had taken this very seriously, as they deduced that this made them princesses, like Elizabeth and Margaret Rose. One jolly summer, they had dressed up one of the dining room chairs as a throne, and she and Billie had spent a happy morning making a crown, sceptre and orb for him out of cardboard and gilt paper and whatever else they could find, and made him sit with a sign on which they printed in ornate letters *King of St Elfwy*. Mama had been designated court photographer, and she had taken several photographs but Daddy refused to be serious and made silly faces throughout. They'd kept the one where he was crossing his eyes and grinning stupidly. She was glad now, because it showed he was far from pompous, making a joke of his kinghood. But if he had been king, then she must now be the island's queen, the ruler of all she surveyed. What still stood on the island – the cottages, barns, tumbledown outbuildings, the abbey ruins, the old jetty and the house – was hers, as well as what was falling down.

When they went out for their walk, Boris leaping about them, she pointed out the signs of civilisation. 'When Daddy bought this place, it was in a state. The rabbits had taken down the banks and ledges and walls, burrowed them away. The buildings were in complete disrepair and the house not fit to be lived in. But gradually, summer after summer, we brought it back and did things like add the plumbing. There's no electricity, of course, but we're used to that! I suppose there will be one day.'

'I hope that's a very long time away,' Jack said fervently. 'The simplicity is enchanting.'

'Well,' Grey said, with a little laugh, 'I'd quite like a telephone. And perhaps a refrigerator. Other than that . . . well, this privacy is divine.' He reached for Jack's hand. 'We can't often do this, can we, dearest?'

'No. Or this.' Jack tilted his head upwards and put a kiss on Grey's lips.

Grey looked to Veronica. 'No one would think twice if we were regular sweethearts. But in London . . . we'd likely be beaten to a pulp. Then thrown in jail. Just for loving each other.'

'It's wrong,' Veronica said firmly. 'I know it, even if lots of people don't feel the same way. Perhaps in the future, by the time there's electricity here, things will be different.'

'We can hope,' Grey said, still holding Jack's hand.

They walked away from the main settlement area, and higher up over the plateaus, where the wind was stronger and the molinia grass bent in the wind while the ground flowers trembled, their petals riffled. Bees, butterflies – white fluttering ones and elegant orange ones – and emerald-bodied hoverflies were everywhere, along with the ubiquitous rabbits and, of course, the birds.

'So many birds!' cried Grey. 'What are they all?'

'The largest you'll see are kestrels and buzzards, and gulls of course – all sorts. The puffins are about to leave. They move in such regularity and order that the locals believe they are under orders from a king puffin and his council. There are choughs and rock pipits and skylarks and petrels and shearwaters and . . . I can't tell you how many there are to see!'

'An ornithological heaven,' Grey said. 'I like birds – up to a point.'

Jack was gazing around with joy. 'It's marvellous, quite marvellous. There must be thousands and thousands of birds!'

Just then the roar of engines could be heard and approaching from the south-east came a great aeroplane, soaring out and over the island, directly over their heads, until they were nearly deafened and the grasses shook, and the birds squawked and fluttered in panic. A moment later, it was gone, flying out over the Atlantic, a whirring dot in the sky.

'That was a German plane!' yelled Jack, outraged.

'They are coming more and more,' she said. 'I never expected them this far from London!'

'Damn them,' Grey swore. 'Damn their black hearts and their filthy bombs. Not our boys, God bless them. They're the bravest, they've proved that already. I mean theirs.'

They stood together and watched the dot disappearing.

'It's not over, is it? We thought it might be,' Veronica asked softly. There had seemed to be a victory of sorts, thanks to the airmen who had battled in the skies against invasion only days before. But that was not the end. It was only holding them off. They were coming and coming and coming.

'It's not over,' Grey agreed. 'It's barely begun. Come on, let's not think of this on this beautiful day. Show us the rest of the island.'

They walked over the brow of hill to the western side of the island. While the east looked back towards the mainland and the great channel between the island and the shore, and was sheltered by the rise of the island, this side looked west to the great stretch of ocean. The coast of Ireland could be glimpsed on a fair day, beyond the uninhabited lumps of rock that littered the miles of water before them. Those rocks must have their own colonies of birds and wildlife, their own nests and burrows. The sheer numbers were overwhelming to imagine. Better only to think of Elfwy, and its puffins who liked to stroll among the sea campion and pick up feathers and straw in their orange beaks, and yawn in the afternoon sun. She loved to watch them take off from the water, their wings whirring and their little feet hanging behind them like small orange paddles.

Veronica pointed down at the ruins. 'That's the old monastery.'

'The old what?' shouted Grey. The wind had blown up and tossed her words away. 'The old monstery?' He laughed. 'How appropriate. That's what it shall be to me now. The monstrous old monstery.'

'You heathen,' Jack said fondly. 'When was it built, Veronica?'

'Oh, centuries ago. This was a religious foundation for

years and years. There was some sort of frightful abbot here, who ruled the place with a rod of iron. Famous for being a tyrant. They got rid of him in the end, then made him a saint, of course. Look, when we walk down there, I'll show you.'

They walked down towards the ruins, a mass of stones and half-standing walls, still laid out in regular lines and showing the outline of the monastic building. One or two smaller buildings were half standing, and even a double-height wall with the remnants of a floor halfway up, and the shapes of arched windows that once would have held glass. Here and there on the ground were patches of stone floor, nearly obscured by grass. One lone tower stood half complete, a stone staircase curving up just a few treads before it vanished.

'Goodness,' Jack said. 'There was quite a place here.'

'It must have been cold,' Grey remarked, looking about. 'Very, very cold.'

'It might have been holy.'

'Perhaps. But I doubt it.'

Veronica led them away from the ruins to the area that would once have been the enclosed gardens of the monastery. 'They knew enough to keep their plants warm,' she said. 'And they probably grew a lot more on our side of the island too. Lots of our buildings were probably originally cow sheds, pigsties, sheep pens and stables. I suppose with the fish and crab and lobsters, they probably ate very well.'

'Better than we are!' Grey said sardonically. Then, with a sliding gaze to Veronica, 'I don't suppose we can get lobster, can we?'

'Plenty, if we want it. Jim weaves lobster pots all the time

271

and sets them. He and I split the profit, as they come from island waters. I usually trade it for all the other things he can get me.'

Jack laughed. 'How wonderful. Now real Welsh lobster would be something to please me, that's for sure.'

'As long as it's thermidor,' Grey rejoined. 'What did you want to show us?'

She led them to the far cliffs, where a small path, nearly overgrown, wound down towards the sea.

'Good God, what's that?' exclaimed Grey. 'Some sort of suicide walk?'

'It leads down to the caves,' explained Veronica. 'You can see them much better from the water. I can take you there in the dinghy one day if you like.'

'And what are these caves?'

'They're called the Singing Caves. You see, when a monk had been disobedient, or was suspected of being insubordinate or whatever, he was taken down to the caves. They're rather beautiful on a fine day, arched like natural cathedrals, with the most gorgeous turquoise water. Seals paddle around them occasionally. In the middle is a rock, tall and pointed, rather slippery and nasty. The bad monk would be put on this rock and left there overnight. He would be told to pray and sing, and if he was still there in the morning, that meant that God knew he was innocent and had saved him. But if he was gone . . . well, that meant he was guilty and had been taken to his punishment.'

There was a pause as they all looked over the edge to where the waves slapped foamily against the cliffs.

'Oh dear,' Grey said.

'It sounds like a witch trial,' Jack said grimly.

Veronica nodded. 'I don't suppose you had a chance if the tides and the weather went against you. I can't imagine what it would be like down there in a storm.' She paused and they all stared down again. 'And they say that you can hear, sometimes, the singing of hymns coming up from the caves – the ghosts of those poor monks.'

'Miserable bastards,' Jack said feelingly.

'That abbot should have been shot,' Grey said firmly. 'And all like him. All dictators. All cruel autocrats.'

'No guns then,' Jack said bleakly.

'No. But we have them now, thank God.'

Back at the house, they were all suddenly tired, but there was still dinner to cook. Veronica would stay with them until later, when she would make her way to the cottage, with her torch dimmed. As it grew late, they lit the fire and the candles and dropped the blackout blinds. Jack had offered to cook and he got busy with some fish that Jim had left them, and some goodies from the various tins and vegetables from the garden. Grey made martinis with the gin and vermouth, and they left Jack in the kitchen and went to the sitting room with their drinks.

Grey sat by the fire and smoked as they talked. 'But what are you really doing with yourself, Veronica? You can't rot here. Everyone needs a purpose.'

'I'm learning to live – to grow things, and cook and eat and take care of myself.'

Grey looked impatient. 'All well and good, my darling, but you need more than that. That's caveman stuff. Even they were drawing on the walls in their spare time! What are you doing?'

'I'm writing,' she confessed.

Grey looked relieved. 'Well, thank the maker for that. What are you writing? Books?'

'Plays.' She shrugged. 'I can't change the fact that I grew up in the theatre. Something must have gone into me. I'm going to write something good. I'd like it to be important but I'd rather it were good. Years ago Mama said something I've not forgotten. She said about the play we were watching: we've come to be entertained, not improved. And that's what I'm aiming for. I don't want moral lessons and highfalutin language and gasping poetry or obscure discussions. I want people to be engrossed and moved and then, maybe, to learn something about themselves and all of us.'

Grey laughed loudly, throwing back his head. He put his cigarette between his lips and applauded. 'Well done, young Veronica. Georgie will be proud, wherever he is. Damn it, *I'm* proud, come to that. You've got it. Got it in one. Good luck to you and if I can help, let me know. I love to write plays myself, delicious bits of fluff with iron at their core. I find it easy, but whether my plays are important – that's for the future to judge. I don't care. People will hear anything if they can laugh while they do it, or cry or feel passion. Well done. But one condition . . .'

'Yes?' Veronica said, feeling absurdly pleased that her ambitions had not been shot down. 'What?'

'It's quite simple, darling. Never write anything better than I do. That's all I ask. Now, let's see if Jack is ready. Whatever he's making smells divine.'

They were finishing up Jack's meal when they became aware of the noise outside: a wail that at first Veronica thought was the night sounds of the shearwaters. When Grey said, 'What on earth is that?', she realised that it was too deep and urgent for bird call. And the wail was punctuated by bangs and rattles increasing in volume.

They went outside. It was not quite dark yet so there was no need for torches but at once they saw lights and flashes on the mainland, some way off, on the other side of the point. The August night carried sound and light for miles, so that they had no idea exactly where it was, but the tumult was obvious. The sky was pierced with shafts of light as searchlights strafed it. Over the top of the screech of sirens and air-raid warnings, the buzz of planes could be clearly heard and occasionally they saw black winged dots illuminated as they soared around, dipping and banking, swooping and lifting, delivering flashes of gunfire. There was an air battle going on. Amid the pounding of barrage bombs, shells burst in the air, exploding like fat balls of lava.

'A raid,' Jack breathed in awe. 'A big one!'

'Where is it?' Grey asked, a trace of anxiety in his voice.

'It must be a way off,' Veronica said. 'But they haven't come this close before!' She clutched at Jack's arm. 'The people . . . I hope the people are all right.'

At that moment, a ghastly boom filled the air and

everything changed. A bright orange light flashed and spread over the ground like a blanket flicked over a bed, while a column of flame rose up over a hundred feet in the air, clearly visible at this distance. It seemed to touch the clouds and set fire to them too before sinking back. The clouds glowed and roiled like flames themselves and against their illumination, Veronica could see that the sky was filled with something else that seemed like black rain that was spattering the clouds and now falling back to earth. The noise went on in a great roar that drowned out everything else.

'What is it?' she cried. 'What can it be?'

'It must be the docks,' Jack said grimly. His face was set like stone, lit by the orange glow. 'They've hit something, oil tanks I should think. My god. What a disaster.'

They watched in horror as the flames crackled and flickered. How great must the fire be at its source?

The enemy planes, having hit their target, began evasive action but the stubborn Spitfires refused to let them go, and the dog fight continued with rattles of machine gunfire in the orange and black sky until at last the enemy craft escaped southwards and the raid was over.

The fire on the ground was fierce as ever. Vast clouds of acrid smoke billowed up above it.

Veronica realised she was sobbing and Jack put his arm around her, his face white in the reflection of the great fire. 'The poor people,' she said, covering her face with her hands. 'The pilots. I can't bear it.'

'I never thought it would come to us,' he said softly. 'I don't know why. Our beautiful Wales. What do they want with us?'

'The same as they want with us all,' Grey said. 'I'm going to have a cigarette and damn the light. With that blaze going like that, it hardly matters.'

The three of them stood watching the inferno, still hearing the wail of sirens and the clanging of bells over the miles that stood between them.

'Sleep in the house with us,' Grey said gently. 'Don't be on your own tonight.'

'Yes,' Veronica said gratefully. 'I think I will. Thank you.'

The next day, despite the sunshine and clear sky directly above, they could smell the acrid smoke. Veronica went out early with Boris for a walk after a sleepless and panicked night. The flames were still visible, flickering in the distance even if reduced in impact by daylight.

It is real then, she thought. *Real and terrible.*

Bombs had begun to fall on cities, a few lone raiders at first. But they would be coming in greater numbers, she was sure of it.

She thought of Billie and Mama in London. Mama had been reluctant to leave entirely the home that had been gratefully accepted by the War Ministry, and had stayed on with Billie in the cottage at the end of the garden.

They must come here, it's safer. I'll write to Billie today and get Jim to post it as soon as he can.

The days that followed had a sense of calm and security, perhaps because they felt that there could be no raid now for a while longer.

Jim arrived from the mainland with post and freshly woven lobster pots to set, and snares to check. Rabbits were usually a winter crop, but with the shortage of meat, they had become desirable all year round, as long as they were well cooked. He put down his sacks in the kitchen and groped in his satchel for the post.

'What happened, Jim?' Veronica asked as he set down her letters. From the sitting room came the tinkle of the piano where Grey and Jack were composing another song. 'We saw the fire. It looked awful.'

'Docks,' he said grimly, shaking his head. 'They hit the oil tanks, twelve thousand tons. Fire's still burning; they've got over sixty men trying to put it out. Explosion blew all the windows out round about. Two houses fell down.'

'That's terrible. Were many people hurt?'

'Five firemen killed, a woman in one of the houses.' Jim seemed to take a grim satisfaction in the telling.

'Oh no!' She felt distraught.

'Could have been worse,' Jim said laconically.

She bowed her head. 'I suppose so.'

'They don't think the fire'll be out for days yet. Weeks, maybe.'

'All that precious oil too. It's too awful.'

'They'll be opening up new airfields round here, I'm hearing,' Jim said. 'To protect the coast.'

Despite her sadness, Veronica felt oddly comforted. The thought of planes and pilots taking up their posts all around to guard the ports and waters was the only thing that could quell her fears. Mastery of the sea and the air seemed to be what stood between them and utter disaster.

One afternoon, Grey declared he needed a sleep after his furious creativity, and an hour or two to work on dialogue after that. Veronica and Jack went out together for a walk, heading up over the brow of the island. They sat together in the ruffling breeze, talking easily about Jack's boyhood in Wales and his musical education as a choirboy.

Jack is so lovely, she thought. *He isn't like Grey, who's so cynical and knowing. Grey's witty, charming and charismatic, but so extremely defensive. One always has to be on one's guard.*

Jack had his natural beauty, which acted like a love potion on nearly everyone who saw him, but more than that, he had a sweetness that gave him enormous appeal. Perhaps it was because he seemed so unaware of his great physical perfection.

'My mother is a force to be reckoned with,' he was saying, plucking bits of grass as he talked. 'She always wanted the very best for me. It was she who put me into the cathedral choir and from there I won a scholarship to a top school, which helped me lose my Welsh accent and gain the veneer of a gentleman. But music . . . that was our shared love. We had a piano in almost every room of the house. Her dream was that I became a serious musician, a conductor at Covent Garden! She's proud of what I've achieved, of course, but she always says I write music for housemaids and cabbies.

She'd rather I composed for dukes and duchesses and the like, but I don't have it in me. Instead, I write about them – my musicals are all about lords and ladies falling in love in far-off kingdoms. They're light as feathers, but people seem to like them.'

Veronica looked over at him, admiring again the Grecian profile and the long lashes sweeping his cheeks. 'How did you come to be so famous?'

'Ah . . .' Jack laughed and then sang suddenly: '*A vale of violets! A vale of violets for you!*'

Veronica laughed and threw a handful of grass seed that she'd been pulling off nearby stalks towards him.

He went on: 'One lucky song. I hardly knew I was writing my life's success story, but that song took me all the way to Hollywood. But I hated it there, hated being in front of the camera, and hated the tedium of film work. Give me the stage any day. Even so, I'd rather write than perform.' He looked over at her with a smile. 'You are terribly easy to talk to, Veronica. I do love women – perhaps because my mother and I were so close.'

'I fell in love with you as soon as I saw you!' Veronica said with a laugh. To hide her embarrassment, she picked up some white campion flowers and began to inspect them carefully. 'I'm sure you knew. And I know I was hardly the only one.'

Jack looked modest. 'It is a hazard of what I do.'

'It's a hazard of being you!'

Jack laughed. 'I do seem to appeal to women, and it's awful of me, but I like to seduce them from a distance, to make them feel those wonderful feelings of excitement and passion, to give them something to dream about in lives that can be very hard . . . even though . . . as you understand . . . I don't have any real interest in them.'

'Of course! I understand.' She squinted hard at her flower, thinking of how she was one of those females once who fell in love with liquid eyes and a dream, and how powerful and sweetly agonising it had been. She was glad she didn't feel like that any longer and that she had fallen in love with a real person instead – stronger, sweeter and more painful though that was. She looked up at Jack. 'You know, Billie and I used to call men like you "seahorses". I'm not sure why. It was something to do with the way seahorses are so pretty, so delicate, but also masculine-looking. I saw some in the aquarium once, a pair floating in the water with their tails curled around each other, and thought they looked like two male friends holding hands. So when Billie and I understood more about some of Daddy's theatre friends, we called them that.'

Jack looked at her, smiling. 'I rather like it. And do you know that male seahorses give birth?'

'Do they?' Veronica asked, amazed.

'Oh yes, they carry the eggs and give birth when the time is right.'

'Amazing!' Veronica laughed. 'And rather suitable. How funny. And talking of giving birth, how is your musical going?'

'It's going very well.' Jack looked away, squinting out towards the sea beyond. 'It's a little hard to get a word in sometimes,' he admitted. 'Grey is very powerful and forceful, teeming with ideas. He leans towards modern sophistication

281

and wit while I'm a romantic at heart. He likes bouncy, clever songs; I like soaring melodies and sentiment. We're different like that.'

'But it's working?' Veronica ventured.

'Just. Yes, it's working. I have just enough say to keep it going.' He looked back at her with a ravishing smile. 'But we might not do this too often in the future. We have a contract and a theatre booked for next year, so . . . And Grey's got this marvellous opportunity, to write a film for the war effort. He's itching to get on with it, and he wants to get this finished so he can move on.' He laughed suddenly. 'Grey says we have to do something to combat the ENSA on Drury Lane.'

'ENSA?'

'Entertainments National Service Association. Entertaining the troops, in other words. They're auditioning and rehearsing plays in the Theatre Royal to send all over the world to amuse the soldiers, poor loves. Something appalling every night, Grey says.' He looked sheepish. 'I'm only joking. It's wonderful work and I'm sure it brightens the lives of the boys marvellously.' He sighed. 'Grey wants to be in films. That's his dream really. He hates performing the same thing every night, it bores him. He could make six different films a year, instead of endless identical performances, and earn six times as much.'

'It sounds like you want different things,' Veronica said slowly. 'I mean . . . if you don't mind my saying.'

'Of course not.' Jack shrugged. 'We're different people.' He stood up. 'Come on, let's go and see your dinghy. Can you really sail it? Take me down to the beach and show me.'

Chapter Fifteen

1941

'It's bad to be in London just now,' Jim said solemnly. He had put the newspaper, already some days out of date, on the kitchen table and its front page was dominated by a photograph of the appalling damage inflicted on the city by the Luftwaffe.

Veronica picked it up and gasped. 'Oh my goodness! That's simply terrible!' She began to scan the news report anxiously, looking for the details and the numbers of dead and injured. As always, she sent up a silent prayer for Billie.

Their vanity is wounded, Veronica thought, as she looked at the awful photographs. *They thought we'd be a pushover, but we haven't been. So now they're going to destroy our city in revenge.*

Despite the relative quiet of Hampstead, Mama had been too terrified by the raids to stay in the cottage. The fire storm inflicted by the enemy at the end of December had been the last straw for her, and Veronica had come home to bring her back to the island for good.

'Won't you come too, Billie?' she'd asked, as they tidied and shut up the cottage together.

Billie shook her head. Her hair was tied up under a knotted headscarf to keep it clean while they dusted, and she wore a yellow apron over her plain dress. 'No. I'm not going, Vee. I've got my work. And I like it here. Margery's found me a place in her women's lodging house in Battersea, very handy to walk to work, better than here. So I'll have a friend.'

Veronica smiled at her sister. 'You seem so much older than you are. You're still a kid, really.'

'We're all growing up fast. And I'm old enough to get married, if you don't mind! I'm not just a kid.'

'Of course not. But look after yourself, Billie, won't you?'

'We're the same,' Billie said stoutly. 'We can look after ourselves, and we jolly well will. Now, you scrub that floor and I'll do the windows.'

Since then, Billie had written at least once a week so that Veronica knew she was safe, keeping her tone chatty even though she now had the dangerous job of being an air-raid warden. She'd sent a picture of herself wearing overalls, sensible shoes and a tin hat with a W on it.

My sector has been lucky so far, but who knows how long that will last. We've had a few smaller hits. I've made friends with a cabbie called Bill. Confusing for both of us. His taxi got requisitioned as a fire truck by the AFS so instead of being a cabbie, he's now a fireman, gets paid for it and everything. He's super at it because he's got the knowledge and can get his buckets

and things there before the standard boys have worked
out where they're going. He's shown up twice now to
help out with the fire fighting. Nothing too terrible has
happened, though it feels hairy when it all kicks off.
Keep your fingers crossed for me, Vee. I wear lots of
lipstick, that helps. Look after Mama.
    Love, Billie x

In some ways, Veronica felt wretched that Billie was so far
away, and guilty that she wasn't there too, but she knew it
would make no difference if she were. She was doing better
work on the island, growing food and sending it to the mainland, along with all the natural bounty she could find. She
spent hours combing her beaches for cockles, winkles and
clams, with lava and gutweed to be found as well, putting
the harvest into baskets to be taken into town, along with
the masses of lobster and crabs, not to speak of the endless
supply of rabbits. Jim used the oars to save fuel and when
she saw his little craft bobbing away, carrying it all to the
mainland, she felt that she was doing something to help.

It was different with Mama here now as well. She was
more lost and forgetful since Daddy's death, but her spirits
had lifted, and though she moved more slowly now, she was
able to help around the house. She was certainly a better
cook than Veronica, who had never learned any such skills
and simply muddled by as best she could on what she did
know.

'Rabbit again,' Mama would sigh, as she started to prepare their evening meal. 'I know we're spoiled and it's better

than starving, but it's so hard to cook this lean meat without fat! It needs cream and butter. Get Jim to get us a goat, won't you? I'm sure I could learn to milk it.'

There wasn't much in the way of dairy products otherwise, with only powdered milk and egg instead to enrich the lean rabbit. Jim had brought a flock of chickens and helped make a run for them, so there were now brown eggs most mornings and, very occasionally, a chicken to cook once it had stopped laying for good.

At least spring was coming but the war looked to be worsening if anything, its dark tendrils spreading out across the world, strangling everyone with its awful might.

Looking at the photographs of poor bombed London now, she wondered how it could end. Victory seemed so very far away. But what else was there to do but keep up the struggle?

As Jim slipped out of the kitchen, heading for the barn where he lit a fire against the wintery cold, she turned a page and gasped. A headline read:

TRIUMPH FOR OSWALD-BANNOCK COLLABORATION
- THE SEAHORSE *CHARMS AUDIENCES AT THE MAYFLOWER*
- *RECORD-BREAKING AUDIENCES AT LUNCHTIME PERFORMANCES*
- *EACH SONG A HIT!*

Underneath was a tiny blurry picture that she could make out as Grey and Jack, smartly dressed in suits and hats, smiling at the camera, Grey holding up his cigarette in salute.

They were business partners now, they could be seen out and about respectably. Up to a point, of course.

'*The Seahorse!*' she said out loud and laughed merrily. 'So they've finally managed to stage it.'

'What is it, Vee?' Mama asked, coming in at that moment. She looked very far from the elegant Hampstead lady now, in her plain dress and white apron over it, but she still had her hair and make-up perfectly done, and her voice was as refined as ever. 'What are you laughing at?'

'Look,' she said, holding out the paper. 'Grey Oswald and Jack Bannock have a hit – a sparkling comedy based around a love triangle. Daring, provocative but essentially good-hearted, they say here. Isn't that nice? We must listen to the wireless more, we might hear one of the hit songs they wrote. They're sure to be wonderful.'

Mama looked over, interested. 'I see. Goodness. *The Seahorse.* I wonder why they called it that?'

'Who knows?' Veronica said with a laugh. She felt light-hearted for the first time in many days.

She took her usual walk around the island that afternoon for the first time in a while, as the storms had prevented them from going out, except close to the house to see the chickens. When the storms had passed, the days were very short and there wasn't long to go about everything that needed doing. Jim was busy with rabbits, for it was now the best time of year for them, and the large hauls needed to be got to the mainland for sale. She and Mama seemed to spend most of the day looking after the house and preparing their meals, as well as collecting driftwood for the fires. Only as darkness fell did she turn back to the work she loved most, sitting at the little desk in the drawing room and working on the play she was writing. She had begun with the structure and concept in Rupert's original draft but had transformed it so often and so far that it was now something completely different altogether, although still set in a lonely house in some woods, far from anywhere, where travellers crossed paths for a night in circumstances that were eerie as well as comforting, frightening as well as reassuring, and with a twist in the end that she was still trying to discover. The only problem was that she wasn't sure that she liked it. It didn't inspire her in the way she'd hoped.

She had written on every sheet of paper twice to save scarce resources, writing longhand rather than typing, as she had heard Grey doing in his room, the sounds echoing out like miniature gunfire as he tapped out his dialogue.

'You know me,' he would say when she remarked on him rattling away seemingly without a pause. 'I write it all in the noggin first, and then let it come pouring out through my fingertips. Doesn't everyone?'

'I don't think so,' Veronica would laugh, thinking how she slaved over lines, crossing and recrossing, trying to find the perfect way to say what she meant. 'And I find it so hard to make it turn out the way I want.'

'It turns out as it was meant to turn out,' Grey said carelessly. 'Try not to think too hard about it. The infinite possibilities of storytelling can end up acting like a gag rather than anything else.'

She thought of that now, standing on the brow of the island, battered by the fierce winds. Out beyond the view of the ruined monastery, the sea was rising and falling in a great tumult, swelling up in foamy peaks as though a titan were rolling restlessly about underneath. The water was iron-grey and formidable under a sky thick with charcoal-coloured cloud. The wind roiled around her, whistling in her ears. Boris sat beside her, his ears blown back and his eyes half closed against the fierce air, enduring the experience for her sake.

She missed the birds. So many had gone on their winter travels. The shearwaters were, she believed, feasting on anchovies in Brazil. The puffins had gone on their mysterious voyage; many smaller species had departed for the warmth of Africa, including the little storm petrel. The rock pipits stayed, though, and the wrens, roosting together for warmth, along with other natives, but many disappeared only to visit occasionally in good weather as if to check that their nests were still in good order. She feared that the gales had blown the remaining birds completely away but somehow, they always returned from wherever they sheltered, to take up their familiar places on the island.

Snow is coming, she thought, gazing out to sea. *Perhaps that will keep the bombers away. Please God it does.*

The snow did come, coating the land in a white blanket. Veronica watched the robins, blackbirds and starlings pecking up the breadcrumbs she threw out for them while the gulls swallowed scraps from the rubbish tip, pecking away at the snow to find them. But the winter weather appeared to do nothing to deter the bombers, and they seemed to have the towns, cities and villages of South Wales in their sights. Jim fought his way over the choppy waters to tell them of attacks on Cardiff and Swansea and their surroundings, awful stories of whole streets being wiped out, of fire killing people in their shelters, of schools being bombed beyond repair.

At night, they heard the engines sometimes when they could see nothing through thick cloud cover. Veronica felt safe enough; their little island, nothing but a black dot, was surely of no interest. Their danger really came from any mistakenly dropped or discarded bombs, and so far they'd come nowhere close to explosions.

It was more dangerous at sea. One peril that lurked half hidden in the waves was the deadly floating black sea mine, while under the waters were minesweepers and U-boats, even now sliding beneath the surface looking for targets. Steamers and trawlers made their way in and out of ports, carrying passengers and vital freight, achingly vulnerable to the bombs and missiles of the enemy. Veronica had seen them steaming away across the Atlantic, sometimes guarded by an air convoy, other times by armed escorts and patrol boats. But she found most heart-wrenching of all the sight of the fishing smacks and trawlers, most creaky with age, going out to fish the waters. The North Sea was almost unfishable now, thick with mines and U-boats, and strafed by planes at all hours, but the western coasts were a little safer and here, those vessels not requisitioned went out to fish for desperately needed food. Veronica would see them heading out early, old and battered, their nets and winches ready to drop, and coming home late with as much of a catch as they could muster. But she knew that over the months, many had not come back. She had heard, on more than one occasion, a distant boom that told her a fishing boat had hit a mine or been torpedoed – although it was said that U-boats couldn't be bothered to waste a torpedo on the creaky old Welsh fishing boats and preferred to use gunfire to sink them.

Veronica and Mama stayed inside in the worst of the chill, burning up the last sacks of coal from the store Daddy had put in years ago and that they had thought would last more or less for ever. It was cosy in the sitting room with Mama embroidering by the fire, or mending clothes and rips in sheets, while Veronica wrote. They listened to music and sometimes Mama played the piano. The wireless was not much good in bad weather, they found, with the static and the signal dropping up and down.

One night, when the wind dropped and they had a clear signal, she heard Grey on the Light Programme singing a selection of songs from his new hit with Jack, *The Seahorse*, and it gave her a wonderful thrill to hear the songs written at the piano in this very room. One about a girl with 'sapphire eyes and flaxen hair, a pouting mouth and stubborn air' made her laugh, wondering if they had meant her.

'They're very good, dear,' Mama said absently, but she didn't appear to have really listened.

It was a frightful blowy afternoon and not far from darkness falling completely when Veronica felt she simply had to go out for a walk.

'Are you sure?' Mama said, in the warmth of the kitchen. 'How can you want to go out in this?'

'My brain is completely stuffed up,' she said. 'I need to blow it clear, that's all. I'll just take a quick turn with Boris. I might check on Jim.'

Jim was staying over as it was too rough to make the return crossing and had settled himself in for the night already in the barn, apparently perfectly happy with his fire, tobacco and a couple of rabbits to skin, gut and fry.

'I'm sure he's fine,' Mama said. 'But don't be long. I don't like you out in this.'

Which was one of the reasons why she had to get out, Veronica thought, putting her hands in her pockets and whistling for Boris as she pulled the door shut behind them.

She strode out along her usual route, skirting the island and climbing the gentle slope until she was standing near the top of the northern point. Below her were the remains of the monastery and the old abbey, and beyond that the sea. Far out, she could see a large ship steaming inwards from the Atlantic, heading for the larger port some miles away, accompanied by a small patrol on either side of it. Just as she noticed the patrol, she heard the roar of an engine. An angular but nimble Halifax aeroplane soared over her head and dipped away over the island towards the ship.

The air boat, she thought jubilantly. *Come to bring the ship home.*

She was heartened by the sight of the protectors flocking to help. The Halifax, in its khaki colours and with the RAF roundels on the side, performed a large circular recce, taking a course out to sea behind the ship before banking to make the return trip, swooping downwards to survey the water for mines and U-boats.

Suddenly she noticed four black dots appear on the horizon. Twin-propellered German bombers were approaching in tight formation, preparing to attack the ship.

'Oh no! Oh no! Look, do look!' Veronica began to jump up and down in panic, yelling and waving her arms, and then stopped. What good could she do? She mustn't distract them, even if they were taking a blind bit of notice. 'Please see them!' she begged.

A moment later, it was obvious that the Halifax had seen, and the aircraft began its manoeuvre to attack the little convoy of enemy planes and draw their fire. The rattle of machine gunfire began, and there were flashes in the sky as the planes began to engage.

How can one plane take on four? It's impossible!

The gunners on board the ship were already pounding shells upwards, which forced the German planes apart. Meanwhile the Halifax darted between them in dives and circles, gunning hard from both turrets. The next moment, one of the enemy planes had taken a shell from below, ripped open across her lower fuselage and burst into flames. In an instant, it had fallen into a burning, twisting dive and vanished into the sea in a whirl of smoke.

'Oh yes! Oh yes!' shouted Veronica and then she felt ashamed. Some mothers' sons were on board that plane and this very moment they were dying.

But it's them or us. It has to be them. It has to be.

She was unable to do anything but watch the air battle, as the planes swooped and dived, releasing volleys of fire upon each other. One escort boat took a barrage of bullets and disappeared in an explosion of fire, smoke and seawater. Veronica moaned in horror, but still watched as the Halifax, now smoking from a strafe of bullets along its side, rolled and gunned down another enemy plane and then, miraculously, another.

'It's going to win!' Veronica cried, in disbelief. 'One against four!'

The remaining two planes buzzed around one another, ratcheting out gunfire, then the Halifax holed the tail of the other and took another volley of bullets to the fuselage, before inflicting a series of fiery shots on its opponent. The two planes both seemed desperately wounded but still locked in combat as they twisted and turned to gain the advantage.

'Come on, come on!' cried Veronica. The whole battle had taken less than ten minutes. Dozens must be dead or dying. The Halifax, tipping back and forth and firing ceaselessly, took the enemy head on and delivered a deathly volley. But, as it twisted into a death spin, the enemy sent back a last blast of machine gunfire. The Halifax somersaulted away and then righted itself only in time to take a soaring dive towards the sea.

'No, no, no!' Veronica shouted. Against all odds, the single plane had taken on a quartet of the enemy and won. Now it too was defeated.

She watched as the plane almost hit the water and then

righted itself and found a blast of power that took it skimming over the surface. But the high deadly whine in the engine grew louder. The Halifax was facing the island now, its nose pointed towards the cliff as it soared towards her, far too low. Before she had time to think, the plane skimmed over the water at an unbelievable rate, heading straight for the island cliffs on the north-west side.

What? she thought, calm all of a sudden. *But it's coming straight for us. What will it feel like when it strikes us?*

It would be stronger than the storms that shook the cliffs, she knew that. Would it shatter them? Could it break the island? Could they even sink? It would hit and explode in a fireball. Would the island go up in flames?

The air was full of noise: the roar of the engine, and the whine of its injury. As the plane flew towards her, it was hard to believe it had ever been a dot in the sky. Now it was a great machine, a marvel of steel and glass and rivets and technology. As the cockpit and towers soared into sight, she saw the men inside, just for a second, and then, when it was inevitable that the plane would explode on the side of the island, it managed somehow to bank to the right, its wing tip dipped in the water, its underbelly exposed, and it veered left, skirting the body of the island and passing it on the far western side. But in another second, it hit one of the rock stacks just beyond the cliffs, broke off a wing, and flew up onto its side, bouncing onto another rock stack and spinning off out of sight. She heard a roar and a crash, a high-pitched whistling, a kind of huge thump and a grating noise. And then it was quiet.

She let out a shaking breath. Out at sea, the ship and its remaining patrol had turned for the port, limping and wounded, trailing smoke. Smoke and burning black debris was engulfed by the waves on the surface. The Halifax, now on the south of the island's edge, could not be seen.

Veronica raced across the island and stood on the far cliffs looking down. The light had waned even more in the short time that she had been watching the battle and now it was hard to see the murky water below. She thought she could make out the shadow of an aeroplane tail in the water but she could not be certain.

I have to see if they're all right!

Of course it was most likely they'd be dead, but she had to be sure. The path downwards was the one that was almost overgrown, the monks' walkway to the Singing Caves. Barely thinking of what she was doing, Veronica began to climb downwards, slipping slightly at times and clutching at the vegetation on the side of the cliff. She couldn't think of danger, after what she had seen.

The light was fast disappearing. As she rounded the tight curves of the path, she was aware of the gathering gloom and the rising chill of the water beneath. The water was a little calmer in the area between the rock stacks and the caves, which acted as natural breaks, but still the waves gathered and slapped against the island in ceaseless motion. As she stumbled round the last bend so that she could peer back towards the caves beneath the island, she saw the tail of the plane first, spattered in bullet holes, and the strange crossbar at its rear, which was floating at an angle in the dark water.

Both wings were broken off and the fuselage was battered and strewn with bullet holes. The plane had come to a halt with its front propeller broken off, and the nose and what was left of its cockpit in the cave was pressed up against the rock in the centre. It was extraordinary that it had lasted even this far, with the amount of holes dotting it. It was still floating but the gurgle of water indicated that it was slowly sinking.

Veronica scrambled forward towards it. 'Hello!' she called. 'Is anyone there?'

The engine was dead, doused by seawater no doubt, which had also killed any flames. But there was no sound and no sign of life. The cave was full of the acrid scent of fuel, smoke and salt water.

Veronica stood there, helpless, overwhelmed by the sight of the wrecked craft, only minutes ago soaring through the air and now a ruin that would never fly again. The mechanical design and mastery, the complex engine and the marvellous construction were gone for ever. But more than that, what of the men inside it?

'Hello?' she called again.

There was still no sound. Tears rushed to her eyes. They must be dead. It was awful, those brave boys. She had seen them in their last moments as they worked frantically to avoid the island.

Then she heard a groan that echoed through the chamber over the sound of the waves.

'Is anyone there?' she called again, pushing forward as far

as she could along the slippery path, clutching the cliff plants to hold herself firm. Had she imagined it?

Then another sound, an unmistakable groan, and Veronica squinted into the gloom of the cave. There, on the rock in the centre, she thought she could see a shape. The nose of the plane was pressed to it, the cockpit lid open, and she could make out a figure, bulky in flying gear, sprawled on the rock, held there by the nose of the plane.

'Wait, wait!' she called. 'Wait, we're coming! We'll be there as soon as we can!'

She turned and stumbled as fast as she could back up the path to the top of the cliff.

Jim pulled hard on the boat's oars, his stocky body fighting against the strength of the waves. It was almost dark now, but he knew his way around the island with his eyes closed. They had left the jetty and skirted the southern side of the island. As they neared the caves, Jim looked back over his shoulder and glimpsed the vast body of the plane, lower now in the black sea. He murmured in shock then said, 'Hope she doesn't block the way in.'

As they rounded the last outcrop, Veronica saw that there was a way to approach the plane from the furthest point and she pointed it out to Jim. 'Can we get in there? Is there room?'

'I reckon,' he said, looking back, 'but we'll have to drift in and push ourselves out.'

As soon as they were sheltered by the cliffs, Veronica got out her torch and shone it into the cavern, standing up as best she could as the boat swayed and lifted on the waves.

The light immediately sent a riot of strange shadows onto the walls of the cave, and the wrecked body of the plane looked more dreadful than ever, the dull colours of its fuselage now apparent. Veronica sent the beam onto the rock, where a slumped figure lay across it, flying mask hanging loose.

'There he is,' she said, and then called, 'Hello? We're coming!'

An answering groan echoed around the chamber.

'He's still alive,' Veronica said, excited. 'Come on, Jim, get us as close as you can.'

The water was icy and the walls of the cliff radiated cold as Jim manoeuvred the boat into the narrow entrance, pulling the oars in and using the cave walls to push them closer to the rock. 'Be careful,' he warned. 'It'll be slippery. I'll jam us in there, between the rock and the walls, and we can try and get him down.'

He got the boat into position as best he could, while managing the swell and drop of the waves. 'I have to hold her here,' he said to Veronica, 'or she'll move away, there's nothing to anchor to.'

'All right,' Veronica said. 'I'll just have to get him down as best I can.'

She moved to the prow of the boat and from there she could see that the airman was positioned so that his legs were on the other side of the rock. There was no way they could get around there. She would have to pull him down towards her and hope that she could get him into the boat. She put one foot on the rock. It was horribly slippery.

'Here,' Jim said, 'take this. And give me the torch.' He

handed her a rope from the bottom of the boat and she slung it round her neck. 'There's a hook on the end, see? Get up if you can and hook it on 'im. We'll haul 'im down.'

Veronica handed him the torch, which he focused on the black outline of the airman, and took a deep breath. She was nervous of the swelling waves, the cold and the darkness, but began to search for foot and hand holds on the wet rock, grateful she was wearing her rubber-soled boots. The man on the rock moaned again and shifted slightly.

'Stay still!' she called. 'I'm coming but you mustn't move, you might fall off.'

She stood for a moment, one foot on the rock, the other on the boat, feeling it move beneath her, and got a horrible sick feeling of dizziness and the sensation that she was about to plummet into the water, then took a deep breath and lifted her other foot onto the rock.

I don't have to go so very far, she told herself. *It's not a huge climb.*

But it felt enormous as she inched her way upwards. Her hands were quickly numb with cold, which at least meant that the pain of the sharp rock and the barnacles stuck to it didn't hurt as much. She would have to be quick, though, she knew that. She couldn't stand this for long.

'Come on now, you can do it!' urged Jim, holding the boat as still as he could beneath her.

His words gave her strength. She managed another step upwards, and then another. Her hands were hurting now despite the numbness and she feared that soon she would be unable to handle the rope in any useful way at all. Panicked, she took another climb upwards, then glanced back. She was far enough up the rock to slip not into the boat but into the sea. She took another deep breath to push away her fear. She was close to the airman now, and could see his flying mask hung down the rock. His arms were flung out on either side but that at least meant she had access to his harness. Fumbling for the rope, she got it from round her neck and managed to get the hook into her stiff fingers. A moment later, after a few wild attempts that threatened to destabilise her, she had succeeded in pushing the hook under the harness and securing it.

'I've done it!" she called, relieved. She knew she would not be able to use her fingers in any practical way for much longer. The cold was creeping into her now, chilling her limbs. Her feet were numb too, despite the sheepskin lining of her boots. She had to get down quickly. If she fell into the water, she would have only moments before hypothermia took her.

'Come down,' called Jim, and she began to edge back down the slippery rock, inch by inch, finding her foot and hand holds as she went.

When she found the prow of the boat with her foot, Jim put up a hand to guide her. 'Now we pull 'im,' Jim said. 'Not the best way but it's all we got.'

They both pulled on the rope, trying to be as gentle as they could. The airman seemed comatose now, not moaning any more. As they pulled on his considerable weight, he edged towards them but then, suddenly, just when it seemed he would not give, he rolled around the rock and began to slither downwards, missing the boat altogether.

'No!' cried Veronica, seeing him slip towards the water.

'It's all right, look!' Jim said. 'The plane is gonna stop him.'

He was right, the nose of the Halifax stopped the airman rolling into the water. Now they could edge a little way to the left and pull him into the boat.

'Oh, thank goodness,' she said. 'I think we can do it! I'm sure we can.'

A few moments later, with the airman safely stowed in the boat, Jim was pushing the craft out of the caves and into the swell of the open water. The sea was rougher now and he had to fight with his oars to keep them on course as they returned to the jetty. The wind had leapt up and was howling around them, as they managed to get back and tie up the boat. Between them, they dragged the man out and hauled him up the slope and then up the stone steps towards the white house, where Mama was looking out anxiously for them, standing outside in the dark, taking care not to let any light escape from the house.

When she saw them, she gasped in relief. 'Come in, quickly! It's freezing! The storm is coming up fast.'

A moment later they were in the warmth of the sitting room where the fire was burning brightly. They gently put down the heavy, sodden body of the airman.

'Poor boy,' Mama said. 'Let's get him out of these wet things. Jim, can you help me get him out of this kit?'

Veronica watched as they began to struggle with clips and buckles, trying to get off the uninflated life jacket, the heavy flying boots, and the helmet with the goggles and the mask hanging free. She looked at the face of the airman, a pale white oval covered in bloody scrapes and scratches from the rocks, framed by his helmet and oxygen mask. He had a dark moustache and his eyes were closed. He could be anyone. He could be dead.

'Go and fill all the hot water bottles,' Mama said to her, 'and fetch more blankets. He's very cold. We must warm him.'

'Is he alive?' Veronica asked in a small voice.

'Just, I think. Go on now.'

Returning with the hot water bottles and blankets, Veronica saw that Jim had been dismissed now. The flight jacket and clothes below were off and she could see a grey vest and pale shoulders emerging from under a Welsh rug. Mama was leaning over him, cleaning the wounds on his face and talking softly to him as she did. 'There's my boy,' she said in a sing-song voice. 'You're going to be all right, you know, you'll be just fine.' She pulled away to look at Veronica. 'Do you have the hot water bottles, dear? He's warming up a little now.'

Veronica didn't answer. She was staring at the airman, who was still unconscious. She looked at his dark lashes curled on the scraped and bleeding cheeks, the slender moustache across his top lip, and his mouth. Despite the wounds, she knew the face so very well.

'André,' she said in wonder. 'It's André.'

Chapter Sixteen

That night, the tempest rose up from the sea as if in fury at the malice and waste of mankind, pursuing its dreadful and futile war. Jim had tucked himself away in the barn with his fire and his tobacco, well satisfied by the rescue that he and Veronica had pulled off. The rain came in torrents, lashing the island and its buildings, pelting the rocks and the sea that rose up to meet it in yawning waves.

There was no chance of anyone official coming on a rescue mission to find the Halifax and any survivors, even if they knew where to look. She would be assumed sunk, not lost in the caves beneath the island and, by the end of the storm, she probably would be sunk. The waves would lift her up as the rising tide filled the cave and then she would roll away and disappear into the depths, carrying with her the rest of the dead crew.

Meanwhile, André lay sleeping on the sofa in the sitting room, the light from the fire playing over his face, swathed in blankets, hot water bottles restoring some warmth to his frozen limbs.

'Will he be all right?' Veronica asked anxiously. She sat in the opposite chair, warm now herself after changing her wet clothes and taking a small but hot bath in the tin tub in the kitchen. She was dressed but in her dressing gown and slippers, a towel around her damp hair, crouched forward in her chair so that she could watch André at every moment.

'We'll know when he wakes up,' Mama said.

'I'll stay and watch him. You go to bed and rest, Mama, in case he needs you again.'

Mama looked over at her. 'So, Vee, are you going to tell me how you know this man?'

Veronica was beyond blushes. All that seemed very childish now. 'I met him in Paris.'

'Paris?' Mama looked surprised. 'Is he French?'

'Yes . . . André. Of course he's French.'

'Some Englishmen have French names, it's not unknown. But why would a Frenchman be flying for the RAF?'

'I suppose we have Poles and Czechs. There must be Frenchmen as well.'

'Yes, I suppose so . . . And how do you know him?'

'He's the brother of my friend, Irène. Remember, the lady who took me out for tea every Sunday.' For a moment, she saw Irène, charming, beautiful, vividly in her mind's eye. She had heard nothing from her in all these months, not since the Germans had marched into Paris. That was no surprise. She could only hope that Irène was surviving, keeping her head down in the little garret and somehow managing to find food and coal and stay safe.

But here, miracle of miracles, was André, brought to her

island in a roar of flame and a hail of bullets, left for dead in the cave.

And yet, he survived. Like the monks who sang and prayed and made it through to morning. He has survived.

And somehow, he's found me.

Veronica had fallen asleep and then woke with a start, sitting bolt upright and staring over at the sofa, half confused. 'André?'

He was lying there, still white as a ghost, but his eyes were open. The only light came from the fire and his brown eyes glowed orange with the reflected flames. 'Yes,' he said in English, his voice low. He blinked at her. 'Am I dead?'

She laughed softly. 'No, you're not dead! The opposite.'

'But I was in a plane. And now I'm here with you. And you look like my little Véronique but it's impossible that you should be her.'

'It's impossible that you should be flying in a plane off the coast of Wales, right over the top of my island.' She smiled, her eyes shining at him.

He blinked at her in the firelight. 'You are saying it's true?' he asked wonderingly. 'You are Véronique?'

She nodded, not trusting herself to speak.

'It can't be true. I hoped I would find you somehow, but I never thought it would be like this.'

'I know. It can't be. So, what's happening?'

'I like this dream,' André said.

'Are you hurt?'

306

'Like hell, all over.' He winced. 'What's my face like? It's very sore.'

'You've been badly scraped. Is anything broken?'

He closed his eyes for a moment and seemed to take stock of himself. 'No . . . I don't think so.'

'You were lucky then.'

He winced again, then made to sit up as if in a panic and said, 'Where are the others?'

She got up and went over to him, kneeling beside him and taking his hand in hers. She gazed into his dark eyes. 'I'm so sorry, André. You were the only one to make it out of the plane.'

He said nothing, but his fingers tightened around hers. His eyes darkened and he closed them, turning his face away from her.

'I'm sorry,' she whispered again.

'I tried to save us all.'

'You were flying?'

He nodded, his eyes still closed.

'You did your best. It's a miracle you made it as far as you did – you beat four fighters singlehanded. And you stopped the plane from hitting the island. If it had, you'd be dead too.'

'I wish I were,' he said bleakly.

'Don't say that, André! You're here for a reason.'

His eyes flicked open and he looked round at her, furious. 'And they are gone for a reason? There is a reason for the others to be dead, and not me? Why did they have no reason and I did?'

She faltered in front of his sudden rage. 'I don't know. I'm sorry. Perhaps it is meaningless. But that doesn't make life any less precious. Maybe more precious.'

André closed his eyes again and turned his face away. For long minutes, she held his hand and waited, and at last she guessed he was asleep.

Mama came in the night, and gently urged Veronica to bed. When she woke, it was to a sense of disbelief. André was here, in her cottage. How? What had happened to bring him to her like this?

Outside, the storm continued, the wind wailing around the house and the rain thumping against the roof and walls. The grasses waved frantically in the tempest. The birds were deep in their burrows or in the cliffs, sheltering from it as best they could.

Veronica got up, dressed and brushed out her thick hair, then went down to the kitchen where Mama was making breakfast. 'How is he?'

'He is still asleep. We can take him something to eat soon.'

'I can't think how he came here.'

'He didn't say?'

'No. He was devastated by the loss of the crew. He was flying, you see.'

'Ah. Poor lad. You must be kind to him.'

'Of course!'

'I know you will. I simply meant . . . you cannot talk someone out of grief. Let them feel it. Let it be. That's all I mean.'

Veronica was quiet for a moment as she absorbed this. 'Yes. I understand. Can I take him some tea?'

'Yes. The pot's brewed. Take some now.'

Veronica went into the sitting room with a cup of sweet milky tea. André lay as she had last seen him. Mama had quietly stoked up the fire and the room was warm. His facial wounds looked red and raw in the grey, stormy daylight. He must have hit the rock with some force, and the journey back down it, dragged by a rope, must have made it worse. Even so, he still looked like her beautiful André, and it was a miracle that he was there.

She put down the tea and went away to let him sleep.

When she went back in, he was awake and sitting up, sipping on the now cold tea with a scowl.

'I don't like to be ungrateful,' he said as she came in, 'but what is this filthy stuff?'

'Tea with milk and sugar. We made a whole pot with fresh leaves just for you.'

He put the cup down. 'I am most grateful. But is there any coffee?'

'Not real coffee,' she said apologetically. 'We've got chicory.'

'I'll have that, if I may, as strong as you can make it.' And he lay his head back against his pillows and closed his eyes again.

She didn't take in the coffee until later when he had woken up, and looked fresher despite the state of his wounds.

'Thank you,' he said, as she put it down beside him, and managed a smile.

'Are you all right?'

'No. Not really. And I need something to wear.'

Veronica gestured to the pile of clothes on the side. 'Some of Daddy's old things. They might not fit but they'll do for now.'

'Thank you,' he said simply. 'You and your mother are very kind.'

'We'd do this for anyone but I'm so happy I can do it for you.' She sat down in the armchair opposite him. 'Do you think you can tell me how you came to be here? I'm so desperate to know. I last saw you in Paris before the war and now . . . here you are.'

André looked over at her and his face softened. 'Forgive me for shouting earlier. The losses I've suffered are not your fault. Your mother told me that you and the fisherman rescued me from the cave. I have been . . . rude.'

'Of course not. You've lost your friends, your crew. How could you be anything else but agonised?'

He smiled wanly. 'You have a feeling heart, Véronique. Thank you. Yes, I last saw you in Paris. How could I forget? I never have, of course. Not for a day. But I had my duty to my country.'

'Irène told me in her last letter that you were in the Armée de l'Air. It was the only thing she really said about you. I was desperate to know more, but she wouldn't tell me.'

André looked thoughtful and, after a moment, he spoke. 'I trained as a pilot during my national service. I loved it, so

310

it made my service very enjoyable. It was natural I would return to the air when recalled for mobilisation. But everything was a disaster. The air army was in a terrible state: ancient craft, and not enough of them. Nothing worked. The bombers even arrived without bomb sights. If we could get enough planes into the air, we didn't have enough ammunition in any case. Our preparations for war were so bad, it was no wonder we lost so easily. Twenty bombers went down in a hopeless cause, trying to stop the Germans advancing. I knew that France was going to be invaded and conquered, so I decided to save what I could. The government ordered what was left of the fleet to North Africa, to the colonies, to regroup and prepare for combat. But it was obvious that as soon as we were occupied and the government had capitulated, the French air force would be commandeered to fight for the Germans.' His eyes burned for a moment. 'I would die before I flew for Goering. I took a plane, a Farman, and a tiny crew and I left.'

Veronica listened wide-eyed, astonished at his daring. Was this the reckless mission that Irène had written about?

'We flew to Berlin, just the single plane, then circled low over the city as many times as we could to create the impression of more than one plane, trying to put the fear of God in them, and also to laugh in the face of Goering, who'd said that Berlin would never be bombed. They weren't ready for us as a result. It was easy enough. We dropped our bombs on factories to the north of the city and then flew for the Netherlands, to join the Royal Netherlands Air Service. But it was almost too late; the Germans had already

311

invaded, the air force was about to be commandeered there as well. The Dutch had already decided to make for Britain and join the RAF. One of my co-pilots in the Armée de l'Air had also stolen a plane in France – he flew himself and twenty friends to Britain to join the Free French here. It was suddenly quite the fashion.'

André stopped talking, exhausted, and reached for his coffee. He took a sip, made a face and then laughed. 'This is actually better than I was expecting. Thank you, my sweetheart.'

She felt a bubble of joy lift inside her at this endearment, and she flushed. Perhaps she was not quite so far past blushes as she had thought. 'You joined the RAF . . .' she said, wonderingly.

He nodded and then looked suddenly bashful. 'If I was going to come to Britain, then I wanted to try to find you. I guessed you would be on your island – or, at least, I hoped you would be. And so I told them that we should make for Wales. I'd heard that the coastal command at Pembroke needed reinforcements and I saw on a map how close it must be to your island, from what you'd told me of it.'

She almost laughed. 'You came here because of me?'

'It seemed unlikely I would find you, but I managed to persuade the Dutch that this is where we should go. And so we flew here, to a very warm welcome from the RAF. They needed us badly.'

Veronica shook her head in amazement. 'You persuaded a foreign air service to let you fly to Wales – because of me? But when?'

'A few months ago.'

'So . . . you've been in Pembroke all this time? While I've been here on the island? We've been only miles apart.'

He laughed again. 'I suppose that we must have been, yes.'

'But that's extraordinary!'

'I wanted to come and look for you, but I never had the leave. I always planned to, as soon as I could. On every mission, I looked out for your island, and I thought I'd seen it several times. I always wondered if you might be on it.'

She was overcome that all this time, he had been so close, that he'd been thinking of her and looking for her. She whispered, 'And now we are back together.'

He looked at her lovingly. '*Chérie*, you saved my life.'

'You've saved dozens.'

'It's different.'

'Not so very.' She gazed at him, her heart swelling with love for him in a new way. 'Can you stay?'

He smiled. 'For a moment.'

'A moment?'

'Of course. I must go back to the squadron. I'm needed now more than ever. You saw what we are facing getting ships in and out of the ports and safely across the oceans. If we can't do that, the nation will starve, our ships will go down, we will lose the war, all of us. More than ever, we have to fight. Every one of us. You for Britain, me for France, and both of us for Europe, the world and freedom. I fight in the air, you in other ways. You fought tonight to rescue me, and you'll fight other battles too, whatever they are.'

She thought of Billie scouting for fires and looking out

for her sector. She thought of the food she carefully cultivated and gathered and sent to the mainland. She thought
of Grey and Jack lifting spirits with their songs and their
plays, and the actors and actresses rehearsing in the Theatre Royal to take their shows to entertain the troops. She
thought of the men and women using the house in Hampstead for intelligence gathering and secret operations. They
couldn't all use bombs and guns and planes. Some of them
had to use words, and ingenuity and talent and laughter,
and a multitude of tiny acts of faith, charity and kindness to
defeat the enemy.

Veronica looked at the weather outside, still raging, battering the little house and whipping up the sea. 'But you
can't go anywhere right now. You need to rest and get your
strength up. You can do that here, can't you?'

'Yes.' André was looking at her with soft warm eyes. 'I
can. We can have this moment together, in the storm. For as
long as it lasts.'

The storm around them raged for four long days. Mama
seemed to know instinctively to leave Veronica and André
alone as much as she could. Within a day, he was able to
dress in Daddy's old things, and move gingerly about the
white house as his bruised limbs recovered. But there was
no question that anything could happen between them with
Mama in the house, even if she did retire diplomatically to
her room. Besides, they were no longer that young couple
brought together for the briefest of encounters in the little
garret. They had seen life since then, and witnessed what had

once seemed impossible. André was different, she could see that, and she was full of awed admiration for his strength and courage. After his initial rage and grief, he took the loss of his crew on the chin.

'We will find them if we can,' he said solemnly. 'They died heroes.'

Veronica watched the progress of the storm, the raging sea and whipping rain, hoping both for the calm to come and that the storm might never stop. She knew that André would be determined to leave the first moment it was possible.

Jim, who was happy enough whiling away his hours in the barn or walking in the rain, had come in to say that the next day was set, at last, to be fair.

'If you would be so kind, please take me back to the mainland,' André said. 'I must report for duty as soon as I can.'

'Ah.' Jim nodded. 'We'll be able to row the tide in, I reckon.'

'Good, good. And from there, can I get over to Pembroke?'

'We'll get you there, sir,' Jim said. 'I know someone who'll take you that way, and more'll help.'

'Thank you, Jim.'

After lunch, with the storm already dying down, Mama went upstairs. Veronica and André sat on the sofa, pressed close together, André's arm around her, his other hand holding hers. He looked down into Veronica's eyes, his own solemn. 'This was meant to be, Véronique, you know that, don't you?'

Veronica nodded, burning with happiness at his nearness and the sensation of his hand holding hers. She felt perfectly content. *I want to live in this moment for ever. I never want it to pass.*

'Even if we never meet again, we were meant to be. Will you remember that?'

She turned to face him, stricken. 'Don't say that, André! We will meet again!'

'I hope so. But there is a long way to go in this war. Anything could happen.'

She tucked in beside him again, leaned her head on his shoulder and sighed. 'I know.'

'Let us make a plan just in case. Remember my sister's flat?'

'Of course. She is there now, isn't she?'

'Yes, I hope so. I have heard nothing from her, but that's to be expected. She doesn't know where I am and I can hardly write to tell her. Well . . . if we are separated and I cannot reach you . . . then here is a plan. If we do not manage to speak or meet before, we will meet on the first New Year's Eve after the end of the war. We will meet in Paris at the garret.'

Veronica nodded. 'Yes, I understand. I'll be there.' She squeezed his hand. 'But what if the war is lost?'

'If the war is lost, there is no future,' he said simply. 'And you will never see me again.'

Then he bent his head and kissed her.

Chapter Seventeen

In the end, Veronica did not spend the entire war on St Elfwy.

The last she saw of André was in Jim's boat. He was wearing his flying gear, mended and restored by Mama, waving at her from the little craft as they set out towards the mainland.

Watching him go was one of the hardest moments of her life. Veronica stared and stared until the boat was just a dot in the distance. Then, she went back into the cottage, lay on the sofa in the sitting room, covered her face and wept. As she sobbed, she felt her mother sit close to her, and reach out to stroke her.

'I know you love him, Vee,' she said gently. 'Tell me, did you love him before, when you were in Paris? Because I always sensed you were different when you returned.'

Veronica nodded, her face still hidden, tears seeping out between her fingers.

'I thought so.' There was a pause, then Mama said gently, 'I loved your dear father, despite all he did to upset me. Even though he was often impossible, he was never dull. Our life together was my great joy. If you've found something similar, then I'm so happy for you.'

Veronica got control of her sobs and began to calm. Eventually she said, 'I do love him, and I think we'd be happy. If I ever see him again.'

'I'll pray you do. I can see he's everything for you.' Mama reached out to clasp her hand. 'And he is a fine man. A brave man. The kind of man I'd want for you.'

Veronica sniffed. She took her hands away from her face, and smiled wanly at her mother. 'Even though he's French?'

Mama laughed, wheezing slightly and wincing with the pain of the sudden tightening in her chest that she now mentioned more often. 'Yes. Even despite that. Who cares where he's from, as long as you love him and he loves you.'

'Daddy wouldn't have thought that,' Veronica said.

'No. He wouldn't. He was always so protective of you girls. No one would have been good enough. Even a man like André. But you're free to love where you wish, and that's a great privilege.'

'Thank you, dear Mama.' Veronica reached up to embrace her mother, taking comfort in the familiar warmth and the sense of safety it always gave her.

When Jim returned a few days later, Veronica pressed him for every detail of André's return journey. Jim told her that he'd arranged a lift to St David's and from there, people were ready to help André back to his squadron. A few days later, a patrol came to look for traces of the Halifax, so she knew that André had made it back and informed them of the plane's fate, but he was not part of it. The storm had done its work: the wreck had been washed away from the caves and was most likely out to sea, gone for ever.

Mama grew progressively weaker, the pain in her chest increasing along with breathlessness and spells of dizziness and fainting. Eventually, Veronica took her to the doctor in St David's, who took her blood pressure and diagnosed heart disease. He prescribed some pills for when her heart raced and advised that she avoid salt, but there was not much to be done except rest as much as possible.

'I'm a burden to you,' Mama said unhappily, as she sat watching Veronica manage the house and garden alone, unable to do much more than some gentle cooking and sewing.

'Don't be silly, of course you're not. I'm young and strong and more than capable,' Veronica said briskly. The worst of the winter was over and the coming spring was lifting her spirits, which had been very bleak after André left. He had sent her cards for a while but they had abruptly stopped, and she was finding it difficult to remember the joy of their reunion in the misery of their renewed separation.

After a moment, Mama said, 'I do miss Billie. It's been so long since I saw her.'

'She could come here?' Veronica suggested, peeling potatoes at the sink.

'Perhaps. But you know . . . we could always think of going home.'

'We are home!' exclaimed Veronica.

319

'St Elfwy isn't home, much as I love it. London is home.'

Veronica was baffled. 'But I thought you wanted to leave London – with the raids and the bombs . . .'

Mama nodded. 'I did. But now I miss it. And I miss Billie. We could think about going back for a while . . . perhaps?'

Veronica stopped peeling and looked over to her mother. Perhaps she was right. Life was hard on the island at the moment, and Mama's health was clearly more precarious and she could receive better care elsewhere. Besides that, it was hard to think about how much she missed André. A change of scene might be best for them both.

'I'll think about it,' she said slowly. 'You might be right, Mama. Perhaps it's time to go back home.'

Once Veronica had decided they should return to London, it took some weeks to make the necessary arrangements. She needed to safeguard the island in their absence, and eventually she had the white house shut up and the island itself let as pasture to a local farmer. Then, as the spring bloomed towards summer, they finally made the move to a small house in Chelsea, not far from the river. Billie would give up her rooms in a lodging house and join them.

It was strange to see the island growing smaller as they left it behind. Veronica sat in the aft of the motor boat surrounded by cases and boxes and stared back at dear Elfwy, wondering when she would see it again.

'I'll be back one day,' she promised the island.

But she also knew it was time to leave, at least for a while.

*

Mama seemed to regain some vitality back in the bustle of London, buoyed by having Billie there as well. She appeared to feel closer to Daddy here, in the world of the theatre, and thrived with more people around her. Veronica took her as often as she could to the lunchtime performances, concerts and matinees still going on. The worst of the Blitz seemed to be over, and there were fewer raids to make Mama anxious. Although the arrival of the V2s, the targeted bombs with their chilling mosquito whine that went silent as they were about to fall, was desperate and terrifying, they seemed to bother Mama less than the previous raids.

Veronica missed the solitude and beauty of Elfwy but the real hardship was that she was now far from the last place she knew for certain André had been posted, and there was no way to let him know where they now were. It was ages since she'd last received a card. She had read the ones she had so often that she knew them by heart – they were the last things she looked at every night before she went to sleep.

Needing something to do, she took up a job in a local Chelsea bookshop, which suited her very well. She loved to read, and enjoyed selling to the customers, telling them about the latest releases. Anything particularly popular she would advise be bought quickly, for the paper shortages meant that no book could be sure of reprint, though somehow the wily publishers seemed to find a way.

During the quiet times, Veronica took out her notebook. Writing was coming more easily to her, thanks to the long months on the island learning her craft. But, even though she was not displeased by the result, she had finally discarded Rupert's play entirely. She had enjoyed writing something with a supernatural element and an atmosphere of oppressive melancholy, but she knew that she needed to be inspired entirely by her own creative forces. She took up a fresh notebook and started something quite new. To her surprise, she found she wanted to write a comedy, and as she sat in the bookshop, leaning her notebook on the counter and scribbling, she found she was writing about a rich heiress lost at sea after a shipwreck, who finds herself on a raft with three other survivors and a talkative, somewhat philosophical parrot.

Well, of course, there had to be a bird, she thought, laughing to herself.

It flowed from her pen: a spare, bitter-sweet allegory that also seemed to work as a human drama. Sometimes she was frustrated and disappointed, and couldn't make it work, but at other times she thought that she might actually have written something people might enjoy. It wasn't ready yet, though. She kept working on it in the odd hours she had to herself.

Time in London certainly seemed to move faster than on the island, and the months melted away for Veronica, with her work and with Mama to care for. Billie was there for chats and jokes and stories from her work, and there were plenty of distractions to keep her from dwelling on her own troubles too much.

One day she took her mother to see a new production of *The Seahorse*, which they both enjoyed hugely, and afterwards she wrote to Jack to let him know that she was now in London. He was delighted and they met occasionally for jolly teas, but life was very different for him. Grey was busy making films now, and Jack was writing musicals by himself again. He was busy and happy, and though he always loved to see Veronica, it didn't happen so very often, and not at all after he and Grey went out to Hollywood – travelling separately for appearances' sake – for Grey to appear in a feature film.

Alongside all of this, Veronica followed the course of the war as best she could, desperately trying to glean where André might be. She had no idea where the war had taken him. She knew that pilots had the shortest life expectancy of any combatant but she tried not to think about that. André had already been lucky. His luck only had to hold out and all would be well. It was frustrating, though, knowing so little about where he was. All she could cling to was that the course of war, gradually, was changing in their favour.

She was almost dizzy with excitement and relief when Paris was finally liberated from its years of occupation, and watched all the newsreels as often as she could in that summer of 1944. The footage showed the official cars carrying the military leaders and government ministers down the Champs-Élysees. The crowds gave them a rapturous welcome, in wild celebration that the hated enemy had been driven from the city and the long years of occupation were over. Over the next few days, there were huge victory parades, with cheering and flags and triumphant marches through the city. Veronica went several times to watch the newsreels, so that she could scan the waving crowds for either André or Irène, but of course, she saw neither.

When victory finally came, the country was giddy with delight and relief. London might be a mass of bomb sites, ruins and piles of debris, but it had triumphed. The sweetness of victory was only very slightly marred by the lack of any word from André. She had long ago made arrangements for any post from St Elfwy to be forwarded to her, but very little ever came, and certainly nothing from André.

He doesn't know where I am, she reminded herself.

And what could she do? She couldn't even send a card to the garret. She knew where it was, but not the address. Surely either André or Irène would write to her, now that the war was over? It was desperately disappointing but there was nothing she could do but bear it and be patient. It was hard but the sorry sight of a mass of refugees trudging home, and the suffering of so many others looking for lost family helped keep her own troubles in perspective.

As winter came and there was still no word from André, Veronica pinned all her hopes on their arrangement. No matter what, she would be there. It was surely her last chance ever to see him again.

I will be at the garret at New Year as we arranged. I'm sure I can find it again, I know the way perfectly.

She looked out the key that Irène had given her, which she kept safe in her purse. It was her last link with André, her last hope of seeing him again. It sat in her palm and she stared at it. She had no idea if the garret even still existed.

Well, soon she would find out.

After a quiet Christmas in their Chelsea cottage, Veronica packed her bag and explained to Billie and Mama that she would be visiting a friend for a few days; she had no desire to share this strange rendezvous with them until she knew its outcome.

On the last day before New Year, she made her way to Victoria for a train to the coast. The boat train was no longer running, but the ferry was taking civilians and soldiers still in service from Newhaven across the Channel. At Boulogne, after a rocky night's crossing and feeling far too anxious to sleep, she took the train to Paris, arriving mid-morning in a city she had last seen six years before. It felt different and yet gloriously the same. She drank in the sights and smells and atmosphere she knew so well and loved so much, as the bicycle taxi took her south from the station towards the garret. It was lunchtime when she arrived, on the last day of the year. She was too nervous to go directly to the flat so she went instead to a cafe and ate rich onion soup with a scattering of cheese and some bread, knowing that this was an unparalleled feast by recent Parisian standards. It was still a feast to her, with the watery and thin rations available in London, and she savoured every mouthful.

When she had finished, she smoked a cigarette nervously, even though she rarely touched them, and then walked slowly along the boulevards to the apartment building, clutching her suitcase. It was still there, grimier than before but otherwise the same. She stood outside, gazing up at it. High up were the garret windows with their views over the city. Was he in there already, waiting for her? Was she perhaps only moments from seeing him again?

The thought filled her with joy and terror at the same time.

But worse, what if he was not there and never came?

Perhaps Irène would be there. Delightful, glamorous Irène, with her jokes and laughter and determination to live life on her own terms. She would be more than just a consolation if André were not there.

At last Veronica mustered enough courage to ring the bell, and waited, breathless, until the concierge answered.

It was the same grim-faced woman who had been there before, apparently not changed at all. '*Oui?*' Then she recognised Veronica. 'Oh, it is you! The little visitor from before the war.'

'You remember me? I must be so changed! It was so long ago,' she said as they stepped through the doorway and into the courtyard beyond.

'Not so changed. And yes, a long time. I suppose you've come back to the apartment. I'm glad someone has.'

'So isn't Mademoiselle Irène here?'

The concierge looked startled and then her demeanour became stonier. 'No.'

'Do you know where she is?'

'No, I do not. I have not seen her in a very long time. It is over a year now.' The woman turned and went into her lodging, closing the door rapidly behind her.

Veronica stared at the closed door, worried. Surely Irène would have been back here at least once or twice since the end of the war. Unless fate had taken her away from Paris, and she was somewhere else. America, perhaps – she would fit in well there. Or perhaps she had gone to the south to be with Philippe in his chateau. There were plenty of possible explanations. It didn't have to be the worst.

She turned for the inner staircase that led to the upper apartments, mounting each stair slowly, her footsteps echoing in the stairwell. Each step brought back a vivid memory of her hours in the garret with André.

Will he be here? Will he keep his word?

At the door to the garret, she knocked and waited, but there was no answer. Well, now she knew that Irène would not be here. And André was not here either.

Yet.

She put the key in the lock, her hands trembling. The door opened under her push and, as she had expected, there was only silence within. But the cosy neat apartment of her memory was not what greeted her. Instead, it looked as though the occupant had simply walked out, leaving everything disorganised and messy. The chair was at an angle to the table, which still had things on it – salt, pepper, coasters, a book, some papers. The little kitchen was untidy, with dishes in the sink, a saucepan still sitting on the cold stove top. In the bedroom, it was the same: the bed was unmade, and clothes and shoes were scattered about. This room made her most uneasy. Irène had been a tidy person, a careful dresser who treasured her clothes. Something in the atmosphere here

327

told her that Irène might have left the apartment in a hurry. It was dusty, though. This had taken place some time ago.

Oh, Irène, she thought, looking around, stricken. *What's happened? Where are you?*

There had been many losses in the war. Rupert had been killed in the jungle. Friends and relations had been lost in bombs and battles and accidents. But somehow she had always imagined that pretty, charming Irène would be all right. Somehow in Veronica's imagination, she was simply whiling away her happy days in the Pompadour apartment, reading her books and amusing herself. In that way, Veronica had kept Irène safe. Now she had to confront the possibility that she was not safe at all.

I can only pray that she left in a hurry to save herself.

Veronica put down her bag, took off her coat and began quietly to clean up the mess.

It was dark by four p.m. The city began to sparkle below her. Lights in the darkness still struck her as a novelty after the years of blackout. It remained silent in the garret, though. She felt sure that André wasn't coming. Surely he would be here by now, on the last day of the year, as they agreed?

Still she tidied and cleaned, feeling that restoring order to Irène's world was the least she could do for her. Not only that, but touching her clothes and shoes and possessions somehow brought Irène back to her for a short while, connecting them again. Her worry for her friend grew each time she wiped away a layer of dust or found an abandoned shoe. Gradually, the flat began to look more as she remembered, though full of Irène's intimate possessions which had not been there before. Veronica was hungry but had brought no food and she couldn't risk going out. What if André came?

By nine o'clock, she had finished. She was exhausted. There were three hours left of the year.

He isn't coming.

She went into the bedroom and threw herself down on the bed, miserable. Why had she made this futile journey? It was a fantasy that had kept her going all these years, a dream she had stayed true to in the face of reality. André was likely dead, and perhaps Irène too. That was what happened in wartime. Even if he weren't dead, the chances he could come to her were tiny. She had wasted her time.

Veronica curled up into a ball on the bed and wept, her hands over her eyes.

'Well, now,' said a voice. 'What's this, *petite*? Tears? Why are you crying?'

She stopped crying at once, and slowly opened her damp eyes. The lamplight was too bright for her to see clearly after she had been crying. There was a large shape in front of her. Then it resolved. André stood there, in a dusty flying uniform, wings on his arm, a cap on his head. He was smiling broadly although he looked exhausted.

She gasped. 'I thought you weren't coming!'

'I couldn't get here till now. As it is, I had to beg for leave. I've driven all the way from Italy in a requisitioned jeep. Just to get here to you, like I promised.' He looked around. 'It's the first time I've been here in years.'

She realised that the flat now looked nothing like it had. There was no evidence of Irène's long absence. She opened her mouth to ask him where his sister was, but just then, he pulled off his cap and threw it aside, then took her in his arms, lifting her from the bed and banishing all thoughts from her mind but him. 'My darling, I knew you'd be here. I just knew it.'

She started to cry again. 'I thought you were dead!'

'I'm not. We're alive. And here we are.'

Then he kissed her. After a moment, holding her tightly in his arms, he said, '*Ma chérie*, there are three hours left of this year. We say goodbye to the old misery. How shall we spend these last hours of the year?'

Veronica smiled. 'Perhaps . . . like old times . . . ?'

'That, my sweet, is a very, very good idea.'

PART FOUR

Chapter Eighteen

ROMY

Romy closed the cover of *L'Amant de Minette*, and sniffed. Her jaw was wet from the tears that ran down her face as she lay on the sofa, engrossed in the slight novel.

'Oh my gosh,' she said to the room, her voice wobbly. 'That was absolutely wonderful.'

She'd been afraid that her French would be too rusty for her to enjoy the novel properly but after a slow start with lots of pauses to look up vocabulary, she'd begun to find her way and soon she was reading the French as naturally as she had all those years ago, when she'd been studying for her degree.

The story was simple enough, told in Marguerite Heurot's spare, elegant prose, so precise that it was almost closer to poetry. The hero meets the beautiful but mysterious Minette in Paris during the war, and they fall madly in love. For a while he is ecstatically happy, but Minette proves elusive and, eventually, faithless. The ending was desperately sad and full of yearning for what might have been if only Minette had been true to him.

No wonder Veronica loved this novel so much, she thought. *And no wonder it was regarded as a masterpiece.*

The character of Minette – beautiful, elegant and utterly seductive – was unforgettable. She stepped out of the pages as a real person, unusual and enigmatic and unpossessable, no matter how much the hero wanted her.

Romy had decided to read the novel through, ignoring the scribbled annotations as much as possible, and that had not been hard, as she had been so intensely absorbed by the print. She had also left untouched the sheaf of typed paper in the back of the book. Those things waited for her like a stocking on the end of the bed on Christmas morning – she hoped they contained lots of wonderful treats. What would Veronica have to say about this novel? It would be fascinating to understand why it had meant enough for her to write notes inside it.

What was more, this novel was so unlike anything Romy would have expected Veronica to obsess over. Veronica Mindenhall was primarily known for writing *The Last Song of Winter* with all its gothic horror, but before then, she'd written a play called *The Raft*, which had been a smash hit after the war but was largely now forgotten, although there were rare revivals. Romy had read *The Raft* expecting something like *The Last Song of Winter* – a similarly gory story with lots of tension and an atmosphere of the macabre – but it had not been like that at all. It had been a clever comedy with a cast of shipwrecked survivors and a philosophical parrot, witty and wise at the same time. In fact, nothing else Veronica had written was anything like her famous film, which was exactly why Romy was so intrigued by her. And here was another unexpected piece in the puzzle.

Romy got off the sofa and went to her laptop. Before she reread the novel and studied the annotations, which she was sure were in Veronica's own hand, she wanted to find out a little more about the author, Marguerite Heurot. While she had read the novel for her degree, Romy hadn't focused exclusively on it and she'd not read any of the author's other work so knew next to nothing about her. She typed the name into the search engine and scrolled to the most likely result.

Marguerite Heurot, she discovered, had had an intriguing career as one of France's most decorated and beloved female writers. As a person, she seemed austere and solitary. After escaping a violent first marriage, she had lived alone from then on, devoting herself to writing. She had written half a dozen slim novels, all considered important, but her last work, *The Lover of Minette*, published a couple of years after the end of the war, had been hailed as her masterpiece. Marguerite had been inducted into the Academie Française and, on her death in the 1950s, she had been buried in the Pantheon alongside literary luminaries like Dumas, Voltaire, Victor Hugo and Émile Zola. Even now, few women enjoyed that honour.

I must read all her work, Romy thought. *She was obviously a genius.*

Another detail leapt out at her. During the war, Marguerite had been gripped by a paralysing fear. She had shut herself away in her comfortable apartment in the Fifth Arrondissement, and had not come out for the entire duration of the occupation. She had carried on working and writing, but she had not emerged until the enemy had been expelled.

Imagine not setting foot outside for four years! Was it fear? Or was it a kind of refusal to accept the situation and give the enemy the satisfaction of acknowledging their presence? That is pretty stubborn.

She summoned up some images of Heurot. Most were of her in middle age: grey-haired, stern-looking, slightly hunched, peering over her spectacles. But there were images from the thirties and forties as well. The younger Heurot was plain except for her slightly upturned, cat-like eyes, and her expression – blank and inscrutable – gave no impression of the rich emotional life that must have existed in order for her to create the story of Minette.

However, Romy reminded herself, Heurot was not the focus of her research. This was all about Veronica, and the question now was why she had taken so much time to study this short French novel.

I suppose she did live in France after her marriage, Romy reasoned. The internet pages on Veronica and her daughter's memoir all recorded that she had moved to Paris with her husband after the war, and remained there for some years. That was where, Romy thought, she had most likely written *The Raft*, which had its debut in 1948. Veronica must have been able to speak French to a good standard, so perhaps it was natural for her to take an interest in a book that was clearly considered a great work even in its day.

Well, the annotations and perhaps the papers will tell me more.

She would reread the novel, and study them as she went along.

I just have the strangest feeling that this ties into The Last Song of Winter, *though I don't know how.*

Just then she realised she was hungry and that it was already past lunchtime, so she shut her laptop and left her work for the time being.

As she made her simple lunch, Romy felt she was beginning to learn the ways of the cottage and the island. She felt at home, pleasantly surprised to find that, so far, it had been relatively easy. The isolation was not as bad as she'd feared; she was managing that very well, enjoying the peace and quiet of her own company while still feeling connected to the outside world via the internet and chirpy messages from Flo and various friends. She had a session with Caroline her therapist coming up. They had reduced from daily at the very worst of everything to once or twice a week depending on how she felt, but it was definitely time to check in.

Then there was the safety of her routines. They were so useful to help her maintain control, but whenever she felt too anchored to the schedule, she would break its grip by playing forward the consequences of not sticking rigidly to it. Meanwhile, she continued filling in her forms and emailing them back to her family and to the professionals who had care over her.

It's working, she thought happily. She'd feared any number of setbacks, so it was extra pleasing that, so far, all was well.

She had just finished clearing up after her meal when there was a loud rapping at the door.

She looked round towards the door, startled, then relaxed.

I wondered when Richard would turn up.

She'd not heard from him since their walk, but then she hadn't given him her number so he would have to wait for her to message him or come around in person. She had seen him motoring back to the mainland the previous day, and then returning in the afternoon with bags of shopping. She was glad he had left her alone; she was sure that he valued his privacy as much as she did hers.

Going to the door, she opened it and Jesse stood there on the doorstep, holding a bunch of violets. He bared his teeth in a wide grin, his pirate eyes sparkling at her. 'Well, hello. How are ya doing?'

Romy blinked at him, still startled to see him. 'Er . . . I'm fine.'

'I think these are for you,' he said, holding out the violets. 'You think they are?'

'I guess so.' He burst out laughing. 'They're not from me! They were here on the doorstep. Don't tell me you've already got a secret admirer. How the hell did you manage that on this rock?'

Romy took them, and buried her nose in them. 'They're gorgeous. Richard must have put them there. I noticed a ton of violets around the house.' She glanced down at the step and saw a white postcard that the flowers must have been resting on. She bent to pick it up.

*Hey, Romy. I picked a few too many violets than I've got
vases for. Thought you might like them for the cottage.
They don't last long. Hope all's well and the shearwaters
haven't been keeping you awake. R.*

'Little lover's note?' Jesse said sardonically.

'No,' she said, 'of course not. I barely know him. It's nice
to see you, Jesse. Do you want to come in?'

'Sure, thanks.'

She led him through to the kitchen and got some chilled
ginger tea out of the fridge. 'Would you like some of this?'

'Yeah, great.'

They sat down together at the kitchen table. Now that he
was sitting here, he seemed rather awkward, as though he
hadn't quite thought through his reason for coming. Then
he got back some of his breeziness. 'So, how are things? Are
you settling in okay?'

'Yes, really good actually. Better than I expected.'

Jesse grinned, showing those extraordinarily white teeth.
He seemed to know the power of that smile of his, how
disarming it was. 'So glad to hear that, Romy. And you've
crossed paths with Richard, have you? How was that?'

Romy considered what to say. She didn't want to share the
details of her time with Richard. And there wasn't that much
to say, in all honesty. Since their walk, she'd enjoyed her own
rambles on the island more, with her newfound knowledge
of the birds' behaviour. She had observed the mating rituals
and considered how the birds were building up their relationships, either new or established, and learning to bond with

339

one another. Caring for their egg and chick would be a two-bird job and they needed complete faith in one another. It was quietly inspiring. Or not so quietly. She'd been listening to the nocturnal shearwater parties as well, until she put on her headphones to shut out the noise, wondering how they could keep going so late when they were out at sea all day. Richard had given her that information and it had, in a very small way, enriched her experience. 'It's fine,' she said at last. 'He seems all right. He came round to apologise for yelling, and then we chatted about the birds. He certainly knows his stuff.'

Jesse blinked his dark eyes at her. He was casual today, in board shorts and a faded T-shirt printed with an advertisement for boat tours, his dark hair loose around his shoulders. The short-sleeved T-shirt revealed sinewy strong arms with a darkly etched pattern of tattoos that stopped a little short of his elbows. 'He hasn't been bothering you?'

Romy shook her head. 'Not at all.'

'Ah, okay. That's good.'

She gave him a quizzical look. 'You say that like you think he might.'

Jesse made a face. 'We had a bit of an issue last year with a girl who was here. Bit older than you, though. Artist. She'd come to paint seascapes and birds. And Richard got a bit keen on her, apparently. She left early in the end, and I was told that he was reprimanded. Told to keep a lid on it where the female visitors were concerned.' He shrugged. 'I guess it's understandable. He must be lonely here.'

'I suppose he's not married . . .'

'Nuh uh. And if he wanted to meet someone, this is not the biggest dating pool in the world, unless you get crazy for guillemots.'

'Or gulls,' Romy said. 'If you were the only gull in the world . . .'

'What's a nice gull like you doing in a place like this?'

They laughed at their weak jokes, then Jesse said, 'But seriously. He clearly likes ladies. And here you are stuck on this rock with him.' He glanced over at the violets which Romy had stuck in a mug until she could find a better container for them. 'And he's given you flowers.'

'I don't think you can read anything into that. Any more than you coming to say hi means anything.'

'Ah. Yeah. You're right.'

'Do you visit all the people who stay on the island?' Romy asked.

Jesse's face softened for a moment. 'Only the ones I'm worried about,' he said quietly. 'There's something about you, Romy. Kind of . . . I don't know . . . damaged?'

She gazed back at him. She hadn't expected that. He seemed like such an easy-going, laid-back person. Perhaps she was underestimating him, judging him on his beach boy accent and the sense of carelessness around him, but she hadn't thought he might have perception like that. 'I have had a bit of a tough time lately,' she said slowly.

'I thought so. I've got a nose for it. Don't ask me how or why, but I can always tell when someone's suffering. My old grandma was a clairvoyant, a sort of medium. You might not believe in that shit, but she knew stuff that was completely out there. She wasn't faking. When my auntie died, my grandma said, "Jodie's gone, I know it. She just came and said goodbye." Jodie was travelling in India at the time. She was killed when she was hit by a car. The police report gave her time of death at the exact time that my grandma said those words.'

'That's spooky,' Romy said with a shiver.

Jesse nodded. 'Yeah. And I get some odd feelings myself from time to time. And really often, I'm right. I get weird vibes from Richard. There's something bad hanging round him, you know?' He leaned forward. 'I heard that his wife and kid died in mysterious circumstances. That's why he came here five years ago. 'Cos he'd lost everything, just like that. And he needed to escape his grief. I don't know how they died – or even if there's any truth in it, to be honest – but I do get a sense of something not right about him.'

'That's awful!' Romy said, horrified. 'Poor Richard! He lost his wife and child?' A wave of sympathy rose in her. 'How could he get over that? No wonder he needed to get away.'

'Like I said, I don't know, it's a rumour,' Jesse said quickly. 'Maybe he was never even married. It's not exactly something you can ask about, is it? The weird vibes I get are not exactly grief. Not sure what they are. And you . . . something is coming off you in waves. Like you've been sick? Not sure. That's what I'm picking up.'

Romy didn't know what to say. Perhaps he was fishing for her to give him more information. In the end, she said, 'That's really interesting. Maybe you have a talent – or maybe not! So, are your tours picking up at the moment.'

He gave her a sideways look to let her know that he had seen her evade his question, but he let it go and started chatting away about the boat tours that were his bread and butter. 'I can recite the script of this place in my sleep,' he said feelingly. 'All the shit about the rock formations and the birdlife and the seal nurseries and the wicked bloody old monks. They love it. They lap it up. Every time I talk about the fact that gulls are so oily that the monks just used to stick a wick up the bird's arse and set light to it for a lantern, they laugh like drains but I can't even see a flicker of humour in it any more. I'm too jaded.'

Romy drained the last of her ginger tea. 'It sounds like maybe you've had enough of the tours? Is it time for a change?'

Jesse sat back in his chair. 'Yeah, maybe it is. I might head off to Ireland soon, get a change of scene. Think about wending my weary way back to Australia one of these days as well. Listen, I've got a day off tomorrow. Would you like me to pop over and collect you? I could take you further up the coast and we could land up there and go into town. If you want to do some shopping? Maybe scout out the town? St David's is a cool little place. It's the smallest city in Britain. Just this tiny little place with the most enormous cathedral, like an ant carrying a piece of bread five times its size.'

Romy laughed. 'I've been there. It is cool. I'd like to take another look around and get some supplies. Great.'

'I'll text you in the morning to let you know what time I'm coming,' Jesse said, 'but it will be quite early. There's a storm coming in tomorrow evening, so we'd better make the most of the sunny weather while we can.'

He stood up. 'Thanks for the tea. Nice to see you, Romy. Take care, okay.' He suddenly leaned over the table and grasped her hands. 'Make sure you look after yourself. Don't . . . don't panic, okay? Remember . . . you're in control . . .'

She was so startled that she could only stare at him speech-less, letting him hold her hands firmly inside his warm ones.

'See ya,' he said, flashing that smile at her, and he went out the back door, crunching off down the path on his way back to the jetty.

Romy was surprised and a little disconcerted by Jesse's remark. She decided to go and have a bath to relax, and while she was running it, she sat on the edge thinking about Jesse. Was it just a lucky guess that he had said those words? She'd had the distinct impression at times that he was trying to get some information out of her. But maybe he was right, and he was clairvoyant in some way, like his grandmother. It was strange in any case.

Watching the water, slightly brown from the island peat, gushing into the old bathtub, she wondered how she felt about Jesse. She had had boyfriends like him before – attractive, with a touch of something mischievous, even a bit devilish, about them. In fact, learning to avoid people like that had also been a part of her therapy. Her perfectionism sprang, she had learned, from a sense of low self-esteem. She was seeking approval, from herself and also from others.

She was never happy unless she got top marks, or managed somehow to be the best at things – not so she could lord it over everyone else but so that she could feel, for a moment, a sense of ease and acceptance. For a minute, just one brief minute, she could relax and feel that there were no peaks to scale, no mountains to conquer, no tests to pass.

When it came to her relationships with men, all that neediness bubbled up in the form of a desperate desire to please and be given all the love and approval she craved so much.

'It is another form of self-comforting,' Caroline had said in one of their sessions, 'but it's probably the most damaging of all, because you're attracted to exactly the people who will reinforce your deep feelings about yourself – that you're unworthy and unlovable.'

Romy had wept. 'Why do I do that? What's wrong with me? Why am I so rubbish at relationships?'

'You're doing it right now,' Caroline had pointed out gently. 'Those guys, particularly like Theo, they are the ones who can do the worst damage. They can sense your vulnerability and they home in on it. Then the two of you get into a very dark and damaging relationship, full of manipulation and exploitation.'

Theo had been the great love of Romy's life, who had put her through the worst pain she'd ever known. It was his rejection of her that had brought on the final crisis. For months during the recovery, Caroline had let her talk about Theo, about what made him act the way he did and why he had treated her as cruelly as he had. Finally, Caroline had said, 'Theo is Theo. Who knows why he is like he is, and who cares? Can we talk about you? Because if you truly want to heal from this, and avoid anything like it again, we need to understand you, not all the Theos that there are in the world – and there are a lot. We need to make you Theo-proof.'

Romy had seen the sense in that. She definitely wanted to be Theo-proof. Flo agreed that this was an excellent idea.

'Just promise me,' she said to Romy, 'that you won't tell a guy about what you've gone through until you really know and trust him. Because lots of shits want to take advantage of someone vulnerable, and in the past you've been the kind of girl who goes up to a vampire and says, "You're going to like me, I'm a fantastic bleeder."'

Romy laughed. She could see it when Flo put it like that. 'I'm trying to keep my brilliant bleeding under wraps,' she said. 'I'm learning to keep that a secret.'

I mustn't forget that, she thought now. She had to keep her vulnerability concealed and stay on her guard. *If Richard is the kind of person to make a play for the women who come to the island, it's good to keep my distance.*

She tested the water with her fingertips, letting it swish pleasantly over her hand. It was nearly ready.

If Richard is a menace, why does the trust keep him on as warden? Surely they wouldn't allow it if he upset the visitors?

She had the vague sense that she needed to be on her guard against being pulled into a conflict between Richard and Jesse. It was obvious that the two men didn't like each other very much. And she sensed that Jesse hadn't liked the flowers on the doorstep any more than Richard had liked the idea that Jesse was planning to visit.

Romy turned off the taps, undressed and then climbed into the steaming water, letting the heat soak into her bones. The good thing about a Welsh summer was that a hot bath was still an enjoyable pastime. She let her mind drift as she relaxed into it.

She didn't bother getting dressed again after her bath, but wandered about the cottage in her dressing gown, cleaning up, tidying and wondering if she had enough laundry to justify a wash. She sat out for a while in the late afternoon sun for a while, doing some meditation, then came back in to write some emails, fill in her form and send it off, while listening to music and humming along with it. Tomorrow she would go on her trip with Jesse. She was looking forward to it. It would mean no work on her book in the morning.

There you are, I can challenge the routine. I can break it. No problem.

She was looking forward to reading Veronica's own words, perhaps being the first person to do so, but there was no rush. She had plenty of time. It would be a good idea to get some fresh supplies, especially if a storm was coming. If it went on longer than expected, she wouldn't be able to get any more shopping for a while. Better to be prepared.

A message from Flo popped up on her phone.

Hi doll, well done for sending your forms. Delighted to hear you're doing so well. How do you feel about me coming for a visit at some point? I'd love to see the cottage and all the fab things you've told me about. No

rush, when you're ready. And only if you're feeling like it.
I'm not checking up on you, honest!
   Take care.
   Love, Flo xxx

Romy laughed. She wasn't fooled for an instant. Flo was most certainly wanting to check on her but was also no doubt intrigued to visit the place that Romy had been so gushing about.

She went to finish off making her supper and was stirring a vibrant sauce through her salmon and spelt pasta when her phone buzzed again and she saw Richard's name flash up. She picked up to read the message. It was very short.

Did you like the violets?

She felt a jolt of embarrassment as she realised that she hadn't thanked him for the bunch he had left her. Quickly she typed out a message.

Yes, thank you! Really kind of you. They're brightening up the kitchen right now.

And she made a resolution to find a vase after supper as the poor violets were still sitting in a mug of water on the side.

It was only when she was eating her supper that a thought popped into her mind.

That's weird. Because I never gave him my number. I'm sure I didn't. So how did he send me a message?

348

Chapter Nineteen

Jesse messaged her to let her know that he'd be at the jetty at 9.30 a.m. and she went down to meet him in the bright morning sunshine. Richard was sitting outside in the garden of Cliff House, drinking coffee with Martha perched, as usual, on his shoulder, which meant he saw her as she came down the path. He waved, smiling broadly, and stood up.

'Hey, Romy! How are you? Want to join me for coffee?'

Romy waved back, smiling. When she came level with the back gate, she stopped and gestured to her backpack. 'Sounds great! But I can't . . . I'm heading onto the mainland to do some shopping.'

'You should have said, you could have come with me when I went,' he replied, his smile falling slightly. 'How are you getting in?'

'Jesse's coming to collect me,' she said brightly. She wasn't going to be drawn into whatever problems the two men had between them. She could be friends with both and wasn't going to be forced to choose. 'He says there's a storm coming?'

'A bit of rain this evening, nothing to get excited about it.' Richard smiled again, apparently fine with her outing. 'Have a great time. See you later.'

'Okay, see you later.' Romy carried on her way, buoyed up by how easy that had been. Maybe she had imagined the issues. She hoped so.

At the jetty, she could see a small motor boat powering easily over the channel. Jesse brought it in in a wide circle and came to a stop at the jetty's edge, where he tied up. 'Aloha,' he called.

'Different boat,' Romy remarked.

'It's my day off. I can't use the tripper. This is better for the two of us in any case. Hop on board and off we go.'

Once she was in, with her life jacket on, he grinned at her. 'We'll take the scenic route.'

He powered up the boat, roaring the engine into life and opening the throttle, the powerful strumming noise filling the air. Then he turned the boat and took her into another looping circle before flying out into the channel and taking a wide course around the southern side of the island.

'Where are we going?' cried Romy, laughing. Salt spray flew up when Jesse accelerated, and the wind buffeted her face. The sensation of the little boat riding the waves, almost bouncing along on top of them, was exhilarating.

'You'll see.'

As soon as they had rounded the rocky outcrop of the island, Jesse brought the speed down to slow and they putt-ered into quieter waters. Here, there were more rock towers and great boulders emerging from the sea, acting as breaks on the waves.

'Look,' Romy cried, pointing, as though Jesse might not have seen what she could see: a large cave under the island, with a series of openings that looked almost like arched doorways. Inside it, under a rocky ceiling dripping with water, and covered with sediment and mineral deposits, a large domed rock emerged from the water, almost in the dead centre of the cave. 'What an amazing place!'

'We can go in, but not far.' Jesse manoeuvred the little boat to edge into the space between the entrance and the rock. The sun was not yet on this side of the island and the water was dark and uninviting. 'These are the Singing Caves.' Jesse adopted the pose of an opera singer, one hand on his chest, the other held aloft, and sang in a cod opera voice a few lines of nonsense. His voice was surprisingly good and the tones echoed in the natural vault of the cave.

Romy applauded. 'Why are they called the Singing Caves?'

'The poor monks who lived here used to get stranded on that rock overnight as a test of their virtue. If they were good, they survived. If not, they drowned. So they sang a lot to persuade God they were one of the good guys. Not sure how effective that was. But you know . . . lots of myths and legends around all that.'

'Poor monks,' Romy said sadly. She imagined some young lad shivering in a robe, stuck on the top of that damp and slippery rock with the tide rising in the cave, singing his heart out to stop from being washed away. 'That's barbaric.'

'They didn't think so. They thought it was the opposite.

Anyway, we've better ways to deal with mental health issues now, thank God.'

Romy shot him a look to see if he had meant anything by what he'd said, but he was concentrating on reversing the boat carefully out of the cave. Once they were clear, he turned them to face the open sea, steered carefully between the stacks and rocks and then took them out nearer to open water. As they went past the cliff walls, he pointed up to the streaks of different colours that ran through the rock. 'Interesting fact. See the different rock strata in the cliff there? You've got white, grey, copper and all the rest running in layers. That's the geological pattern of the local formation in the order it happened by eon. Except that it's upside down. The oldest is on the top. That means the island was probably formed by some sort of volcanic activity when it was thrust up from the sea bed and turned over. So you've got reverse order.' He grinned at her. 'Free information. Just one of the many benefits of travelling with me.'

Romy laughed. 'Thanks, that was actually very interesting.' She gazed up at the cliff, feeling awed by the age of the natural world in comparison to the human tenure in it.

'Now,' Jesse said, 'hold tight.'

He opened the throttle and powered the boat away from the island, heading out into the open water beyond. The noise was too great for talking and she sat back to enjoy the sensation of the little boat racing over the waves, lifting and dropping like a fairground ride, spraying her with water as Jesse took some fancy turns. The sky was full of birds, and some of them began to follow the craft.

'They think we're fishing!' Jesse yelled, gesturing up at them. 'And they'll hunt whatever we churn up in any case.'

Romy watched the birds for a while, as they floated on the currents, their wings stiff and outstretched. Their upper bodies were dark grey, almost black, but their bellies and the undersides of their wings were pure white, and they tipped and banked as they glided, flashing black and white. 'Are they shearwaters?' she called.

Jesse raised his eyebrows. 'Yeah, that's right. Good spot! They kind of shear the water when they tip like that. They'll be looking for fish mostly: whitebait, sand eels and fry. Beautiful, aren't they?'

She nodded. Jesse had left the island behind now and they were bouncing along parallel to the mainland, heading around the point which stuck out into the sea like a long rock finger. On the clifftops she could see houses and campsites, where brightly coloured tents were already pitched despite the early season, and fields that held row after row of pale green holiday caravans, all facing out to sea. Further ahead, she could see a long stretch of pale sand, a few tiny shapes moving about on it. This was prime holiday territory. No doubt a lot of income for the area came from the tourist influx from spring to early autumn and it was just kicking off.

After about twenty minutes, Jesse turned the craft for a small harbour, steered in and found a place among the many boats moored there to tie up. They climbed up onto the harbour wall and walked along it towards the village.

'It's a bit of a trek to St David's from here,' Jesse said. 'The coastal shuttle bus comes along here all the time so we can catch one of those if you like.'

'Okay. Let's do that.'

The shuttle turned up a few minutes later and they boarded for the fifteen-minute drive to St David's. As soon as they arrived, Romy remembered how it had looked years before when she'd come here with her family. The town was a bit slicker now, with fewer old-fashioned shops and more art galleries and delis. The huge old newsagent's that had once sold plastic buckets, spades, windbreaks, surfboards, beach shoes and windmills was long gone; a cafe with organic coffee, vegan cakes and high-vibe lunches had taken its place.

She and Jesse arranged to go their separate ways while they shopped and meet up for lunch there in two hours.

Romy had a happy time wandering about the town centre, doing her shopping and topping up her supplies. She was in the cafe, reading a novel she'd found in the second-hand bookshop, when Jesse came up.

'You're a right book worm, aren't you?' He flung himself in the seat opposite her and looked at the menu. 'What are you having?'

'The hummus and pepper flatbread. You?'

'The beetroot and feta tortilla looks good. I'll have that.' He poured himself some water from the bottle she'd ordered. 'I just popped into headquarters. The tours are based here.'

'Oh? How's it looking?'

'Good. Very good. They mint it in, to be honest. The tours cost a packet – a family of four will spend about two hundred pounds on the hour-long boat ride. Fill up a tour boat and you're making a healthy profit, even taking the fuel and wages into account. And then they run the river days, kayaking, orienteering, and all that. Pricey stuff. So they're doing all right. They don't really pay enough; they rely on people like me who are just passing through. I wondered about setting up a rival operation but they've got it covered really – all the marketing, the website, the online booking, the craft and kit, plus the shop on the high street to lure them in.' Jesse shrugged. 'Besides, I'm just not sure I want to put down roots here.'

Romy said, 'To be honest, it does sound as if you are thinking of moving on.'

'Maybe I am.'

The waitress came and took their order, and they chatted about the town until the lunch arrived. Once it was set down, Jesse poked at his tortilla with a fork and sighed. 'Truth is, I'm a bit lonely. When I first got here, I had a ton of mates. But they moved on after a bit and now I'm the grizzled old hand and they're the young kids who want to stay up drinking all night and can still go out first thing on a tour.'

Romy laughed. 'How old are you? You make yourself sound ancient!'

'I'm thirty-one.'

'That's nothing.'

'Too old for this lark. My idea of fun is staying in with a nice bottle of wine, a good dinner and a movie.'

'That sounds great . . . Everyone likes that, don't they?'

'Yeah . . . but it's lonely.' Jesse grinned. 'So, you know I've been telling you about that film they made on Elfwy, *The Last Song of Winter?*'

Romy said neutrally, 'Of course.'

She cut another piece of flatbread slowly, pushing some pomegranate seeds onto it with the blade of her knife. She was still reluctant to confess her reason for being on the island. It felt important to keep it to herself.

'Have you seen it?'

'Oh yes. You can't forget that ending.'

'I'm a bit of a super fan to be honest.'

Of course you are, she thought wryly. But it occurred to her that this could be useful. Maybe he knew some things about the filming that she didn't.

He leaned towards her, eyes bright. 'Wanna see it again? It's going to be a rainy evening, you could come over to my place – I promise my caravan is a lot more comfortable than it sounds. I can make us a curry or something and we could watch the film and soak up the atmosphere.'

Romy's spirits sank as he talked. It had been a pleasant day so far but this wasn't a development she welcomed.

He looked wary. 'I can see from your face that you don't like that idea.'

Romy was about to protest that she liked the sound of the idea very much but she stopped herself. *Take a pause and think about your own needs.* That was what Caroline had counselled her over and over. *You don't owe anyone anything – not your time, not your approval, not your love. Those things are yours to give, not theirs to take.*

A casual suggestion to watch a movie together seemed like

nothing but, in fact, this was exactly the time when she had to consider herself.

Jesse looked impatient with her silence. 'Hey, it wasn't anything. It was just an idea, okay? There's no need to take it too seriously. I wasn't asking you to marry me! Just watch a film and have something to eat – no biggie.'

'Okay,' she said slowly. Her mind was turning it over.

But this is how it starts. I go and do this harmless thing. Then you want another harmless thing, and if I say no, you want to know why. You get upset that I didn't like your movie and your curry, even though I liked it fine but that was enough for me. You press me to do another thing, another casual thing, and suddenly we're dating, according to you. Now I owe you something, for the curry and film and hours you've spent with me. And you will have encouraged me to talk about myself, so now you were the guy who spent time listening and helping me. So I owe you for that too.

She had been through it too many times, finding herself tangled up with men who claimed she had led them on, when she'd been doing what they wanted.

'Boundaries,' Caroline had said. 'It's called boundaries. You need to learn to say a firm no. And you need to learn not to care about their hurt feelings. Their feelings are not really hurt. It's a manipulation. And why do their feelings matter more than yours, in any case? A healthy person recognises and respects the other person's wants. It's a bad sign when they can't do that.'

Romy looked over at Jesse, who was still waiting expect-antly for an answer. And once more, the other voice in her head said exactly what Jesse was saying: *But it's just a film and a curry! Maybe don't overthink it . . . it's not a big deal.*

Jesse smiled his most charming smile. 'Look, if it's coming to my van that's the issue . . . I can come to you. I'll bring my tablet, it's got the film downloaded on it. Honestly, Romy, I'm a nice guy. Ask anyone round here, they all know me. I'm not a creep. I'm decent and honest and I treat women well. I can treat them as friends, not potential girlfriends. And I think that's what we are: friends. Aren't we?'

She stared back at him. He did look warm and trustworthy, and he'd been kind to her so far.

He leaned forward. 'Maybe I've given you the wrong impression. I'm sorry. You're just such a lovely girl and I feel like we've connected. As friends. Also, I do sense that you're a bit vulnerable and you're stuck out on the island with that creepy old man – I can't help feeling a bit protective of you. I know that's not my place, and I need to deal with that because I can also see that you're strong and independent and don't need me shoving my nose in.'

'That's very nice to hear,' she began, but he cut her off.

'Look, I don't want to make you uncomfortable or unhappy, so just forget I said anything about the movie, okay?'

She shifted awkwardly in her seat and took a mouthful of her lunch to give herself some thinking time.

'If I come to you,' he said lightly, 'then I can just head off afterwards, no worries. The weather's not so bad this evening. Or another night, if you like.'

'Okay,' she said at last. 'Maybe another night then.'

'Great,' Jesse said with one of his broad smiles. She felt its fizzing energy. Maybe she was wrong to try and squash the idea of anything happening between them. After all, he was attractive. He clearly liked her. Should she really judge all men by the likes of Theo and his ilk? 'That's great. I'll look forward to it.'

After another trip around the town, together this time, they headed back to the shuttle bus loaded up with bags, Romy's backpack crammed full of the heavier supplies. They had chatted easily all afternoon with the awkwardness of the lunch behind them, Jesse keeping her entertained with stories of his large family and his crazy friends out in Australia, where life seemed to involve a lot of drunken adventures, the beach, bonfires, cars and boats.

As they pulled into the island jetty, she felt light-headed from the exhilarating ride back and the laughter they'd shared.

'That was really cool,' Jesse said as they walked up the path loaded with her shopping.

'Really cool,' she agreed. 'Thanks so much for taking me.'

'Any time.'

'When you're not doing the tours.'

'Of course.'

They got to the front door of Clover Cottage. Romy fished out her key to unlock it. Jesse laughed.

'I can't believe you're locking your front door on Elfwy.'

'Force of habit. I guess it's psychological. All my stuff is in there – my work, I mean.' She opened the door. 'If you can just drop it all there, that would be great, thanks.'

'Aye, aye, my lady.' Jesse put the bags down and then loitered slightly in the hallway. He gave Romy a sideways look. 'So . . . are you going to ask me in?'

'Well . . .' Romy wrinkled her nose. 'I guess not? I've had a lovely day but I really need to do some work now. Is that okay?'

'Sure. Of course.' Jesse made a tragic face. 'I'll just go back to my caravan and be all alone. It's fine.' He pointed out to where the sky was darkening and thick grey clouds heavy with rain were gathering. Beneath, the sea was turning steely and choppy. 'When the rain comes, it's like being trapped in a tin can in a hailstorm.'

Romy laughed. 'You must be used to that by now. I mean, five years, isn't it?'

'Don't rub it in. Have it your way! I'll wend my lonesome way back. But if you change your mind, give me a call? Okay?'

'Okay,' she said firmly. 'Thanks, Jesse. And see you later!'

'Sure thing. Bye.' He turned and began wandering away down the path. Romy closed the door behind him and went to unpack.

It was rather lovely to be back in the quiet of Clover Cottage after her trip to the great and bustling metropolis of St David's. Romy sorted out her shopping, put a casserole in the oven to cook slowly and poured a glass of wine to take with her to the sitting room. Despite turning down Jesse's invitation, she was in the mood to curl up and watch something with her supper and she was going to choose a film to download. Outside, the light had dropped dramatically and the wind was blowing up. The first light patter of rain had hit the glass of the windows. It wasn't cold but Romy was tempted to light the stove to get the maximum effect of cosiness when the rain really started falling.

She sipped at her glass of wine as she scrolled through the seemingly endless variety of things on offer. Just then, her phone vibrated twice in quick succession. She picked it up to see that Jesse had messaged her.

> Hey. Send me your email and I'll share that film with you. You can watch it on your own if you like! But I don't recommend it, it's super creepy. Great to see you today. Catch up soon. Jx

That's nice of him. She felt obscurely that he was apologising for trying to pressure her into watching it with him.

The other message was from Richard.

> Hi, Romy, just checking you got back safely from your trip. The storm is coming in but it's not going to be a big one. It should have blown itself out by morning. Take care. Richard

Another decent message, not pushy, not patronising.

Romy sat back and sighed.

Even here, on the edge of nowhere, it was impossible to

escape the subtleties and pressures of human interaction. She had thought that she would be free of all that. She worried she would miss it.

I shouldn't be so spoiled, she scolded herself. *I have people looking out for me. That's good. I just have to learn how to hold them all at arm's length.*

That, she knew, was the survival skill she needed most. Holding other people and the world in their rightful place, and taking her own with strength and confidence. She would get there. It would be fine.

Her choice for evening viewing was an impulse one. She'd been thinking of watching a comedy or a drama when her eye was caught by a documentary on Sir Grey Oswald, the great national treasure who had died in the 1970s after a lifetime in showbusiness that spanned the stage, film and music. Romy had a soft spot for music of the forties and fifties; she could sing along with quite a few of Sir Grey's waspish hits, and she'd seen a production or two of his plays. They'd been provocative in their time but were now very dated. What must have seemed funny then came across much like cruelty now.

I'll watch that, she decided. Perhaps the forties were in her mind, with her research into Heurot and what was happening in Veronica's life at the same time, as it opened up into the era of her real success.

When she'd returned with her supper, she set the programme playing and watched while she ate as Grey's life story unfolded in a montage of old film and stock shots to evoke the period when there was no footage of Grey himself. He'd come from an ordinary background but had somehow got himself onto the stage while quite a young boy, and once on it, had never left. These early years were told quickly, and soon Grey was in his twenties, smoking his trademark cigarettes and quite the dandy, as he pumped out play after play and song after song. His work ethic was strong, to say the least.

The programme touched, too, on his romantic life.

'It was during the war years that his relationship with musical theatre heartthrob Jack Bannock really took off,' said the voiceover, and a photograph of the most beautiful dark-haired man appeared on the screen. His eyes were soulful with an extraordinary melting quality, and his lips formed a perfect masculine pout. Romy couldn't remember hearing his name before and yet, this face looked oddly familiar. A tune she knew began to play over the soundtrack. 'The origins of the love affair are lost to us, but soon Grey Oswald and Jack Bannock were an item, and not just as lovers. Composer of the hits "A Vale of Violets", "Fear No More" and "The Last Song of Summer", Bannock was almost a match for Oswald's talents and the two collaborated on several musicals which helped raise morale during the war years. One show, *The Seahorse*, was written in just a fortnight in the summer of 1941. But the relationship, a secret at the time, didn't last, and came to an end a short time after the war.'

Another photograph came up on the screen, showing Jack and Grey together that summer.

Romy was already sitting up straight, her eyes wide. She

put down her plate and went to rewind the film a few seconds. Had she heard that right? And was she seeing what she thought she'd seen?

The Last Song of Summer? What?

She listened again and, yes, she heard that right. It was 'The Last Song of Summer'. And the photograph . . . She was sure that she not only knew where they were standing, but that she had seen that very photograph already, just a few days ago.

It had been in Richard's hallway, framed and on the wall.

She grabbed her phone and opened the short film she had taken of the photo gallery in Cliff House and watched it in slow motion. Yes. There it was. The same photograph. Grey Oswald, right here on the island in the summer of 1941, writing a musical with his lover – she'd never heard of it, it must have been one of Grey's few forgettable productions.

She thought of the passage in the memoir of Veronica by her daughter. According to that, Veronica had spent the war years mostly on Elfwy – at least the early part of them. Perhaps she even took this photograph, and sent a copy to Grey.

Romy shook her head in disbelief as she zoomed in on the photograph in Richard's hall. Grey Oswald, right here, with his secret lover.

But who on earth was Jack Bannock? And how did he come to write a song called 'The Last Song of Summer' . . . years before Veronica wrote her film of almost the same name? I don't understand.

Ignoring her cooling supper, she turned off the documentary and went back to her file of the old film. She opened it just at the end, as the credits started to roll, then freeze-framed them, and began to read carefully, inching forward a frame at a time.

The cast and crew names unrolled for long minutes and then . . .

Yes, here it is!

She froze the page.

Music. Original song 'The Last Song of Winter' – Jack Bannock. Adapted by Seth Horton.

She sat back, releasing a long breath.

So he wrote two songs of almost the same name. Okay . . . that seemed quite odd. Then her eye was caught by another of the credits.

Story and script by Grahame Hall based on the original play by Veronica Mindenhall.

How had she never noticed that before? Veronica's name was on the title credits before the film started. Now, here at the end, it was clear that she hadn't written the film at all.

Romy stared at the screen, puzzled. Things were supposed to be clearer but instead, they seemed to be getting more tangled.

Chapter Twenty

VERONICA

1948

'Miss Mindenhall? This way, please.'

'Thank you very much.' Veronica followed the guard through the clanging doors until they reached a bare, awful room with strip lighting and plastic-coated tables, mean little chairs tucked under them.

'Please sit,' said the guard.

'Where? Here?' She gestured with her fur muff to the nearest table.

'Yes, ma'am. There will do nicely.' The guard turned and walked away, to stand at the side of the room, staring balefully into space.

'Very well,' she said, and sank down onto one of the low chairs. In her Parisian clothes, she was exotic enough in England, let alone inside a prison. London was a mass of bomb wounds and deprivation, the women dressed in various shades of brown, grey and khaki, the men in demob suits, the children tatty, and everyone looking dazed and shocked even three years after the general victory. Veronica felt almost guilty, in her beautifully cut suit, silk stockings, fashionable hat and furs. But what could she do about it, really?

She sat, looking about the empty room, and coughed self-consciously. After a moment, a door opened at the far end opposite to where she had come in. Another guard entered and behind walked a figure in prison overalls, shuffling and looking utterly broken.

Veronica went to stand, but the other guard motioned at her and she stayed on her seat. The prisoner was brought over and observed as he also sat. Then the guard retreated a few feet to watch proceedings.

Veronica reached out her gloved hand, even though she couldn't possibly touch the man opposite.

'Jack,' she said yearningly. 'Oh, Jack.'

'I wish you hadn't come, Veronica,' mumbled Jack, unable to meet her eye, staring at the tabletop instead.

'I had to come. You know that.'

Jack glanced up for a moment, those dark brown eyes still liquid and melting despite everything. 'I don't know that. But you're too kind.'

She stared at him. It was so hard to see bright, handsome, stylish Jack reduced to this shadow of himself. He was faintly stubbled, his moustache straggly and untrimmed, his skin sallow and his eyes dull. She desperately wanted to reach for his hand, and had to clench her fist to stop herself. 'Darling Jack. This will pass.'

'I'm so ashamed,' he said wretchedly.

Veronica leaned forward, her tone intense. 'You do know that you don't deserve this, don't you?'

'I must,' he said, unable to meet her eyes again, twisting his hands together on the tabletop instead.

'No. I read the court reports. That magistrate was punishing you for being who you are. It had nothing to do with the petrol coupons. He knew how you love and he wanted to demean you, make an example of you. It was completely obvious.'

'I broke the law,' Jack said wretchedly.

'You didn't know.'

'It's no excuse.'

'Oh, Jack!' She could see it was pointless but she was desperate to convince him that he was not the miserable criminal he seemed to think he was. 'I read your testimony in the paper. And the whole tone of what they wrote was sympathetic to you. Remember the crowds outside the court! I saw the photographs.'

'Silent crowds.'

'They did not condemn you. They were there to support you.'

Jack looked bitter for a moment, recalling that day two weeks before. 'The magistrate said I should have managed on the ration, I had no need of the extra coupons . . . But I'd driven to stop Grey from leaving me for ever. I had used up all I had, trying to save us. But it was no good. I was weeping outside Victoria station, because he'd gone and I knew somehow that he'd never be back. There I was, with the useless Rolls, my heart broken. When that good-hearted woman came up, all excited to see me, and found out my situation, she acted from the best of motives. I should have thought!

I should never have taken the coupons from her. But at the time, she seemed like my guardian angel.'

'It was harmless, really,' Veronica said firmly. 'No one was hurt, you didn't understand it was wrong. And very bad luck to be caught, my dear Jack. Think of the terrible crimes in the war, the profiteering, the exploitation! You accepted a gift of a couple of coupons without thinking. And if you hadn't been Jack Bannock, you most likely would have got away with it.'

'Well, my life is over now. My family are ashamed, even my mother finds it hard to speak to me. My career is finished, my name mud . . .' He raised his eyes to her, misery in their depths. 'I've lost Grey as well, Veronica. I have no idea why. Can't you see? Life is over for me. I have nowhere to go. I can't stay in London to be a figure of contempt.'

Veronica felt a prickle of fear. 'You're not thinking of doing anything stupid, are you, Jack? You do know this awful time will pass . . . You're still young, just as talented as ever . . . We will still need your songs and your musicals and all the joy you bring to us.'

Jack gave a wan smile and shrugged.

'I mean it, Jack. You have so much to live for.'

'If you say so, darling.'

Veronica stared at him, feeling at a loss. How to comfort him? How to give him hope? 'When do you get out?'

'Another two weeks in this infernal place,' he said grimly. 'But perhaps a week if they decide to let me out early. They might as well. They've thoroughly destroyed me already, what will another week achieve?'

'And where will you go?'

He shrugged. 'My flat, I suppose. That's one thing that managed to survive intact at least.'

'And then?'

Jack looked suddenly exasperated. 'What do you care, Veronica?'

'Of course I care! I'm worried about you.'

'That's all very nice, but please don't be. Enjoy your wonderful life. Your play is a hit, on Broadway and in the West End, and being filmed in Hollywood. Your father would be ridiculously proud. You're married, you live in glamorous Paris. You don't need to bother yourself with my problems.'

'Don't be so silly, you're very precious to me.' She noticed one of the guards shifting a little on his boots. Her time was no doubt coming to an end. 'Jack, listen. I was going to offer this in any case. Why don't you go to the island? The house is there, it's empty. I can ask one of the regular girls to look after you, I have a little rota of them again. You can have some peace to recover from this terrible ordeal and in privacy too. And perhaps even write some music.'

Jack frowned. 'Elfwy? Beautiful Elfwy?' Suddenly his eyes filled with tears. 'Where Grey and I wrote *The Seahorse*. What a happy time that was! I don't know if I can go back there. It's too sad. Too much.'

'I understand. But the offer is there. I want you to be safe and to get better from this frightful depression. If Elfwy can help, then it's yours.'

He looked up at her from under the lashes that had

once enchanted her so deeply. 'I appreciate that, Veronica. I really do.'

'Think about it and let me know. It's yours for as long as you need it.'

'Visiting time is over,' called the guard from the side of the room.

Veronica stood up. 'I must go, Jack.'

'Are you doing anything nice?' Jack asked wistfully, and she was struck by how far he had moved from his old world of glamour and fun.

'Just some publicity for the play,' she said vaguely, not wanting to make him feel worse.

'I'm so proud of you, dear girl. You can't think. What you've achieved! I've heard *The Raft* is quite brilliant, no wonder you're sold out. I wish I could see it – I will one day. I always knew you could do it. Georgie would be pleased as Punch.'

'Thank you.' She smiled, warmed by his generosity in thinking of her when he was so low. 'It's been very exciting. I must go, dearest. Do think about Elfwy, won't you, and let me know? I really believe it could help.'

'I will. Thank you for coming to this ghastly place, Veronica. I'm eternally grateful.' He smiled for the first time. She was delighted he was a little brighter, but her heart still ached to see how much he'd changed, how beaten he looked.

'I couldn't come to London and not see you, you know that.' She smiled. 'Goodbye, darling Jack.' She kissed her gloved hand to him, and turned to go.

*

371

The theatre owner greeted Veronica like visiting royalty. She was escorted into the foyer with a fawning delight, the theatre staff lined up for her inspection.

'We've been breaking all sorts of records with your play, Miss Mindenhall,' the theatre owner said breathlessly. 'It's an honour to have you here.'

'You're very kind. I'm just so pleased it's been a success for you,' Veronica said. It was very odd to be in a London theatre like this, hailed as a kind of star herself despite never appearing on the stage. She could never have imagined it when Daddy was the celebrity and she was the fierce-faced, blunt-haired girl who hated all kinds of attention. But if she had to have fame, then this was a kind she could manage. She could walk unnoticed in the streets and go about her business as she liked, but her name was selling tickets, bringing in a healthy income, and more interesting opportunities were coming her way as a result. Somehow her play had captured the public imagination and soared into unforeseen success.

The manager took her through to the stalls and up onto the stage, where the director, crew and backstage team were waiting to make Veronica's acquaintance. This was the second cast, taking over from the first sell-out run, and she had been invited to watch a dress rehearsal, to give her stamp of approval to the new players. She shook hands with them all and then took her seat at the front of the stalls to watch the rehearsal.

Despite the effort the actors were putting into impressing the distinguished lady author, who had come all the way from Paris to watch their performance, Veronica found she could not concentrate. Besides, she knew the play so well, she could recite the whole thing from memory in any case. Nevertheless, she tried to be attentive. The players were very good, and she could see her play was in safe hands within the first few minutes, but she wanted to pay them the compliment of her support and encouragement.

But her mind wandered to poor Jack. His disgrace had been all over the papers, awful photographs of his stricken face as he went into the Bow Magistrates' Court to be tried for his crime of the misuse of petrol coupons. She could entirely understand how innocently he would have accepted those coupons in a moment of desperation, without even wondering if it was the right thing to do. And how could he have been thinking straight if his heart had been broken?

Damn Grey! she thought, suddenly furious. *His star is still high, he is a huge success. Why on earth did he abandon Jack like that? He loved him so desperately. And not a word from him throughout this horrible mess. How could he?*

Grey had, in fact, written to her, but had not mentioned Jack at all. He sent a card with a huge bunch of lilies addressed to *The Magnificent Miss Mindenhall* – ignoring her marriage but using her professional name. He wrote:

Well! Little Veronica only went and did it. Just remember that promise – don't write anything better than I do. Congratulations, my angel, and welcome to the world of success. You've earned it.

The card hadn't made her happy at all. She sensed condescension and the repetition of that warning joke bothered her. She had tucked it away in a notebook and tried not to think about it, but on some level she was relieved that she lived in Paris, and wasn't obliged to meet Grey in the social round, as she would in London.

She was still brooding on it when the play came to an end, but put it from her mind as she went to congratulate the cast and director. Then Billie arrived to take her away to supper.

They went to Wheeler's for oysters.

'You have given my career a shot in the arm, and no mistake,' Billie said. She looked like a glamorous film star herself, with her hair perfectly styled, a chic hat perched on the side of her head, and bright red lips, rather than an agent who created stars for the stage and screen. 'Everyone knows you're my sister. So thank you for that!'

'You're doing perfectly wonderfully without my help,' Veronica said, smiling. 'You've completely reinvigorated the agency. No wonder Mr Cunningham felt he could retire and leave it all in your hands.'

'Perhaps.' Billie smiled. 'I love the work, I suppose.' She gave her sister a warm look. 'You do know that Daddy and Mama would be so proud, don't you? And we've only just started, really. Who knows what heights you'll climb?'

'Proud of both of us,' Veronica said quietly.

Mama had died of a heart attack last year, the heart disease finally taking her. Both sisters had felt that she had been waiting for something to take her so that she could join

Daddy. As a result, they mourned her but not with the depth of sorrow they might have otherwise.

The oysters came and they were absorbed with their supper and swapping theatre gossip. It was only when the meal was nearly finished that Veronica raised the subject of Jack, describing her visit to the prison and his state of mind. 'Billie, you've got your ear to the ground as far as all this is concerned. He was so adamant his career is over, and that he's finished. Do you think this scandal has ruined him?'

Billie frowned, eating the last mouthful of creamed spinach from the side dish. 'I don't think it's really harmed him. He was so well loved. It might have been different if he'd been caught in something that truly revolted the public.' The sisters swapped glances. 'But it was obvious it was a simple mistake. If anything, I think public sympathy might be on his side. They'll certainly forgive him, if that's what you mean. Especially if he writes a song that enchants them.'

Veronica sighed. 'That's what I thought. But I couldn't persuade him.' She looked over at Billie. 'You don't know why Grey dumped him, do you? They were such a partnership. I always felt that if anyone was going to do the chucking, it would be Jack. He's so handsome, he could have anyone!'

'Oh no.' Billie shook her head. 'I don't agree. Jack has the looks, but he's the gentle, soft one who needs love like he needs air. I could always tell that the power lay with Grey.' She smiled at her sister. 'You loved Jack, didn't you? Perhaps not as a potential lover when you saw that he was of the seahorse variety, but you always loved him. Grey is not so easy to love, and I don't think he loves many people either.'

'He loved Jack.'

'Did he?'

'Yes,' Veronica said obstinately. She twisted her water glass on the tablecloth, watching the liquid inside shimmer as she remembered all the affection between the two of them, Grey's naked adoration of his handsome lover. 'I'm sure of it.'

'I wouldn't be. Grey is not like the rest of us. I can't say why, exactly. But he isn't.'

'So he just got rid of Jack when he didn't want him any more?'

'The word is that someone came between them. The ghastly man Grey spends all his time with now. And there was some kind of business issue. I don't know really, I'm afraid.'

'All so sad.' Veronica sighed. 'I've offered for Jack to go to St Elfwy.'

'That's a good idea. He can lick his wounds in peace.'

'I just hope he takes up the offer, that's all.'

'Poor love. I do too. Now . . . tell me. How is life in Paris? Where have you been shopping lately? I've been admiring that hat and your blissful suit for the last two hours!'

It was strange, Veronica thought, that London didn't really feel much like home any more. The house in Hampstead had not been returned to them. Instead, the government had forced a sale and kept it. Veronica suspected that it was useful in the new post-war world as a training centre, or safe house, or both, for the secret government services. She didn't mind, she had no desire to go back there, although she did take a trip to the heath and then to the cemetery to see Daddy and Mama's graves. It felt like the right thing to do, considering she did not intend to be back very often.

Making her way back down the hill, she saw poor wounded London laid out in front of her. Thank goodness so much had survived, but still . . . the wreckage and destruction was frightful. It seemed unfair that Paris, occupied by the enemy, had escaped with so much intact, while London, victorious in the end, had been so destroyed and was still beset by shortages and rationing. She had a flash of memory, recalling the air battle she had witnessed in 1941, when the Halifax piloted by André had beaten four planes and then died in the moment of triumph.

That won't happen to London, she thought. *It will come back, it will grow again. It will take time, that's all. And my life isn't here but I'm cheering her on. If the play can help . . . well, that's all to the good.*

Over the next two days, there was a round of dinners and drinks and parties, as she mixed and mingled with friends and business associates. Her literary and theatrical agents were keen for her to make useful contacts in the film and publishing worlds, and she knew it was part of her job now. She could not entirely enjoy the glamour and sense of being feted, though, knowing that Jack was shut up in Wormwood Scrubs, lonely and miserable.

On her last morning, after she had packed up her things and was waiting for the hotel porter to take them down to the lobby, she sat down at the desk in her suite and pulled out some hotel writing paper. In her strong hand, she wrote out a quick note.

Dearest Jack,

You must go to St Elfwy. It's the only way. As soon as you are home, let me know and I'll get the house ready for you and have a boat standing by to take you over. You need it, my love. Take it. It's yours.

Promise me?

All my love, Veronica

She put the letter in an envelope, addressed to *J. Bannock Esq, HMP Wormwood Scrubs, W12*, lifting her eyebrow at the strangeness of such an address, and handed it to the hotel maid to post.

Then she went down to get a taxi for the boat train at Victoria.

Veronica's spirits lifted whenever she crossed the Channel and knew that she was in France again. There was only one place in the world that she felt she belonged other than St Elfwy, and that was Paris. They could not be more different, of course, and yet they both contained vital elements of her character.

It was a relief finally to arrive in a taxi outside the doors of their grand St Germain flat, concealed by glossy green gates. The concierge opened the gate for her; a maid was there to curtsey and greet her at the apartment door, and a footman was on hand to go out for her luggage and to pay the driver.

Life was very different for her and André now. They had come a long way from the little garret, and in such a short time.

As the maid came in to collect her coat, Veronica asked, 'Is Monsieur le Colonel in?'

The maid replied that he was not in and no one knew when he was expected back.

Veronica nodded. 'I see.' She started to take off her gloves. 'Tea in the salon, please, Marie. In the English style, as I like it.'

She went through into the salon, with its view of the garden beyond. She loved this view in particular, and the way it was hidden from everyone. You would not know this oasis was here in the middle of Paris unless you were lucky enough to be invited behind the glossy green gates. This was what the success of her play had bought them: this luxury and pleasure and comfort. She must write another, and soon, to keep their standard of living up. They had eight staff, this elegant apartment and a busy social life with all the entertaining and dressing that required. It took a lot of money to maintain it.

Veronica looked around and sighed. She'd been hoping to see André, she'd missed him, but he was so busy these days. He was one of the youngest and most decorated colonels in the French air force.

When he had left Veronica, he'd returned to Pembroke but his time on the coastal command was over soon afterwards.

The rival French government was now fighting its own battles and needed André's services. He spent the rest of the war as a Free French pilot, flying mission after mission over Germany, and returning almost every time, except for one crash and capture and a spell in a prisoner of war camp. He had escaped after six months and, with the help of the Resistance, made it back to England to resume his flying duties. Towards the end, he was involved in the liberation of Europe, which was how he ended up in Italy for some months after the victory. And now, he was enjoying a celebrated post-war career in the government.

'But I do not miss flying,' he would confide to Veronica. 'I have the funniest feeling that my luck has reached its very limit, at least as a pilot. I do not think I will ever fly again.'

He had developed a reluctance to travel by air at all, preferring to drive or take the train and boat to get to his destination. After their swift and sweet wedding in a Paris *mairie* in the spring of 1946, they had motored to the south of France, and then into Italy and down to Venice.

'I prefer this kind of travel too,' Veronica said, hugging his arm as he drove. The countryside was war-torn, and there were endless streams of people heading in different directions across Europe, making their way home or seeking lost family. They saw dreadful, pitiful sights. But there was a sense of rebirth.

That was almost two years ago. Since then, Veronica had settled into her Parisian life with André, and she could not complain. Her mornings were spent working, and then she lunched with André when he was free or with friends when he was not, or worked on if she needed to. The afternoon was generally spent shopping or at the hairdresser's, planning their social life, running the house and writing letters. The evenings were often spent out, as André was in high demand.

'And so are you, my clever, successful wife,' he would say, dropping a kiss on her shoulder. He was proud of her triumph with her play, probably much more than she was.

She was very happy. Married life was wonderful; she adored André and he loved her back. Life would be close to perfect, if it weren't for not knowing what had happened to Irène.

'She is dead,' André would say simply, his eyes darkening and his shoulders rounding with sorrow.

'We don't know this for sure,' Veronica said one night, as they lay together in the darkness, talking of her.

'She was most likely taken from her apartment by the Gestapo in 1944, as the liberation of the city approached. Dozens were hauled away and shot. She must have been one of them. I can't find anything out, no matter who I ask, no matter their connections.'

'But why on earth would they take Irène?' Veronica asked, holding his hand tightly.

'You don't know what she was really like,' André said. 'She was brave. Very brave.'

'I don't know about her. Or about you. You've never talked about your early life,' Veronica said in a low voice.

'It was hard. Traumatic. My sister always looked after me, though. She was the strongest of the strong, despite that outward look of frivolity. Our parents died when we were young and she made it her business to bring me up. By the time you met us in nineteen thirty-nine, we were polished, civilised, comfortable citizens of France. But it wasn't always that way.'

'Will you tell me more? I want to know. Perhaps it will help us understand what happened.'

She felt André turn away and he said bleakly into the darkness, 'We'll never know. She is just one of the many, one of the millions erased by the war. A tiny tragedy among the thousands and thousands of tragedies. She's gone, and she will never come back. We must make our peace with that.'

I want to help him so much, Veronica thought now, going to the window of the salon and looking down into the garden. André's grief for his lost sister and the ignorance of her fate somehow kept them apart in a way that saddened her deeply.

If only I could find out what happened to her. But if André can't, with all the strings that he can pull in his job, then I don't see how I can.

Absent-mindedly, she stroked her fingertip over the pearls at her neck one by one on their string.

Oh, Irène. How we miss you. Please, somehow . . . come back to us.

Chapter Twenty-One

1949

Veronica went into the hallway and dropped her hat and muff on a chair. Some letters and packets awaited her on the marble console table, and she idly flicked through them. As usual, there were gifts of books from publishers, and she tore open a small packet to reveal a hardback book in a plain ivory cover, the title in elegant block capitals:

L'AMANT DE MINETTE par Marguerite Heurot

Veronica scanned it and looked at the summary on the inside of the cover. She had heard of Heurot, of course, but not read her work. This was another offering from a publisher who no doubt hoped she might sell some translation rights to them, but this novel was not her kind of thing really. She preferred the classics of adventure and drama: *Les Misérables*, *The Count of Monte Cristo*, and the works of Zola. But these very spare, short novels were becoming more fashionable.

She put it down without interest. She would look at it another time perhaps.

'Madame?' The maid called out to her. 'The colonel has asked me to tell you that he will not be at lunch today. He has an appointment.'

'Thank you, Mathilde.' Veronica walked into her study and turned back to her notebook where she was working on her next play, but the words were not coming to her today. Instead, she looked through the long windows in front of her desk out over the garden and the giant chestnut tree that rose nearly three storeys. She loved being able to see it and to look out over the garden, and felt sorry for the residents who did not have access to it.

Veronica jumped as the telephone on her desk rang with a sudden shrillness. She picked up the receiver. '*Hallo?*'

The voice on the other end said in French, 'A call for you from London. Putting you through now.'

A moment later, she heard a familiar voice on the other end. 'Hello, Vee!'

'Billie? How lovely, this is a treat! How are you?'

'I'm all right, darling! I won't be long but I wanted to be in touch with you quickly, as it could take an age otherwise. I've had a letter from Evans, the farmer who's leased the land at St Elfwy – you know, grazing the cattle there.'

'Yes?'

'He says he's concerned, that's all. About the man in the house.'

'Jack?'

'Yes. You know he lost his mother last month.'

'I know. I wrote to him, poor boy. What does Evans say?'

'He says Jack is wandering around the island at all hours. Doesn't seem to know where he is or why half the time. Jim and other fishermen have seen him too. They all have an instinct that he's not right.'

Veronica sighed. 'Oh dear. I hoped that the island would help get him back on his feet. Perhaps that was the wrong thing. What should we do?'

'Darling, if you can, I think you should go there and make sure he's all right. If he's any kind of danger to himself, you need to know. I don't think he should be there alone, that's all.'

'You're right. I'll get there as soon as I can.'

When the call was ended, she stared out of the window for a while. Perhaps a trip to the island would help her find some fresh inspiration for the play she was writing. It was stuck in the early stages and she couldn't find what she needed to give it an impetus.

Yes. I'll go to the island. It's always been a place where I've found what I need to know.

Before Veronica could leave for St Elfwy, she had to make plenty of arrangements for André's care while she was away – ordering his lunches from the kitchen, making sure he had the right uniform and clothes for his various functions and checking they would be laid out correctly on the right day, and reminding him of his social engagements – and she had to fulfil her own obligations or make excuses for some of the many events she had in her diary. But there was no immediate hurry.

She wrote to Jack that she intended to visit, wondering if she might even reach the island before her letter did.

'I wish you were not going,' André said mournfully, a few days later, tying the bow tie on his evening dress as they prepared for a dinner in one of the grand residences of Paris. 'I don't like you to be away from me. How long will you be gone?'

'I don't know – a week, I suppose? As long as I'm there, I'll see Billie and some friends, and get some business done as well. And of course, I must see Jack, that's the whole point.' She rustled over in her evening dress to kiss him, putting her pale arms around his dark jacketed shoulders. Their reflection glittered back from the mirror: she looked like a sophisticated Frenchwoman, in her long, elegant gown and dazzling jewels, her blonde hair no longer unruly and frizzy but smooth and styled into elegant waves, and her lips no longer in a sulky pout but painted an alluring dark red. André looked the handsome Frenchman with his slicked-back hair and slim moustache. He had filled out quite a bit over the last year but it suited him.

'You are so beautiful, my love,' she said.

André smiled at her. 'Not as beautiful as you are.' He kissed her. 'Is there time to go to bed?'

She laughed. 'No! But later . . .'

'I can't wait.'

She kissed him again, thinking how lucky she was. The

early years of married life had been bliss. He was keen for children but she wanted to wait another year, and finish another play, before she began that part of her life. He had agreed, a little sulkily, to wait.

He murmured into her ear, 'Stay, will you? Don't go to Wales.'

'I must. But I'll hurry home, I promise.'

The soirée was a grand affair. A ballroom full of people drank champagne and conversed, the hubbub bouncing off the many gilt mirrors. Veronica was talking to an Italian count and a distinguished-looking Frenchwoman in an elegant red gown. The count was pulled away by a passerby who knew him, and the two women were left alone.

'You are married to the celebrated colonel over there, I believe?' the lady said, nodding in the direction of André, whose dinner jacket sparkled with medals across his chest. 'A national hero indeed.'

Veronica smiled proudly. 'Ah, yes. He is too modest to say it himself but I am certainly very proud.'

'You should be,' the lady said.

'I'm sorry, madame, I didn't catch your name?'

'Duprès. Estelle Duprès.' The lady had a mature face, her dark hair streaked with silver threads. 'And you have more than one reason to be proud.'

Veronica assumed she meant the success of her play and was about to thank her new friend kindly for the compliment, when Madame Duprès added, 'I knew your husband's sister quite well for a while.'

Veronica blinked at her, startled. 'You mean, Irène?'

'That's right. Such a beautiful girl. I could quite see why Philippe adored her. We all could. He was a lucky man to possess her for as long as he did.'

'I'm so sorry, madame, do I understand you correctly? You knew my husband's sister? . . . Was this before the war?'

'No, no. During the war. I worked with her.'

'Please . . . explain. I know nothing of what Irène did after I last saw her in nineteen thirty-nine.' Veronica's heart had begun to race. This was extraordinary. Was she about to learn something of value at last?

'I hope I haven't raised your expectations too high. I didn't know her well. She arrived at Maison Gillarde early in nineteen forty, and took a position as a reader and assessor of manuscripts.'

'The publishing house?'

'Yes. Owned by the Du Crois family.' Madame Duprès gave her a meaningful look.

'I'm so sorry, that means nothing to me.'

'Philippe Du Crois? Irène was his mistress. We all knew that was why she had been given the job; he had arranged it. But she proved very good at it. She was promoted and began to edit the manuscripts and liaise with authors. Again, she was excellent at this. No one begrudged her this position as a result. Not even I, and she was promoted over me in a matter of months.' Madame Duprès smiled ironically. 'It was hard not to be charmed by Irène. She had a very clever line in appearing superficial and delightful, while being extremely sharp. Extremely.'

'So, how long did you work together?'

'Well, that was the very odd thing. Irène left before the year was up. She had become the editor of Marguerite Heurot. Perhaps you've heard of her?'

In her mind's eye, Veronica saw at once the ivory-coloured hardback book on her hall table, the one that had arrived just a day or two ago. 'Yes, I have . . . There was a connection?'

Madame Duprès waited while a passing waiter poured more champagne into her glass before continuing. Her voice was low and Veronica had to lean in to hear her amid all the chatter. 'Heurot was an odd character. No one liked working with her much. She was demanding, complained a lot and could be, quite frankly, insulting. None of us, apparently, was good enough or clever enough to understand her art. She was so sensitive that no one dared to edit her work in any real way. Of course, she was brilliant and she could get away with it but only up to a point. None of her early books fulfilled their potential completely. And then . . . Irène arrived with her legendary charm! She was the only one who could calm down the creative genius and make her listen to ways to improve her work. As a result, her next book was markedly better received. And that is when Irène left.'

Veronica frowned with surprise. 'Really? Where did she go?'

'To work with Heurot. The woman famously never left her apartment. She didn't come out for the entire occupation, if you can believe that. She wanted Irène to become her private secretary, dictation-taker and editor, and for Irène to devote herself to that work solely and completely.'

'Irène agreed to that?'

Madame Duprès nodded. 'She did. It surprised me too. What was she thinking of? How could she want to spend her days with that difficult woman? Perhaps it was to please Philippe – Heurot was the great literary hope of Gillarde, you know, capable of turning their fortunes around permanently. I am sure he had an eye to the business post-war, assuming we won. Perhaps he asked her to take the job. Who knows? But she did.'

'And what happened next?'

The other woman made a sorrowful face. 'I'm afraid I don't know. I never saw Irène again. And I left myself not long afterwards, I was too strained by the situation in Paris to work. But I've often thought of her. Can you tell me what happened to her in the end?'

'No one knows. You are the first person who's offered any news.'

'Perhaps you should speak to Philippe, if you haven't already. I believe he is back in Paris.' Madame Duprès raised an eyebrow. 'Or speak to Heurot herself. She has just published a book, you know.'

'Yes, I know of it. *The Lover of Minette.*'

'You should read it. I hear it is very good.' Just then, the gong sounded and Madame Duprès put down her champagne. 'Ah. It is time for dinner. It has been so nice to talk to you. Please do give my regards to your husband.'

She walked away, leaving Veronica staring after her, her mind spinning over all she had heard.

*

Supper was served in the great dining room, hung with crystal chandeliers and sparkling with glass and mirrors. Veronica talked to an old ambassador on her left, and a very young attaché on her right, but didn't really pay much attention to either of them. She was longing to talk to André, but he was seated far away at the other end of the table.

Then she heard a familiar voice and, glancing down the table, she saw to her surprise the elegant figure of Grey Oswald. He was some distance off but holding court over his part of the dining room, easily keeping those around him in gales of laughter. He held his wine glass high as witticisms flew off his tongue, ignoring his food to sip on his chablis. Veronica watched him, both glad to see him and somewhat melancholy at the sight. Despite thinner hair and a thicker middle, he looked in fine fettle, as though life was treating him well. It must be, if he was at a dinner like this. She already knew he had a new musical slated for the following year, and he had appeared in at least two wartime films, one of which he'd written. There was word that a famous and beautiful star wanted him to appear with her in a musical that he would write. Life must be full of glamour and excitement.

While poor Jack is trudging about the island, desperate and lonely.

Gazing up the table at Grey, she decided, *I will talk to him. I must.*

In the end, though, it was Grey who came to her. As supper was nearing its end and people were moving between seats to greet old friends, Veronica was still talking to the elderly diplomat, struggling a little with the old-fashioned and formal French, when she felt a hand lightly on her shoulder.

'Well, if it isn't my little partner in crime from Wales,' Grey drawled lightly. Then he smiled winsomely at Veronica's neighbour. '*Excusez-moi*. I must steal this young lady to dance with me, not least as I'm told they are going to play one of my songs any moment now.'

Veronica was delighted to be rescued, though she apologised to her neighbour with great regret. Grey tugged her insistently away. As they walked through the gallery towards the ballroom, he said under his breath, 'What a lot of terrible old corpses they are! Most of them are barely alive. How did they make it through the war? They were all supposed to exit stage left, as gracefully and quietly as possible.'

Veronica laughed. 'It's lovely to see you, Grey.'

'Of course it is,' Grey retorted. 'That's not in doubt. But will it be lovely to see you? That is the question, my dear.'

'I hope so.'

'Good. Then you mean to behave.'

She gave him a glance but he wouldn't meet her eye. She guessed he meant that she wouldn't mention Jack. *Well, we'll see about that.*

As they reached the ballroom, Grey said, 'Here we are. Ah, yes, they're about to play "The Lane Where We Wander". Not my best, but serviceable for a waltz. Are you ready?'

Veronica picked up her train as Grey put his arm around her back and clasped her other hand. 'Yes.'

'Then away we go.'

Grey could certainly dance, and they moved gracefully across the floor, stepping and turning in perfect time.

I've come a long way since foxtrotting with my friend Mary.

Dancing was divine, and she soon lost herself in the pleasure of the music, especially as Grey sang along as they waltzed, giving her a private performance of his own number. It was over too soon.

As the music drew to a close, they stopped, Veronica smiling and breathless. 'Oh, that was lovely!" she exclaimed. 'André doesn't dance, at least not like you.'

'Would you like another spin?' Grey said, obviously pleased at her enjoyment.

'Yes, I would!'

'Then we will.'

At that moment, the band struck up again and they began to dance, but as the music resolved into a familiar tune, Grey's face hardened. 'Oh. What a shame.'

'It's "A Vale of Violets",' Veronica said, in surprise.

'I know *that*, dear.'

'It's a beautiful song.' She hoped it might in some way touch his heart. At least it might be a way to begin talking about Jack, even though he clearly didn't wish to.

'I dare say.'

There was a long pause as they danced, then Veronica gathered up her courage. 'Grey, what happened with Jack? You know he's heartbroken, don't you?'

'My very dear Veronica, Jack has only himself to blame for whatever has happened to him. He knows that. I'm sorry, of course, that he was sent to prison. But it was hardly my fault.'

'Of course you had nothing to do with his prison sentence . . .'

'Absolutely not!'

'But while he feels terrible about that – and you must know how he's suffered, how sensitive he is – he is broken-hearted because of what happened between you.'

Grey's eyes went icy and his grip tightened slightly on Veronica's hand. 'These things happen,' he said at last. 'It's between Jack and me.'

'But he doesn't seem to know what went wrong. Couldn't you tell him? Couldn't you put his mind at rest?'

'I'm sure that's a very bad idea.'

Veronica was at a loss. She knew how stubborn Grey could be, and also that this was her very last chance to speak to him about it. She was sure he would avoid her from now on, if he possibly could. 'Please, Grey. I'm very worried about Jack.'

'I thought you were going to behave.'

'Just hear me out and then I'll say no more. Jack is on St Elfwy all alone. He is desperate and miserable, and so low that even the farmer has written to Billie to say he fears for his well-being. He can't seem to find any peace, and I think it's because he doesn't know why you decided to leave him. He has never been able to close that chapter of his life. Can you understand that?'

Grey's jaw was clenched and rigid. 'Perhaps.'

'Don't you owe him something, Grey? To tell him? You

were so happy together. You once told me that the most beautiful things in the world were Jack's eyes, and your talent. Remember writing *The Seahorse* together? And what wonderful songs you created? I was so proud of you both.'

'It was a terrible idea to work together,' Grey muttered. 'We really were better off doing our solo projects. In fact, that was the last time. We never worked together again, not really.'

'Then it was an even more special time there on the island. How happy we were and how much he loved you.' She gazed up pleadingly into Grey's eyes. 'I'm going to St Elfwy myself, I'm leaving on Monday. Why don't you come with me? Come with me to the island and we'll see Jack together. It will be the three of us again. Even if you can't love him any more, at least tell him why.'

They turned together for a while in silence, Grey lost in thought and Veronica afraid that the end of the song was approaching and with it her last chance to speak of this to Grey ever again.

She said quietly, 'Will you come?'

Grey said, 'Vincent will never allow it.'

'You can do whatever you want. You're Grey Oswald.'

He looked at her quizzically for an instant and then burst out laughing. 'You're right. I am. And perhaps I do owe Jack something. I did love him. Very well. I will come.'

The band drew the song to an end of the quivering last line of Jack's song: '*A vale of violets for you . . .*'

'Thank you, Grey,' she said, filled with pleasure. 'I'm sure it is the right thing. I really am.'

'Hmm. We will see about that.'

In the car on the way home, she told André what Madame Duprès had told her at the party. 'Isn't that wonderful?' she asked, excited. 'We have some news of Irène at last.'

'Yes,' André said, taking her hand. 'Thank you, my love. It is lovely to hear something of Irène's last years while we were parted.'

Veronica's smiled faded a little. 'Is that all you can say?'

'I should have spoken to Philippe myself if I had known his surname. But I never met him and Irène never said it. She was very good at keeping secrets without you even noticing. I did know that he had abandoned Paris before the invasion, and I was very sure he had abandoned Irène as well. It is a comfort to know that he attempted to help her in any way that he could.'

'Shouldn't we speak to him? And even to Heurot?' Veronica persisted. 'They might be able to give us a little more detail.'

'Perhaps we could.' André shrugged. 'I doubt Du Crois knows anything considering he wasn't here. Heurot – perhaps. We could try that. I'm not sure.'

'You want to know what's happened, don't you?'

'I know what's happened. She's dead, for sure. How she died . . . only the enemy can tell us that, and I don't believe they ever will, even if they know.'

'But these people might be able to tell us a little more

of her life, before whatever took place happened. Isn't that worth something? I loved hearing about Irène's life in the publishing house and how clever she was! How talented.'

'Of course.' André hugged her close. 'But it is also painful. I knew that already. And it hurts so much to think of her. I want to know her fate, but nothing else.'

'I don't understand,' Veronica said helplessly. It went so against the way she felt and thought.

'Then don't try. We're nearly home.'

As they went into the hall of their home, Veronica saw the hardback book still sitting on the console table where she had left it. She had meant to take it to the study but here it was.

André was already heading to his bedroom. Veronica lingered for a moment, peeling off her long evening gloves. Then she picked up the book.

Something told her she should read it as soon as possible.

Chapter Twenty-Two
ROMY

The weather was cold and blustery on St Elfwy. For three days, Romy hardly ventured out, except for some morning walks to stretch her legs. She wrapped up warmly in her waterproofs and put on her stout boots, and marched along the paths, taking the force of the battering wind in her face in one direction and at her back in the other. The rain whipped and stung her face when the wind blew it there, and she walked past the colonies, now hardly visible in the bad weather, while the waves crashed and roared below. The birds, just dots on the cliff sides and the stacks, looked miserable huddling on their nesting spots, often whirling off to ride the storm for a while as if to get a change of scene.

The rest of the time, Romy was inside. She had started to go down a Grey Oswald wormhole and spent hours watching his films, and listening to his songs, of which there were many. For now, she had put off rereading *L'Amant de Minette*, and was thinking instead about Elfwy and what role it might have played in some of the best-loved music and plays of the last century.

Perhaps I should think of writing my book as a biography of the island . . . monks, Mindenhalls, Oswald and Ban- nock, The Last Song of Winter . . . *think about how it all fits together, how one place can be completely inspiring in so many ways . . .*

She liked this idea and started to write up notes for it while she watched yet another film of wartime propaganda, with the script by Oswald, the music by Oswald, performed by Oswald, directed by Oswald and also starring Oswald.

He wasn't shy, she thought, laughing to herself. *He did everything but play the leading lady.*

She had quite a lot of thoughts amassed before she had to check in to an online counselling session with Caroline.

'How is island life?' Caroline asked, once they were connected.

'It's going well,' Romy said honestly. 'And I'm really absorbed in what I'm doing.'

'So everything is all right there?'

'Yes. I'm sleeping well, walking a lot. I feel perfectly safe. In fact, safer than I have for a long time.' It was true. She had seen nothing of Richard but his dark-coated figure out on the island in the distance, but only in the afternoons. There had been no further messages. The dark smoke curling out of the chimney in the evening had been another sign that he was there but that was all. Jesse too had gone quiet and the rougher sea meant that the tours were cancelled and he hadn't come by in his motor boat.

The fact that everyone had backed off a bit had reassured

her that she was managing the situation well and there was no need to bother Caroline with it.

'I've looked over your forms,' Caroline said, smiling. 'It looks like you're doing really well. Eating, sleeping, working. Taking your meds. Well done, Romy. I'm really proud of you. You said this would be a stepping stone to normal life and I think you might be right.'

Romy smiled back, pleased to have her approval.

'Do you have any concerns?'

'No.' Romy shook her head. 'I really don't. But ask me in another week!'

'Oh, don't worry, I will. See you then, Romy.' Caroline's picture vanished and the session was over.

The afternoon was wet, but she had had enough of watching films and investigating the religious foundation on the island, and wanted to walk again in order to process everything. She put on her coat and boots, tied on her hood against the blustering wind, and headed out for a couple of circuits of the island, walking further inland to avoid the slippery muddy paths by the cliff. As she went, she thought about Jesse in his caravan, and whether he was getting bored of the rain as well. It was certainly losing its novelty as far as she was concerned. She wondered if the rain meant that he couldn't earn any money doing the tours, or if he was paid anyway. It would be a precarious life if it relied on it not raining in Wales.

Back at home, she took off her wet things to dry and had a hot bath. She was pondering what to make for her supper when her phone twitched with an incoming message.

Hi, Romy. It's miserable weather! I'm used to it but I wondered if you could do with some company. Would you like to come over for something to eat later? I'm roasting a chicken, you could share it with me? Richard.

She thought for a moment. Why not? I would like some company.

She texted back:

That sounds great. What time do you want me?

*

Her walk to the white house that evening wasn't the pleasant leisurely stroll of last time but a struggle against the blasting wind and rain. Romy arrived shiny with rainwater, her boots sodden and the label on the bottle of wine she was carrying almost soaked off.

'For you!' she said, breathless, holding it out to Richard as he stood in the warmth and light of the hallway.

'Thanks. Come in, for goodness' sake! Get those things off!' He beckoned her in.

'I'm dripping everywhere.'

'That's what stone floors are for. Here, I'll get you a towel.' He went off and returned with one. She'd already divested her coat and boots and had hung the coat to dry, and changed into the dry shoes she'd brought in a bag.

'Thanks.' Romy wiped her face and rubbed at her hair. 'It's something else out there. It's like the world is made of water.'

He waited until she was a bit drier, then took the damp towel from her. 'Come on. Come through.'

The kitchen was full of the warm aroma of roasting chicken, and the vegetables were set out ready to put in the oven. It was neatly organised, with the table already laid. Richard got two glasses out of a cupboard and opened the wine she'd brought. 'I think it's fairly chilled after your walk,' he joked. They took their wine through to the sitting room, where the stove was lit and the fire blazing behind the glass doors. Martha the raven sat on a perch in the corner, apparently asleep, although she opened her beady eyes from time to time as if to make sure that everything was running satisfactorily while she napped.

'So how are you getting on in Clover Cottage?' Richard asked as they sat down opposite one another. 'Any problems?'

'No, it's fine. Except . . .' She went through a small list of snags she'd experienced with the cottage and a few repairs she'd seen that needed doing and for a while they talked about the cottages, their modernisation and how it had been done.

'These places need constant upkeep,' Richard said. 'The sea air means you have to keep on top of it, like you would on a ship. You have to wash off the salt, it's very corrosive. Keep the paint fresh and the woodwork repaired. You've probably noticed all the holiday caravans on the mainland? The pale green ones?'

Romy nodded.

'They disintegrate after about ten years. The weather and the salt water does for them, they start to rust away. They have to be replaced regularly. It's a good lesson in what the water can do. Apparently a plane was wrecked on the side of the island in the war, got washed away, and nothing was ever found. I'm sure it just rusted away to nothing but some bits and pieces.' Richard stood up. 'Let's go back through and I'll finish off the dinner.'

Back in the kitchen, she sat at the table while he set about putting the vegetables on to cook.

'So,' he said, 'tell me a bit about your work. What are you writing? You said something about a history of the religious community?'

'That's right. Monks, crazy abbots, pilgrims, and all the rest.'

'How's it going?'

'Oh . . .' She thought quickly. She still didn't want to mention her interest in the film, at least not yet, and she'd been researching Grey Oswald and Jack Bannock all morning and her head was full of it. She thought fast. 'I'm expanding it actually, towards examining the island itself as a refuge and place of retreat.'

Richard looked interested. 'That's ambitious. Will you get it published?'

'I have no idea. I hope so. But it's in the really early stages. There's not a lot to tell right now.'

'Well, good luck,' Richard said. 'I'll be interested to know more when you're a bit further along.'

She felt guilty for a moment, knowing that she wasn't being entirely candid. 'Thank you. Me too.'

A few minutes later, Richard served up their simple but

well-made dinner and sat down with her to eat. Romy asked about how the weather would affect the birds and Richard told her that a really severe storm could have very detrimental effects on the colonies, to the point of decimating them. But this kind of storm would be fine.

'As long as it doesn't go on much longer. They need to be mating. They don't like mating in the rain.' He smiled at her. 'I guess we can all sympathise with that.'

She smiled back at him, a little awkward again, and nodded. 'So what happens if the eggs are delayed in being laid?'

He started to explain about the incubation periods and the time available for laying. 'Sometimes a breeding pair might lose an egg and lay another, or even another. So nature does build in time for inclement weather or accidents. It's clever that way.'

While Richard cleared away, she went to the loo again and this time resolutely didn't look at the photographs on the wall. Now that she knew him better, she was feeling bad about being sneaky and not getting his permission. But on the way back, she stopped long enough to look quickly at the framed photograph of Grey Oswald and Jack Bannock on the island together. She was tempted to take another photograph of it, but decided against it. She was going to be good from now on.

When she got back, he had finished clearing, and they went back to the sitting room with more wine and a bar of good dark salty chocolate to share as pudding. Richard put some music on the sound system and she noticed a guitar propped up against the piano, a chestnut-brown old upright that had clearly been there a long time.

'So you headed off to the mainland with Jesse the other day,' Richard said lightly as they sat down. 'Did you have fun?'

Romy felt slightly on her guard but said in just as light a tone, 'Very nice. St David's is quite chichi now, isn't it? Not like when I was last there. Lots of artisan pizza and goat's milk ice cream, that kind of thing.'

He laughed. 'You're not wrong. So you had a good time?' She nodded.

Richard frowned, looking down into his glass of wine. 'There's something about that guy. He really doesn't like me but he's sort of . . . I don't know . . . interested in me.'

Romy remembered what Jesse had said about Richard: the unusual interest in the visitors, the reprimand from the trust. Somehow he didn't seem like that kind of man – but that didn't mean he wasn't. She said, 'He seems a bit wary.'

'I don't know why. I mean, I'm not his biggest fan either, we're just very different. But I'm happy just to stay out of his way, you know? But he always seems to be in my eyeline, one way or another.'

'He said . . . ' She hesitated.

Richard looked over quickly. 'What? What did he say?'

'He said you'd had a pretty bad tragedy in your life.' She spoke fast as he looked away again. 'I'm sorry if that's too prying. You don't have to tell me or explain anything. I just wanted you to know that he'd told me. No details. Just that you'd had a big loss.'

There was a long pause and she felt agonised. Should she

405

have brought it up? It felt like the right moment. And it had been on her mind since Jesse had told her, consciously and unconsciously. She now saw Richard as someone labouring under the weight of great grief and it was making her want to reach out to him and to let him know she knew.

'Be careful,' Caroline had said, 'of trying to fix other people's problems for them. Watch out for feeling their pain more than you feel your own. It might feel like a good thing to do, a caring thing to do. But you can't fix other people, that's not your job. If you want to help them, you let them know you're there, that you care for them in their struggle, that you have faith in them getting through it. But that's all.'

She thought of that now. *But I don't want to fix him. I just want him to know that he's seen. That's what Caroline was saying.*

But she was also worried that she'd gone too far and trespassed on Richard's private life, considering how little she knew him. She waited, nervously biting her lip and clutching at her wine glass.

He looked up at last, his expression pained. 'It's hard to talk about. But yes. I lost my wife and son six years ago. We were on holiday – not here, abroad. She came from the Caribbean and we were visiting her family. She and my boy were swimming and he was caught by an undertow. She tried to swim further out to save him. I was on the beach and when I saw they were in trouble, I started swimming out, desperately trying to get to them, but I couldn't reach them in time. And then . . . well, it was too late. It was astonishing how quickly it was over, how little time it took to wipe them out. I was about to go under too when someone came along in a boat and hauled me in it. I was barely conscious.' He gave a bitter laugh. 'I curse that person every day. Every bloody day.'

'I'm so sorry,' Romy whispered, appalled.

'They got my wife and son, got back to the beach and they did CPR, trying to get them back. The emergency services arrived. I lay on the sand, just disbelieving. I couldn't believe it. And you know what? Six years on, and I still can't believe it.' He shook his head. His skin had flushed and his shoulders drooped. 'Every day, I wake up and have to remind myself that it happened. It's my normal now. But it wasn't for a very, very long time. It was my abnormal, my living nightmare. My hair turned white in three weeks.'

'Oh, Richard. I can't say how sorry I am.' Her eyes filled with tears thinking of his suffering, and of the terrible bad fortune that had taken the lives of his wife and son.

'Thank you.' He smiled wanly. 'I'm only here because I knew my wife would never forgive me if I killed myself, much as I longed to be with them. I decided to devote myself to the birds instead. That's what brought me here.'

'I understand – I mean, as much as I can.' Her heart ached for him. She felt so sorry for what he had been through and how much he must have suffered. 'I can't really imagine it, of course. I haven't been married or had a child. It must be the worst thing.'

'The very worst,' Richard said simply. 'You wonder what the point of living is. I never knew that was possible. Intellectually I knew people felt that way. But I couldn't comprehend it until it happened to me.' He looked over at Romy, his eyes full of deep sadness. 'I hope it never happens to you.'

She looked down, unable to meet his eyes. She had been in a very dark place herself, but it was nothing like what had happened to him. She felt suddenly spoiled, as though all her troubles were simply self-inflicted. 'I've been ill,' she said after a moment. 'I don't know your pain, but I do know desperation and misery brought about by illness.'

'I'm sorry to hear that,' he said after a moment. 'Are you well now?'

'Getting better. I'm just saying that so you know . . . that I don't know your suffering, but I do know suffering.'

'There's no hierarchy,' he said with a small smile. 'And you know what? Something I've learned is that everyone knows suffering, one way or another. Everyone you walk past in the street, or sit next to on the bus, or who's drinking a coffee on the next table in the cafe . . . they're all suffering. And if they're not, then they have been, or they will be. Pain helps you learn to be human, to accept other people's humanity. If it doesn't do that, then you have a big problem. The people who feel pain and become less human and less kind – those are the people you need to avoid. Now, I'm going to put one of my favourite jazz bands on, and we're going to talk about something more cheerful, okay?'

Romy stayed until eleven, enjoying the conversation, the music and the slight fuzziness of drinking more wine than normal. What Richard had said had struck a chord with her, and she had found herself relaxing. She was glad she had raised the subject of his past and it seemed to have created a bond of friendship between them. She felt less wary of him than before.

When she noticed the time, though, she got up. 'I must get home.'

'I'll walk you back,' he offered, standing up as well.

'No point in both of us getting wet,' she said with a laugh. 'I'll be fine, I have a torch.'

'All right then. But text me when you're back so I can mount a rescue if you don't make it.'

'Of course.'

She went out into the hall and as she was putting on her not-quite-dry coat and boots, he said, 'If the sun comes out, do you fancy an afternoon of birdwatching? I've got a spare pair of binoculars. It's a brilliant time to do it.'

Romy looked up from her laces. 'That sounds great. Yes, please. I would.'

'Great.' He smiled. 'First sunny day.'

'You're on.'

The sunny day was proving remarkably elusive.

Romy walked in the rain in the mornings, sometimes waving at Richard in the distance when she saw him, but otherwise keeping to herself. She found herself thinking often of the terrible story he had related. No wonder he had needed the isolation of the island. It made complete sense.

Six years. It's nothing really. How could you ever get over a loss like that?

And yet, he was usually cheerful and friendly. She felt a

kinship with him now, as though they had both joined the community of people that the island had tried to heal. And she liked the way he had said there was no hierarchy of suffering – hers was as valid as his, just different.

But even though she felt she had made a friend, it was important that they kept their distance and maintained their privacy, in a tiny place like this. So she waved but stayed away.

Instead, she thought about her new idea of a history of the island and its place as a site of creativity and inspiration of all kinds. She might have to get the trust's approval but that would only be if she got anywhere near being published, and it wasn't even written.

One late afternoon, she noticed that the weather had cleared at last, and decided to go out while it was not raining, this time going down to the beach to explore. It was too early in the year for the seals to be giving birth, but she still saw some grey heads and whiskery faces popping up in the water around the island, as well as the usual host of birds wheeling in their circles and figures of eight above it.

She looked over at the mainland, where the last tourist boat of the day was preparing to go out. Rows of people sat in the high-backed orange seats, their life jackets on, preparing to be driven out to the island and then around its sights and features. She wondered if Jesse was on board this one, and waited until it had zoomed over the channel, taking a few sharp loops to amuse the passengers on the way, and was approaching the beaches.

Once again, she could make out the voice over the

loudspeaker, giving the tourists the well-worn patter about the flora and fauna of the island.

Definitely not Australian, she thought.

She felt suddenly guilty about Jesse. Maybe she had led him on a bit. They had had a really nice lunch together and he'd kindly taken her on that trip to town. She could afford to be nice to him, all she had to do was keep her distance.

I must remember to text him. A coffee or something couldn't hurt.

The next morning was bright if cloudy. Romy got a text early from Richard telling her he was heading off into town and asking if she wanted to join him.

She said she would and they met by the jetty half an hour later, where Richard was revving up his small motor boat.

'Jump in,' he said. 'Let's get going and beat the crowds!'

'I thought we were going birdwatching when it was sunny.'

'Oh, we will! But I need some supplies first. And it's worth waiting for a really nice day to see the birds.'

They didn't talk until after the motor boat had roared across the channel and Richard had moored her at the opposite side near the lifeboat station. From there, they climbed up the steep steps that Romy had descended on the day of her arrival, which felt like an age ago.

She followed Richard up to a small parking area.

'I keep a car here,' he said as they climbed into a battered old VW. 'It's a bit of a necessity. I've had to sleep in it before now when there's no way I can get over to the island.'

Romy looked over the fields, with their stunning view of

the island and the sea, and noticed quite a few of the pale green caravans, wondering which one might belong to Jesse. They did look cosy close up. Then she climbed into the car for the short journey into town.

Richard parked behind the cathedral. 'Right. I'm going shopping. Very dull things including twine. Meet you back here in an hour? We can go and get something to eat. I want to hear about your research.'

'Sounds good,' Romy said, smiling. She liked the way he was not at all pushy. She would talk about her research into the island's monastic foundation; perhaps he might be able to help her with some information. She might even mention *The Last Song of Winter* and her interest in it, now that they were friends. 'I need to do some shopping too. See you later.'

She went for a wander around St David's grocery shops and delis, picking out delicious-looking fresh produce to supplement her tins and packets. At some point, she'd need to do a proper restock but things were ticking over quite nicely right now. As she went back down the high street, wondering whether to buy an oggi, the Welsh version of a Cornish pasty, she saw the headquarters for the island tours, the poster showing the distinctive yellow boat that took tourists out to the islands. On impulse, she wandered in. It was a single bare room, decorated with posters of the local beauty spots and wildlife. There were lots of pictures of birds, some of which she could now identify, which pleased her very much.

Behind the long wooden counter, which offered leaflets for all the many tours and activities, two young people, a man and a woman, were working intently at screens. The young man with a mop of curly hair and glasses looked up as Romy approached. 'Can I help you? If you want a tour to St Elfwy, we're all booked out for today. The weather has meant we've got a rush on. The soonest I can do you is probably Thursday.'

'No, that's okay, I don't need a tour. I live on Elfwy.'

The man gaped at her. 'You live there?'

'Temporarily.' She smiled. 'I'm spoiled, I know. And I'm pretty familiar with your tours as well. I just wondered if you can tell me when one of your guides is working.'

The young man shrugged. 'Sure. I'm jealous by the way. I'd love to live out there for a bit.'

'It's great, I recommend it. The guide is an Australian called Jesse?'

The man looked blank. 'I don't know her.'

'It's a man.'

'I don't know a man called Jesse either, I'm afraid. Sorry. We don't have a Jesse working for us.'

Romy frowned, puzzled. 'I'm sure he said this was the place. He does tours on a yellow boat like yours.'

'Well, I can take a look on the system, but I really don't think we have anyone called that working for us.'

The young woman behind the counter had gone still and now looked over. 'I think I know who you mean. We did have a bloke working here last year. But he got fired.'

Romy blinked at her, startled. 'Fired? Jesse? Are you sure?'

'Yep, if you mean an Australian guy with long hair and tattoos?'

'That's him. But why was he sacked?'

413

She looked around guiltily as though Jesse might be hiding somewhere. 'I'm not supposed to say but the boss was really fed up with him. Something about unreliability? Or . . . inappropriateness? The actual sacking was last year before I started. But I know about it because there is some kind of ongoing issue to do with returning our gear. The boss is pretty upset about that too. Jesse's got keys to the motor boats and won't give them back. He's running renegade tours from time to time. The boss has been talking about getting the police involved if he doesn't stop.'

'I see.' Romy stared at her for a moment longer. 'Thanks very much. You've been really helpful.'

Richard was waiting for her at the car when she returned to dump her shopping.

'I thought we could take a look around the cathedral,' he suggested, locking the car once her things were stowed away. 'And then I could treat you to an early lunch in the cafe.'

'Sounds good,' Romy said, putting her uneasy feelings about Jesse out of her mind for now. It wasn't a subject she wanted to discuss with Richard. They walked down the hill to where the cathedral lay, magnificent in its situation below the town. It was a soaring achievement that was quite out of proportion to the rest of the city, which was really a small town. They went inside, wandering around the chapels and admiring the ancient windows, ceilings, carvings and grave monuments. Then they passed into the modern extension where there was a light, airy cafe for visitors.

'So . . .' Richard said when they were finally settled with

their lunch at a table by the window. 'How do you like the place?'

'I love it. I've been here before but I don't do quite as much colouring in or have such an interest in ice creams as last time I was here.'

He laughed. 'Glad to hear it. I mean, ice creams are great. You should try the peach melba at the stand in the high street. It's fantastic. But I wouldn't want it every day.'

'You truly are a man now.'

They laughed together.

She said, 'Seriously though, it's been good for my research to see the cathedral.'

'If you're looking for more material about the monastery on the island, you might find the second-hand bookshop useful. I bet that will have loads of gems for you to get your hands on. There's bound to be a lot around the cathedral and island and the monks.'

'Great tip, thank you.'

Richard took a bite of his sandwich, and after a while said, 'I'm not all that keen on the ruins and the abbey and all the rest of it. It's not my area of interest. And there's another reason why I'm not so into it . . . that bloody film and its bloody ghost monks.'

Romy looked over at him across her soup, trying to appear neutral and not go pink. 'The film?'

'That's a reason why I like you, Romy, among others, because you haven't once mentioned that dreadful film, *The Last Song of Winter*. It was filmed on the island.' Richard made a face. 'An absolute pile of old tripe. No one cared for years but in the last decade or so it's become what they call a cult classic, and it's made life a misery, with twice as many people wanting to visit the island, most desperate to get ashore and look about, preferably inside my house.'

Romy looked down into her soup now, feeling the colour rising in her cheeks. Perhaps she wouldn't admit her real interest in the island after all. 'Well, actually, I do know it . . . I've seen it. It's got that macabre ending, hasn't it?'

'God, yes. That's the other thing. If they're not trying to get ashore, they want to hang out in the caves. It's not safe in there. But more to the point, they'll risk destroying it. We've already had some nutter trying to graffiti in there. Jesse doesn't help, with his bloody tours, taking people into the caves without permission. I've complained about him last year to the island tours but they don't seem to do anything about it. I've given up now. I agreed to two tours a season, that's it. Jesse seems to think I'm spoiling his fun for the hell of it. I'm sure it's a nice earner for him, but the island comes first.'

'Okay,' Romy said slowly. Richard appeared to think that Jesse was still working for the tours when she knew that he no longer was. Unless Jesse was now with a different outfit? With similar boats? She would have to find out. 'So you don't get any more money from the island's association with the film?'

'Not from the tours or the visitors, no.'

'But . . .' She hesitated and then said, 'other ways?'

He looked up at her sharply. 'What do you mean?'

'I guess, if it was filmed on the island, you might get some royalties or something? I don't know.'

Richard looked distant for a moment. Then said, 'I suppose the trust would. But whatever it brings in, it's still a massive pain.'

'I suppose it must be.' She smiled at him. 'It's a shame that the ghost monks don't scare them off. Maybe you could dress up and pretend to be one, to frighten them away.'

'Ha!' Richard laughed. 'Sounds like a *Scooby-Doo* plot. I'd get some pesky nosy kids on the island, and eventually they'd pull back my cowl and say, "So it was the bad-tempered warden all along!"'

Romy laughed too. 'I'd watch that one, definitely.'

As they talked on and finished their lunch, she thought, *So that's that. I absolutely can't confess that I want to write about the film, even if it's only a part of my new idea.*

Heading back, Richard negotiated the car park exit and took the turn for the coast. As soon as they were up the hill and out of the town, he sped up and the little car whizzed along the narrow road lined with hedges and cow parsley. They were forced to stop a few times for oncoming traffic, Richard nestling the car over to the side as much as he could so that they could pass. It took a pick-up truck ages to edge past them. Romy watched as the two vehicles managed to pass one another without scraping, and just as they were about to be free, she saw that someone was sitting in the trailer at the back, and the next moment her eyes met those of Jesse.

He was wearing a reversed baseball cap, one tattooed arm hanging over the side of the truck.

She widened her eyes in surprise as he stared straight at her and then at Richard, but before she could do anything else, the two vehicles were clear and the truck accelerated away as Richard pressed down in the opposite direction.

She didn't think he had seen Jesse and she decided to say nothing about it.

Chapter Twenty-Three

The sun came out on a sky so fresh and blue it seemed newly cleaned. The morning was alive with birds and insects, all seemingly in a high state of excitement. Richard texted while she was having her breakfast outside, basking in the already warm sunshine.

It's a beautiful day! Want to come and spy on some eligugs?

She felt a pleasurable warmth. Aside from the slight moment of awkwardness in the cafe the previous day, she had really enjoyed her time with Richard. They talked so easily and laughed a lot. He seemed to wear everything lightly, from the scars of his grief to his evidently enormous knowledge about birds and the natural world, and she liked that. She had come across enough overt show-offs and covertly arrogant types to value this kind of modesty when she found it. So often those other people really had nothing much to be so superior about.

When they'd reached the jetty on the way home, Richard had seen that she was perfectly capable of getting back, said a friendly goodbye and then hugged her. To her surprise, the hug had affected her quite strongly. She hadn't been hugged since she'd arrived, she realised, but it was not just that. She'd felt the strength and sincerity in his hug as he pulled her to him and embraced her. He really meant it, not with any sleazy overtones, but as a moment of intense human connection. She appreciated that, and had not quite been able to put it out of her mind.

She would very much like to spend the afternoon with him, and spying on birds actually sounded pretty fun, put like that. She texted back yes, and they made a plan to meet after lunch.

Richard was waiting for her on the path to the cliffs with the binoculars and a rug, wearing a pair of shades against the bright sunshine. The air was rich with insect noise and birdsong, and dozens of birds wheeled overhead and around the cliffs and stacks, shrieking in the sunshine. The atmosphere was rich with a kind of excitement, as if the good weather had started a spontaneous party and they were all getting carried away with it. Out in the bay, boats buzzed about or tacked slowly under sail, and out at sea, great liners and ferries drifted along the horizon.

'Isn't it gorgeous?' she breathed.

'It's like the famous song in the Bible,' Richard said as they walked along. '*Arise, my love, my fair, and come away . . .*

for the rain is over and gone and the time for song is here.
Or something like that.'

'That's beautiful,' Romy said.

'And appropriate. Listen to them!'

They walked along the path, alongside the hedges and
wildflowers until they reached a patch of grass that was
just about opposite the main stacks. The rocky towers
had looked craggy and inhospitable in the bad weather,
but the sun had brought out tufts of green and even tiny
speckles of pink flowers on them, among the hundreds of
birds jostling for position and crammed onto them wing to
wing.

Richard lay the rug out and sat down on it, beckoning
Romy to join him. He passed her a pair of binoculars. 'Have
a go with these and see what you can see.'

Romy took the glasses and put them up, working
with the focus dials until the birds on the stacks opposite became sharp and clear. She could see now how much
like little penguins the guillemots were, with their black-
and-white backs and heads – the black actually more like
a chocolatey brown – which seemed to be held back at a
permanent tilt. She observed the way their wings folded
back, giving them a long white chest, and she noticed their
flat webbed feet. They were constantly shrieking and calling
to one another in loud, grating sounds, their yellow bills
stretched open.

'It's like some kind of festival,' she said with a laugh.

'And they've all turned up in their dinner jackets,' Richard replied. 'But they don't really have the first idea of good manners, all that pushing and nudging and squabbling.'

They sat in companionable silence, sometimes exclaiming or pointing out a particular bird, watching through their binoculars. There was plenty to see besides the guillemots. Wide-winged gulls soared about, landing here and there, looking for prey and watching the goings-on. Out on the water, shearwaters were hunting in small packs, seeking the tiny fishes. A small pod of porpoises passed by, curving up and down in the water as they swam. Romy was entranced, amazed at how much there was to see.

'Look,' Richard said, pointing at the stacks. 'They're mating.'

Romy turned her binoculars to where he was indicating. She could see a bird bending forwards on its nesting spot, pressing its breast onto the cliff and raising its tail, cawing loudly, while its mate went behind it, keeping steady in a whirr of wings. 'Oh yes, I can see.' Now she could see that there was mating going on all over the stacks, in whirring wings and prone females.

'The next generation is on its way,' he said softly.

They carried on watching. Richard put his binoculars down but Romy kept on observing as he talked very gently beside her.

'You should see the puffins. There isn't a large colony here any more but there used to be. I've seen them, though, on the island just over the way, billing and cooing. They spend ages in great excitement, rubbing noses together, courting and wooing one another, performing mating dances and generally just having a fabulous time. And then they'll start the deed itself. Shameless. Out there in the open air. The other puffins are thrilled. They'll gather round to watch and chatter their encouragement and it's all just the most brilliant love-in. That's what it's like at this time of year . . . just full of love and sex and excitement.'

Romy put her binoculars down and looked at him. Her heart was beating faster and she was filled with a strange sense of excitement herself. Perhaps it was because they'd been watching a couple of hours of what was bird porn – the thought made her want to laugh – but there was something else. Ever since that night at Cliff House, she had been thinking about what he'd said about suffering and pain. There was something in the clarity with which he had expressed it that had touched her. She had found herself summoning him to mind: the green eyes that could be cool or warm depending, but which had been mostly warm lately. And the white hair, that now seemed like an outward sign of his deep grief and, she felt, his humanity. His face had a softness to it that at first had seemed a bit featureless but now seemed to show his gentle side. She had dreamed of him too, not in any way she could remember, but with a sense of connection and comfort. The hug that she had felt as a connection deep within her. And she had been looking forward to this, the birdwatching.

She looked at him now and he was gazing straight at her, looking deep into her eyes. 'Do you feel it too?' he said slowly. 'That . . . feeling in the air? The spring rush?'

Her heart was racing now, and she couldn't speak. She

was overcome with a sudden shyness and also a sensation of whirling excitement, as though she was standing on the stacks with the guillemots, buffeted by spring breezes, held up by currents of warm air, part of the cycle of mating and breeding and creating. She nodded and whispered, 'Yes, I feel it.'

'So do I.'

They were both very still, close together on the rug. Neither moved until Romy reached over, pulling his face to hers, pressed her mouth onto his, and kissed him.

Romy lay on the bed in the white house, Richard's sleeping form beside her. It was dark outside but the shearwaters were moaning and wailing into the night as usual. The fine weather had set them afire as well.

What just happened? she wondered. *Was it real?*

She played it all over in her mind, step by step. She had kissed him. How audacious of her! She had never done anything like that before; she'd always been the conservative type who waited to be asked, not the rash kind to take risks. Risk meant the possibility of rejection and she had never wanted that. But somehow, yesterday, she had known that he would never impose on her and that only if she made the first move would anything happen.

Which was odd, bearing in mind what Jesse had said about Richard coming on strong.

She put that out of her mind. It wasn't how it had been. She remembered the magic of that first kiss. It had been so long since she'd touched anyone like that, and as soon as she'd put her hand to his face, and found that the stubble was not coarse but soft, she felt its utter rightness. His mouth on hers had fitted perfectly and once they'd kissed, they were both utterly absorbed by it, lost in the pleasure of one another.

Almost immediately, they'd been carried away. Romy – her heart racing, her skin alive, every nerve tingling – had not felt anything like it since her early days with Theo, before the mind games and manipulation had made all their lovemaking a kind of combat instead of a union.

Kissing Richard, letting her excitement flourish like a new flower opening up to the sun . . . it all felt like something fresh and new, even though it was so familiar – not just to her, but to lovers of all kinds through the ages. It was a primal memory that guided all creatures to follow their instincts, continue in the age-old patterns.

There on the rug, in the sunshine, they had let their bodies and desires guide them, and where they had watched the birds in their rituals, now the birds watched them.

It was much later when they had gathered their things together and walked back to the white house, talking in low voices, hardly able to meet one another's eyes, but when they did, finding a mutual sparkle there. They were half embarrassed and half delighted, trying to find out how they felt, and how the other felt, about what had just happened between them.

Without much discussion, Richard set about making them some supper and they ate it sitting outside in the evening sunshine, over a bottle of cold white wine. When the meal was over, he leaned towards her, took her hand and said intently, 'I want to make love to you again. Will you let me?'

'Yes.' She hadn't even had to think about it.

So they'd gone up to his bedroom, shut away from all the hundreds of eyes that had observed them before. Only Martha watched them go up and she cawed loudly, shaking her tail feathers as they passed her, but Romy couldn't tell whether it was in protest or not.

Now here she was.

In bed with the warden!

She laughed internally at the thought, but then felt a prickle of anxiety. Had she just been the biggest fool in the world? Did he seduce all the girls who came to the island? Maybe Jesse had been right and the woman who complained was just one of the few who said no. After all, no one came here without some sort of issue or vulnerability, surely? It must be a happy hunting ground for Richard.

But no. She thought back over what had happened between them. She started it. It had felt very real. She hadn't dreamed the connection.

What now, though?

She rolled over and stared into the darkness.

She had come here for quiet and work and recovery, and she had barely been here a fortnight. She had weeks to go. This could be extremely awkward.

I shouldn't have done it.

But she had. And now she would have to deal with it. There was nothing to do at this moment, in any case.

She closed her eyes and drifted off to sleep.

She woke in the morning to Richard coming in holding two mugs of coffee.

'Morning,' he said brightly. 'You're awake!'

'Yes.' She yawned.

He put down the mugs and got back in the bed beside her. 'How are you? Are you feeling okay?' He looked at her tentatively. 'I mean, I'm feeling on top of the world. Absolutely amazing. But . . . how do you feel?'

'Okay.' She sat up, pushing the pillows up behind her, and pulling the duvet up around her chest.

'Ah. Only okay.' Richard laughed lightly. 'Fair enough. I'm a bit out of practice.'

'Not about that,' she said quickly. 'That was . . . very, very nice. You know it was.' They exchanged shy smiles. 'I mean, I feel okay. I'm not feeling like I regret it. But it is also a thing. And I'm not sure where it goes from here.'

He took her hand and raised it to his lips. 'Let's not overthink it or rush it. It was lovely. We can be glad about it. There's no pressure from me.' He let go of her hand and passed her a cup of coffee. 'I was thinking this in the kitchen and so I'm going to say it now. Please don't think I'm expecting anything. I'm not. You've got weeks more on the island, and you have your work and everything you need to do. I'm not going to be hassling you in any way. Okay? Your time is your own. Whatever happens next, if anything . . . well, it's organic. You decide. You've come into my life like a little beam of beautiful light and I'm just happy you've shone on me for an instant. I'm not expecting anything more.'

She sipped her coffee, feeling happy. Looking up at him over the rim, she smiled.

'Thanks,' she said. 'That sounds just perfect to me.'

Romy didn't stay for breakfast but went back to Clover Cottage, delighted to be back in her own space, but also feeling elated and energised. Her body was enjoying the unaccustomed feeling of being held and caressed.

Basically it's been given a thorough and very satisfactory seeing-to, she thought with a smile. After a bath and some breakfast, she went back to her desk. When she stopped working, it was well after lunchtime and she was ravenous. She went to the kitchen to get something to eat and saw a message on her phone. It was from Jesse.

Hey, did you survive the storm? Hope you're doing well. The sun is out, and I'm finishing work in a couple of hours. Howzabout I zoom over with some beers and that curry and we watch the movie?

Romy looked at the message, feeling uneasy. She knew that Jesse would not be at all pleased at what had transpired between her and Richard. It was none of his business, but that made no difference. He would still be unhappy. There was no need to tell him, but even so. He had seen them together in the car, she was sure of it, when they'd passed him in the pick-up truck, although he'd said nothing about it now. She might not be in any kind of relationship with Richard but she was still reluctant to do anything with anyone else right now and she had to admit to herself that Jesse very likely had some intentions towards her. It wouldn't be right to lead him on with anything that could be construed as a date. A suggestion of a cosy night in with a movie was not hard to read.

And then there was the fact that Jesse wasn't working for the island tours outfit after all. She couldn't entirely remember what he had previously said about it, and perhaps she had misunderstood him, but he definitely hadn't mentioned falling out with the boss and not giving back the keys to the boats, let alone running renegade tours for film buffs to St Elfwy.

Or did he hint at all this, and I didn't understand? He said that he did film tours, I just assumed they were part of his other job. But maybe all along he's been telling me what he's doing and I just misunderstood . . .

She would need to ask him outright but the prospect wasn't appealing. She had a feeling he wouldn't like her finding things out about him, and that in itself was troubling. She thought for a while as she made herself some soup and then, sitting down at the little table with her lunch, she wrote back:

Hi, all is good here. To be honest, I'm not really up for a movie. I'm doing a lot of work and I'd like to carry on. But we can maybe meet up in town for a coffee or something? I need to do some shopping at some point.

There was a long pause and then a message flashed up. It was one word.

Okay.

She looked at it for a moment, disconcerted. Then she pushed the phone away. She'd been polite but she'd said no. There was nothing wrong in that. Even if she gave Jesse the benefit of the doubt over the boat quarrel, she had a feeling it might be better to keep him at arm's length.

In the afternoon she went for a walk around the island, drinking in the beautiful sunshine and glorious views. The birds were as excited as the day before and she felt a kind of kinship with them now. Soon the eggs would be appearing, and then the chicks.

No worries about a chick for me, she thought with an inner chortle. She had an implant that made sure of that, even if Richard had not taken precautions.

On her way back, she saw him out with his binoculars, noting down observations in a book. She went over to say hello and when he saw her, she was touched to see that he flushed pink with pleasure.

'I'm trying to spot our banded birds,' he said when she reached him. 'They're the ones that we monitor for our base information. There are too many to band, but I'll get as many chicks as I can when the time comes. We can track them all over the world now.' He closed his notebook. 'I'm just about done for the day. Fancy coming back for a cup of tea?'

'Yes . . . lovely.'

'Great.'

They went back to the house, chatting easily, although with the tingling undercurrent of what had happened between them always present. It was not spoken of, though, at least not yet.

Richard began to make tea for them in the kitchen and Romy asked if she could go through to the sitting room. 'You've got a piano through there, haven't you?'

'Sure, go ahead. Do you want to play it?'

'I can never resist a piano.'

'I thought we might sit outside when the tea's ready – unless it's a bit warm.'

'Lovely. Call me when you want to go outside. I don't think it's too warm, it's balmy out there.'

She wandered into the hallway, still feeling a frisson when she saw the gothic mirror from the film, and went to the sitting room. The piano was there against the wall and she went over, and pulled out the stool from under the keyboard to sit on. Lifting the lid, she looked at the very yellow keys, then picked out a few notes. They were very twangy and out of tune. No one had looked at this instrument for a long time, she suspected, and, like everything else on the island, the sea air had no doubt taken its toll.

But she had remembered only that morning how apparently Grey Oswald and Jack Bannock wrote their musical here and it had occurred to her that they might have

431

composed it on this very piano. And if they composed here, then there was a chance, perhaps a faint one, that Jack wrote 'The Last Song of Winter' on it. That would be amazing. And so far as she knew, she was the only one who had put the pieces together and come up with all these connections. She was sure there was something more to find out, something here in this house, though how she would find it, she had no idea. Romy played a short piece from her childhood piano lessons, but the piano was so discordant that it sounded awful.

It certainly sounds like it hasn't been played since the 1940s.

On impulse, she stood up and tried to lift the lid of the piano stool but it was locked.

Just then, a loud caw broke through the air, and Romy shrieked, jumping violently. Martha was staring at her balefully from the perch in the corner.

Richard shouted from the kitchen, 'Is that you, Martha? Come here, you naughty girl, and stop scaring Romy!'

Martha stared for a moment longer and then flapped up off the perch and flew out of the room to find Richard.

'Oh my god!' Romy said out loud. 'I nearly had a heart attack!'

She left the piano and walked slowly back up the hall towards the kitchen, wondering what was in all the other rooms that she hadn't yet seen. Stopping outside the door to the lavatory corridor, she paused and then called, 'Just nipping to the loo.'

'Okay!'

432

She went down the hall and used the loo, and then coming back, she stopped again. These photographs were fascinating to her. She would love more time to look at them. She had examined her film of them, only to find that her hand had been shaking at times and some of them were out of focus.

I'll do it again, she decided, and got her phone out. She was less anxious now, even if Martha had just sent her adrenaline levels shooting up, which meant she would be steadier. She started at the photos closest to the loo and carefully filmed them, walking slowly up the hall, doing the lower ones on her first pass and the higher ones on the way back. Her attention was pulled to a black-and-white photograph from the 1930s of a beautiful woman, with polished black hair, a flawless face and ropes of pearls around her neck. She gazed straight into the camera with a candid, open, yet direct look that showed a strong character and, Romy suspected, a stubborn streak as well.

Who is that? she wondered and went to have a closer look. *She's absolutely stunning.*

I need another picture of this one, a proper one. It's obviously a professional studio portrait.

She stood in front of it, carefully positioning her phone to minimise the reflection from the glass, and turned off her flash to prevent it obscuring the photograph before getting ready to take the picture.

'What the hell are you doing?'

Romy gasped and turned to see Richard standing in the doorway. She dropped her phone down guiltily.

'Are you taking photos of the pictures on the wall?' he

433

said coldly. His green eyes had turned as chilly as they were that first day he had shouted at her. 'Because that's what it looks like. There aren't many explanations for why you would do that. And they are all bad.'

She stared at him, unable to say anything, feeling miserable and guilty.

'Well, Romy? I'm waiting. Because if it isn't good, then I want you out of here, and off this island. Right away. Do you understand?'

PART FIVE

Chapter Twenty-Four

VERONICA

Veronica and Grey couldn't get a passage together for the journey home so arranged to meet in London. From there, Grey would pick up his car and motor out with Veronica to the far coast of Wales, where the boat would be waiting to take them across to the island, weather permitting. It was becoming wintery again, when crossings were less reliable and more uncomfortable, when visitors were likely to be stranded for days at a time, just as André had been.

'I had better not get stuck on that rock,' Grey warned as they climbed into his Daimler in Belgravia. 'I won't have it, you understand!'

'I understand.'

They drove west from London towards Bristol, and then, with the weather still fair, they took the Aust Ferry across the Severn into Wales and set off again towards the far west coast of Pembrokeshire.

On the way, Grey told her something of what had happened.

'It didn't work, you know, Veronica. To work together.

Jack doesn't think like me, and I don't think like him. It's not a criticism, it's just how it was. Jack agreed with me. In one way it worked, and in another way it didn't. I knew by the end of *The Seahorse* that we would never write anything more together. He simply loved his hearts and flowers too much. Violets here, violets there, violets bloody everywhere. I like my acid. My slices of lemon. My cruelty and cynicism. That is how I am. And after that I began to sense that Jack is not well. He really isn't. I am many things, but I am not mentally weak. If anything, I am too strong. Too strong and selfish for most people, almost for myself. And, you see, I can't bear people loving me too much, relying on me too much. I don't like it at all. It's fine if they are supplying me with what I need – which is, you won't be surprised to hear, adoration – but if they become needy and desperate, I can't love them any more. That's all there is to it.'

Veronica listened aghast, looking at his stony profile as he watched the road. She'd had no idea that Grey knew himself so well and was so capable of understanding his own actions. 'So you stopped loving him because he loved you too much?'

'No, no,' corrected Grey, his gaze sliding across to her from the road and then back. 'Because he *needed* me too much. It's quite different.'

'I see. Oh dear.'

'But perhaps I could have stood it if Vincent hadn't come along. You haven't met Vincent. Oh, he's nothing compared to Jack. Second-rate. Not very good-looking. Not beautiful and talented and a magnet for every man and woman in the

438

world, like Jack is. Not my equal at all, except for one thing. He is as selfish and ruthless as I am. He is prepared to devote his iron soul to my needs and give me exactly what I want without asking for anything for himself – nothing emotional, I mean. As long as I provide for his wants.'

'What are they?' Veronica asked faintly.

'Money, mostly. A career, up to a point. But I can't work miracles. And a glamorous life enjoying what I enjoy – good food, fine wine, travel, luxury, mixing with high society. Success, in other words.'

'It sounds very empty. Your relationship, I mean.'

'Oh, it is. But it's safe. I get the full force of all his attention – and I mean, *all* of it – while having to give nothing at all to him. It is less pleasant than what I shared with Jack. But it is much less trouble.'

'That isn't really all it is, is it?' Veronica asked in dismay. This was more desperately sad than she had guessed. She'd hoped it was a misunderstanding, or a quarrel or a simple falling out of love. But the idea that it was because Grey was too selfish to love was terrible. She thought of Jack eating his heart out for the sake of someone who had discarded him so easily, and she wanted to weep.

'No, that's not all.' Grey drove on in silence for a while and then said, 'I told you, Jack isn't well. I can't cope with it. I'm sorry, but I can't. And then there is his hopelessness with money. He was helping himself to far more of our *Seahorse* royalties than were his. Oh, he probably didn't know. He would have given back whatever he owed, I'm sure. But I hated that incompetence. The petrol coupons were the same thing. Anyone would have guessed that it was illegal to take someone else's coupons, but not Jack. Too innocent, too silly, too thoughtless. I can't have that kind of liability on my hands. I just can't. I fully intend to be knighted one of these days. What if it's discovered that Jack and I were lovers? He's just the sort to give it away, to anyone who asked. And how could I be partners with a man who's been to prison, who has a criminal record? Business or otherwise. I can't. You must see that.'

Veronica stared at the road ahead as it disappeared under the wheels of the Daimler. Suddenly she feared she was doing entirely the wrong thing. She had once dreamed of a reconciliation but now she saw that not only was that impossible, but it would not be at all in Jack's interests. He wasn't tough enough for someone like Grey. She could only hope that a kind resolution, an explanation, would do the job and help Jack find peace. Grey was insistent that Jack wasn't well. Perhaps he wasn't. He had certainly suffered from Grey's treatment, but it was possible there had been something wrong before that. Although no doubt he could get better, and this farewell must surely help? At last she said, 'You will be gentle, won't you?'

'Of course,' Grey said. 'I want to see him one last time. You don't need to worry. I won't be cruel.'

They drove on for hours, stopping for coffee and buns, then pressing onwards so that they could make the crossing to the island before dark, all being well. They made good time, and arrived at the boat with over an hour of daylight left.

Grey parked the Daimler safely out of the way and covered it with a tarpaulin. Jim was waiting with the motor boat, which was going to be far faster than the sailing boat and oars he'd had to use for most of the war. They were able to sit in the little cabin to keep warm and dry during the short journey.

'Does Jack know we're coming?' Grey asked, sinking his chin into his scarf.

'I think so. I did send a card after you'd said you'd come. It all depends if it arrived.' She shivered. 'I wish I'd brought my furs.'

Grey looked apprehensive. 'I am beginning to wish that I didn't come after all. I hope this wasn't a terrible mistake.'

'I'm sure it wasn't,' Veronica said heartily but secretly she was wondering the same.

Jim had tied up the little craft so that they could disembark and Grey was offering his hand to her from the jetty when she caught sight of Jack coming down the path from the house towards them. He was wrapped in a large black astrakhan coat with a red leather hat that strapped under his chin to prevent it from being blown away, but even in this odd outfit, he was still unmistakeably Jack Bannock, the handsome heartthrob and star of the stage and screen. Looking up at him, Grey's face softened. For a moment, Veronica's heart lifted in hope, but then she remembered what Grey had said in the car. It was so uncompromising and so clear. There was no way he would take Jack back and that was no doubt best after what he had said.

'Hello, my dears!' called Jack, waving as he approached

441

them. His eyes were sparkling and his cheeks were glowing pink. 'Hello, Jim, my old love. Thanks for bringing my pals over the water. Inside, everyone, the wind is coming up!'

When he reached them, he landed smacking kisses on Veronica's cheeks and then on Grey's. Grey was admirably relaxed, accepting the kisses as if completely normal and as though he and Jack had parted only a short time ago on the best of terms.

'Jack, how lovely to see you. How are you?'

'Can't complain,' Jack said brightly, thrusting his hands deep in his pockets. 'Enjoying myself on my ownsome. Come on, come on!'

The next moment, they were going into the familiar old house.

'Daisy has done us dinner!' Jack said. 'I told her to make something nice. She's gone back to the cottage now. It's jolly useful having her around. You're an angel to sort her out, Veronica.'

'I'm very glad she's helpful,' Veronica said, taking off her gloves. She noticed the half-empty bottle of whisky and the sticky glass beside it on the kitchen sideboard.

'More than helpful, I depend on her. Now!' Jack rubbed his hands together as Grey took off his coat and hat. 'What shall it be? Tea? Wine? Something stronger?'

Grey had already lit a cigarette. 'I say, a scotch would be just the ticket.' He had obviously also seen the bottle on the side. 'Shall we go through to the sitting room and have it there? Let's be civilised, while we can.'

'Of course,' Jack said. 'You go, I'll bring the drinks.'

Veronica and Grey went through to the sitting room and Grey set about stoking up the fire into a nice blaze, adding more coal and driftwood to set it burning and crackling.

'He's drunk,' Grey said bluntly. 'I know the signs. I'm afraid, my dear, that this was a bad idea.'

'You're probably right,' Veronica said miserably. She should have come alone, she saw that now. 'But let's be kind. It's all we can do.'

At that moment, Jack came in with a tray, his cheeks more hectic than ever, and, Veronica noticed, the level in the whisky bottle a little lower than before.

'Well, how nice this is!' Jack set down the tray and began to pour out the measures of scotch. 'I had no idea I'd be entertaining like this until yesterday. I'm rather rusty. Forgive me if I'm very bad at it.'

'You're wonderful, dear,' Veronica said, smiling up at him and accepting the glass of whisky he offered.

'How are you, Jack?' Grey had sat down in an armchair and was lighting another cigarette. 'I was so sorry to hear about your mother.'

Jack handed him a glass of scotch, his gaze flicking over him. 'Yes, the poor old dear. Far too young. But there. I wish you'd met her. That was the plan, do you remember? But it never happened.'

'A great shame. My condolences.'

'And Vincent, does he send condolences?'

There was a pause as the atmosphere turned to ice. Then Grey said in a voice of forced lightness, 'Of course he does. He's very fond of you.'

'Oh, I don't think so.' Jack sat down on the opposite end of the sofa to Veronica. 'He was never fond of me. In fact, he hated me, and he drove us apart.' He looked full on at Grey for the first time, now with a look of defiance as though daring Grey to respond. 'Don't you remember we were supposed to come to Wales, to see where I grew up? Instead, you sent Vincent to meet me, to take me for lunch and to break the news that you never wanted to see me again. I call that cruel, Grey. Don't you? Didn't you owe me a little more than that after all our years together?'

'I probably did.' Grey concentrated on tapping the ash from his cigarette.

'Well, did you?'

'I did.' Grey shrugged. 'But that's in the past. I can't change it. I'm sorry if I disappointed you.'

'It wasn't disappointment, it was devastation.'

'Like I say, I'm sorry.' Grey's voice was curiously flat and unaffected.

Does he mean it? Veronica wondered. She could feel Jack's misery and anger coming off him like an energy. But the more he seemed to glow with his emotions, the flatter Grey became.

'Wasn't I worth more?' Jack persisted.

Oh, don't, Veronica begged silently. She suddenly saw that Jack would never get what he wanted. Grey, she felt, was almost enjoying the game of raising his hopes and dashing them. She was sure that Jack had expected penitence, and perhaps a desire to make reparation. Why else would Grey make the grand journey to the island? And yet, she could now understand, Grey never meant that at all. In her heart, she feared that in fact Grey was relishing this opportunity to drive the blade home, to make sure of his power over Jack. *Does he hate Jack?* she wondered. But no, it wasn't that. It seemed more complicated and nuanced.

He doesn't hate him. Any more than he loved him. It is all about what Jack does for him. And by collapsing, Jack is doing something even more wonderful than loving him. He is proving Grey's power over him. That's why Grey came. To see his power in action.

She felt horrified. She had brought Grey here believing he felt pity for Jack, and a desire to be kind. Now she felt sick with the fear that she had enabled Jack's worst enemy to come here to make him suffer.

She looked over at Jack, who was still waiting for a reply. 'Wasn't I worth more?' he repeated. 'Than that?'

This wasn't the way, Veronica could see that. Begging for reassurance and value from Grey could never work.

Grey coughed lightly. 'Of course, my very dear Jack. You were worth far more and I was a rat, quite simply a rat. You've found me out. You're better off without me, if you didn't guess.' He stood up and stubbed out his cigarette, then wandered to the piano. He sat down and began to play the music that was on the stand. 'Ah, "The Last Song of Summer". Very nice. One of your best, my dear.' He played a few bars, humming along.

Jack was staring at him, his face a rictus of agony. Veronica looked at him, her own heart bleeding at the sight of his pain.

'Jack . . .' she said, reaching a hand towards him. He glanced at her and for the first time, she saw the liquid chocolate eyes hard and bitter.

'Veronica . . . perhaps you'd better leave us.'

She looked at him imploringly. 'Are you sure?'

'Yes. Grey and I need to talk and we need to do it without you. Would you mind checking on the dinner? Daisy left it in the range.'

She stood up. Grey was still absorbed in the piano. 'Of course. Take all the time you need.'

She went through to the kitchen, feeling quietly desperate.

Veronica remained in the kitchen of the white house, keeping the stew bubbling away while she waited for Grey and Jack to finish their talk. She heard voices raised and then lowered. She even heard laughter, quite a lot of that. She heard music too. Grey's unmistakable piano-playing and his light but enunciated voice. She heard Jack's honeyed tones, and the ripple of delicate melodies that marked his compositions. It was mystifying. She had expected storms and tears, but not this.

What on earth are they doing? she wondered, pacing the kitchen. Glad she had brought cigarettes, she puffed on several herself, trying to calm her nerves, wondering how long she could keep the potatoes from disintegrating entirely.

And then suddenly, the sitting room door opened and Grey and Jack came bustling into the kitchen, their demeanours quite changed. They were full of energy and excitement.

'Well, I think it will make a wonderful show!' exclaimed

446

Jack, taking his place at the kitchen table. 'Sorry we've been so long, darling! But we're both starving.'

'It's a marvellous idea,' Grey declaimed, also sitting down.

Veronica stared at them both, astonished. Had there been a reconciliation? 'This sounds very exciting!' she said merrily. 'What have you decided?'

'We're going to work together again,' Jack said, his cheeks flushed and his eyes bright. 'We're going to write a wonderful musical!'

Veronica was flooded with relief. It was going to be all right after all. 'Oh, that's marvellous. What is it about?'

Grey and Jack exchanged excited looks. Grey said, 'It's a daring concept. It's set here, but in the original monastery. There are two timelines. It's a love story – concealed, of course – and a story of rebellion against tyranny. It's going to be beautiful.'

Jack smiled at him. 'So very beautiful.'

Veronica hurried about, getting the supper on the table, as Grey said, 'You will be so excited by it, darling. We want you to help as well, of course.'

'Here's the thrilling thing,' Jack said. 'In the present day, our lovers will sing "The Last Song of Summer". They are the girl and boy, of course. But in the past, our monks will sing their chant – almost the same song, but like a psalm, the key more melancholy. And with altered words, of course. It will be called "The Last Song of Winter".'

Veronica clapped her hands. 'That's superb! What a brilliant idea.'

'I do like the sound of that, Jack,' Grey said. 'Have you written that one yet?'

'No, not yet. But it's coming. I can feel it.'

Veronica scooped out stew and potatoes onto plates. They had somehow rescued victory from the jaws of defeat. She put the food in front of them, and they both began to eat heartily, still talking about their wonderful idea and all it would bring them both.

Veronica watched in wonder. There was no sign of the brittleness and resentment of earlier. Now, all was joy and collaboration.

'Will you write our script, Veronica?' asked Jack.

She looked over at Grey. 'Well, Grey is more than capable . . . he has dozens of hits to his name.'

'I can always use some more help,' Grey said solemnly. 'I'm not perfect, though it pains me to admit it.' He smiled, showing his small teeth. 'I would welcome your help.'

Veronica leaned back in her chair, smiling broadly with relief. 'I can't tell you how happy this makes me, boys. It's like old times.' She lifted her glass to them. 'Here's to you both!'

'Here's to us all!' Jack declaimed.

'Hear, hear,' said Grey, knocking glasses with him.

Just then, Jack's face tensed. 'Do you hear that?' he asked.

Veronica frowned, listening out. 'Do you mean the wind?'

It had leapt up and was howling around the house.

'No,' Jack said impatiently. 'Not that. The singing! Can't you hear it?'

Grey and Veronica swapped swift glances and both listened hard.

'I can only hear the wind,' Grey said decisively.

'The same,' Veronica said, looking over at Jack.

He looked confused and then smiled. 'Well, good. I thought I was hearing something. I'm obviously not.'

'You need to listen to the music in your mind, not the wind,' Grey said. 'Shall we go back to the piano? I'm eager to get to work!'

'Yes.' Jack stood up, smiling. 'Back to work!'

After supper, Veronica tidied up, listening to the hubbub of talk, piano and singing emanating from the sitting room. The visit had not been a mistake after all. Instead, it was another creation. They were like the male seahorses who give birth, she thought with an inner laugh.

When all was done she was exhausted, but she stood outside the sitting room door, smelling Grey's pungent cigarette smoke from within, and hearing their chatter about choruses and rhymes, and turned and went up to bed, taking her bedtime oil lamp with her.

It was a grey and milky dawn when Veronica woke to the sound of knocking on her bedroom door and Grey's voice. 'Veronica, wake up. Wake up, can't you?'

She scrambled out of bed, pulled on her dressing gown and opened the door. Grey stood there in his pyjamas, his face drawn and eyes worried. 'What is it?'

'Jack's gone,' he said briefly.

She knew at once that this wasn't right. Anxiety prickled all over her. 'Has he gone for a walk?'

'At this hour?'

'Perhaps not.' There was not even the excuse of Boris now; he had been adopted by a farmer's wife during the war when Veronica had moved away. She'd known he would never have been happy in the city, much as she missed him. 'But what else could he have done? Taken the dinghy back to the mainland?'

'Get dressed,' Grey said. 'We'll have to look for him.'

'Why did he go out, Grey?'

'I have no idea. Get dressed. I'll see you downstairs.'

A few minutes later, in their stoutest clothes and boots, they met in the kitchen. Veronica was mystified and anxious. Grey was holding a sheet of music in his hands.

He said, 'I've just been to make sure he wasn't sleeping in the sitting room. I thought he might have slipped down to carry on working and then passed out on the sofa or something. There was only this, on the table. It wasn't there last night.'

Veronica took the paper he was holding out. It was a completed version of 'The Last Song of Winter' and at the top was a scrawled sentence:

Darling Grey, for you, for always. Jack x

'This is good,' Veronica said in relief.

'Is it?' Grey replied curtly.

'Well . . . yes . . . isn't it? A gift for you. He wants you to be together always. Now that you're reconciled.'

'But we're not.'

'But I thought . . .' Veronica looked at him, bewildered. 'You're not? What about last night? . . . The musical, the songs . . . You were getting on so well . . . and you spent the night together in the same room . . .'

'Yes, yes, but there was no question of our resuming our affair. Jack knew that. I was very clear. That was over.'

A dark foreboding began to rise within her. 'When did you say this?'

'I made it clear,' Grey said impatiently.

Veronica sensed a certain fear in his manner, a desire to be setting the record straight already. 'But when precisely was it made crystal clear? Before you started writing the musical – or after you went to bed?'

'What is the point of these questions?' Grey said testily. 'Hadn't we better get on with looking for him?'

Veronica pulled on her hat, her sense of foreboding getting stronger. She knew that she had her answer. She had been right the first time, and horribly mistaken the second, when she had thought everything was restored.

Oh, Jack. The last twist of the knife. To raise your hopes and dash them again. I bet he did it so easily and so casually too. Tears and apologies and regret might have helped you survive it. But he wouldn't have done that. The simple careless cruelty, the lack of anything for you to hold on to and treasure . . . that is what destroyed you.

'I think I know where he is,' Veronica said simply and sadly.

She saw in Grey's face that he knew too, but he was

451

resisting it. Perhaps he did have a conscience after all. 'How can you know that? It's ridiculous. We must look everywhere. He's very likely not to have been able to sleep, gone for a walk and slipped. We'll find him on the path with a twisted ankle, desperate for a cup of tea and a warm bath.'

Veronica said nothing. She could guess that Jack had been gone some hours. The torch by the back door was missing for one thing. 'Come on then,' she said. She ought to be frantic and yet somehow she was not. 'We'd better make a start.'

At Grey's insistence, they went to the outbuildings first, leaving the barn where Jim was no doubt asleep on his driftwood bed, and looked inside. There was no sign of him.

'You know where we should go,' Veronica said urgently. 'I'm not going to waste any more time.'

'What are you talking about?' Grey said hotly. 'I have no idea where he is! If you're so sure, you go wherever you want, but I'm going to walk the island. He's probably up by the ruins, having tripped over a rock or something.'

Veronica stared at him, suddenly furious. 'How can you be so pig-headed?' she shouted. 'You know very well! If he's still alive, we need to find him quickly! If I didn't think better of you, I'd suspect you're delaying on purpose!'

Grey gasped, outraged. 'How dare you, Veronica? How could you say such a thing of me? I wish I'd never seen you at that dinner party, let alone agreed to come on this ridiculous errand to help a washed-up old has-been, a convicted criminal and a miserable soak!'

'So that's how it will be,' Veronica said grimly. She wasn't afraid of Grey. She could see everything clearly now. 'You acted out of the goodness of your heart? I don't believe you. You came here to torture him one last time, to see if you could exert your power over him if you wished. And you could. You gave him hope – of a brighter future, a new career, a musical renewal. And perhaps even of love. Then you snatched it all away again, but worse this time. You didn't come here to do your best, you came to do your worst. And you have succeeded.'

Grey's face twisted in indignation. 'How dare you?' he shouted again. 'I won't listen to these dreadful accusations! It's lies, all of it. All of it!' He stormed away, heading up the slope of the island.

Veronica turned and went quickly down to the beach, where her dinghy had been pulled high up and out of the way of the autumn tides. She uncovered it, and dragged it down the sandy shingle to the water, then jumped in and pushed away with her oars until she was deep enough to row. The sea was unusually calm, the waves docile little things running into shore with light foamy tops, and she rowed easily enough around the island, venturing into deep water to row around the rocky outcrops at the south-eastern edge. A few minutes later, she was coming round to the stacks and towards the cave. The last time she had made this journey, she had been searching for the wrecked Halifax. Now she was looking for Jack.

She pulled around so that she was approaching the great arched caves, the natural cathedral that lay beneath the island where the monks had sat on their rock, sang their hymns and prayed for deliverance. Feeling frightened for the first time, she stopped rowing and looked over her shoulder to the rock in the middle of the cave. There was no one there. She didn't know whether to be pleased or miserable. In an ideal world, Jack would have been sitting there, cold and wet no doubt, but safe, waiting for her to arrive in her little boat. Perhaps he would even have been singing in that beautiful voice of his, which always took on its original Welsh lilt when he was on St Elfwy. She could hear him now, lifting his voice in 'The Last Song of Summer', the way he had on the day of Daddy's funeral.

With a sudden onslaught of grief, she knew she would never hear Jack's voice again. He had not been able to take the last blow that Grey had handed him. He was already broken, and then he shattered. She began to weep. The boat drifted with the waves into the cave and she pulled the oars in, crying hard now, letting it go where it wanted.

Despite being almost blinded by tears, she saw the dark shape floating face down in the cold dark water at the back of the cave.

'Oh, Jack, Jack.' She was sobbing bitterly now, reaching a hand towards him. 'My darling Jack. It's over now. Just like you wanted. No more pain.'

Chapter Twenty-Five

The funeral for Jack Bannock was enormous. It featured on all the newsreels and several of his songs went into the hit parade again, on both sides of the Atlantic. The great and good of the stage and screen turned out to pay their last respects to one of their own.

Everyone had expected that. But no one quite expected the great tide of people who came, bearing bunches of violets, to stand in solemn silence outside the crematorium, watching as the hearse, decked in flowers, pulled up before it. The white coffin, covered in wreaths, was carefully lifted out to a sigh of sadness from the watching crowds, and carried into the chapel. Thousands, from all sections of society, thronged the chapel grounds, listening to the service as it was relayed to them by loudspeaker, and more were in the streets beyond, some climbing on walls for a better view. They placed their violets and other bunches of flowers – lilies, roses and lilac – in great banks along the chapel walls and the hedges that surrounded the ground. Many faces were etched with grief, some impassive, others solemn.

The words of the chaplain echoed across them. 'He helped us through our darkest days with music and laughter and song. He gave us words of hope. He reminded us of a better life, and renewed our faith in love.'

Veronica, inside the chapel, found it deeply moving. Whatever Jack had done, he had been forgiven. If only he could have known how deeply he was loved and what a legacy he had left. She bowed her head as the organist played 'A Vale of Violets' in a melancholy key and Jack's coffin disappeared from view.

Grey was not there. She had guessed that he wouldn't be. She had only seen him once more after their words on the morning of Jack's death, when he walked down to the jetty with his bags so that he could be taken to the mainland. She knew he had to be interviewed by the local police in order to give a statement, but that had been the end of his involvement in Jack's death. It had not even made the news reports that he had been there the night before. It was accepted by all that Jack had drowned himself while the balance of his mind was disturbed. His behaviour in the preceding weeks made that all too likely.

And that is what happened, she reminded herself. *Grey didn't actually kill him.*

But in her mind, she found herself thinking all the time that Grey had killed Jack. He might not have planned anything so wicked, but in effect, he had destroyed Jack for the sake of his own vanity. She could say nothing about it, not even to Billie, who accompanied her to the funeral that day and who dabbed away tears as the coffin slid out of sight.

She would say nothing, Grey didn't have anything to fear about that. But she could never forgive it. Never.

Now, she thought, as she took a taxi to Victoria, *I have to think about forgiving myself.*

The guilt over what had happened to Jack was frightful. Rightly or wrongly, she felt that she had somehow brought about his heartbreak.

I will make it up to you, Jack, I promise.

In her suitcase was the final composition of his life: the music and words of 'The Last Song of Winter'.

Somehow, she would make it his legacy.

In her study in Paris, Veronica was searching in her attaché case for something when she found the slim ivory-coloured volume that she'd taken on her voyage out to England, meaning to read it. Somehow she hadn't started it after all, always distracted by something else.

Since that awful visit to St Elfwy with Grey, her grief for Jack had blocked all thoughts of Irène from her mind. All her time and attention had been taken up with dealing with Jack's death and making the arrangements for his funeral, while also doing all she could to help his grief-stricken father. As a result, she had stayed in England far longer than she intended as there had seemed little point in going back to Paris in the interim. She was surprised and moved to find that, apart from a legacy for his father to take care of him into old age, Jack had left all his estate to her. All his rights and royalties would be hers.

It took no time for her to decide that she would dedicate

any income from these rights to St Elfwy and its preservation. The money would support the island and protect its wildlife and natural habitats for as long as it continued to flow. At some point, she would set up a trust of some sort to govern the island and its astonishing birdlife, in honour of the spirits of those she loved who had gone and who she still somehow imagined as birds: Daddy, Mama, Irène and Jack.

More than that, she now owned the copyright to all of Jack's plays and songs. Strangely, through that, inspiration had come at last. She had taken the eerie idea that had grown from Rupert's play and built a new story around it. This play was almost a ghost story, but it was really about the layers of life that can build over a place over time, with all the many aspects of human experience that occurred there. It was about how the same location could be a place of joy, terror, love and despair. And it was about how love could last beyond death and Jack's beautiful, haunting song formed a musical motif to echo these ideas. The supernatural aspects were allegorical, just as *The Raft* had been, and she was certain that audiences would feel the truth of it. It encompassed the grief, fear and despair of existence, as well as its beauty, but the fear was embodied by malevolent spirits of the past, and beauty only sensed at the last moment, as the heroine realised that she would not survive beyond her time on the island. Nevertheless, it was a tribute to hope and love. Most of all, a final tribute to Jack. She was still working on it, but Billie had promised to read it as soon as it was finished.

Now, she looked at the book that she had taken all the

way to England and back without reading it. How could she have forgotten?

Well, I will just read it now. Right now. There's no time like the present.

Veronica perched her glasses on her nose, sat back in her chair, and began.

The book was short, and Veronica read it over the course of that afternoon, finishing not long before supper. When she closed the cover, she stared out of the window at the soaring chestnut tree, dazed.

She had read it in a whirl of emotion, experiencing the story on several different levels. First, of course, Heurot was a genius, that much was clear. With a deceptively spare style, she had created a rich and layered novel that lived vividly in the imagination. The story was deeply moving for its understanding of human nature, the complexity of personality and motive, and how it was possible to love someone and to hate them at the same time. Minette was an extraordinary character, and her lover was everyone who had ever fallen in love.

But it wasn't these things that had caused such inner tumult in Veronica.

It's unmistakable, surely?

She knew the beautiful Minette and yet . . . also didn't know her. All of her good qualities seemed to be Irène's, from her beauty and charm to her bravery and determination to live life as she wanted. But her faithless aspects? Her ability to betray, and her utter selfishness? Was this Irène too?

Veronica got up and began to pace her study, thinking hard. She was a writer. She knew very well that it was possible to draw on a real character and transform or adapt it for the purposes of fiction. She also knew that it was possible to express deep truths or deep emotions that way. After all, what was her new play, *The Last Song of Winter*, if not an attempt to make Jack immortal, to bring him back from the dead and make him live and be happy again?

Could Heurot have done the same thing for Irène? Or is it something darker?

It would be impossible to be sure.

Veronica picked up the book and her pen. She would read it again tonight and mark everything that reminded her of Irène, to see if the pattern that she discerned really was there, not something she had imagined.

It was easier to read the story the second time, Veronica found, now that she knew the outcome and found the emotional aspect less intense. She had brought the book up to bed with her and now sat propped against her pillows, pen in hand and trying not to get black ink on the sheets.

Now she was reading in a businesslike way, or like a detective, combing the text for all the clues she could.

A bang from outside the room made her look up. It was the front door closing; it sometimes banged like that in a strong wind.

André must be home from that reception at the Élysée.

She was glad she had managed to escape that. The tedium

460

of official functions was something she found increasingly difficult to stand.

A few minutes later, as she'd expected, he knocked on her bedroom door and put his head around. 'Ah, you've retired already,' he said with a smile. His eyes were sparkling, he'd had some champagne. 'May I come and say goodnight?'

'Of course.' She smiled back, put her book down on the side table, and took off her glasses.

He came over and sat down on the edge of the bed, a little stiff and unwieldy in his military uniform. 'How was your evening, *chérie*?'

'Quiet. I've been reading.' She had already decided to say nothing to him about the book and her suspicions. She knew exactly how it would go. He would be unhappy and upset and dismiss what she was saying as the product of her vivid imagination, so unless she had solid proof, she would stay silent.

'Oh? What have you been reading? This, I suppose.' He reached out for the book on her side table. 'The new Heurot. I hear she is very good, though I haven't read her.' He examined the title. '*The Lover of Minette*.' He looked up at Veronica and smiled again. 'Promising! I hope he was a very good one, especially if she only had the one.'

'It's an interesting story,' Veronica replied. 'I'm enjoying it.'

'Good, good.' André opened the book, flicked the pages a little, and then closed it again, staring at the cover. 'A pretty name, Minette.' He seemed lost in thought for a while, and then said, 'I heard it during the war, you know.'

'You did?' she asked, her interest pricking up. 'When?'

André frowned. 'Now, what exactly was it? I do want to remember it correctly . . . You know that the Resistance helped to organise my journey across France and back to England after I escaped that filthy camp I'd been put in?'

'Of course.'

Very occasionally, sometimes when he was drunk and sometimes when he was deeply melancholy, André would recall his wartime experiences and give her glimpses of what had happened to him. The rest of the time, he never referred to them. It might be modesty, or dislike of recalling the stress of the experience, with the death and suffering it encompassed, but it was only in certain circumstances that he would speak of it.

'Did you meet someone called Minette on the way back? Did she hide you, or help you?' Veronica spoke softly, hoping to prod his memory just a little. When his memories came, she always tried to get as much from him as she could, and then write it down later, perhaps for her future children, perhaps for him.

André frowned, staring at the floor and clearly deep in his memories. 'No, I never met anyone by that name. But I do recall, late at night when I was being smuggled from one farmhouse to another, that one of the men helping me muttered in my ear. He said . . . what was it?' His frown deepened and Veronica noticed his fists clench slightly with the effort. 'He said . . . "Minette said to look out for you. She said to take special care of you." Or something like that. I remember thinking, *Well, who is she and why do I need*

462

special care? Then I wondered if perhaps it was a code I did not know. What did it matter? I was taken care of, just like all those who needed help, and I escaped.'

'Yes,' Veronica said carefully, repeating his words over in her mind so that she could remember them as he'd said them. 'That's strange.'

He looked up, his face clearing, and smiled. 'But very long ago. Let's not think of it again. May I come and stay with you tonight, my love?'

'Of course, I would love that.'

He stood up. 'Then I will change out of this wretched uniform and join you.'

Once he had left, she picked up the book and scrawled down the words on the blank pages at the back.

Minette said to look out for you, she said to take
special care of you – André escape 1943/Resistance.

It might mean something, or nothing. But she felt she must remember it.

Veronica strode out of the gate and headed for the Bois de Boulogne, desperate to walk away her agitation.

The morning paper, left on the table by André after he had departed for work, had unexpectedly upset her. On the front page was a large photograph of the serious-looking Marguerite Heurot and a headline announcing that she had been elected to the Académie Française, the most prestigious and exclusive literary body in France.

The Lover of Minette was being hailed as a masterpiece by France's most respected literary critics, and suddenly it was a huge bestseller. All the excitement seemed tied up with a sense that this was a triumph for the nation and a resurrection of its literary might in the post-war world.

The character of Minette had become a byword for seductive beauty, deathly charm and the ultimate faithlessness of women. She was loved and hated in equal measure.

Veronica could not understand why she was so churned up over this. What did it matter? There was all the difference in the world between fact and fiction. Heurot had created an imaginary woman who had aspects of Irène and aspects that were not Irène at all.

Why does it upset me so much?

As she walked, vague answers came. Because Heurot had taken a piece of Irène? Was that it? Or was it because she could have written something true and loving about Irène, and given her an immortality that mattered, the way Veronica was trying to do for Jack?

It's unfair, that's all.

It was also, she realised, jealousy. How many hours had Heurot spent with Irène over her final years? She must have come to know her well. She was the last person to know her that well.

Veronica stopped short in the middle of the street, causing a man behind almost to bump into her. *Perhaps she knows . . . perhaps she knows what happened to Irène. Is it possible?*

She changed direction at once, heading for the river where the little green kiosks sold books and paintings, and at the first one she reached, she scanned the rows of books for what she sought. Then she found it: a book published by Maison Gillarde. She snatched up the volume from the shelf and turned quickly to the copyright pages. There it was. The address she was seeking. She knew the place. It was not so very far from where she was standing. She would go there at once.

'Madame,' said the receptionist on the front desk of the Maison Gillarde publishing house, 'Monsieur Du Crois isn't here and you wouldn't be able to see him if he were, not without an appointment.'

'He would see me,' declared Veronica, still breathless from her stride across town. 'If he knew why.'

'That is not for me to say,' the woman replied, stony-faced. 'But the fact is, Monsieur Du Crois is not here and so you cannot see him.'

'Can you tell me where I can find him?'

'Of course not,' the woman said, affronted. 'That would be most inappropriate! It is bad enough that you want to see him without an appointment!'

Veronica sighed with frustration, but controlled herself. 'Very well. Thank you, madame.'

Outside on the street, she stood and looked about, wondering what she should do now. She was a few streets from the Tuileries and the Louvre, an area she knew well from when she explored it while Daddy was having his meetings in the hotel.

Gasping with a sudden thought, Veronica turned and strode off in the direction of the place she had stayed with Daddy all those years ago.

She knew him at once. He sat at the same table, the one he had occupied with Irène on those carefree afternoons when they had met for coffee or champagne, and she had amused him with her wit and charm. From what she could see, he was still a handsome man, though he looked older than she remembered, and immaculately dressed in a well-cut suit and polished shoes. She went up to him.

'Monsieur Du Crois?'

'Yes?' he said, turning to face her, and she tried not to gasp in shock. A part of his face had been shot away below his left eye, leaving a livid and puckered wound. It had healed badly over the hollow that remained, and now pulled the eye downwards, exposing a red rim. As she looked, he took a handkerchief and gently dabbed it. It must weep all the time, she realised. 'Who are you?'

'Monsieur, good day. My name is Veronica Mindenhall. May I please join you, if I don't disturb you?'

'Yes, if you wish.' He gestured to an empty chair, and frowned. 'Veronica Mindenhall. The author?'

'That's right.' She had used her maiden name on purpose so that he might recognise it.

He smiled, though evidently startled she should suddenly join him. 'I have seen your play, *The Raft*. It was very good. Congratulations. May I offer you tea, or coffee?'

'No, thank you. And I'm very pleased you enjoyed my play. I thought the French translation was excellent.'

'I take it you did not translate it yourself?'

'No, no, I can translate into English well, but not the other way around.' She smiled. 'I'm sure you're wondering why I've joined you. You see, I was a friend of Irène, her young friend from before the war. Perhaps she spoke of me . . .'

Philippe frowned. 'She spoke of her life very little. But now I think of it . . . Wait . . .' He looked astonished. 'But you married her brother! Veronica Mindenhall married Irène's brother André, now so very high up and so successful. You were also Véronique, the little English friend of Irène?'

'Yes,' she said, excited and proud to have been one of the few people Irène spoke of to her lover.

'How strange,' he said in a wondering tone, and dabbed his eye again. 'Well, it is charming to meet you.' He smiled. 'Those of us who knew and loved Irène must stick together.'

'Yes, she can live on in our memories. But . . . you have never contacted André?'

He looked awkward. 'Ah . . . no. It didn't seem appropriate in the circumstances. And out of respect to my wife. It would dishonour her for me to discuss my mistress with someone who is now a war hero and a member of the government, even if he is her brother. But tell me . . .' – Philippe looked suddenly hopeful, the eyebrow above his good eye lifting – 'does André know what happened to Irène? My dear girl. I miss her every day.' He gestured to his drooping eye, and dabbed it again with the handkerchief. 'And now I weep for her every day too, or that's how I like to think of it.'

'We know nothing at all.' Veronica leaned forward, eager to share with him what she had been pondering. 'But one person might. Monsieur, you must have read *The Lover of Minette*?'

'Of course,' Philippe said simply. 'Heurot is the most famous and celebrated author of my company, Maison Gillarde. Who today was announced as a member of the Académie Française. Of course I have read it.'

'And?' urged Veronica. 'What did you think?'

'Quite brilliant.'

'You know what I mean!'

Philippe went still and then took a sip from his demitasse. After he put it down carefully, he said, 'Yes. I know what you are saying.'

'You think so too. It is Irène.'

'Some aspects, undoubtedly. Of course, Irène worked for her, she clearly provided some inspiration. But it is also fiction and that is how I choose to read it.'

'You can see how she feels, monsieur,' Veronica said quietly. 'She felt as we all do. She loved Irène. But you must see what I can see. She also hates her with a passion, a passion violent enough to kill her. At least in the book.'

Philippe took a deep breath, and dabbed his eye. 'I read it once. I tried not to think about it.'

Veronica became suddenly impassioned. As she talked, everything began to make sense; all the things that had bothered her, that had turned over and over in her mind, began to fall into place. 'But don't you see, it is obvious. Everything in the book . . . it could not be written unless she was madly in love with Irène. Do you think Irène would have returned this love?'

'Irène love Heurot?' Philippe gave a bitter laugh. 'Even Irène's talents could not have stretched that far. No one can love that woman. It may not be her fault that she is so unlovable, but she is impossible to reach, almost impossible to like – she makes it her business to be so.'

'There.' Veronica sat back in her chair, staring at Philippe, desperate to make him see what she could. 'There! Irène would never pretend to love. She simply would not. She was the only person who would tell Heurot the truth. What if she told her the truth? That she was a horrible woman no one liked, and that she, Irène, could never love her!'

'She would not be so cruel.'

'Of course not, not those very words. But she would still have told the truth if she were asked. You know that, and so do I.'

Philippe nodded slowly.

'And what if Heurot hated her for this, for the very thing she loved about her? What if she decided that if she couldn't have Irène, no one could?'

'What are you talking about?'

Veronica's mind was whirling over everything she knew, trying to connect things. Last night, André had spoken of a Minette in the Resistance – obviously a code name – who had specifically asked for him to be protected. Surely that might possibly be the woman who had protected him from childhood, who cared most about his safety? Veronica remembered the words Irène had said to her in Paris, and written to her later – that freedom and truth and liberty were worth fighting for and dying for. She had said they must resist these things being taken away. That girlish, feather-brained exterior had always concealed her strength and intelligence. Irène was exactly the kind of person to offer herself to fight the Germans the best way she could: in secret, using brains, stealth and courage.

Minette. The war. The Resistance. The book.

Perhaps Heurot, who loved her, somehow knew Irène's code name and used it brazenly to bring Irène back to life in the pages of her novel. And gave herself away in the process.

'What if Irène had a dangerous secret that Heurot discovered, and so she had the power of life and death over her? And one day, one terrible day, rejected at last and completely by Irène, she decided to use this secret to get her revenge? Monsieur, I believe that I may have proof – or be able to find it – that Irène worked for the Resistance, and helped escaped soldiers cross the country to safety. But she was betrayed. And what if the book you have published is the story of how Irène was loved and then punished for not returning that love?'

Philippe sat very still, staring at the table. A large tear gathered on the rim of his bad eye and began to roll over his wound. He put his handkerchief to his face to dry it away. At last he whispered, 'It can't be true. Surely not.'

'Our great woman of letters, our literary giant . . . perhaps betrayed a Resistance heroine to the Gestapo?'

'No.' Philippe straightened his shoulders and pronounced firmly again, 'No. That didn't happen.'

'I think it did. It makes sense. The novel is the final piece of the puzzle. And now I have said it, I think you believe me.'

He looked straight at her. 'There is no proof. And until there is proof, it is supposition. I beg you, madame, forget this. It cannot bring Irène back. It will destroy Heurot, and my publishing house, and for what?'

'Justice,' Veronica said simply. 'Justice for Irène. Truth for Irène. Recognition for Irène.'

'She is gone,' Philippe said in a broken voice. 'It cannot help her now. I beg you, don't do this.'

Veronica thought for a moment and then said, 'Give me Heurot's address. Arrange for me to see her.'

'Why?'

'Because I want to talk to her.'

'I can't allow that.'

'You must. Here is my deal. If you give me her address, I will go there and I will talk to her. Whatever we say will remain a secret, certainly for as long as she lives. But if you do not allow this, I will find the evidence I need. There will be people who worked with Irène in the Resistance, for I'm sure that's what she did. What's more, Heurot used Irène's actual code name, which was – I'm certain – Minette. A stupid but sentimental thing to do. Once we have these details, then there may be Gestapo papers still surviving that tell us how Minette was betrayed and how she was killed. All of this I will write up as a book and publish.'

'Heurot would sue you.'

'Not if I have the proof. Not if it's true. It would destroy her. Even a whisper of doubt would take its toll. And that would be the justice Irène deserves. Not this travesty . . . It is a monstrosity that Heurot gains wealth and immortality with this book, and the way it portrays our beautiful girl. It is a double monstrosity if she also condemned her to a terrible death.'

Philippe was white-faced, almost trembling. She could see how torn he was. He was with her, emotionally. He wanted that justice for Irène. And yet . . . if it were true . . . the scandal of Heurot's collaboration, her frightful act of revenge and all it would mean for him as well as her . . .

Veronica stared at him, waiting. At last, she said, 'So, Philippe. What will it be? Will you tell me what I want to know, or not?'

Chapter Twenty-Six
ROMY

Romy stood in the hall, staring at Richard's angry face. She had been caught in the act, and she couldn't deny it.

'Did you hear me, Romy? What's the explanation? Because I feel pretty upset right now. I don't want to believe what it looks like.'

'It isn't like that!' she stammered out. 'I promise.'

'Really? Do you know how many requests I get from people who want to come inside this house? Begging and pleading for me to let them in to see where various people got axed or chopped or garrotted by monks' belts or whatever?' Richard's eyes were flashing with anger now. 'I always say no. Always. Because this stuff is private. I can't believe you've invaded my privacy like this.'

She could feel that she was flushed scarlet and her fingers were trembling, her palms prickling with discomfort. He was not entirely wrong, that was the thing that made her feel so awful.

He stared at her, slightly breathless with his indignation,

while she scrabbled for an explanation that would pacify him.

'Well? What are you up to?' he demanded. 'I'm waiting.'

She gazed up at him and saw in his eyes that he desperately wanted to be wrong, to be convinced that she had not wormed her way in here and slept with him under false pretences just to get access to the location of the film he seemed to detest so much. She opened her mouth to make up some explanation that would make him happy, and then she thought, *Just tell him the truth. He deserves that.*

'Can we sit down?' she said, her voice quavering only slightly. 'I want to tell you something. I'll tell you the whole story. From the beginning.'

He hesitated, his anger now mixed with a hurt that pained her deeply. She had done this, when she liked him so very much and he had trusted her completely. 'I don't know . . .'

'Please, Richard, please just listen and if you don't believe me, I'll go today. But give me a chance to explain.'

He frowned. After a moment, he said, 'All right. The tea's ready. We'll sit in the kitchen and you can tell me about it.'

Romy started by telling him how she ended up in the hospital. Throughout her story, he stayed impassive, sipping on his tea from time to time and listening. He asked the occasional question but mostly let her speak.

It was strange to tell such an emotional story into the void like this. She had no clue how he was receiving it, and found it easier to talk to the tabletop or her mug or the bunch of flowers in front of her.

'So then I found myself watching the film. I knew nothing about it, but something touched me. The haunting music, the atmosphere. I don't know. Usually I hate horror but there was something unreal about the horror in this film, as though it didn't really exist, it was all imagined. I watched it over and over and soon I was convinced that the supernatural element was an allegory for grief and that the heroine was not brutally slaughtered at all. I was convinced that she killed herself, under the influence of the violent thoughts in her head. I wasn't alone. Others felt the same.'

She looked up for the first time in a while, and saw Richard staring at her with a strange expression. He was surprised, she could see that. He looked as though he was going to say something, but stopped himself.

Romy took a gulp of tepid tea. 'I got very interested in the whole film, how it was made, and who wrote it.'

'It seems to affect quite a lot of people that way,' Richard said drily.

'Isn't it weird? It really is a cult classic. It obsesses people. And it obsessed me too. I became interested in Veronica Mindenhall, this very proper young lady from a well-off family, who was primarily known for a social comedy that had been a post-war success. And she intrigued me too – her life on this island, the very place the film was set. She didn't live like most of her contemporaries – marrying a Frenchman, retiring to remote Wales, and then writing this famous horror film.'

'She is an interesting character,' Richard conceded.

'But there's so little about her, apart from a memoir written by her daughter which says hardly anything.' Romy decided she wouldn't mention *The Lover of Minette* right now, as she didn't want Richard to have more evidence that she might have been using him to get her hands on Veronica memorabilia. 'Then, quite by chance, I was watching a programme about Grey Oswald.'

'Oh yes?' Richard's eyes hardened again. 'And what did that say?'

'It mentioned someone I'd never heard of – a man called Jack Bannock. He was Grey Oswald's lover. They wrote musicals together, and I think they did it right here on Elfwy! Imagine that. Sir Grey, national treasure, bastion of stage and screen. Writer of the wittiest songs and plays of the twentieth century.'

'And cause of Jack Bannock's suicide.'

Romy looked at him, astonished. 'Really? The programme didn't mention that.'

Richard nodded. 'Jack Bannock died right here. He killed himself in the caves. It's no secret. But not many people care about it, to be brutally honest. They are more excited by some riot of fake blood and a screaming actress than a real man dying down there.'

'Oh no!' Romy said with dismay. 'That's so sad.'

Richard nodded. 'The poor bloke. At least he didn't live to hear what they did to his song.'

'Well, that's the thing. He wrote a song called "The Last Song of Summer" and a song called "The Last Song of Winter" and they are virtually identical, except one is hopeful, if melancholy, and one is utterly miserable. No prizes for guessing which is which.'

'Romy,' Richard said, but with a slightly warmer tone, 'you still haven't explained why you were taking photos of the gallery in the hall.'

'I came here thinking I would write a book about Veronica and how and why she came to write the film, and how it was made.'

'You didn't put that on your application. If you had, you'd never have been accepted. We don't encourage film fans at all.'

'I could tell that from the website. I admit, I did change my project slightly so that the trust wouldn't know what I planned to do – though I would have asked permission retrospectively.'

'Of course,' Richard said, cool again. 'Forgiveness is easier to ask for, they say, than permission.'

'Then I found out about the Bannock connection. And I became fascinated with that too – and you have that picture of Grey and Jack on the wall, and I really wanted to look at it properly, up close, to see them as they were here on Elfwy, while they were in love and composing. And that's why I thought I wouldn't write about the film at all any more, but more about why Elfwy brings such peace and inspiration to people, from monks to authors, actors, composers like Grey and Jack, birdwatchers, and all types of creators and makers. To those who need peace and healing, like you and me.'

Romy looked up properly and saw that Richard's expression had changed again. He looked almost touched.

'That's the book I really want to write,' she said quietly.

'Which, ironically, is pretty close to my application form. And I would never, ever give your pictures away without asking. And I didn't get close to you just to be in the film location – though it was quite exciting in a way. And I certainly didn't sleep with you so I could look at the photographs. I like you. I really, really like you and I'm desperately sorry I hurt you and made you mistrust me. I want so much for you to forgive me.'

Richard breathed out hard, and frowned, clearly torn. Then he looked at her and said, 'But why were you taking a picture of the dark-haired woman?'

'Why?' Romy gazed back at him guilelessly. 'Because she's so beautiful, of course.'

Richard stared at her with an unreadable expression and then suddenly stood up. 'Come on,' he said. 'Let's go for a walk. It's easier to talk outside, I find.'

'All right.' She stood up, relieved to find that he wasn't ordering her off St Elfwy. At least, not yet.

They went out of the house together and began to walk towards the stacks at the far end of the island. The afternoon was dwindling, but still warm and bright. A light breeze played over the island top, ruffling the grass in a friendly way. Despite the warmth, Richard kept his hands in his pockets and walked at arm's length from her. The distance pained her but she still couldn't blame him. She'd broken his trust, even if not in the way he thought. No wonder he was hurt.

As they walked, she looked at the sea. It looked like a tropical lagoon with its marine blue colour, but the Welsh sky above had a deep softness to it, as though to quieten the water down a little and make it remember where it was.

Birds flew and fished and brooded, squawking and singing around the clifftops. Romy took a deep breath and let it out again, tasting salt on the tip of her tongue.

'It's kind of strange that you should have focused in on Bannock,' Richard said at last. 'You're the only one I know who has. He was hugely famous at one point and now, hardly anyone knows him. They can sing a couple of his songs, but they can't name the composer. But he meant a huge amount to Veronica Mindenhall, and she to him. They were very close. When he died, he left her all the rights to his works – songs, musicals, all of it – and that was how she established the trust here. Most of it isn't worth much, but one thing keeps the money rolling in, year after year. It funds the retreats here, the maintenance upkeep, the science, the bills, the wages and all the rest. And that thing is *The Last Song of Winter* – the film, and the song.'

Romy stared at him. How weird. Her stay here was funded by the very thing that had intrigued her so much.

Maybe it was calling me here. It was a comforting thought.

Richard looked back at her over his shoulder as he walked along the narrow cliff path ahead of her. 'If it hadn't been for the film, Jack would be entirely forgotten. And what he earned was nothing to what Oswald made in his lifetime and his estate still makes. His legacy is huge . . . the much loved, much admired knight of the realm. What I'm trying to say is that history doesn't always remember the real heroes. It sometimes remembers the villains.

Sometimes – quite often – the bad guys win. Everyone thinks Grey was wonderful but my grandmother hated him. We weren't allowed to listen to his music, or watch any of his films or plays, until we were grown up and could make our own choices. She said Grey basically killed Jack.'

Romy stopped stock still. 'Wait. What? Your grandmother! But . . .'

Richard stopped walking too and turned to face her. The wind ruffled his white hair, and he scrunched his green eyes against the sunlight. He looked, suddenly, very young. 'I haven't been exactly open with you either. So here's the thing. Veronica Mindenhall was my grandmother.'

She stared at him in astonishment. At last, she stammered out, 'But what's your name then? Mindenhall? No, it can't be . . .'

He shook his head. 'Razinsky. Richard Razinsky.'

Romy frowned. She knew this name and then it popped into her mind. 'Anna Razinsky! The woman who wrote *Memories of My Mother*, Veronica's daughter!'

Richard nodded. 'That's right. My mother. She's still alive if you want to talk to her. I'm sure she'd be happy to.'

'Really?' Romy was still trying to take it all in. 'But you're so reclusive, so private! You won't talk about the movie at all!'

'No, that's not quite right. My grandmother hated the movie because of what it did to her play. The film company bought the rights from her and she signed away all control without realising it. They could do whatever they wanted to her script and still sell it as though she had written it. They took her original play, which was very sad, and slightly ghostly with a beautiful song at its heart, and changed it into a crazy, over-the-top thing that became a laughing stock.'

They were at the far end of the island now, directly facing the stacks, where they had sat on the rug with the binoculars only a few days before. Richard went and sat down in almost the same place, putting on his sunglasses against the glare of the sun on the sea as it moved west. The light was changing to liquid gold as it prepared to sink.

Romy went and sat down next to him, but a little further away than she had the other day. She was still aware that he had not yet forgiven her, even if this revelation was a step in the right direction. She waited until he spoke again.

'The reason we hate the movie so much is because of how much it hurt her,' he said at last.

Romy paused, then said gently, 'It's a classic now, it's had dissertations written about it. Most of her other work has been forgotten and this lives on.'

'She didn't live to see that. All she knew was that Jack had died broken and then was forgotten. Her attempt to rescue him and make him great again failed and failed really dismally. Instead of paying tribute to Jack in the Singing Caves, where he died, people go to see the scene of that gore fest at the end of the movie.' Richard stopped and took a breath. 'Look, I'm sorry. I still get worked up by how much she cared and how little she could do to change things.' He fixed her with a solemn look. 'But you've discovered Jack. And maybe you can help bring him back to where Veronica always wanted him to be – if you really intend to write this book and tell his story.'

'That's quite a lot of pressure,' Romy said in a small voice.

Richard turned and smiled at her. 'I don't mean you have to do this, or even that you can. But you seem to want to. That's the important thing. And I think people may be ready to hear some truths about Grey Oswald despite his national treasure status.'

'I'd be fascinated to research all of it,' Romy said frankly. 'There's a story to be told there.'

Richard nodded. 'There was a lot of sadness in my grand-mother's life. A lot of loss. But there was happiness too. She had this place, after all, and she was able to ensure its sur-vival and its role in protecting the birds here.'

Romy began to realise the implication of what Richard was saying. 'Wait . . . Veronica owned Elfwy, and she was your grandmother, so are you a member of the trust?'

He looked over at her, his eyes invisible behind his glasses. 'I am.'

'So you get a say over what happens here?' She was begin-ning to see why no one interested in the movie ever got a retreat application accepted.

'I get more than a say, I suppose. You see, the island is mine. Veronica left it to me.'

They walked back together towards the eastern side of the island as twilight fell and the breeze grew cooler. When the path branched, one trail leading to Clover Cottage and the other to Cliff House, Romy stopped. 'I suppose this is where we say goodbye,' she said shyly. 'Do you want me to pack and be on my way?'

He took her hand. 'I think you know the answer to that.'

'I'm very sorry I hurt you,' Romy said. 'I really am.'

'I know. I do trust you. I want you to stay.'

Relief and happiness filled her. 'Thank you for forgiving me.'

Richard took off his glasses, his green eyes warm again. 'You're forgiven. And thank you for telling me your story. I was really moved by what you've been through and how you're recovering.'

'I'm nearly there,' she said, smiling. 'The worst is over, I think. But it's cyclical. You can wheel back to the dark times and have to go through it again, and heal again. You just have to keep trying to get better.'

'It's true. And . . .' He gripped her hand a little tighter. 'I don't just want you to stay on the island. I want you to stay with me. Will you?'

She stood there, returning the squeeze of his hand, before she said quietly, 'Yes, please – I would like that very much.'

Everything has changed, Romy thought, as she let herself out of Cliff House the next day. She had left Richard sleeping upstairs and was heading back home, keen to keep working on the new book outline – the one that now had Richard's approval.

I can't believe I was busy getting close to her actual grandson without knowing it, while stumbling on the one connection that meant so much to Veronica herself – Jack.

It feels like fate was busy getting me here as hard as it could. She remembered her thought of the previous day. It tickled her. *Or maybe the island called me.*

The night before, as they lay in bed together, she had asked a little more about his involvement with the island. 'Why don't you tell people that you're the owner? They might be on their best behaviour a little bit more.'

'I prefer not to,' he'd said. 'It just muddies the water. I'm the warden and that's all people need to know. Besides, we usually pick people who are well behaved in any case.'

She could see his point.

He told her about his grandparents, whom he could not really remember together. They had lived very separate lives until his grandfather died in his seventies, some twenty years before Veronica. 'He lived in Paris, working high up in the government. He had a marvellous life really. But after the birth of my mother, Veronica seemed to change a little. She found Parisian life more and more tedious, while my grandfather thrived on it. And I think he started to play around quite a bit.'

'Oh. That must have been hard.' Romy was holding his hand, interlacing his large fingers with her small ones, while his other hand stroked her hair or rested on her shoulder.

'It was more common behaviour then, I think, but Veronica was such a romantic. Love till death, that sort of thing. I don't think she could bear it, and when my mother went off to school in England, she followed and went to live on St Elfwy for good, except for the occasional stay at her London flat.'

484

'That sounds really rather nice.'

Richard nodded. 'It was great for me and my cousins. We spent our summers here, from the time we were babies. This place gets in the blood. Once you're infected, you're never cured of your love for it.'

They lay together in the dark for a while. Outside the nocturnal birds wailed and called.

'It's sad, though,' Romy said after a while, 'that their marriage didn't really last.'

'That might have been partly because there was another sadness that never went away,' Richard replied. 'My great-aunt Irène, Grandfather's sister, disappeared in the war and my mother believed she knew what happened to her. My grandfather just didn't want to know, he refused to listen. That drove a wedge between them. It was pretty sad. But that's how it works out sometimes, I suppose.'

'What did happen to her?'

'I don't know. Another secret. It wasn't spoken of like that. I don't think my mother knew either.'

'Irène is a pretty name in French.'

'She was Russian actually. Irina. She's the woman in the picture you photographed, the dark-haired beauty in the pearls.'

'Really?' Romy recalled the perfect smooth face and almond-shaped eyes. 'She was bewitching.'

'That's what my grandmother said, though she didn't talk about her much. I don't think she knew much of her story, except that when they came to France Irina and Andrei adopted French names. It was completely normal for them, as Russian aristocrats all spoke French like natives. And they slightly tweaked their surnames – because he was Ratzinski and she, a woman, was Ratzinskaya – to become Razinsky. André Razinsky married my grandmother. Veronica Mindenhall. So there you have it.'

'Easy as pie.' She thought for a second. 'But wait, why are you Razinsky, if that was your mother's maiden name?'

'Nothing gets past you, does it, Sherlock? My surname is Fortescue Razinsky, if you must know. My father agreed when I was born that I should carry on my mother's family name as I was the last to bear it, and I have dozens of Fortescue cousins to keep that one going. And I'm glad he did. I like it.' He pulled her close. 'That's enough talk. Come and kiss me again, I'm missing you.'

Romy thought of that now as she walked back from the house towards the cottage, smiling happily to herself as she remembered what it had been like with Richard the night before.

'Looks like you've just had a really lovely cosy night in,' said a voice.

Romy stopped, startled, and looked up from the path to see Jesse standing in front of her. He was dressed as before, in his board shorts, T-shirt and flip-flops, his long brown hair lifted by the wind. But his expression was not the laid-back, smiling one she was used to. Instead, his eyes were cold and he looked annoyed. Romy felt a familiar and unpleasant sense of anxiety – that jittery worry and guilt that she'd upset someone.

'What are you doing here? It's so early.' It was all she could think to say. Inside she was telling herself that she'd done nothing wrong, reminding herself that she didn't need to justify herself or placate him.

'I was just passing,' he said with a shrug. 'You know how it is.'

'Oh, okay. This is private property, Jesse. Are you allowed to just turn up when you want?'

Jesse raised a sardonic eyebrow, crossing his arms as he stood in her way. 'Oh, sorry, do you and your boyfriend get to say who comes here now?'

I thought so. He's jealous. I guess it was inevitable. 'He's not my boyfriend.'

Jesse made a gesture towards the house. 'You're leaving at the crack of dawn. It's obvious you've been there all night.'

Romy paused a moment, wondering how to handle it. He was obviously hurt and disappointed, but he'd just have to get over it. 'To be honest, that's really none of your business.'

Jesse's face darkened. 'Look, you're a great girl. I've tried to be good to you. I helped you when you got here, I warned you about that dickhead Richard. You shouldn't believe anything he says. Honestly, Romy, I just want to help you! I don't want you believing all his lies.'

'What is your problem with Richard?' Romy asked helplessly. "I can't see why you don't like him.'

Jesse sighed and rolled his eyes. 'Haven't you been listening? I told you, he's a creep, he can't be trusted.'

'Well, what about you? You apparently don't work for

the island tours at all and you never said. You let me believe that you did.'

Jesse was silent for a moment, his dark eyes glittering, tense with annoyance. 'All right,' he said at last. 'It's true I've gone freelance. And the reason is that Richard got me sacked out of pure spite, because he hates the tourists and he hates the fact that my tours were so popular. He's got some personal beef about me for reasons I don't understand and to be honest, that hurts. I haven't said anything about it because I didn't want him to look even worse than he is.'

Romy shook her head, confused. 'I don't really understand that.'

Jesse said quickly, 'I just want to be your friend, and more than that, I want you to be on your guard, but you just won't listen.' He stuck his lip out crossly like a petulant child, then said in a sulky voice, 'I've got something important that you should know.'

'Really? What?' She hoped she wasn't showing on her face how anxious she was feeling. Jesse was obviously very worked up about her relationship with Richard and she was still having a hard time working out exactly why. She felt that Richard getting Jesse sacked sounded out of character, but then, he did really dislike those tours and she was sure Jesse would not have hesitated to do as many as he could without bothering with things like permission. Even so, Jesse would just have to get over this upset, and the only way she could think of to help that was to talk calmly and stay firm.

'Okay.' Jesse stood in a half-defiant stance. 'Richard isn't the warden. He's the owner of the island.'

'I know, he told me.'

'He's told you, has he? Well, all right.' Jesse shifted awkwardly, still full of indignation. 'Has he told you that there is no trust? Every application only comes to him and is vetted by him and okayed by him. He already knew who you were when you got here, and all the details of your project and whatever. If you sent in a photograph, he would have seen that too. He probably picked you because he fancied you before you even got here. He might be pretending to be innocent now, but he certainly isn't.'

Romy stared at him now, feeling uncertain. 'No trust?' She remembered Richard's initial lack of interest in her project. Perhaps that was because he already knew about it. And then there was the text to her phone before she'd given him her number. A whisper of doubt sounded in her mind.

'Well, if there is one, it's him, more or less. He's not just some employee. He's the boss. That's what I'm saying.' Jesse could see that something he had said had hit home and he softened immediately. 'Look, you shouldn't trust him, that's all. Don't get too close, too fast. I'm looking out for you. It comes from a good place.'

Romy looked away, not wanting Jesse to see that he had made her feel awkward. 'That's nice of you, but I don't need it,' she said. She turned back in the direction of Clover Cottage. 'I'm going home now, okay?'

'Can I come?' he asked, squinting at her in the morning sunshine, smiling almost shyly. He looked like the Jesse she knew and liked again. 'We could have a coffee or something together?'

Romy sighed. 'I'm sorry. No. I really want to be on my own. Please just . . . leave me alone, Jesse, okay? The more you keep pressing me, the more I really don't want to get pushed into things.'

Jesse looked meek. 'You're right.' He smiled, not quite the megawatt smile that she knew from before, but still with power and charm. 'Sorry if I come on strong. I'm a passionate guy but I act from good motives and, honestly, I'm one of the good ones. You have to believe me.'

'I believe you,' Romy said firmly. 'But I want you to promise me something. Will you promise you won't come over without agreeing with me or Richard first? I find it disconcerting when you just turn up like this.'

Jesse gazed at her, expressionless, his eyes blank.

'Do you understand? No sudden appearances? Make a time with me if you want to meet up. Is that fair enough?'

He nodded. 'Yeah. I get it. I don't want to make you upset.'

'Not upset. Just a bit uncomfortable. I'm here for the chance to be alone with no distractions, so let's arrange in advance from now on.'

'Sure. Whatever you say.'

'Thanks.' She smiled. 'I'm going home now. I'll see you another time. Bye, Jesse.'

She turned and started off back down the path to the cottage, feeling him watch her go. It was some time before she turned round to see if he was still there, but when she did look back, he had vanished.

Chapter Twenty-Seven

Romy was pleased to return to the peace and comfort of Clover Cottage. She felt emotionally wrung out. First, she had almost ruined everything by taking that picture of the photograph in the hallway. But in a way, it had been a good thing. She had been able to confess everything to Richard and he'd done the same. There was a new intimacy and understanding between them despite the rocky journey to get there.

It was Jesse who was bothering her. Why was he on the island so early? Could he possibly have been there all night, keeping tabs on her? That was an unpleasant thought.

No, she told herself. He had most likely motored over first thing and found she wasn't in. There weren't that many places she could be.

Now that she was on her own in the cottage, it all seemed harmless again – a bit of jealousy, territorial males having a very mild battle over her. And she was sure that Richard could explain it all from his side perfectly well.

Managing her tendency to imagine dramatic and catastrophic outcomes had been a key part of managing her

disorder. This was what she had come here for: to find calm
and spend some time following whichever direction her mind
wanted to go.

Right now, she was supposed to be thinking about her new
outline but, in a contrary-minded way, as soon as she noticed
the copy of *L'Amant de Minette* sitting on the desk where she
had left it, she decided she wanted to take another look at it.

Perhaps it was because she had just learned that her new
lover was in fact the grandson of Veronica herself, but she
had a sudden yearning to be close to her, and this book, with
comments and scrawls by the woman herself, seemed suddenly like the way to do that.

After she'd had a bath and changed into clean clothes, she
sat down to start deciphering the annotations and to transcribe
them into a document on her computer while trying to make
sense of whatever it was that interested Veronica so much.

The first thing she noticed was on one of the title pages.
Veronica had ringed two letters so that they made a strange
symbol that she hadn't seen when she first read the book. A
capital A and a capital I had been circled in black ink.

A I

What could that mean?

She noted it down and continued back through the book.
Veronica had underlined and circled details about Minette:
how she looked, for example. The heroine was dark-haired,
fair-skinned with deep blue eyes and elegant brows. She
always wore ropes of pearls at her neck. These things Veronica

had noted, sometimes with question marks, sometimes with arrows that led to a scrawling comment. *This very like* was one. *True* was another that was repeated several times.

Veronica seemed most interested in what Minette gave away about her history: hardship, exile, prostitution. Here, Veronica had written in capitals: *UNKIND. NOT TRUE.*

As she read on, she saw that it was almost always the character of Minette that Veronica focused on, about whom she seemed to have firm ideas. She was less sure about the character of Paul, Minette's lover. References to him were annotated with plenty of question marks. At one point, above a passage describing Paul, she had written *PDuC???*

When Minette finally betrays Paul and leaves him broken-hearted, he has dark fantasies of revenge against her that Veronica had marked with thick zigzag lines in the margin.

Paul's final parting shot to Minette was thickly underscored.

'*You will regret this, Minette. I gave you the purest thing I have: my heart and my love. Who are you to throw it back in my face like this? What makes you so much better than me, that you believe you can stamp on my very soul and not suffer for the most heinous thing a woman can do to a man? Rejection is cruel. It is erasure. It is death. You will learn the truth of this from me or from no one.*'

Veronica had written at the top of the page: *Chilling. She did not deserve this.*

Romy put the book down and stared into space, thinking.

Could it be that Veronica believed the character of Minette to be based on a real person, and that she knew who that person was? Or, at least, suspected?

She was almost at the end, and there were few marks in the pages where the narrative featured only Paul, as he prepared to escape the city and its occupiers. He had carried out his threat. Minette had paid the price.

Romy flicked through to the end and to the pages at the back of the book, looking for any acknowledgements or further clues to the text. Then she saw in Veronica's handwriting a single line, written more clearly than the rest, as though at a different time.

Minette said to look out for you, she said to take special care of you – André escape 1943/Resistance.

André was Richard's grandfather, of course. But the mention of the Resistance was intriguing. What was Veronica thinking when she wrote this down? It sounded as though her theory was right and Veronica had believed that Minette was a real person. But who?

On impulse she went to her search engine and typed in a phrase: *Minette, French Resistance 1943*.

Instantly, a raft of results sprung up, all in French. She could translate them with software instantly but her French was certainly good enough to read them in the original. They were nearly all news reports from a few years before. Some archives had been opened that revealed the existence of a woman codenamed Minette, who had lived in Paris during the war and played a vital role in smuggling escaped French soldiers across Europe to join the Allies. She had been extremely brave and tenacious in her determination to save French lives and outwit the enemy in any way she could.

But in 1944, as the liberation of Paris approached, the Germans launched a last struggle to identify and root out members of the Resistance, to prevent them aiding the Free French and the Allies. More than a thousand had been rounded up and shot. Minette had been one of them, taken from her apartment one summer afternoon and executed within the hour, according to the newly discovered papers. She had been posthumously awarded a medal for her work but as no one knew who she really was, she was awarded it as Minette.

Romy stared at the images that came up with the articles. Only one tattered photograph found in the Gestapo archive had been identified as Minette. It was grainy and hard to make out, but Romy knew she had already seen the face before.

She pulled out her phone and opened the photograph she had taken in Richard's hallway the previous afternoon.

The likeness was unmistakable. It might not be the same person but it definitely looked like it. Proper analysis could no doubt confirm whether it was or was not.

I'm certain the woman in the photograph is Richard's great-aunt, the beautiful Irène.

Romy took off her glasses, her mouth open in astonishment. If this was right, then she had just discovered the true identity of the wartime heroine Minette. And more than that, from what she had deduced, it seemed that Veronica might have believed that the famous literary heroine Minette was a portrait of her sister-in-law, Irène. Perhaps she had made some kind of connection between the two Minettes. But, Romy remembered, it was not known that the real Minette was a Resistance fighter until after Veronica's death. She must have had some inkling, because she had the snippet of information that André's escape had been aided by someone called Minette. Perhaps his sister had spread the word through the Resistance, that if they ever found an André Razinsky, they were to take special care of him, for her sake.

She remembered how Richard had told her that the uncertainty over the fate of his grandfather's sister had driven a wedge between his grandparents, and slowly driven them apart.

Although I suppose that the affairs didn't help.

Perhaps it would have been different if they'd known the truth about Minette and been able to see her honoured as she deserved in her lifetime.

Romy jumped up and hurried out of the cottage, texting Richard that she was on her way as she went.

He was not at home but she soon found him, standing on some of the abbey ruins with his back to her, his binoculars to his face, observing the birds.

'Richard! Richard!'

She ran towards him, shouting, but the wind kept carrying her voice away in the opposite direction. At last, he

THE LAST SONG OF WINTER

heard something and turned to see her. A huge smile covered his face as she approached but it dissolved into an anxious expression as she got closer.

'What is it? Is everything all right?' he demanded, jumping off the wall and striding towards her.

She reached him, breathless, and fell into his arms. He held her tight.

'Are you okay? What is it?'

'I've got the most amazing thing to tell you! And you're never going to believe it!' Romy pulled back so that she could smile broadly, her eyes shining. 'You are not going to believe what I've found out!'

Back in the Cliff House kitchen, Richard got a bottle of champagne from the outside fridge. 'I don't know why I put this in to chill or when – about two years ago, I should think. I haven't had reason to pop it before now, but this calls for a celebration!'

He pulled the foil off the cork and undid the cage. A moment later, the cork released with a satisfying pop and he poured the foaming liquid into two glasses and handed her one of them. 'Congratulations to you, Romy, on a marvellous bit of detective work.'

She took it, smiling. 'I hope I'm right about this! We'll need some proper proof of your great-aunt and Minette the Resistance member being the same person. If I am, I didn't really do anything. Veronica did all the work.'

'No, that's not true . . . you read my mother's memoir, you saw the reference to the novel. You found the novel and borrowed it' – he gave her a mock stern look – 'under false pretences, I have to say, but let's forget that, and deciphered all her comments and made the connection. That's what detective work is. Without you, it could never have happened.'

'Me and the internet,' she said happily. 'That was rather useful. And I needed whoever located the archive that finally named Minette and recognised her work.'

'It's pulling the threads together,' Richard said obstinately. 'And that's what you did.'

She laughed. 'All right, all right! I take your praise. Cheers.'

They touched glasses and drank the champagne.

Martha came flapping in from the sitting room, roused by all the chatter. She landed on Richard's shoulder and pecked at his ear affectionately.

'Jealous,' he remarked, stroking her black-green plumage. 'She's noticed that there's another female in my life.'

'Let's hope she doesn't turn nasty,' Romy joked, noticing the big bird giving her a baleful side eye as usual. But then, she always looked that way as far as Romy could tell.

'She's pretty friendly, to be honest. Lots of ravens can be aggressive but she's been brought up here, she's practically a captive bred bird.' He put down his glass and collected a box from a shelf. Inside was a mixture of maize and dry chickpeas. He put it on the table, and Martha hopped off his shoulder, landing lightly on the table on her two feet, then bounded forward to start inspecting the contents and pick out what she fancied.

'She's clever, isn't she?' Romy said, watching her.

'Oh yes. And she's very generous, she's always bringing me

gifts – moss, twigs, sticks, shiny stones, anything that takes her fancy. If you find odd objects on the table, they're often from Martha.'

Romy watched the bird for a while as she pecked at the food.

Richard sat down opposite her. 'I meant to tell you that I've to go to London today. I've got a meeting there first thing tomorrow.'

'Really? Today?' She was dismayed. London seemed so far away.

'I've got a meeting of the trust.'

'The trust,' she echoed, remembering Jesse telling her only that morning that the trust did not exist.

'That's right. We have to have the occasional meeting. It's me, my two cousins and a couple of distinguished professionals to guide and support us. It's fairly straightforward but it has to be done.' He smiled at her. 'If it's okay with you, I'd like to ask them about endorsing your book and opening the archives to you. All of Veronica's books and papers and diaries and so on. Would that be useful?'

She gasped, unable to speak for a moment, and then said, 'That would be more than amazing. I would be able to write her biography! I could include the history of the island, the story of her family, of Jack and Grey, and . . . of course . . . Irène and what happened to her. It could be quite a revelation.'

'I can't wait to read it,' Richard said, and he lifted his glass to her. 'Here's to your book, Irène's return and Jack's restoration to his rightful place in history!'

499

Romy laughed. 'Wow, that sounds like a lot! But yes! I can't wait to get started.'

'Champagne first.'

She lifted her glass to him again, flushed and excited. 'How amazing that this has all turned out the way it has.'

'St Elfwy magic strikes again,' Richard said with a wink. 'You can't escape it. Now, Martha, outside with you. Time for a splash about in your tub and get those crumbs off your feathers. I'm going to say a proper goodbye to Romy.'

Before Richard left for London, they spent a happy few hours in the white house, talking and laughing, going to bed for a very long and pleasant stretch before Richard walked her back to the cottage.

'Take care, won't you?' he said, as he stood on the door-step preparing to leave. 'I don't want to go but I have to.'

'Don't be silly, I'll be fine. I'm like Rapunzel in a tower on the island.'

'Not exactly. Anyone who wants to can sail over and moor here. Although we do have CCTV at the jetty. Just in case. We've had the odd stag party wanting to go mad here, and more than one conspiracy nut trying to set up an end-of-days commune. So we have to take precautions.' He pulled her to him in a tight hug, the soft stubble grazing her cheek. She rubbed her face against it, feeling comforted by his nearness. He pulled back and stared into her eyes. 'I'm going to worry about you. I can't help it. I don't think you're weak or anything. Just vulnerable. I'll be quite glad when the new retreater turns up. She's an artisan jeweller, I think. It'll be good to know that there's someone else here if you need them and I'm away.'

'I get it.' Romy smiled at him. She felt touched, moved by his concern but also glad that he didn't want to impose a lot of questions on her. It occurred to her that she probably should have told him about Jesse turning up that morning but he had agreed not to visit again without notice, and she was sure he'd stick to his promise. They'd parted on good terms. 'Honestly, I'm stronger than I look. I wouldn't have got this far if I weren't. You're only going for forty-eight hours or so, aren't you?'

'Yes. And I believe you. You're strong.' He kissed her forehead and then her cheeks, each in turn, and then her mouth, wrapping her in that strong embrace at the same time. When they parted at last, he whispered, 'I'll be back soon. Bye.'

She watched him go, feeling that strange wretched delight in both parting and knowing that there would be another meeting. Then she closed the door and went upstairs to run a bath.

After all the excitement, a quiet evening and an early night was just what she needed.

The next day, refreshed, she did some cleaning and tidying, making a list of all her remaining stores and what she might need to get soon. Not long after lunch, she got a text:

Meeting done. News all good. Home later. Rx

She was delighted that he would soon be back.

What does later mean, though? Today? Tomorrow? It takes a while to get back from London. Even if he left now, he might not be back before midnight. I suppose I'll see him when I see him.

Romy went back to work, now concentrating on a new outline that would take all the exciting new discoveries into it. It was absorbing stuff, and she lost herself in it, stopping only to make the occasional cup of tea or stare out of the window. It was early evening when her computer chimed with an incoming FaceTime call and Romy remembered with a start that she had a session with Caroline booked. She put in her wireless ear pods and clicked to accept the call.

'Hi, Caroline!'

'Romy, how are you doing?' The picture was a bit fuzzy, with a slight delay on the call, but she could make Caroline out easily enough as she sat in the therapy room in Bristol.

'I'm doing really well. Really well!' She grinned broadly at her therapist, seeing her own bright smile in the thumbnail of herself on the screen. 'You wouldn't believe what's been happening.'

'Okay. Why don't you tell me?'

Romy started to explain everything that had happened since she had last talked to Caroline, who looked a little dubious when she heard that Richard and Romy had slept together only a very short time after Caroline had urged caution.

'It's honestly okay,' Romy insisted. 'I mean it, I've been

careful, I've kept a bit of distance and I'm on top of it. He isn't rushing me or pushing me. It's all okay.'

'Can you write up some of this on your next form?' Caroline asked. 'Just so we have a record?'

Romy blushed. 'Well, I'd rather not, seeing as Flo reads it.'

'You don't want Flo to know?'

'Not in graphic detail. It's all a bit personal.' Romy had told Flo a little about Richard in her emails, but she knew that Flo's early warning system would go off as strongly as Caroline's had and she was convinced that it wasn't necessary, so she had kept the extent of their burgeoning relationship under wraps.

'Okay, I get that. You could do an addendum that you send to me for now? I want you to keep a record of your emotional journey with all this.'

'Yes, I'll do that,' Romy said. 'And I've also got quite a lot happening on the work front too. But the only thing that's bothering me slightly is this guy Jesse. I mean, I'm sure he's harmless but he's been hanging around a bit and getting slightly overemotional about things.'

'Uh-huh. Tell me more.'

Just then there was a loud rapping on the front door. Romy jumped.

'What is it?' Caroline asked, seeing her sudden movement.

'Did you hear that?' Romy asked.

'No, I can hear your voice, but nothing else. You've got your pods in.'

'There was a knock on the door. Hold on, I'll just answer it.'

'Who else is on the island?' Caroline asked.

'No one right now.' Romy stood up. 'But I think another visitor might be due here soon. Richard said something about a woman arriving, a jeweller or something. Perhaps it's her. I'll be right back.'

She went to the front door and opened it. Jesse was standing on the doorstep, two carrier bags dangling from his hands. He grinned at her as soon as he saw her, and held them out.

'Tadaaaa!'

Romy's heart sank. She had had a bad feeling that it might be Jesse but she had hoped it was not. 'What are you doing here? We don't have any kind of arrangement and you promised you wouldn't just turn up like this.'

'I know that. But you know what, I really want to watch this movie with you and have that curry and I'm pretty fed up of waiting. It's not so much to ask, is it?'

She stared at him, exasperated. 'How did you get here?'

'In the tour boat, of course.' He laughed, his dark eyes sparkling with that slightly manic energy that was alternately alluring and alienating. 'I wasn't going to swim here! Or row. Too lazy for that.'

'How come you're still using the tour boats? I don't think you're allowed to, are you? They told me you're refusing to return the keys despite being asked for them.'

Jesse went very still. Then he stared down at the doorstep and heaved a great sigh as though he was immensely weary. After a moment he said in a reflective voice, 'Now that's disappointing. I didn't realise you were not just checking up on me but also believing all the bullshit. I guess you might be more like Richard than I thought.'

She lost patience. 'Look, I don't want to go through that again. I'm sorry, I know you've come all this way, but I'm busy right now. I have to go.' Romy went to close the door but quick as a flash, Jesse stuck his foot against it and easily stopped her from moving it.

'I don't think so.' His voice was suddenly more menacing than she had ever heard it. 'I'm coming in. Don't worry, I'm not going to hurt you. I just want to come in, okay?'

His eyes were glittering now and she had the sudden and inescapable feeling that she mustn't thwart him when he was in this mood.

I'm alone on the island. I can't risk making him really angry.

The powerful urge to placate him came over her.

'All right,' she said, trying to hide her reluctance, 'come in. Come into the sitting room.'

He followed her in, his mood lighter again, his voice cheerful now that she had capitulated. 'Great. We can watch the movie. I bought some tinnies. The food will need a bit of a reheat, it's been a while since it saw the inside of an oven, but that's okay.'

Romy walked ahead of him, keeping herself between him and the computer on her desk, her eyes on the screen where Caroline's face was still visible, looking anxiously out as she tried to make out what was going on in the room beyond.

'Can you hear me, Romy?' she said quietly, her voice coming down the ear pods directly into Romy's ears.

505

'Yes,' she said firmly, and then added, 'We can reheat the food. Do you want to take it to the kitchen?'

'Yeah, sure.' Jesse put the bags down and made no move for the kitchen. 'I brought my tablet with the film downloaded.'

'Who is it?' Caroline said. 'Are you all right?'

'Okay, Jesse,' Romy said. 'It was a good idea to bring the movie.'

Jesse looked up from where he was unloading the bag, his expression wary. 'Yeah, I thought so.'

Caroline said, 'Are you worried that you're in danger?'

'Hmm,' she said, trying to work out how to answer. 'I like movies. It's a good idea. A movie and a curry and then you go home. I think that will be okay.'

Jesse stared at her, warier still, then frowned. 'Are you listening to music or something while I'm talking to you? That's not very polite.'

'Oh yeah, sorry, just some music. I can hear you fine.'

'I think you should take those pods out,' Jesse said softly. 'Are you talking to someone?'

'Of course not.'

'It's not fucking Richard, is it?' he said with a sneer. 'The Lothario of South Wales? The Casanova of bird sanctuaries?'

Romy tried to hide her anxiety and stay entirely calm, outwardly as least. Caroline could still hear her, but not see Jesse or hear what he was saying. 'If you want me to, I'll take my ear pods out.' Then she said quickly and brightly, 'So you want us to have the curry and watch *The Last Song of Winter*, right? That's sounds nice. Then you'll go? 'Cos I have a lot of work to do.'

'While Richard's away, the little cat won't play,' Jesse said in a sing-song voice. 'You can take a night off, can't you?'

'I'd love to but I can't, I have a deadline. So you'll go after the movie?'

'Sure,' Jesse said with a shrug. Then his eyes hardened again. 'Ear pods out, please.'

'Okay, as long as that's agreed. I'll take the pods out.' Romy turned around to the screen where Caroline was staring out anxiously. She was still concealing the call from Jesse, who couldn't see the computer, or be seen. Slowly she lifted her hands to her ears. 'I'm sure we'll have a nice evening,' she said, staring straight at Caroline. 'And you've promised to go when it's over.'

Jesse said impatiently, 'Are you talking to someone? 'Cos you sound pretty strange right now.' He stepped forward as she was lifting the ear pods from her ears, and she made a wide-eyed, frightened face at Caroline. Just as Jesse pushed around her to look at her desk, Caroline leaned forward and cut the call. The screen went black and Romy spun round, looking Jesse right in the face and distracting him.

'I'm all yours!' she said brightly. 'Just had to get my head out from my work. Shall we go and heat up that curry?'

He looked at her with a trace of suspicion but seeing her open expression and smile, he relaxed. 'Sure. Let's do that. I'm starving.'

*

In the kitchen, Jesse sat at the table with a can of beer while Romy put the curry in the oven. Her phone began to buzz and she saw that Caroline was calling her, but she ignored it. She couldn't take the call with Jesse there.

'So how did you find out about the tours and the boats?' he said in a conversational way.

'Just by accident. I went in to see if you were working and they told me.'

Jesse shrugged. 'That was a bit of a pain, if I'm honest.'

'What happened?' she asked lightly.

'Ah, we just didn't see eye to eye. My ex-girlfriend worked there, that's how we met. Once we broke up, you know how it is. She went with her big sob story about how awful I was, and they swallowed it whole. No question that maybe she was the one to blame considering she was the one cheating on me. No, sirree. The guy is always at fault. I'm the villain of the piece. They took her side. So when Richard complained, the bosses used it as an excuse to sack me.'

'But you wouldn't let them?'

Jesse looked gleeful. 'Correcto! I wouldn't let 'em. They can't just sack me when I haven't done anything. I wasn't going to let fucking Richard win. And I need compensation, at the very least, that's just fair. So we've been in a bit of stalemate but they can easily get out of it. Just pay me what's owed, and I'm off.'

'And your ex went off?'

'Yeah, in a big "boo hoo hoo, this town's not big enough for the both of us!" kind of sulk. Good riddance.' Jesse smiled at her. 'She was fucking nuts anyway. Massively unfaithful. You know the kind.'

'I suppose I do.'

'Have a tinnie,' Jesse offered, pushing a can of beer across the table at her. 'And tell me a bit more about this work of yours. 'Cos you sure do love it.'

While the curry was heating, Romy tried to keep him occupied with general chat. Her phone buzzed with more calls, but there was no way she could answer. Every time she even glanced at it, Jesse stiffened and looked alert. After half an hour, they loaded a tray with the food and took it back through to the sitting room. Romy unloaded while Jesse closed the curtains against the evening sunshine and got the tablet set up for the film showing.

'I'm excited about this,' he confided. 'I love this movie.'

They sat down with the food and Jesse started piling up his plate enthusiastically as the opening credits played.

Romy felt too sick to eat but she tried to make an effort. She had about an hour and a half while the film was playing to try and decide what to do. It was just possible that Jesse would stick to his word and go. But she had a horrible feeling that this movie-curry-chill night was not something that he was going to give up on easily. He had obviously really wanted it, and been determined to get it and wasn't going to take no for an answer, no matter how she felt about it.

She thought of Richard's words suddenly. What had he said? Something like: *The people who feel pain and become less human and less kind – those are the people you need to avoid.*

Yes. That was it. And she had the feeling that Jesse wasn't just less human himself, he was treating her as less human. As though she wasn't allowed to make her own choices.

As she thought this, she watched the film's opening sequences, filmed in evocative black and white with an eerie soundtrack, and there was the island.

Jesse said, 'Amazing to think we're on that very island! Isn't it great?'

'Yes,' Romy said weakly. 'Great.'

The film played on. Jesse ate heartily, his eyes fixed on the screen, not seeming to notice that Romy barely touched her food. Once they'd finished, he pushed his plate away and sat back on the sofa, pressing closer to Romy. After a while, he put his arm along the back of the sofa so that it wasn't quite around her, but she was in a kind of hands-off embrace. His lips, she noticed, were moving along with the dialogue. His eyes were glassy in the reflected light of the screen.

She got up. 'I'm just going to the loo.'

'Sure,' Jesse said. 'I'll pause it.'

'Okay.' She went to pick up her phone but he was too quick for her, scooping it up before she could reach it.

'No distractions!' he said cheerily. 'You need to hurry back.'

'Right.'

Romy went off to the loo, and locked herself in. She stared at her frightened face in the mirror. *What the hell am I going to do? I'm not going to be able to call anyone. He said he would go when the movie is over. I've got no reason to disbelieve him, he's always just gone off before.*

She looked directly at herself and asked the question: *Do you really think he's dangerous?*

After a moment, she answered her own question.

No. He's a bit emotional but I think he knows where to stop. He's lonely and he wants company, and he's a bit jealous. But I don't think he's really dangerous. I can handle it.

She went back to the sitting room, her palms still a bit clammy, and sat down as far as way from Jesse as she could without looking rude.

'Great,' Jesse said, starting up the film again. 'It's just getting to the good bit.'

The movie was still chilling, even now, but she felt more bothered by sitting here with Jesse, and by the melody of 'The Last Song of Winter' which was beautiful and haunting but warped into a terrifying crescendo of discordant sounds in which the original song could still be heard. Romy watched the heroine as she desperately fled the malevolent presence on the island, stumbled down the cliff side and met her terrible fate in the caves.

The film ended with the music echoing in the caves, the film lingering on the wide-open dead eyes of the heroine.

Jesse jumped up to turn it off. 'Oh my god, that was fantastic! Did you like it?'

'Yes,' she said, her heart racing, her stomach full of nausea. The bit of curry she had eaten sat there, sickening her. 'It's great.'

'It's a masterpiece! Can you believe old Richard's grandma wrote that? What a gal!'

'You know about Richard's grandmother?'

'Course I do. We all do. It's part of the tour information! The old bird who wrote the film lived here in the war, she owned the island and she gave it to the dickhead.' Jesse seemed jubilant somehow. 'If Richard wasn't so devoted to the fucking birds, he could make a total mint out of the film fans. He could have themed vacations here, the lot. And someone's bound to want to do a remake or a sequel or something. Honestly, he's missing a trick. I wrote a script myself and gave it to him but of course he wasn't interested. Far too grand for that! His fucking money came from that film, he has no reason to be so high and mighty about it.'

Romy stood up, feeling shaky. 'Jesse, I'm really not feeling well. I'm tired and I ought to get to bed.'

Jesse looked instantly contrite. 'Ah, sorry, love. I didn't realise. You want me to put you to bed? I could stay here if you like? On the sofa, of course. Your virtue is safe with me.'

'No . . . no. I would like to be alone. Do you mind going back now?'

Jesse stared at her, and his expression changed. All the jubilation dropped out of his face and his eyes went blank. 'You don't seem to mind being with Richard,' he said. 'You're spending a lot of time with him. He's your boyfriend now, isn't he?'

She opened her mouth to deny it but then thought, *Well, maybe this will help break the spell and make him leave.* 'Yes,' she said firmly. 'He's my boyfriend. He wouldn't like you staying. So could you please go home? I really need to go to bed.'

'He wouldn't like it,' echoed Jesse. 'He doesn't want me near you.'

'It's not that, but he wouldn't like you staying if I don't want you to. And I don't. It's nothing personal. I'm just tired. Okay?'

'Oh, sure.' Jesse said. He seemed to start back into life. 'Sure. Yeah. I'm gonna go now then.'

'You are?' Relief coursed through her. 'Okay. Well, thanks for coming! I enjoyed the movie and the curry. Just give me a bit of notice next time.'

'Yeah. So, gonna walk me back to the boat?' Jesse was gathering his things, getting the tablet.

'I'd rather not, I'm so tired . . .'

'Come on,' he said. 'Five more minutes and I'll be on my way. It's a gorgeous night out there.'

'Well . . . all right.'

Romy put on her coat. This wasn't the worst option. He hadn't put up a fight. He was leaving. Just a few more min-utes and she'd be alone again. He wasn't that bad really, a tiny bit odd and set on getting his own way. But essentially harmless. It sounded like his breakup had hit him hard, much harder than she'd realised. But he'd accepted that she wasn't the answer to that, she was convinced of that now.

They stepped out of the cottage together. The moon was full overhead, glittering on the water below. The birds were silent, as though they still thought it was somehow daytime.

'It is beautiful,' Romy said.

'Yeah. Reminds me of nights like this with my girlfriend, before we broke up. It's the night for romance with a moon like that, isn't it?'

Romy said nothing, wishing she hadn't mentioned the beauty of the night. They walked down to the jetty, and Jesse climbed into his boat. He turned on the engine, which sounded loud and intrusive in the quiet night air. Romy stood back on the jetty, watching him prepare to leave. Just a few more minutes now.

'Can you untie that rope?' he called to Romy, gesturing to the mooring.

'Of course.' She went forward, bent down and unknotted it, then stood up to hand it back to Jesse. He was standing close to her in the boat, and as she stood up, he pulled very hard and very suddenly on the rope and the next moment she had tumbled forward. He caught her and swung her round, depositing her into the interior on her back. Romy gasped, shocked, and tried to scramble up.

'The night isn't over yet! I want to take you on a tour of Stix Island! With a special *Last Song of Winter* add-on. So hold tight. You won't need a life jacket for this one! This is just for you, Romy!'

With that, he opened the throttle, reversed and spun the boat round, sending Romy toppling back into the bottom of the boat, winded.

Jesse turned his face to the full moon, and whooped. 'And we're off!'

Chapter Twenty-Eight

'Please take me home, Jesse,' Romy called in a shaking voice.

The noise of the engine was loud in the night air and she had to shout to be heard over it, but Jesse wasn't listening to her.

He was, she realised, conducting an island tour. She had heard these very words before, floating up towards her on the afternoon breeze: the information about the geological formations and the birdlife.

'Of course, we can't see any birds right now, they're roosting, or they're inland, tending to their burrows. Shearwaters are pretty useless on land, they're made to be on the wing. At this time of year, you'll find them tipping and falling about all over the place as they try to walk about on legs used to flying. Right, now, ladies and gents, let me take you round to see the low-hanging caves.'

Jesse spun the boat around and took them to the north part of the island. He pulled out a torch and, as they glided under the dank dripping roof just above them, Romy felt her first real chill of fear. It was dark in there. The tide was

515

high, and they were only just clearing the roof. In another few minutes, they might be stuck there. Jesse's torch beam played over the ceiling of rock, which glittered and glowed black and orange in the light. He was talking on about the rock formation and composition, all in a sing-song voice that revealed it was just a patter he had learned.

She wanted to ask him to leave the caves, but she had a feeling that anything she said would have the opposite effect to what she wanted, so she kept quiet. Maybe he would take her back when this crazy tour was over. She mustn't provoke him, that was the main thing. No sudden moves, no shouts or screams, and surely he would take her back?

That's what you thought before. About the movie. About the meal. About him going home. One more concession and he'll leave you in peace.

She tried to still the voice in her mind. For years, she had battled with terrible, intrusive thoughts. Her obsessive thoughts had taken her to the darkest places where she had believed that she was capable of terrible things, that she might kill other people, hurt innocent children, cause car crashes or plane crashes or natural disasters. She wouldn't want to do these things but she might not be able to help it, by not being perfect or not being able to control herself. Control became her religion. Controlling everything so that the terrible things would not happen.

Her journey had been a long journey back from believing she was responsible for things that happened in the world.

And now here she was, in the kind of nightmare she had dreaded for so long: out of control and on the edge of what she feared might be a disaster. There was nothing she could do. And the spiteful internal voices that had once told her that the way out of catastrophe was to perform a thousand push-ups or to refuse food or to run ten miles had nothing to offer her now.

What would Caroline say?

She remembered Caroline's face on the screen earlier. As far as she knew, she was going to have a curry and a movie. She might not think the situation merited any intervention.

I should have been clearer about how I felt. About what was happening.

Well, it was too late now.

I have to stay calm. It's all I can do. She began to practise her breathing and tapped lightly at her hand. *Calm, calm, calm. That's important now.*

To her relief, Jesse put the engine into reverse and steered the boat out of the cave and onto the open water.

He turned around to grin at her, where she was now sitting on one of the passenger seats, her arms wrapped around her, nursing what she thought might be a bruise on her arm. 'Now for the highlight of the tour!' he cried. 'The film location visit! The glamorous bit. Lucky you. This is my special add-on.'

As he steered the craft around the island, the engine purring low as they crawled through the calm waters, he said conversationally, 'I fucking hate Richard. Did I tell you about my ex-girlfriend?'

'A bit,' Romy said in a small voice. 'You said she was unfaithful.'

'Yeah – and guess who with! Richard doesn't have a problem getting the girls. I wonder what attracts them to the guy who owns an island plus the rights to a cult movie? Er . . . you tell me!' Jesse laughed. 'They all turn to mush at his feet. My ex was no different and he fucking loved it. They had this wild and crazy affair right under my nose. It was humiliating. And when I tried to stand up for myself, I was the bad guy. Oh yeah, me! Not the creepy old guy who can't keep his dick in his pants around someone's girlfriend. No, everyone loves him around here, or they love his money. Or they're afraid of him. Who cares? It all comes out the same way.'

Jesse steered the boat around the rocky outcrops of the island, weaving a slow path between the stacks as they rounded the south-west edge of Elfwy. Romy knew where they were. They were approaching from the opposite direction to the one that she'd come before, but she knew. She had only just seen this spot, on the screen. It was the Singing Caves. Jesse himself had brought her here before, but he didn't seem to remember that.

'Here we are, film location time!' Jesse cut the engine and they drifted forward towards the arched opening of the caves. He turned to look at Romy. 'So here's the thing, Romy. I thought you might be different but you were just like the others. The ones who always leave me and who always go to him. I just couldn't believe it when I saw you were spending the night at his place. I thought, *Not you too! Not Romy!* I was sure you wouldn't fall for it. But I guess I was wrong.'

'Jesse, please let's go home,' she said in a clear voice. 'You can take me back to the jetty now. I've enjoyed the tour but I'm cold and I want to go back.'

Her phone was in his pocket. He had not given it back after taking it when she'd gone to the loo. She looked at its outline, wondering if she could make a grab for it, but knowing that she wouldn't be fast enough to do anything with it before he took it back.

'You wanna go home? But you haven't had the full experience yet.' He grinned at her, his white teeth shining eerily in the reflected moonlight.

She looked at him warily. 'The full experience? What's the full experience?'

He came forward, gently, still smiling, his eyes looking deep into hers. Then, in a rapid movement, he seized her round the waist, hauled her up and over to the side of the boat.

'This,' he said firmly, and he threw her over the side.

The water hit Romy, freezing and bitter, and jolted her with a huge shock. She was in a mass of icy bubbles, her clothes quickly pulling her down, but she reacted instinctively, holding her breath, closing her eyes, and kicking as hard as she could for the surface. She could hear a loud roar in the water and she broke through in time to see the motor boat with Jesse at the wheel powering away into the distance, heading for the mainland.

Gasping, she fought to stay afloat, able to sense that the water was very deep beneath her. Terror rushed through her but she had no option but to do her best to control it. Otherwise, she knew she would not survive. She was not many minutes away from losing her ability to stay afloat. Turning towards the cave, she could see that she was only a few metres from the rock at its centre, and she kicked towards it, grateful for the moonlight that meant she could see quite clearly. Usually she was a good swimmer but she wasn't used to swimming in icy water in her clothes, and she could only make slow progress, kicking towards the rock and moving her hands in a kind of doggy paddle fashion that was very inefficient but at least got her moving closer to the rock.

As she neared it, she was able to reach out and pull herself the last metre or so. The rock was freezing cold and painful to touch, covered in sharp edges and barnacles.

I just have to bear it. Either that, or give up. I'm not giving up.

As she fought to drag herself up, she thought suddenly of her sister. Flo had always been there for her. She had been the one who had said for ages that Romy was ill, even when no one else had noticed. And it was Flo who, finally, had got her to hospital the day that she had the final breakdown. She talked her through the process step by step remotely over the phone, at a time when Romy could barely remember how to do the simplest things. Romy could still hear her sister's voice, calm yet urgent. 'Get down to the street, Romy, the taxi is waiting. I've paid in advance for it. They know where you're going. Tell him your name and he'll take you there. Okay? Can you do that?'

'I think so,' Romy had said, and she had.

It had been Flo who had demanded an end to the poisonous social media that was feeding Romy's quest for perfection, her dissatisfaction with herself and her addiction for setting endless new goals.

'You need to enjoy your life as it is,' Flo had said. 'Just as it is. That's all.'

She had assembled the team that had dedicated itself to saving Romy, getting her back on her feet and away from the mental bully who had tormented her for so long.

It's not going to come to an end here, she told herself firmly. *I'm not going to drown here in this cave. Okay, so I have no phone. No one knows where I am. Jesse has gone. I'm wet and cold and exhausted. But I'm still alive and I'm going to stay that way.* Suddenly she laughed to herself. *I can always sing!*

She had managed to pull herself up the rock, slowly, her hands cut and bleeding, and now sat on the flat seat-like outcrop she remembered from the film. It did make rather a good seat, now she was on it. Those monks had needed somewhere to perch to last all those hours. She wondered how high the tide would rise and was grateful for the calm sea. At least she wouldn't be washed off.

I will sing, she thought. *Why not?*

She began to hum the tune to 'The Last Song of Winter', and then sang a bar or two of the chorus. It echoed around the cave and she shuddered. *What am I doing? Am I insane? That's the last thing I can think about right now.*

She needed to think about other things. Her nieces and

nephews. Her parents. Flo and her husband Ted. Her friends – the ones she had left after her long illness and hospital stays. Her home. Her work – the book that might make her a success. And . . . there was Richard. She thought about his warm arms, soft kisses, and the pleasure she'd found in his bed.

How annoyed he'd be that Jesse had turned up and caused so much trouble.

She closed her eyes and thought about Richard, wondering where he was and what he was doing right now.

I hope I can last till morning. Maybe someone will come and find me then. I really don't want to end it all here. I'll be a sort of footnote to the movie. The girl who finished up like the heroine of The Last Song of Winter, *only a bit less bloody.*

Despite the cold weight of her wet clothes and the deep chill seeping into her bones, Romy felt fatigue coming for her. Perhaps she would just fall asleep and slip off the rock. She was sure that had been the fate of some of the poor monks. She would have to stay awake somehow, or it would be hers as well.

For a moment, she thought she heard the distant buzz of an engine and she became alert, listening hard. She was sure she could hear something, and the noise seemed to be getting louder, but then it died away and the silence returned.

False alarm. Is anyone looking for me? I don't expect so. No one even knows I'm missing.

She thought about Richard again. He would be back tomorrow at the latest. He would wonder where she was.

He might come looking. It was a forlorn hope but it was all she had.

I just have to hang on till then.

She woke with a start, struggling under freezing water, desperate and confused. What was happening? She had taken a breath under the surface before she'd realised she was submerged and now began to choke.

The calm she had worked so hard to preserve deserted her. There was no way out now. She was choking, too wet and cold and weak to get to the surface.

You fell off the rock, scolded a voice in her head, one of the bullies she knew so well from the past. *You are so stupid and useless. You couldn't even stay awake till morning.*

Her longing for oxygen was filling her brain, exploding inside her head.

Useless and stupid. You deserve to die.

For a second she thought dully that the voice was right. What was the point in fighting any more? She'd spent so much of her life struggling for survival against her imaginary foes. Now there was a real struggle. And she had wasted so much time and energy. Perhaps she should give in and let go.

No! I will not let this happen.

She kicked as hard as she could, reached out, flailing her arms, and found the rock. She seized what she could of it, and pulled herself upwards, finally bursting through to the surface with a dreadful spluttering gasp. Coughing and choking, she sought air around the water clogging her throat and lungs.

Clinging to the base of the rock, she managed to regain her breathing, still coughing and panting. There was no way she could climb back up. She was too wet and weak. The water was very cold and her hands were numb and hurt from her previous climb.

I can't stay here for much longer.

There was a limit, she had to acknowledge that. She had nearly reached it.

What did Jesse think would happen?

She heard a noise in the distance, a droning sound.

He's coming back!

Had he had second thoughts? Maybe he was stricken by remorse? Or maybe he wanted to finish her off in a proper tribute to the film and he had just gone back to get the proper tools to do it.

If he has, I won't have a chance. I can't fight him. I'm too weak.

The noise was still so far away. She was getting weaker and colder by the second. There was not much time left before she would not be able to hold on any longer.

You have to try.

The buzzing sound grew louder and closer.

When the boat came nosing around the side of the caves, its engines down to a murmur, she knew she was on the point of passing out. She couldn't speak and could barely open her eyes. She knew that the boat was close now, almost too close, the water swishing and slapping on the hull. She managed to open her eyes and saw that the torch beam from the boat was playing over the top of the rock, looking for her there.

'I'm here,' she whispered.

'Romy? Romy!'

It was Richard's voice, full of panic, but he still hadn't seen her.

'Romy, are you there? Romy? Where are you?'

She couldn't summon her voice. It was gone. He could be on the point of giving up, revving the engine and leaving. She couldn't let that happen. He had to hear her.

Dipping her head, she took a mouthful of seawater and tried to swallow it. Instantly her body rejected it and she coughed it up loudly, choking and spluttering all over again.

The torch beam swung down towards her, the bright light blinding her.

'Romy? Oh my god, oh my god, there you are! I've found you!'

Romy lay shivering violently in the bottom of the boat as Richard powered it round the island and back to the jetty. He was on the phone the entire time, evidently alerting people to the fact that she had been found. When he had moored, he helped her out onto the jetty, then picked her up and carried her up the steps to the white house.

A few minutes later, he had a warm bath for her and was helping her into it, still answering the calls that kept coming.

'She's okay, I think. We don't need to go to the hospital right now. She's cold but I'm warming her up. We can have her checked on in the morning. Don't worry, I'm looking out for her.'

After the bath that put some warmth back into her limbs
and stopped her shivering, Romy was wrapped up in blankets and put on the sofa by the stove with a hot drink at
hand. She was deeply tired but unable to sleep, comforted
by the sight of Richard moving about purposefully, caring
for her. He sat down beside her and took her hand, his face
still etched with worry.

'I can't believe this happened to you. I should never have
left you alone.'

'You weren't to know.' Her voice had returned, hoarsened
by the seawater and the choking. 'This was Jesse's fault, not
yours.'

Richard's eyes glittered. 'That lowlife piece of shit. I had
no idea he could be this evil.'

'How did you find me?'

'I had a strong feeling that I wanted to get back as soon as
I could, so I skipped lunch and got in the car. I thought I'd
surprise you by coming back early. Halfway along the M4,
your sister called me.'

'Flo?' Romy was surprised. 'How did she have your
number?'

'She messaged me ages ago, before you arrived, and gave
me emergency contact details and took mine. She didn't give
away any details, she just said she wanted to have another
contact as you were on your own. It made sense.'

'Is that how you had my number?' Romy asked. 'I wondered about that.'

'That's right, I forgot your detective skills.' He smiled at her. 'Flo said she'd had a call from your therapist who was concerned because you'd had a visit from someone called Jesse and you were on your own with him and something didn't sound right. I told her to call the police, and I put my foot down.'

'The police?' Romy was surprised. 'I never saw any police.'

'They must have arrived after Jesse took you off in the boat. They didn't see him either, or any tour boat.'

'He spent quite a long time giving me a private tour. We were at the back of the island for a while, in the low-hanging caves.'

'Right. So they came, had a look around, concluded you'd gone to the mainland together and went away.'

Romy shivered. 'He took me to the Singing Caves and then . . .' She closed her eyes, still disbelieving. 'He threw me in.'

Richard reached for her and held her tight. 'My poor girl. What a terrible experience. You must have been terrified.'

Romy opened her eyes to look into his concerned ones. 'The strange thing was how calm I was. For most of the time, I just focused on getting through it. It was only when I slipped in again that the panic really came.' She clasped his hands tightly. 'How did you know where to find me?'

'When I got to the jetty, I saw the tour boat moored up there. So I knew Jesse was back. Flo had rung again to tell me that the police had visited and found nothing. So I went to Jesse's caravan, where he was in the middle of packing his things. We had . . . a little chat. From that, I learned that he'd

527

dumped you in the caves. I locked him in the caravan, rang the police to collect him.'

'How did you manage that?' Romy said, shaking her head.

'Jesse is your typical weakling. And I'm stronger than I look, and also I used to box.' Richard smiled at her. 'I think he underestimated me.'

'I don't know. His jealousy for you is incredible.'

'If he didn't like me before, he's going to hate me now. But you know what? I couldn't care less.' Richard stroked his thumb across the top of her hand. 'I was terrified about where you were and what was happening to you. I got in the boat and headed over, not knowing how long you'd been in the caves but guessing it had to be a while.'

'I don't know really,' Romy said, suddenly exhausted again. 'It could have been hours or just a few minutes. I lost track when I fell asleep.'

He hugged her again. 'You could easily have died.'

'But I didn't. Thanks to you.'

'And to your courage.'

'I'm so tired,' she said and yawned.

'Come on.' Richard stood up. 'Let's get you to bed. You need to sleep.'

'Yes, please,' she said longingly, suddenly desperate to close her eyes. 'But one thing . . .' She looked up at him pleadingly. 'You won't leave me, will you?'

'No. I won't. You're safe now.'

On the way upstairs, she said, 'Did you actually steal Jesse's girlfriend?'

'What?' Richard made a face. 'No! I didn't know he had one. I never met her if he did.'

She sighed. 'Oh, good. It seems that I'm always glad when it turns out you don't know things.'

Romy slept late but had to get up, rather dozy, to talk to two police constables who came to take her statement about the events of the night before. They listened carefully, asked her questions and got her to sign what she had stated. She would need to go into the station the following day. They returned her phone, which they had found on Jesse.

Before they left, one of them said, 'This Jesse's been causing some problems for a while. We didn't think he was capable of this, though. It's quite an escalation. But he won't be bothering you again.'

There would be charges brought against him, there was no doubt of that. Time would tell how serious they were.

Once they were on their own again, Romy had to make a series of calls to reassure everyone she was all right. She thanked Caroline for alerting Flo to the situation. But her talk with her sister on a video link was the most emotional.

'I can't believe it!' Flo said, weeping. 'I said you shouldn't go to that island!'

'Not because of a crazy Australian with a grudge against the owner and who got jealous when I started hanging out with him,' Romy said. 'Quite different reasons.'

'It all comes to the same thing!' Flo wailed, putting a tissue to her eyes to wipe the tears. 'We nearly lost you.'

'You've nearly lost me a lot of times. But I'm okay. And

there was a very important difference. I didn't want to die. I really wanted to live and I don't think that's going to change. I think I might be almost better. I did one last battle with that bully who lived in my head, and I won.'

Flo stopped crying and sniffed. 'That's good.'

'It is good.' Romy smiled at her sister. 'I want to live. Life is good, nature is good. It's all very, very good.'

Flo managed to smile back. 'I've wanted to hear you say that for a long time.' She started to cry again.

'What now, lovely? Are you still sad?' Romy asked, worried now, leaning into the camera.

'No.' Flo smiled through the cascade of tears. 'I'm happy now. I can't tell you. So happy.' She reached her own hand out towards the camera. 'Dear sis. I'm so happy you want to live. I'm so happy you've won your battle at last. I always knew you could, my strong girl. And now you have.'

It was late the next day, after a lot more sleep and a visit from a local doctor to check her over, that Romy returned to Clover Cottage.

Richard had asked her to move in with him full-time and she had agreed that she would stay with him for at least a week, to be looked after and get her strength back. But she wanted to collect her material from the cottage so that she could carry on working.

They went back together, letting themselves into the slightly musty cottage. There was still the faint aroma of curry in the air from the abandoned curry dishes that still sat on the table. Romy shivered at the sight of Jesse's empty beer cans.

'This is chilling,' Richard said grimly, seeing her expression of horror. 'I'm going to clear this stuff away right now.'

'Okay. Thanks.' Romy opened the front door to air the cottage and rid it of the curry smell.

While Richard cleared up, she collected her laptop and packed her backpack with everything she needed. Picking up the copy of *L'Amant de Minette*, she thought of what this book had done for her, and what it might achieve in the future. The problem was that Veronica's comments were so opaque and provided no real detail. She would have to do a lot of research and hope that she found the link to bring it all together and prove it.

Richard came through from the kitchen. 'Are you ready to go back?'

'Almost. I've got to pack some things upstairs, then we can go.'

'Great.' He looked around. 'I'm getting the creeps in here.'

'Says the man who lives in the famous white house of horror.'

'That's the difference between real and pretend, I suppose.' He grinned. 'Now, grab your things and we'll get on our way.'

They walked back laden down with Romy's things. The sky was a pure blue with grey-white clouds floating just over the horizon. The sun was shining and the hedges buzzed with life.

Cliff House, white and welcoming against the blue, looked like home, she realised.

Richard let them into the kitchen and put Romy's things down as Martha came swooping in from outside and landed on his shoulder. Romy followed in behind, weighed down with her backpack and books.

'Hello, hello,' Richard said, walking over to the kitchen table. 'It looks like Martha's left me another little present. Some moss and something shiny this time.' He leaned over and picked something off the table. He held it up, frowning. 'Look. A little key. I wonder where she found this.'

Romy put down her things and went over, looking at the key he was holding up. It was gold but scratched and stained. 'That's odd. It looks old.'

'But it doesn't look like a door key. It's too small. It's like something for a jewellery box or a safe.'

'Or a filing cabinet,' Romy added. A memory stirred in her mind. 'Or . . . or a piano stool.'

They looked at each other and then went quickly to the sitting room where Richard pulled the stool out from under the old piano.

'I wondered if this is the instrument where Jack composed his famous song,' Romy said, excited. 'I thought it might be. There might be music inside the stool!'

Richard knelt down by the piano stool and put the key in the tiny lock. It scraped and stuck, and then turned. 'You're right,' he said, looking up at Romy, almost gleeful. 'Let's take a look inside.'

The stool was full of sheet music and books. They hauled them out to have a look.

'I'm sure these are the working notes of Jack and Grey,'

Romy said, as they spread them out across the table in the kitchen. 'Look, two different hands, lots of scribbles, lyrics in the margins . . . This is absolute gold, it's an archive. The creative process of two great talents!'

Richard shook his head. 'Amazing. All in the piano stool, just waiting to be discovered.'

'The answers often are right in front of you.' Romy pushed aside more of the scribbled-on sheets. 'Overlooked and forgotten.'

A thought came into her head, bobbing to the surface of her consciousness like a cork. She gasped.

'What's wrong?'

'Something I've forgotten.'

'What?'

Romy didn't reply but jumped up and went over to her backpack. She took out the ivory-coloured hardback novel and opened the back cover. From under the jacket, where she had tucked it, the sheaf of typed paper at the back fell out. How had she not read this already?

She picked up the tissue-light typed pages, unfolded them, and began to read.

PARIS 1949

TESTIMONY OF VERONICA MINDENHALL

THIS IS TO RECORD THE CONTENTS OF MY
INTERVIEW WITH MARGUERITE HEUROT WHICH
TOOK PLACE YESTERDAY. I WENT TO HER APARTMENT
IN THE FIFTH ARRONDISSEMENT IN ORDER TO
CONFRONT HER WITH MY SUSPICIONS REGARDING

THE FATE OF IRÈNE RAZINSKY. I WENT WITH THE
AGREEMENT OF PHILIPPE DU CROIS, WHO PROVIDED
HER ADDRESS ON THE PROMISE THAT I KEEP THE
OUTCOME A SECRET. I THEREFORE CANNOT DIVULGE
WHAT I HAVE LEARNED BUT I CAN WRITE IT DOWN
HERE IN THE HOPE THAT IT IS ONE DAY FOUND AND
MADE PUBLIC BY SOMEONE WHO HAS NOT SWORN
THE OATH THAT I HAVE.

Romy looked up from the pages, her heart pounding. She
looked over at Richard, who was watching her, confused.

'Here it is. The answer. The proof we need to link the
Minettes together and show that Irène was the heroine of
the Resistance.'

'Oh my goodness,' breathed Richard, staring at the paper
she was holding out to him.

'Yes. Here it is. And, just like the music, it was here all the
time. We just didn't know what to look for.'

Chapter Twenty-Nine
VERONICA

'Do you know that they believe a storm petrel is the soul of a human who was lost at sea?' Veronica asked.

She and Billie were sitting on the grass just above the abbey ruins, watching the children run about, shouting and chasing one another.

'No,' Billie said, shading her eyes against the sun in the west. It was beginning to turn the sky into mackerel clouds of pink and silver as it made its way to rest in the Atlantic.

'Yes,' Veronica said, 'each bird a drowned soul. That's why sailors find them so unlucky, I think. But they're beautiful. I hear them purring in the crevices of the stone walls at night. You know, they make me think of Jack and his beautiful drowned soul.'

Billie put a hand to her. 'Dear Vee. You're still grieving him.'

'Yes.' Veronica managed a wan smile. 'I'm still grieving Daddy too. I know that seems silly from a middle-aged woman, when her father died years ago, but I do. I think he's here but I see him as one of those noisy gulls, always on the hunt, very loud, very fearless, taking up a bit too much of the sky and keen to swipe the helpless chicks for himself.'

Billie laughed. 'I wonder where you get all that from! And of course it's natural to mourn him. I do too. I think of him often.'

'Yes . . . I suppose so. My grief for Jack is different.'

'Well.' Billie ran her hands through the cool grass and then squinted up against the glare of the sun, checking on the children who were running along the ruined walls and shouting. 'You loved Jack. Like a lover.'

'Better than a lover. Because my love for him would never fade or die, not like my love for André.'

'André has proved . . . a disappointment?'

'I suppose he's human. We are all disappointments. But I have been hurt. Very hurt.'

'I'm sorry, dear Vee. I have my ups and downs with Ronald, but he is faithful. I will give him that. And I can't bear the men who are not. I had thought better of André but perhaps I shouldn't.'

Veronica sighed. 'I think part of the problem is that he is always looking for Irène and yet doesn't want to find her. He can't ever forget. I can't either, but with him, it's something else. All his young lovers seem almost to be a way to reach her somehow, as though she is in the past and they are a way back to her. Even though they are the future and he is the past.'

'They don't look like her, do they?' Billie asked, making a face. 'His lovers?'

'Oh no. Some are fair, some not. It isn't that. It's a spirit.

536

That's what he wants.' Veronica sighed again. 'It's so sad. But when I got older and further away from Irène, I lost some of my appeal, I think. I will never know. Perhaps he doesn't like my work, my success. Perhaps he feels neglected. I tried to be a good wife, perhaps I wasn't.'

'I'm sure you were as good as any wife could be.' Billie smiled at her. 'You did your best, I know that.'

'I tried. I even tried to give him what he wanted most – the answer to Irène's fate. But he refused it. And in the end, we wanted different things. A different life.' Veronica gestured to the island. 'I have this, of course. It would be different if I didn't. I might just have to make the best of things and be a French government wife turning a jaded eye away from her husband's increasingly ridiculous escapades. As it is . . .'

Billie nodded. 'Did you ever find out what happened to her?'

Veronica said nothing for a while, letting the wind blow her thick hair over her eyes. Then, eventually she said, 'Ah. Well. I can't say. Not yet. One day.'

Some of us can bear secrets, some of us can't.

That was what she knew ever since the day she visited Marguerite Heurot in her grand apartment, the one she had not left for four years during the war. Philippe had requested the interview for her, and Heurot had said yes, not realising the connection between the English playwright and Irène, her one-time secretary and editor.

Veronica was shown into the salon by the maid, and had time to take in a room filled floor to ceiling with books across an entire wall. The furnishings were plain and mis-matched, almost purposefully at odds with the high-ceilinged elegance of the room itself. The art was good, but everything else in the room was ugly. Opposite the wall of books was a large desk with a typewriter on it, a metal filing cabinet with open drawers that spilled papers, and more piles of books, some holding dozens of scraps of paper as bookmarks. There was little in the way of comfort: no flowers, or pretty rugs, or plump cushions.

How could one spend four years in a room like this? she wondered.

By the window, in a plain suit and a polo-necked jumper, was a short, plump figure looking out over the street below. As she turned, Veronica recognised the bespectacled face of Heurot.

'Good day, madame,' she said. Heurot was not married but she had been, and even if she hadn't, she would have merited the more dignified title. 'Thank you for agreeing to see me.'

Heurot gave a small smile. 'It was a favour to Du Crois but I have to admit that I'm intrigued to meet you. I haven't seen your play but I've heard of its success, of course. You must be very pleased with it.' She gestured to the couch. 'Please be seated. May I order you coffee?'

'No, thank you, I don't want anything.' Veronica sat down, ill at ease. She felt Irène closer to her than she had for a very long while but in a way that made her uncomfortable. The atmosphere of the room was bad. She could not imagine Irène being happy here. How many hours had she spent here with this woman? She sensed conflict. But that could be her fancy. There was no proof.

Heurot came and sat down in the armchair opposite. She pulled out a packet of cigarettes and lit one, smoking rapidly, drawing lungfuls of smoke down and expelling them in a steady stream, as though powering herself with it. 'Are you here to interview me? Ask advice? You might want to learn how to move from frivolity to seriousness, and that would make sense.'

Veronica said coolly, 'I will come straight to the point, madame. I want you to tell me everything you recall about Irène Razinsky, your secretary.'

Heurot stiffened and her expression hardened. 'What?'

'You heard me. Tell me everything about Irène. I want to know and that's why I'm here.'

'What impertinence!' Heurot scoffed at her. 'You can get out if you're going to talk like this. I was going to give you the benefit of my experience and literary achievements, but I don't think I will now.'

Veronica leaned forward, summoning all her dignity. 'Before you refuse to speak, madame, and send me away – and believe me, I cannot wait to leave here – I should warn you that if you do not tell me what I wish to know, I will make it known to the world what you did.'

'What I did?' Heurot gave a mocking laugh and blew more smoke towards Veronica. 'What did I do?'

'I believe you condemned Irène to death.'

Heurot went very still.

'Yes,' Veronica went on. 'I know it, and so do you. You

discovered she worked for the Resistance and you betrayed her.'

'This is utter nonsense,' Heurot said scornfully. 'You cannot prove it.'

'I don't need to, you have proved it yourself. Your novel is the story of your desperate love for someone who could not return it. And like Paul in the book, you were so enraged by Irène's refusal to love you in the way you loved her that you took the same revenge on her. You wrote it all down – your emotions, your reasoning, your desires and your actions.' Veronica gave a bitter laugh. 'We authors are stupid that way. We keep writing our stories and telling the truth about who we are and what we believe.'

'You might, madame, but I do not. I am heartily offended by what you've said, and I must request that you leave.'

Veronica stared at the tight face opposite, with all its signs of repression: the stiff lips and jaw, the drooped lids, the lined skin revealing tension and scowls. 'I will go in a moment. But madame, you forget that you dedicated this book "A I". To Irène. You used her Resistance codename as her character. And I think that records will show that she left your apartment on the morning that she was betrayed, and perhaps some record somewhere will show that the call to the Gestapo came from here. I will make it my business to find out.'

Heurot went deathly white, still smoking rapidly.

'One day I will find out,' went on Veronica. 'And I will explain to the world how you sent a heroine to her death because she refused to sleep with you, and then turned that action into a monument of literature to ensure your own greatness. It sounds disgusting, doesn't it? That's because it is. And everyone with a scrap of humanity will agree with me. They will look at the pictures of beautiful Irène, murdered because of you, and they will be repulsed and revolted. Your legacy will be dust. Your books will be erased, just as you erased Irène and replaced her with Minette. You know this. You know that all you've ever achieved will be forgotten.'

There was a long and dreadful silence before Heurot said, 'What do you want?'

'A confession.'

'Never. I refuse.'

'There will be a condition. This confession would be for my peace of mind, and mine alone. If you agree to make it, then I will swear never to tell anyone. You will retain your honour and your reputation.'

Heurot stubbed out her cigarette in an ashtray on the table next to her and immediately lit another. 'I don't understand why you would do this. You could destroy me, even without proof. Even the hint of a scandal like this would undo me.'

'I have my reasons. I've made promises. All I want is to have the truth confirmed and then we can both rest easy. Will you do it?'

The little woman eyed her suspiciously but her shoulders unstiffened slightly. 'I would have your solemn word? Your promise? You would never reveal a thing?'

'Yes. But in return, I want every detail, every memory, every fact. That is my bargain to you.'

There was a long silence. Veronica thought longingly of

Irène, imagining her elegant beauty in this ugly place. She could imagine now the hungry gaze of Heurot wanting to possess and devour her, Irène's discomfort as she realised the extent of the other woman's passion, her realisation that the denouement must occur and that she must reject it. She could not have guessed the depths of Heurot's rage and what she would do in revenge.

At least, I hope she did not.

Heurot spoke at last. 'Very well. I will tell you everything, as long as I have your oath never to tell anyone what I say.'

'You have it.'

'Then . . . let us begin.'

When she left two hours later, exhausted and miserable, Veronica knew she would carry the weight of this secret alone. André would never be able to bear it, although she would not break her oath and tell him. She would take it with her through life and then she would leave it for the future, a time when Heurot was gone, André was gone, and she herself was gone.

The future could possess it and make of it whatever it wanted.

She went home and sat down at her typewriter.

Now Veronica and Billie sat in companionable silence for a while, breathing in the soft air of St Elfwy and contemplating its ever-changing beauty. The birds chattered overhead as they rode the warm currents, wheeling over the jewel-green island with its carpet of wildflowers.

Billie turned to her sister. 'What about your writing? Have you finished that play yet, the one you're writing for Jack?'

Veronica plucked some flowers from a little skein by her hand and began to examine the delicately veined petals. '*The Last Song of Winter*? Not yet. I'm getting there.' She smiled over at Billie. 'Remember that play of Rupert's, the one he was writing all those years ago when he came to our house and I fell so in love with him? I've used that as inspiration. It's nothing like it – not that he would care now – but it's inspired by it. A sort of ghost story. It's about the tortured soul and how it can destroy itself. And about how love lasts beyond death. That's how I feel about Jack. That my love for him is eternal and deathless and that one way or another, he'll come back to me. A little storm petrel riding on the wind for ever.'

'That's beautiful,' Billie said.

They watched their children playing in the sunshine, their hair ruffled by the sea wind, their arms glinting against the dark blue sea. Birds wheeled and soared overhead, calling and shrieking.

Billie said, 'It's always hard to imagine the winter in the middle of summer, isn't it?'

Veronica nodded. 'Especially here, in this beautiful place. But one thing we know for sure is that winter always comes in the end.'

'And so it goes on,' Billie added.

Veronica nodded. 'And so it goes on.'

Chapter Thirty

ROMY

'This is terribly exciting for all of us, particularly as you've decided to give your first exclusive interview to us here at the Llangwm Literary Festival.' The interviewer, a well-known journalist, smiled winningly at Romy and then he turned to the audience gathered in the large white tent. 'Aren't we lucky, everyone? Please welcome Romy Razinsky!'

There was a noisy wave of applause that settled down quickly as the audience prepared to listen to Romy.

'We have a lot more people than normal,' the interviewer declared. 'And a lot more press than we usually get here. That is just a small indication of how much interest your book, *The Story of The Last Song of Winter*, has generated.' He opened a hardback copy of the new book. 'It's the extraordinary story of Veronica Mindenhall, Jack Bannock and Irène Razinsky – or, as we all know her now, Minette, the heroine of the Resistance. There is so much in this, Romy, but one of the major talking points is the fact that the great writer Marguerite Heurot was actually a collaborator. Can you tell us more?'

'Of course.' Romy glanced out over the audience, who were looking up with rapt faces. At the back, she could see Richard, who refused to sit at the front because he might put her off, even though she said that he wouldn't. 'Can I say first, I came here to talk about this for the first time at Llangwm because Pembrokeshire has such a dear place in my heart, and in the heart of my husband and his family. Our lives have been bound up in this place in more ways than we can really understand, even now. And the real-life story that unfolded as I investigated the history of St Elfwy and all that happened there was so startling. I did not expect it to lead me to wartime France, a grande dame of literature and the revelation that my husband's great-aunt was a real-life heroine. Though he wasn't my husband then.'

The audience murmured with surprise and interest.

'The twists and turns keep coming,' said the interviewer. His fingers, slightly ink-stained, turned the pages of the book. 'This reads as grippingly as any novel. But there's no point in trying to keep your discoveries a secret, is there? Because they've already made headlines around the world. Not least in France.'

'Yes.' Romy laughed. 'I'm not sure when I'll be welcome back to France again after this. Perhaps in time.'

'But it's a very serious charge,' the interviewer said, 'about a very famous and honoured woman. That she betrayed her secretary to the Gestapo.'

'She confessed everything to Veronica,' Romy said. 'We have all the details in her own words, as told to Veronica, and all the evidence from the new archive corroborates her story exactly. Heurot did it.'

'She was in love with Irène?'

'Yes. According to Veronica's account, which came straight from Heurot herself, Marguerite was deeply, madly in love with a beautiful and enchanting woman who could never return her passion. We don't know how much Irène knew about the feelings Marguerite had for her until at last Marguerite declared herself.'

'Did she know that Irène was a member of the Resistance?'

'It seems not at first. Not until later, just before the end. When she did find out, she was delighted: her beloved Irène was a heroine, a soldier, a goddess of valour and courage. That was probably the point at which she confessed her love and was rejected.'

'She told Veronica that?'

'Oh yes. She was tortured by the rejection, utterly humiliated and cast down. She found it frightful that the balance of power had been reversed. She was the great writer, the powerful woman, and Irène was the secretary, the society butterfly, the mistress of a rich man, the no one. And then Irène proved to be strong and mighty, a woman of infinite lovability – at least for Marguerite – and Marguerite was the supplicant and then the spurned, rejected lover with nothing left to live for.'

'So she took her revenge.'

'Yes. Her terrible revenge. She betrayed Irène to the Gestapo, who took her from her flat. She had no warning before they arrived and dragged her away. She was never seen again, mostly likely shot almost immediately.'

The audience gasped and murmured again.

The interviewer looked solemn, frowning, before he said in his mellifluous voice, 'And yet, Marguerite Heurot got away with it.'

'She was never caught. She was instead honoured when she wrote her famous book about her love for Minette.'

'Marguerite was telling on herself,' mused the interviewer.

'I'm sure she was. It is actually very hard to keep secrets. They tend to find their way out in the end.'

'This is fascinating stuff, no wonder you've caused shock waves in the literary world,' the interviewer said. 'But that's not all. You've also uncovered truths about another hero, Grey Oswald, and his role in the suicide of a much-loved composer, Jack Bannock. So, let's start at the beginning. Tell us a bit about St Elfwy and how it links all these amazing people.'

When the event was over and Romy had signed dozens of copies of her book, Richard was waiting to drive her back to Elfwy.

'You were brilliant,' he said as they got in the car.

'Was I?' She was suddenly exhausted.

'Yes. I was so proud.'

'This is just the first of many. I've got months of events.'

'Don't knock it,' Richard said. 'Lots of authors would kill for that kind of schedule and all the publicity you're getting.'

'I know. I'm glad about it. Not so much for me as for Irène. In the nineteen thirties she was just a giddy mistress, a clothes horse, a kept woman. Within a few years, she was one of the bravest of the brave. You should be very proud of her.'

'I am,' Richard said. 'The whole family is. I wish my grandparents could have been around to see what you've done. It's incredible. Not only that, you've rescued the island from the clutches of that dreadful film.'

'I don't think so. You'll still get hordes of film fans!'

'But they'll know the truth. That matters. For Veronica and Jack.'

They drove in silence through the late afternoon sunshine, heading west towards the coast where the boat was waiting to take them over.

Summers were always spent on Elfwy. Richard went in April. 'For the beginning of the sexy season,' he would say, twinkling at her. He never let her forget that it had been an afternoon of birdwatching that had brought them together. Even now he would suggest birdwatching when he meant a few hours in bed.

Romy would join him in May or June, and then Elfwy would be their base for the golden months, before they returned to their other life, in the house near Bristol, where Romy worked on her research for a new book and the master's degree she was completing and Richard, temporarily giving over the care of the island to others, oversaw the work of the bird trust and his grandmother's estate. It was better for Romy to have the contrast. Even though her mental health was now very much under control, she needed to keep an eye on it and watch out for feelings of becoming too isolated.

Despite her stoic attitude to what had happened with Jesse, she had suffered some after-effects, not least nightmares about the caves. Jesse pleaded guilty to his charge so Romy had not had to appear in court. After his prison sentence, he'd left the country, apparently returning home. Knowing he was likely on the other side of the world had helped Romy, and her trauma over that night was subsiding. It helped that she spent a lot of time with Flo and her family on the island. The children's joy and excitement and pleasure on Elfwy helped to wipe it all away. She just never wanted to go back to the Singing Caves, if she could possibly help it.

Besides their summers on the island, Romy and Richard would always go back there for Christmas. In the cold days of late December or early January, they would wrap up against the bitter winds and go across the island, past the abbey ruins, to the stacks to watch out for the guillemots to return.

'It's called the Christmas Dance,' Richard told her. 'The birds appear out of nowhere in the middle of winter to perform a sort of giant sexless mating ritual. No one knows why. Once it's over, they disappear again until spring.'

Every year they would look out for the return of the guillemots. The birds would gather in their hundreds to observe their riot of water dancing, diving and swimming, before they vanished again till spring.

'There, you see, they're having a ball!' he would say to Romy. 'Singing and bonding like they've turned up to their own Christmas party.'

She would smile at him and hug him as they watched the eligugs performing their excitable water games.

Richard hugged her back against the biting wind. 'You see, Romy? It's not just spring. Even in the depths of winter, we need love!'

Romy leaned her head on him. 'Maybe that's when we need it most of all.'

They watched the birds until it grew too cold, and then turned to go back to the white house on the cliff.

Acknowledgements

A huge thank you to Richard, Judy, Becca and Tim Sadleir, who shared their beloved holiday spot in Pembrokeshire with us, and passed on the love for an amazing and beautiful place. That gift has enriched our lives enormously and we are forever grateful. Thank you too for your equally precious love, support and friendship over many years.

I am very grateful to Harry Mount, for taking such a generous interest in the book and pointing me in the direction of invaluable research; showing me the famous guillemot stacks and telling me about their Christmas dance; and arranging a boat ride around Skomer Island for me to see the puffins for myself. Thank you also to Julia Bueno and David Horspool for warm welcomes and wonderful walks along the coast. The Llangwm Literary Festival has provided happy days of fascinating talks by terrific authors.

My super-agent, Lizzy Kremer at David Higham Associates, is always a rock, and her support and editorial insight is second to none. Thanks too to Maddalena and Orli for so much help and guidance.

I would like to thank Wayne Brookes, who commissioned my first book for Pan Macmillan and went on to publish me tirelessly for twelve more. I'm enormously grateful. Here's to more lunches and laughs and chatter.

Thank you to Lucy Hale, who has guided me so carefully over the last few months, and Katie Loughnane for taking me on with so much enthusiasm and excitement – I'm looking forward to working with you and Maddie Thornham. Huge thanks to all the marvellous Pan Mac team, especially to Kate Tolley and Meg Le Huquet in Managing Editorial, Neil Lang in the Art department and Ana Taylor in Marketing. I'm hugely grateful to Susan Opie for a sensitive structural edit and to Lorraine Green for her encouragement along with insightful copy edits. And thank you to Nicole Foster for proofreading the book so expertly.

Thanks to all my readers – you make it all worthwhile.

Thank you always to my dear friends, wonderful family and to my children, Barney and Tabby, for their marvellous company, love and support.